THE
JULIA LEGACY

MAZE INVESTIGATIONS –
THE GENEALOGY DETECTIVES: BOOK 3

M. K. Jones

THE JULIA LEGACY
Maze Investigations – The Genealogy Detectives - Book 3

© 2023 Mary Kathryn Jones

Fourth Paperback Edition, 2023 – re-published by M. K. Jones
Cover by Alison Morgan, Alicat Design

Category: Historical, Crime & Mystery

ISBN: 978-1-7392284-3-9

Published by M. K. Jones

Chapter 1
Cornwall 1736

The house was in silent uproar. All day the servants had moved around only when necessary, keeping to the shadows, trembling at the very idea of encountering their mistress, fixing their gaze on the floor. Anger, rage, fear. Mostly fear. They spoke fleetingly in whispers until the end of the day when, knowing she was finally asleep, they could give vent to their feelings.

Edward Steelfox, the head servant, sat in front of the kitchen fire, staring intently at nothing. His grief was still too raw to speak of his feelings. His wife, Emma, sitting herself down beside him, had no such qualms. "If I ever pray again, it will be that the old bitch dies a horrible death," she said.

Edward shook his head. "Won't make no difference. Can't bring him back, can it? Nor her."

She put her hand on his shoulder, felt his body trembling through the wool tunic. He moved forward to put another faggot of wood on the open fire.

A voice spoke quietly behind him. "You should let the fire go out, now the mistress has gone to bed. You know she doesn't like the waste."

"And that's all we be, isn't that right Mistress Pencarrow? Waste, just waste." He jumped to his feet, kicked at the embers. "My brother was waste, and his betrothed girl. And their child. All just waste."

The housekeeper, Julia Pencarrow, kept to her seat at the table at the back of the kitchen. "You know that I am as sorry as you be for what happened to your brother, Master Steelfox. And the news this morning concerning his girl and the child was indeed terrible." She paused for a moment as all the servants in the kitchen stopped what they were doing to listen to the exchange.

"We all did what we could," Julia Pencarrow replied, "but they gave the verdict."

"Nothing we said would have made no difference, anyway," said a rough voice from the back of the kitchen where the shadows hid the face of the speaker. "She wanted rid of Peter. Don't understand why, though."

"Jealousy," said Edward Steelfox. "My brother was popular and liked by all."

There was a murmur of assent, and whispers of "Aye," and "A good lad."

"You must not say these things out loud, Master Steelfox. You know how talk carries."

Julia Pencarrow stood and moved towards him. Despite the compassion in her soft voice, he shrank from her outstretched hand. He glanced over at his wife, whose eyes were fixed on him. She flicked them at Julia and gave a tiny, abrupt shake of her head. He turned back to the fire and put his hands out to warm them. The gesture was lost on no one.

Julia Pencarrow put her hand back to her side and turned her back on the fire. "You should all retire now," she said, staring at the back of the kitchen but looking through the people. They stood as one and left silently.

"Come, Edward," said his wife.

"No, not yet. I shall not be able to sleep this night," he replied. "I think I shall walk."

"You must take care," Julia said, still looking at the rear of the room. "Easy to lose your way on such a night. The mist will thicken yet."

"And that be your doing perhaps, Missus?" Emma Steelfox murmured as she leaned in to kiss her husband. He hushed her.

"I know the pathways well, Mistress Pencarrow. I would be alone with my thoughts."

The housekeeper assented. "You will be safe."

Emma Steelfox gave her husband a quick, fearful glance, then walked in a wide berth around the housekeeper. Edward could not prevent a half smile. "My mother valued your advice, Mistress. As do I."

Julia Pencarrow returned his smile, acknowledging his meaning, then left the kitchen, blowing out the candles on the servants' dining bench.

Chapter 2
Cornwall 1736

In the courtyard the mist had thickened into a smothering fog. The collar of his coat was as close to Edward's neck as he could pull it and he had wound his muffler around his head. But he couldn't avoid inhaling the thick air. Ahead he could barely make out the arched entranceway at the centre of the house. Turning, he made his way to the formal garden, then down to the path to the rough patch of land that led to the sea.

He had walked this path many times with his brother Peter. Born in the county of Shropshire, they had been brought to Cornwall by their mother as young boys, when she had decided to return home after the death of her husband. She had been lucky, as she told them often, to find work in the house at Penwith. Her own mother had worked there. Lady Vyse had remembered her mother, and taken her on, providing accommodation for her and her boys. They were put to work in the stables, where Peter had shown an aptitude with horses.

But not me, Edward thought as his feet followed the path in what he knew was a seaward direction. *Not horses for me. I was good with people.*

The little boys had never seen the sea. Their mother had described it to them many times, but nothing prepared them for their first walk to the cliff-top, half a mile from the house. There, they looked across the cliffs at the boundless body of heaving water, whose size was beyond their imaginings. Seeing the enormous Atlantic breakers, hearing the seabirds screaming above them, smelling the tang of salt and seaweed, both were enthralled, bewitched, and knew they would never leave this place.

But Peter was gone now, probably never to return. And the girl he had loved was dead. She had thrown herself from the cliff onto the needle-sharp rocks at the head of Sennen Bay. The child she carried, dead with her. All because of a ring.

Edward stopped and twisted his head from side to side. Yes, still heading in the right direction. He looked down at the path but could no longer see his feet. The fog had snaked around him as he walked, enveloping him in a shroud. But he was sure of his way. And he was sure of Julia Pencarrow. She had said he would be safe. If she said it, it would be so. Despite her reticence, all about knew that she was a cunning woman as were her forebears.

The path took him through the unlit hamlet of Penwith. He passed Julia Pencarrow's long, dark house, and he bore left, taking the path past the old church to the cliffs.

A sudden swirling around his head shifted the air for a moment and Edward felt the sea. He must be close to the edge of the cliff. Yes, here it was, a sucking and pulling of water in and out of the rocks. No breakers tonight. No birds, either. Another swirl of air thinned the fog for a few seconds, enough for Edward to see the cliff edge in front of him and hear the water way below his feet.

He stopped and sat. He must have walked more quickly than he realised, or else his thoughts, or the fog, had taken away his sense of time. He put his hands around his knees and rested his head on them. Then he gave way to sobbing.

Chapter 3
Cornwall 1736

Back at the house, Julia Pencarrow prepared to return to her own home. Although she felt sorrow and sympathy for the Steelfox family, she knew that the mistress of the house was unmoveable. She also knew that the mistress was a liar. But the only person who could prove the lie was dead. She left one candle burning in the grate, so that Edward Steelfox would have light when he returned. She carefully put another small log on the embers. It would be a long night.

**

Upstairs, in the small bedroom next to the sumptuous main chamber, Sir John Vyse lay on his back, unable to block out the penetrating snores of his wife from the four-poster bed in the room next door. There was no longer space for him in that bed. Since their marriage he had felt himself shrinking as she had grown. The former Mildred Denys was a substantial woman, both in height at six feet tall, and in girth, when they'd wed. But her unappeasable greed had bloated her head and body. He had let her have her way when they moved to the master bedchamber after the death of his mother. Mildred's money had put right what his mother, for all her great dowry, could not support. It had been a marriage of convenience; he admitted it to himself when he could not sleep. But her need, her greed for dominance, which had led to the recent outrage, had brought him to despair. He had advised her, then begged her, then warned her, not to practise her love of punishment on the servants.

Poor young Peter Steelfox, the innocent target of her enjoyment, was now on a convict ship, heading to the American colonies, all because of a silver spoon. Sir John knew that Peter had told the truth. That his mother, the now-deceased Lady Johanna

Vyse had known and indulgently ignored that he had taken the little silver spoon to make a ring for his fiancée. Shy, pretty, little seventeen-year-old Julia Treseder. But Mildred Vyse had accused the boy of theft, and had, Sir John was certain, paid the gardener Michael Weston, to attest to the theft in court. And she added the charge of assault she claimed Peter had made upon her person.

Mildred lay on her back, spread out on the great bed, mouth open, the spoon ring on a chain around her neck for the servants to see. The ugly symbol of her triumph; and how they now regarded Sir John. They all blamed him, especially Julia Pencarrow. He had a fearful respect for Julia. His mother had made sure he understood Mistress Pencarrow's 'abilities'.

Sir John wanted his servants to respect him as they had his mother. But he knew that it would never happen as long as his wife ruled his household. He wanted to be liked and respected amongst his neighbours and the local gentry. But he knew that whatever face they presented to him and his wife, behind his back they laughed and pitied him.

Anger made his fingertips claw and tingle. Someone must do something.

Chapter 4
Cornwall 1736

At the edge of the cliff, Edward Steelfox leaned unsteadily over the abyss. Close to this spot little Julia had thrown herself in despair onto the rocks not two days before. It was the morning after Edward had returned from Bristol, with the news that his entreaties had fallen on deaf ears and that Peter was manacled in the bowels of a convict transport ship. And just after Lady Mildred Vyse had dismissed Julia for being pregnant to a convict, saying that her condition would bring shame upon the household and that she could not appear to condone such behaviour.

Peter and Julia were to marry the day after his arrest and the servants knew his detention was timed to prevent the marriage. The woman had no shame. She had gone to the Assizes in Bodmin and told her tale. She'd lied to the Magistrate about how she had caught the villain with the ring made from the silver spoon he had stolen, and how he struck her when she attempted to take it from him, corroborated by the weasel gardener, who had since disappeared.

Peter was condemned to death for the theft of the spoon and for grievous assault, but the sentence was commuted to transportation. He was taken from Bodmin to Bristol, where he had been in jail for six weeks while the transportation ship waited for enough human cargo to depart.

Edward had spent the past week in Bristol, tried everything he could to explain how his brother had not stolen the spoon but had had implied permission to take it. But the testimony of the woman and her gardener was incontestable. Edward had stood on the dock and watched, in a state of misery, as the shackled prisoners were paraded from Bristol Gaol through the streets to the dock before boarding. Poor Peter could hardly stand. He had never been a strong boy. The weeks of confinement had so emaciated him that Edward at first found it hard to pick him out. He was filthy, his hair bedraggled, his clothes in rags.

Families watched and waited and wailed on the dockside. All knowing it was unlikely that they would see their loved ones again. Edward knew that most of them had been condemned to transportation to the colonies for theft, for items worth only a few shillings. But that was the law. It was better than hanging. Or was it?

He had taken with him all the money he had, hoping to buy Peter's reprieve. When that proved impossible, he approached his brother closely enough in the melee to push what remained into his hands, hoping he could to buy extra provisions on the journey. He hoped that it would be safe from the dubious-looking crew who prodded and shoved the prisoners onto the ship. For them, transportation was a money-making opportunity.

The brothers wept, Peter begged Edward to take care of Julia and the child he would never see. Edward promised, and blessed his brother. They had had less than two minutes together, then Peter was gone.

Edward turned his back on the sea. Dawn was breaking over the rough tor. He thought there was lessening in the clotting thickness of the fog. He set his feet on the path back to Penwith. Now he was resolute. Now he decided that something had to be done.

Chapter 5
Cornwall 1736

After staring into the kitchen fire's dying embers, Julia Pencarrow put on her cloak and walked across the heath to her house in Penwith. She insisted on living in this house, though it was most unusual for a housekeeper to live out. It had been in her family's ownership for ten generations. The fire she had left smouldering was almost out, but she'd placed dry gorse on the woodpile before she had left before dawn. As soon as she threw it on the fire it sparked, then roared into life. Once the flames were strong, she put on a fat log. That would keep it going for as long as she sat there.

She ran her hands up and down the arms of her chair, sat back so she could rest her back on the padded cushion, and allowed herself to think about her situation.

Julia had been in the service of the Vyse family for almost thirty years - since early childhood - following in her father's footsteps. She remembered the late Lady Vyse as a good if somewhat scatter-brained woman. But a woman with a good heart. She knew that the spoon, although it was not actually gifted, had not been supposed stolen by that good lady. She had overheard the conversation between Peter and Lady Vyse. The object itself had not been mentioned, but Lady Vyse had been clear in her meaning. Julia remembered smiling with affection for Lady Johanna Vyse. She knew that no one else had been privy to that conversation. Definitely not the gardener. She remembered the warm smile on Peter's face as he left to tell Julia that they had a ring and they could set a wedding date.

What about the gardener? She sat upright in a blaze of anger, but a loud crack from the fire distracted her. She saw a small piece of gorse jump into the air and burn on the hearthstone. She carefully poked it back onto the smouldering log. She must be careful. The servants suspected, but they also valued her knowledge of simples and cures. Yes, they believed her to be a witch, but no one could produce evidence she had ever sought to do harm. There were ignorant people in the village who would denounce her if they could. But all they knew was that she had a great understanding of the use of herbs to cure maladies, from which anyone in need could benefit. Julia was deliberately generous with her skills.

The fire managed, she sat back and returned to the question of the gardener. She knew that he had been paid well for his treachery. She had challenged him. He had threatened her with denunciation. She had laughed at him. After the trial he had returned briefly to Penwith before disappearing. It surprised no one. He was loathed. The other servants were glad to see the back of him, Edward Steelfox in particular, who had uttered many threats in front of the kitchen fire.

Julia was the only one who knew that the gardener's body was lying at the bottom of the old well, after Mildred Vyse had pushed him down there. That would teach him not to be greedy and demand more money for his silence.

Her problem was that it would have been her word against that of the new Lady Vyse. And the main suspect would most likely have been Edward Steelfox.

Lady Mildred Vyse was a dangerous, evil woman. Who would fall into her sights next? Who would she target for destruction? Julia Pencarrow closed her eyes. She sensed that it was almost dawn. Time to return to the house. Something must be done.

Chapter 6
Cornwall 1736

Edward Steelfox and Julia Pencarrow reached the house at the same time. It was daybreak and Sir John Vyse was leaving. He'd had his horse saddled and was walking it through the archway at the front of the house when the servant and the housekeeper arrived. They bowed their heads, but no one spoke.

Once again, it was a quiet day, in so much as there was none of the usual chatter. Mildred Vyse rose at around eleven. She summoned her maid to help her to dress, then descended to the hall to take breakfast alone, on the dais she'd had built at the far end of the room. She sat at the centre of the long table, looking down the hall. The servants had laughed when they had first seen it. This huge, pretentious woman, thinking she was a medieval monarch, sitting above everyone else! No one had ever joined her on the raised platform. Sir John had loudly refused and took his meals in the smaller dining room next door. The rare guests and family who joined them looked at the set-up once, uncomfortably sat through a meal and did not return. Lady Vyse didn't seem to notice. Julia Pencarrow thought the woman didn't really need other people. She was satisfied with her own self-importance. She liked to have her superiority acknowledged, but she couldn't tell that people were mocking her.

There was still the occasional afternoon caller. They were met and entertained in the fine drawing room that overlooked the formal gardens. On this day, the wife of a local squire came with her daughter to take afternoon tea. She'd been a friend of old Lady Johanna Vyse. She had called once before, shortly after Mildred had arrived. Edward Steelfox, who met the carriage and ushered the women into the drawing room, sensed their distaste. As they seated themselves, Mildred Vyse swaggered into the room and heaved herself into an armchair.

"That will do, Master Steelfox." She waved him away. "Ask Mrs Pencarrow to bring tea and refreshments for my guests. And," she added, apparently as an afterthought, "when my guests are leaving, ask Master Smith to see them out. I do not wish your presence to embarrass my guests." She fingered the chain around her neck with the spoon ring, unable to hide the glint of malice in her eyes.

He put his head down and backed out of the door, hiding his fury. A quick glance as he closed the door took in her expression of smug delight, and that of disgust on the face of the squire's wife.

He knew what was coming now. He and Emma were next.

Chapter 7
Cornwall 1736

Dinner that night was a quiet affair. Worn out by the exertions of entertaining guests for an hour, Lady Vyse took dinner in her bedroom, then retired for the night.

Sir John returned home shortly before midnight. He was in a foul mood, shouting at the stable boy who did not wake up and react quickly enough. He took himself to the kitchen where he found Edward and Emma Steelfox and Julia Pencarrow sitting in front of the fire, and he demanded bread and cheese, and beer.

In silence, Emma fetched them for him. Then, to their surprise, he sat down at the servants' table at the back of the kitchen, ate his food and drank his beer. Then he bade them goodnight and left.

Emma cleared the table, raising her eyebrows at Edward. "What was that, I wonder?" she said, taking the platter to the sink.

"I believe it is a very difficult time for him," Julia Pencarrow breathed. "He wanted none of this."

"Then he should stop her," said Edward.

"I don't believe he can," Julia replied.

"Well, someone has to."

"Edward, stop that." Emma spoke in a warning tone. She didn't want him venting his rage in front of Julia Pencarrow. "Come to bed now. You haven't slept for two days."

He nodded, went to stand, but his legs trembled and he had to lower himself back into the chair. Emma ran to him, put a hand under his armpit and pulled him to his feet. He ran a hand through his hair.

"More tired than I realised," he said. "Goodnight, Mrs Pencarrow."

Nodding as they left, she took his place in front of the fire.

Chapter 8
Cornwall 1736

Three days later, at dawn, Edward and Emma rose and went down to the kitchen where they found Julia Pencarrow with a jug of beer and a loaf of bread.

Edward thought she, too, looked weary, but neither acknowledged the other.

All was ready for the usual gargantuan breakfast for Lady Vyse at eleven, but she didn't appear. After waiting half an hour, the maid was sent up to knock on the door, to see if Her Ladyship required anything. She returned ten minutes later, saying she had knocked repeatedly on the door, but got no answer.

"Did you not enter?" Edward asked her.

"The door be locked, Master Steelfox, from the inside. What shall we do?"

By this time, more servants had appeared in the kitchen, realising that something out of the ordinary was happening. Julia Pencarrow appeared.

"Why are you all here?" she asked them.

"Lady Vyse seems to have locked herself in her room and won't answer or come out," Edward replied.

"Fetch His Lordship," Julia said, "he may have another key."

Edward went to the back of the house where he found Sir John in the stables, in conversation with the blacksmith. He explained the dilemma. Sir John seemed reluctant to get involved and needed persuasion from Edward that he should take charge, so Sir John followed him back to the kitchen where Julia Pencarrow confirmed the situation. Sir John agreed that there was a spare key, which he fetched from a cabinet in the drawing room. Edward thought he seemed reluctant to open the bedchamber door, but Julia insisted, almost pushing the man through the great hall, across the porch and up the staircase. Edward Steelfox followed them. They paused in front of Lady Vyse's room. Julia knocked. There was no reply.

"Sir John, I am fearful that some accident may have occurred. Please open the door."

He put the key into the lock. It was rusty, being unused for some time, and it took a few minutes to push out the key on the other side and open the lock.

They entered the room. They could see Lady Vyse in bed, lying on her back in her usual sleeping position. But she was not snoring.

Sir John held back, breathing slowly and deeply. Julia Pencarrow approached the bed. She put out her hand and touched the woman's neck, then turned to the two men.

"Her Ladyship is dead," she said in a voice devoid of emotion.

The two men stumbled forward. Now looking at the dead woman, they saw that her face was blue, her hands at her throat, where a red gash bit into the folds of her neck.

In a room locked from the inside, Lady Mildred Vyse had been strangled by the chain she wore around her neck. The spoon ring was gone.

Chapter 9
Sennen, Cornwall
Present Day

They had been in Cornwall for a week and on the surface, everything was going well.

Maggie Gilbert hunkered down into an armchair on the deck of the beach café above Sennen Bay, hands clasped around a mug of hot chocolate. She gazed through the glass barricade at the sweep of the great curved beach and the Atlantic. She and her son Jack and Janine, her daughter Alice's friend, had spent the afternoon at the beach. Jack and Janine were surfing fanatics. But Alice was no fan of the beach. Alice hated the feeling of sand between her toes and when forced to accompany them, dressed as if it was midwinter and sat under the beach tent, her back to the sea, reading a book. After two such visits they got the message and left her at their holiday home.

Maggie could see that the friendship between Alice and Janine was lessening. Following Janine's episode of running away back in January, from the school they both hated, the girls, forced to return to school until the end of the academic year, had clung together, mutual support against the tidal wave of bullying that the timid Janine had endured throughout their first year at the comprehensive school in their hometown of Cwmbran. But Janine's unexpected prowess at sports was taking her in a different direction to that enjoyed by the more introvert and cerebral Alice.

Most of the families who had spent the day on the beach were leaving now, heading off to evening barbeques, trips to the pub, or out to one of the coastal towns.

She could easily make out Jack and Janine in the sea, riding their boards, waiting for the next big wave, chatting easily together. Maggie waved to them, knowing that there was no chance they

19

would see her, picked up her phone and found the number she wanted. The call was answered immediately.

"Hi Zelah. How's it going?" There was the slightest of pauses, during which Maggie knew that Zelah, her friend and colleague in Maze Investigations, was arranging her face into a smile.

"Fine, thanks. We've just come out of the tin mine. We'll be heading back in about ten minutes. Louisa has just left the gift shop."

"OK. I'm just going to call Nick, see how he and Alice are getting on. Then I'll drag these two out of the sea and we'll head back up. We still having a barbeque tonight?"

"Yeah, fine. Rick says he'll cook it."

"Excellent," Maggie replied. "I got salad and stuff. There'll be plenty to eat. Keep going."

There was just the hint of a snap as Zelah cut the call. Maggie saw she had missed another call while she was talking to Zelah. Nick had left a message.

"Hi Maggie. Alice and I are on our way back. Should be there around six-ish. Had a great time. Excellent stones. See you later."

Maggie glanced at her watch. It was just after five. Time to go down to the beach and offer the alternatives. A lift back to the house now, or stay and carry their boards up the steep hill path.

As she stood and picked up her bags, she felt the stiff breeze that was encouraging bigger waves as the tide moved up the beach. It whipped Maggie's light brown hair above her head as she descended from the café deck. She walked down the boat ramp and onto the beach. As she glanced up, she could see their holiday house near the top of the cliff, far above. Avilion. A seven-bedroom, mini French chateau, with a round turret at each end of the house, each with a little crenelated spire. The house was white with a blue slate roof and two tall chimneys and a conservatory of sorts built between the turrets. This was where Maggie headed every morning, to look out across the short patch of garden to the edge of the cliff and the view of the Cornish sea. She had found it mesmerising from the moment they arrived.

The house belonged to Mabel Trelawney, a friend of a friend

of Zelah's. Zelah herself was of Cornish origin, but this was the first time she had returned to the county in over fifty years. Well, the second time. She had visited a solicitor in Truro back in March when she had first heard about the death of her stepsister and her inheritance.

Maggie reached the water's edge just as Jack and Janine were surfing to a stop. She waved, and they jumped off their boards and ran towards her.

"Time to go, if you want a lift back up the hill. Up to you. You can stay another hour, but as soon as the lifeguards go, you're done."

"I'm coming," Janine said immediately. "I'm knackered. But it's been great," she added, looking for Maggie's approval.

Maggie smiled at the girl and turned to Jack, who was wavering, looking back at the waves that were increasing in size and speed.

"I'll come too," he said.

Maggie suppressed her grin. "Don't want to wear yourself out. Back again tomorrow, I expect?"

They walked together up the beach.

"There's a competition at the weekend," Janine said. "They've got a beginners section. I thought I might try. Give it a go?" Again, the need for endorsement.

"Good for you," Maggie said. "You won't know if you don't try. What about you, Jack?"

"No, I'm not as good as she is," he admitted.

They reached the car, strapped the boards to the roof rack and sped up the narrow, winding hill to the house.

Zelah was already back and in the kitchen making tea. Jack and Janine put their boards in the little outside store, then headed up to their respective rooms for showers.

Maggie sat on a stool at the counter in the kitchen. This room had been an add-on to the original building, slightly back from the main line of the house so it didn't block the view from the turret. Its side windows had a view of the cliffs at the end of the bay where the waves were now smashing themselves against the rocks, throwing up twenty feet of spray.

"Good day?" Maggie asked, waiting for the tirade. Instead, she got a deep sigh.

"It's been OK," Zelah said, her back to Maggie as she poured hot water into the teapot. She went to speak again but was interrupted by the sound of banging doors as someone entered first through the outside conservatory doors, then through the double doors that led into the dining room. Any minute whoever it was would turn left from the dining room into the hallway and into the kitchen.

"I'm looking for some kind of lighting device. I've got the charcoal on ready, but I can't light the damn thing." Rick Matheson marched chest-first into the kitchen and stared around like an angry bulldog.

"Here you go," Zelah said, reaching into a drawer, and tossing him a box of matches. He grunted and left.

"Despite what you may think," Zelah remarked over her shoulder to Maggie, "he is having a wonderful time here."

Maggie liked Rick but had been unsure why Zelah had invited him. When she questioned Zelah, she was at first surprised, then amused. Zelah blushed, something Maggie had never seen in over a year of knowing her.

Zelah had met Rick back in January when she'd gone to Canada, to investigate a client's claim that he was from Nova Scotia. She'd been looking for a woman called Louisa Sturridge, the only direct link to the client. Louisa had been away from home, but Rick was her next-door neighbour.

In a bizarre twist it had turned out that Louisa Sturridge was the only living relative of Nick Howell, the third partner of Maze Investigations. But the client was a fake; he had been dead for over three centuries.

Morgana Hwyl, or Howell, as the family name had evolved over the centuries, had been exacting revenge on Nick's family for seven generations. They had found and deterred her, but not without a cost. Zelah had almost died because of a skull fracture caused by Morgana, or by her mentor and Maggie's nemesis, Eira Probert, encountered when Maggie had first met Zelah and they had together solved Maggie's family mystery. Both were gone, but Maggie knew that they still existed somewhere beyond the living world. And they would probably try to return. Maze Investigations' cases often involved bizarre or unnatural discoveries; for which they were becoming internationally known.

As a gesture of thanks, Zelah invited Louisa to the UK to meet Nick, all expenses paid. But Maggie now appreciated that the timid Louisa could never travel alone, so Zelah invited Rick to travel with her. Devious devil, Maggie thought. She hadn't wanted to make Zelah uncomfortable so had said nothing, but watched with amusement as the ordinarily grumpy Zelah and the taciturn Rick spent time in each other's company.

"And Louisa?" Maggie asked. "Difficult to tell if she's OK."

"Ecstatic," Zelah grunted. "Thank God for Poldark. She's the ultimate fan. But it keeps us conversing. She has nothing else to say."

"Pity she and Nick didn't hit it off," Maggie said. "An hour of enthusiastic conversation, then nothing to say to each other for three days."

"What did you expect? They have nothing in common and the link is generations back. But they're both keeping busy and being polite. Just another couple of days."

"And then do we find out why we're really here?"

"Just leave it for a day, will you," Zelah hissed, as Louisa's head appeared around the door. They hadn't heard her coming down the stairs. Louisa always walked quietly. Small, mousy, and thin with round shoulders and an air of unceasing nervousness that someone was about to shout at her, Louisa pulled back as soon as she saw Zelah, but Maggie called her in.

"We're just getting ready for the barbeque, Louisa. Rick's in the garden trying to get the fire lit. Would you like to go join him?" Louisa nodded rapidly and backed out of the kitchen. "God, what a wuss," Zelah muttered. She was about to say something else but was interrupted by the sound of a car arriving outside. Nick and Alice were back.

"Here come the troglodytes," Zelah grinned.

Alice rushed into the kitchen, followed by Nick who was heaped up with backpacks, boots, and books. "A good day," he said, looking out of the window. "Lots of stones."

"We found all of them," Alice added. "Tomorrow I want to see the Cheesewring. Is that OK? And explore on Bodmin Moor."

"We have to leave that for a few days yet," said Maggie. "Don't worry," she added, as Alice's face fell, "plenty of time yet. Tomorrow we're all going to the Eden Project. It's the last day for Rick and Louisa." She gave Alice a hard stare. The girl looked as if she would complain, then got the message.

"OK. But I can slide down to the bio domes on the rope slide, yeah?"

"As many of you can go down to the bio domes on the rope slide as you want. The civilised ones amongst us will use the transport, or walk," Zelah replied.

"Good," Alice said. "Where's Jack and Janny?"

"Upstairs, showering and changing. We're having a barbeque."

Alice left saying nothing further. Nick moved into the kitchen.

"Who's taking them back to the airport?"

"I am," Zelah replied. "And you're coming. Don't complain. She came to see you."

"And she has seen me," Nick replied. He turned to Maggie and said in a low voice, "I told you families aren't all they're cracked up to be."

"Be nice," Maggie hissed as Nick walked out of the kitchen.

Chapter 10

Two days later, Zelah left early in the morning for London. Rick had been profuse in his thanks, on both his and Louisa's behalf. He had issued an invitation to all of them to visit his hometown of Shelburne in Nova Scotia, the following summer, to which Zelah had enthusiastically agreed.

Jack, Janine, and Alice were at the beach. Alice had gone reluctantly, and after much persuasion. Promises of spending the entire day walking to the extraordinary pile of balanced stones on Bodmin Moor, known as the Cheesewring, convinced her. She had even put on shorts and a tee-shirt. Maggie had taken them, helped Alice to set up the beach tent, and left them with food and drinks.

Back at the house, Maggie now had several hours before anyone would return. Which gave her enough time to start some research. But she had to do it without Zelah knowing.

She made herself a pot of coffee, gazing down at the beach as she went through the motions. She poured a full mug and took it down the three steps from the kitchen into the small office. There was a safe sitting on the floor, a huge sturdy thing. Maggie unlocked the combination lock and took three small black boxes from the top shelf, put them on the desk under the window next to her coffee, and sat in front of them.

Folding her arms and sitting back, she went over how they had got to this point, feeling a growing sense of frustration with her friend.

At the beginning of the year Zelah had received a letter from a Cornish solicitor informing her that her step-sister had died and left her a legacy, which had turned out to be a ring. This had shocked both Maggie and Nick, as Zelah had always claimed to be an orphan without a family. But Zelah had explained that this person was not her sister, not even a relative, but the daughter of the vicar, Charles Hopton, who had brought Zelah up until she ran away at fifteen. There had been no love lost between Zelah and the Hopton family and she had never heard from any of them in over fifty years, until the letter, and then the ring, arrived.

When she received the ring, Zelah had been interested in its history. It had turned out to be a seventeenth century 'spoon ring': a ring fashioned from a silver spoon by a servant to give to his bride-to-be. And, usually, it was stolen from the household in which they worked.

When she showed her colleagues the ring, she said she would be interested in finally going back to Cornwall. This was something she'd previously vowed never to do. Now she wanted to get more information and, as she cryptically put it, "Introduce you to the real Zelah Trevear."

In March Zelah had gone to Truro, alone, to meet the solicitor and had returned with two more rings and, Maggie had since discovered, a letter. Zelah had revealed the rings, but not the contents of the letter. Ever since she had been closed and unapproachable about what had happened.

Zelah had been offered this house for the whole of August by its owner, her friend Mabel, before the solicitor's visit, so felt obliged to take them down for the promised holiday. Nothing was said before or since they arrived about the 'real Zelah Trevear'. Zelah had excused herself to Maggie that with Rick and Louisa joining them for the second of their four weeks, she didn't want to talk about personal things or get into anything complicated before they arrived, but just ensure that they all enjoyed their holiday. Maggie knew this was bullshit. Zelah had never had concerns about what she said, or in front of whom. Now their visitors had gone, Maggie decided it was reckoning time.

Besides, Maggie had already learned the first of Zelah's secrets and didn't think she could keep it to herself for much longer. She took a quick slurp of coffee, then leaned forward and opened the first box. The spoon ring.

It was made for a tiny finger. They'd speculated that this spoon would have been for sugar or mustard, or something for a small pot. The handle was beaten flat and wrapped the length around so that the original ornate crest design wrapped over the flattened end. On the inside was a hallmark. Zelah had dated it to 1690. The crest was not so easy to decipher, having worn down over the years, but it had a flower, with engraved lines curling to and from its stem. Maggie guessed that it might be a family crest, but without dismantling the ring it was impossible to tell. She did know it was solid silver.

She had examined the ring many times since Zelah had first produced it in March. Apart from dating it, she could not discern any clue to explain why it had come to Zelah. By itself it would have been a mystery, an inheritance from a forgotten relative. When combined with the rest of the bequest, there was a story to discover. A significant one.

Maggie put the ring back and opened the second box. As she gazed at it, she smiled, sadly. This ring was exquisite, but she felt a whisper of melancholy when she looked at it. The Roman ring.

She picked it up between her thumb and middle finger and held it up towards the light. The beam of sun coming in from the small window caught the colour in the widest part of the ring. Not a gem, but what might be ivory or bone, coloured red, depicting two clasping hands on a white background, set into filigreed gold. It had marks engraved onto the surface of the gold beyond the centrepiece, on one side what looked like 'I' and 'V'. On the other side no letters were clearly discernible. Maybe a 'C', but it could have been a worn 'O'.

It was a delicate piece of metalwork, given its age, and also made for a small finger.

As she touched this ring this time, she felt a sadness emanating from it again. What age of a girl could have worn such a small wedding ring? She knew that Roman girls could be married from twelve. Had someone tried to marry off a young girl with this ring? High-status Roman marriages were usually political, and gold was only available to the higher classes. There were beautiful examples in museums around the world, some better engraved and more ornate. Her research told her that this was high status, not the highest, but significant. She doubted that they would learn the true story.

After a few minutes she put the Roman ring back in its box and turned her attention to the last of the three. This was easier to date and understand. She picked it out and sat it on her palm. This was a Welsh gold 21-carat wedding band, slightly curved, known as a D band. Solid, yet ethereal. Zelah had taken it to a jeweller and had it dated at 1917. Wedding rings of this size, shape, and gold content today could cost thousands. They advised Zelah to insure it for two thousand pounds.

Maggie had done as much general research as she could. Why these rings had come to Zelah and to whom they might once have belonged, was a mystery. A mystery that Zelah was no longer showing signs of wanting to resolve.

"We'll see about that," Maggie murmured as she put the last of the rings back into its box and returned the boxes to the safe.

She was putting her shoes on to walk up to the small village at the top of the hill, to recommence the next part of her secret search, when her mobile rang. It was Zelah.

"Seen them off, just getting back into the car now," Zelah shouted.

"Why are you shouting?"

"It's very windy here. Back in about four hours, OK? Has he arrived yet?"

"Not yet," Maggie replied. "He said he'd be here about six. Don't break your neck on the motorway, there's no rush," she added.

An exhalation and the end of the call was her reply.

She had promised to check on the kids after a couple of hours, so she walked down to the beach where she found Alice still in the blow-up cabin and Jack and Janine still in the water.

"They'll have hands like prunes," Alice said without looking up from her book. Maggie shushed her aside and sat down with her. It was time to remind Alice what was coming.

"What's that you're reading?"

"It's about the stone circles around here, what they mean." For the umpteenth time Maggie wondered what was going on in the head of a girl about to become a teenager, who wanted to spend all of her time on holiday trekking on moors and reading books with titles *like The Standing Stones of Ancient Cornwall.*

"I've brought sandwiches. You hungry?"

"No, and I know what you're trying to say. I know he's coming today."

"How did you know what I'm trying to say?" Maggie was both amused and exasperated but tried to hold back on the latter.

"You've gone purple. It's your nervous colour."

Maggie sighed. It was proving increasingly inconvenient to have a child with such an exceptional, esoteric ability, one who could read her so easily. She knew Alice was practising more, so she could not only see but also interpret, which Maggie was sure was because of Nick's encouragement of her 'ability'. Would it be good for her as she entered her teenage years? Maggie had an uncomfortable feeling that Alice would need a lot of support. And, equally uncomfortably, that probably meant from Nick, as much as herself. She suspected that Alice saw Nick as a new father figure.

"I didn't think I was nervous, but if you say so… But if I am," she added, "It's because I'm anxious about your reaction when he gets here."

Alice shrugged, reached out for the sandwiches, and ate, eyes back on her book.

"We'll talk again later," Maggie said, looking out to sea. "I'm off for a walk. I'll be back about four." Another shrug.

Back at Avilion Maggie parked the car, walked into the inner porch, and pulled out her walking boots from the heap of footwear on the floor. She sat on the stairs and was tying up the laces when she stopped at the sound of a vehicle pulling up outside. She glanced at her watch. One-thirty. Too early for anyone to be back. Probably a delivery.

She reached out and pulled open the front door to check and saw, half-dismayed, half-delighted that it was a camper van. Bob Pugh had arrived early. He pulled up outside the garage, jumped out and walked towards the front door as Maggie opened it. They each paused for a moment, then moved towards each other and kissed. Wordlessly, Maggie took him by the hand and led him upstairs.

Chapter 11

Later they sat in the garden, Maggie explaining how well the holiday was going, but not as planned, and her growing frustrations with both Zelah and Alice.

Bob had grown used to Zelah's initial aggressive attitude to everyone she met, since he and Maggie had worked together on an inheritance case earlier in the year. Together they had found a descendant of an old friend of Bob's, a Welsh soldier in the Spanish Civil War, who had asked Bob for help before he died. Being no expert, Bob had sought help from Maggie. At first, they had been tetchy with each other, he a Detective Inspector, and Maggie not a fan of authority. But their friendship had continued beyond the end of the case and over the following months had deepened.

"I've got to get her to talk about the rings, at least," Maggie said. "You remember how enthusiastic she was in March?"

He nodded as he took a swig of beer from the bottle he was holding. "It was just the one ring then, though."

"Something happened when she went to visit the solicitor in Truro, more than just getting her hands on the other rings."

"Is she usually reluctant to talk?"

"Are you kidding?" Maggie retorted. "She can be reticent about personal stuff, and Cornwall has always been a delicate subject. But... I thought she was ready. Now, well I just don't know," she mused. "But I have to get her to talk. And there's something we have to do. Soon."

Bob gave her a wry glance. "What?"

"Can't tell you, not right now," she said, turning her head away from him. "Damn, it's after four. I said I'd be back at the beach by now. Back soon." She jumped up and ran into the house, leaving Bob a little peeved, but smiling.

All three kids were ready when Maggie arrived. They quickly

loaded up their equipment and headed back to the house. They were all chattering as they entered. Jack grinned when he saw Bob, who was in the kitchen looking for another beer, and Janine greeted him with a muffled 'Hello', with her head down, as she did with any policeman who crossed her path since her episode of running away earlier in the year.

Alice stopped dead in her tracks as soon as she saw him, scowled, turned, and went up to her room. Maggie went to follow her, but Bob called her back. "Leave her, Maggie. It's still early days."

"You don't know her," Maggie snapped back. "She can dig her heels in so far they'll grow roots."

"OK, but wait until you've calmed down too. If you talk to her now, it'll just end up in a row."

"But it's so rude," Maggie remonstrated. "I've brought her up to be polite, or at least I thought I had."

"She is rude, but... I wonder if there's something else?"

This was something that had been on her mind, too, but she hadn't voiced it. She had thought she wasn't ready to bring up the past. Maybe the past was pushing itself into the present. Not for the first time.

"I don't think this is about her father, if that's what you're saying?" she said.

He nodded.

"OK." She paused, put her hands on the back of her neck and pushed to stretch out the tension, then took a deep breath. "This elephant in the room needs addressing between us, too, I think. Look, I haven't talked much about my – about David. Perhaps it's time. But I honestly don't think Alice's problem is about her dad. It's about Nick. I think she's seeing him as a potential new dad. But she knows that he and I are colleagues. Nothing more."

He walked to her and gently pulled her hands away from her neck. "Talking is good," he said, smiling at her.

She went to speak again, but the sound of a vehicle pulling up outside stopped her. Zelah and Nick had returned. Following the slamming of car doors, Zelah stormed into the house, went straight through to the conservatory, and flopped down on the settee. Maggie shrugged at Bob.

"Just as it was about to get interesting. Never mind." He handed Maggie a cold beer and signalled his head in Zelah's direction. Mouthing 'later' over her shoulder she joined Zelah on the settee and handed her the beer, which Zelah took without speaking and swigged half the bottle.

"Thank God for that," Zelah puffed out, wiping her lips with the back of her hand. "Too much driving in one day. We should order dinner in tonight. My treat. Save anyone cooking."

"Works for me," Maggie replied. "Jack and Janine want an early night. Competition nerves."

Zelah shot her a puzzled look. "What? Oh, yes, the surfing. Jack changed his mind, then? What time tomorrow?"

"Ten. Yes, he did, and I know, early, but you don't have to come. It's tide dependent."

"Of course I'll come," Zelah said. "We should all go." Then, as an afterthought, "And I'll book a table for lunch afterwards. Might as well celebrate, whatever the outcome."

"That would be nice, thanks. But I want to speak to you this evening. We have things to discuss."

Zelah sighed and stood up. "I'll order the food. Usual from the pub?" Maggie nodded and Zelah added, "Good. I'm going up for a shower. OK. Let's talk after dinner. And I want us all to go for a walk, just a short one. Then we'll talk. But just you and me to talk, OK?"

"OK, if that's what you want." Maggie was surprised that Zelah didn't want to include Nick. And that would also mean leaving Bob out. But whatever, it was Zelah's choice. She already guessed the purpose of the walk and was relieved and hopeful it, whatever it was, would come out at last. But there was no chance now of a heart-to-heart with Bob. It could wait, she supposed, but not for long.

After the food arrived, and they'd eaten, Zelah chivvied them all to put on walking shoes, and head off across the field at the back of the house towards the main road that ran down the

Penwith peninsula to Land's End. She marched at the usual Zelah pace, much to the annoyance of Jack who soon fell behind. Maggie drew back to join him.

"What's this all about, Mum? I wanted a quiet evening. I even told Pip I wasn't going to see her tonight." Jack had found a girlfriend, another surfer, who was staying in Sennen with her parents.

She put an arm around his shoulders. "We came here for Zelah to help her get to grips with her past, and to have a holiday. It's important to her, Jack. She's about to tell us all something monumental about herself. It's an honour to be here, you know. To be one of the few people she trusts. I don't believe that she's ever told anyone. Apart from her husband," she added.

He shrugged. "It had better be good."

Reaching the main road to Land's End, they crossed in single file. Zelah led them along a narrow pathway towards a church that stood on a slight rise next to the road. It was small, shabby, and battered by Atlantic winds and storms.

They walked around the side of the church, through the broken lych-gate to the front door. Instead of entering the church, Zelah climbed a few steps up the bank to the left of the door and walked around, following a path through the graves. Reaching the opposite side of the church she stopped and turned to face them as they gathered in front of her.

"I told Maggie, Nick, and Bob in March that I would introduce them to the real Zelah Trevear. I don't think they had any idea what I meant. Well, the time has come. Here she is."

She stepped back to reveal a flat, coffin-shaped stone, raised a few inches above the grass. They all moved forward to read the words carved into the stone.

Here lieth the remains of Zelah Trevear.
Wife of Ezekiel Trevear of Penwith.
Born 1680. Died 1761.

"At age three I was abandoned here. I spent the night sitting on this stone. I had a paper bag in my hand. I didn't know my name, I thought I was called 'kid'. The vicar, not a good man as it turned out, found me. He named me after this gravestone. That's the only beginning I ever knew."

She turned and walked to the edge of the graveyard where the wall bordered the road, jumped down and marched off across the road and into a field.

Chapter 12

When they got back to the house, they found Zelah in the garden. Maggie, Nick, and Bob held back, eager not to upset Zelah. Maggie knew Zelah well enough to know that if she didn't want to answer questions, she could tell them to stop asking. Janine walked straight up to Zelah, put a hand on her arm, and said in a quiet voice, "I'm sorry you had such a troubled time." Then she walked off to the kitchen. Nick followed her and brought her back out.

"Thank you, Janine. You know what it's like to be isolated, don't you?" Zelah said, looking down at the girl where she was now sitting on the grass with a bottle of Cola. Janine nodded. Zelah continued, "It wasn't a good childhood. I ran away when I was fifteen."

"Where did you go?" Janine asked.

"Cardiff," Zelah replied. "Don't ask me why. I think I liked the name. Tiger Bay, actually. Sounded exciting. How wrong was that?"

"Did you have any friends here?" asked Jack.

"I did," Zelah replied. "The vicar got paid to keep me and decided he'd have more of that, so he took in other orphaned children from the same charity. A few were my friends. Made it bearable; but they all moved on in the end."

"How do you know you were three when it happened?" Alice asked. "And what was in the bag?"

"What perceptive questions," Zelah said, "but no more that I'd expect from you, Alice. I can't answer that, I just knew. I suppose someone must have told me. It's the only thing I did know. As for the contents of the bag, I didn't know that until recently. There were three rings and a letter. Well, not so much a letter, more of a note. Plus a few bits of stuff."

"Did you go to school?" Janine again.

"Yes, they had to let me go. But they didn't encourage me in anything. I was clever, too; good with numbers. But they made me leave when I turned fourteen. Sent me to work as a skivvy for a local farmer. And took my wages."

"Vicars are supposed to be good people, aren't they?" asked Jack.

"I guess so. But this one was a real bastard; a vicious, cruel bastard. And his wife. They never got found out as I discovered when I came back here a couple of months ago. They're still thought of as pillars of the community."

All the time she had been talking, Zelah looked straight back at her questioner. Now she gazed into the distance. Maggie decided that this was enough.

"OK, Jack, Alice, Janine. Give Zelah a break now. Go and get yourselves ready for tomorrow."

Maggie had decided not to confront Alice tonight. It needed more discussion with Bob, and she knew Zelah wanted to talk to her, alone.

The sky turned from pale azure to inky blue and the full moon was bright. The breeze that had accompanied them to the church had gone. The air was still, the noisy gulls had left for the cliffs. The sea was a distant roar.

Jack, Janine, and Bob headed back into the house chatting about surfboards and wax. Bob had offered to take them to the beach early to get prepared for the competition and get their boards in good shape.

Alice stood up at the same time as Nick, but then darted forward, gave Zelah a hug, then ran into the house. Nick looked at Maggie, gave her an *'I don't understand what that was about'* face, and followed. Maggie and Zelah were alone in the garden.

"Wait there," Maggie said. She went into the kitchen for a few minutes, then came back out with two cardigans and two large glasses of whisky and ice. She put one on the table in front of Zelah, who immediately picked it up, took a good belt and winced but held onto the glass in both hands.

The sky was rapidly deepening to an intense mauve with stars showing themselves. At the horizon, the last remnants of colour were fading in the far western seascape.

"I have things to tell you," Zelah began. "About my past. Ancient and recent." She was gazing up at the sky and just as Maggie tried to speak, Zelah's hand shot straight up pointing at the sky. "I'd forgotten," She said. "It's the Perseids tonight."

"The what?"

"The meteor shower, ignoramus. Biggest one of the year. We'll get a fabulous view. Keep looking up. It makes it easier for me to talk if you aren't looking at me. Oh, and you already knew, didn't you?"

Maggie picked up a cushion from the floor, put it behind her head and pushed the lounger back. "Yes," she replied. No point denying it. "I walked up to the church last week. You know how I love a graveyard. And I found her. I knew it couldn't be a coincidence; but I was about to drag you up there if you hadn't told us. Anyway, I'm ready," she said. "I presume you don't want me to ask questions?"

"Let me get through this. There will be a few, but let me get it out first, OK?"

"I'll try, but don't shout at me if I have to ask something."

"Right. Well. Then… I left here when I was fifteen. Couldn't get out fast enough. I'd had years of being abused," she paused at the sharp intake of breath from Maggie. "Keep it in. It was physical abuse. And mental. They were evil, the pair of them. He hit me and the other foster kids. She isolated us, made us feel useless and worthless. Did we complain? Some did, not me. No one believed them. In the eyes of the community Hopton was a saint, who took in abandoned children and gave them a home. She ran the local mothers' union, organised charity events. There wasn't an iota of charity in the old bitch's soul. They had a daughter. And boy, did she lord it over us. Tracy Hopton. She was the school bully, and we got the worst of it. She picked on the little ones, pinched, and bit them, then said they did it to each other. That was my so-called stepsister."

She paused and took another slug of whisky as a shooting star flashed across the sky and a chilly updraft ruffled the surrounding grass.

"The three of them made sure we were lonely and isolated. I had a few friends, one in particular, but most of the kids moved on. Apart from me, they didn't want them too long. Just enough time to make money and ship them on again before their stories came to the attention of anyone who should have been taking notice and joining up the dots."

Again, she paused, and Maggie heard the tinkle of ice trembling against the sides of the glass.

"My friend and I stood up for each other, though. He got some terrible beatings for it. Back in those days there was no outcry at a boy being beaten. He never cried." She gave a short bark of laughter. "We used to play tricks on Tracy, hide her stuff, we put treacle in her gloves once. Jay got a hammering and practically no food for days. But it was worth it. Then one day, he just wasn't there when I came home from school. We used to go together, but he had just gone up to High School and I was still a junior. I waited and waited, but he never came home. They said he had run away, but I don't think so."

"What do you think happened?" Maggie asked apprehensively.

"I think the beating went too far. I think they killed him. Probably an accident. But he didn't run away. That I know. I've told no one about this; apart from Martin. And before you ask me how I know, Jay gave me the most precious thing he had, to keep for him. He thought Tracy might destroy it out of spite. He would never have gone away without it. I still have it. Just in case."

They sat in silence, side by side, gazing at the infinite vastness of sky. Three shooting stars flashed across in quick succession.

"I stuck it out for a while, then I made a run for it. I went to Cardiff and, inevitably, ended up homeless. I did some begging for a while. Then, when I was sixteen and knew I couldn't be put back into care, I went on the streets." She paused. "You know what I'm saying?"

Maggie had closed her eyes. "Yes, I think so."

"Two years. Until I was eighteen. Nearly got killed twice.

There are some nutters out there."

"What did the police do about that?"

Zelah's laugh was louder than usual. "Told me it served me right, mostly. They called us cows and whores. Thought we were scum. Until we were useful. You aren't crying, are you?"

"No, I'm just sniffing loudly. And I'm angry, for you."

"Well, as long as you don't feel sorry for me. Because I don't feel sorry for myself. Ever. It was a policewoman who helped me turn things around. Sheila. That's all I ever knew her as. She arrested me when a punter complained that I tried to rob him. Bloody cheek. But she said she saw something in the feisty little kid. She asked me if I wanted to get off the streets. Well, of course I did! Stupid question. That's what I told her. She laughed and let me go. A couple of days later she'd found me a place in a hostel, gave me some money for clothes and got me help to get some benefits and get into college. I'm clever, as you know. She told me not to let her down. I never looked back from there. I ended up being an accountant and set up my own business. But I hated men. Kept away from them. Until one day a new client came looking for help. He was in a right mess. An artist who'd sold his paintings and was terrified of the Inland Revenue."

"Martin?" Maggie asked.

"Yes. I never looked back from there, either. I think I was more contented than I'd ever believed was possible. But I never came back to Cornwall. Couldn't bear to think about them."

"But what about whoever left you on that grave?"

"Not interested, never interested. They had abandoned me. I was three years old. In the middle of the night. Whoever did that was evil, I've always believed. Until Tracy died."

"I know something has happened, Zelah. You were enthusiastic when you got the first ring, but after the second visit here you've been more reticent, and reluctant to talk about it, let alone do anything. Has it changed?"

"No, it hasn't. But… the rings are interesting. Tell me, when you've looked at them – which I know you've been doing when I'm not there – did you ever put one on your finger?"

Maggie smiled ruefully. "I looked at them. But no, I never tried one on."

"Never try and don't suggest to anyone else that they should. It was in the letter from Tracy."

"Are you ready to find out about all of this, now?"

"If you mean my history, no. I decided a long time ago that I will never try to find out who left me in that graveyard. My life has been good, apart from… what I explained. But the rings, as a research project, yes. Intriguing. You up for it?"

"Are you kidding?" Maggie replied. "When do we start?"

"Let's sit down with Nick and, yes, Bob, tomorrow, after the surfing."

"Good." Maggie stood up, then hesitated. "Zelah…" she paused, trying to think how to put the question she particularly wanted to ask.

"If you're thinking about what happened in Cardiff and whether I need help, or do I want to talk? Forget it. I did all my talking to Martin. And, I'm not ashamed. Not at all. It had some good outcomes."

"Really?"

"Ill wind, et cetera. How do you think I learned to walk everywhere on six-inch heels?"

Maggie shook her head and picked up the glasses. "And that's Zelah Trevear in a nutshell," she said as they linked arms and went into the house.

Chapter 13

The following day, Sunday, nine people sat around a table on the deck of the beach café; Zelah, Maggie, Jack, Alice, Janine, Bob, Jack's girlfriend Pip, and Pip's parents. In the centre of the table, in the pride of place, was an enormous trophy, awarded to the winner of the Outstanding New Junior Surfer.

Zelah raised a glass. "To the winner, a brilliant victory." They all raised their glasses and turned to Janine, who blushed and looked at the table.

"I was lucky," she mumbled. "Got the waves."

"No," Maggie said, "you made good choices. You've developed an eye for the good waves, and you have amazing balance." She paused for a moment, then took Janine's hand. "I filmed you, on your surfboard and when you got the trophy. I'd like to put it all on the Cwmbran Life website, if that's OK with you?"

The girl's expression was a mix of elation and terror.

"That should gain you some fans," Alice said.

There was a puzzled look from some around the table at this remark, but Maggie stepped in to move the subject on. She wasn't sure at that moment if Alice was being supportive or malicious. If the latter, a serious discussion had moved up Maggie's list of priorities.

"Well, Janine has to go home tomorrow. Nick's taking her and we have business matters to discuss, so I think it's time to go back up to the house." She stood, and everyone followed suit.

Pip's mother thanked Zelah for lunch, waited while Jack and Pip planned their evening, then turned to Maggie.

"He's welcome to come with us. We're heading into St Ives for a stroll and dinner. We'll bring him back later, if that's OK with you?"

Maggie looked at Jack, who nodded with unnecessary fervour.

"That would be good, thanks. He can come and get changed now and I'll drop him back down in an hour."

Chapter 14

Back at the house, Maggie gathered the adults around the table in the conservatory. Alice and Janine had gone up to Janine's room to pack ready to go home.

"Right, we've got about an hour before I have to take Jack down to meet Pip's family. It'll take him that long to do his hair and choose a shirt. Zelah has decided it's time to find out about her legacy. So, here goes." She turned to Zelah. "The floor is yours."

Zelah leaned forward and put her hands flat on the table. "Before we make plans, I want to make something clear. I have no interest in finding out why I was left in that churchyard or who left me there. OK? And I'm not forcing anyone to get involved. If you want to be, good. If not, also good."

They all nodded.

"I've long since come to terms with that and I don't need to know. But... if – and I say if – something comes out of the research that suggests a path to my history, I will decide if that path is pursued. Is that clear?"

More nodding.

"That's the deal, the bottom line. It's my decision and no one else's." She banged her hands on the table.

"You've made your point," Maggie said. "So how do we go about this research?"

Zelah sat back. "First, are we all in?"

"I'm not here for the next few days, but yes, I'll do my bit," Nick replied.

She turned to Bob. "What about you? Do you want to be part of this?"

"I'm willing to help," he replied, "but I'm not an expert. And I already have a job that can go critical at any time. But I could work with Maggie."

"Fair enough," Zelah said.

"How about we start with some background, Zelah?" Nick's voice was muted, as usual. He was sitting back, gazing out at the cliffs. "Tell us what you've learned already."

"Right. Well, you know that I got that letter in February from the solicitor in Truro. When we visited the International Brigades Memorial in March, I showed you the letter I received from the solicitor and the ring I inherited. The letter asked me to visit him, which I did. And yes, I went on my own. I decided that was best." She paused, keeping her eyes fixed on a point out to sea.

"When I got there, he told me that there was more. Tracy had decided that they should only give me the first ring, to see if I wanted to know more. If I responded positively, then I would receive the rest of my legacy. What a bitch she was, right to the end.

"Anyway, I went to Truro. Not sure what I expected. But what I got was… unexpected. It seems there had been a few bits of old junk in the bag I had been carrying, a stick of carved wood, like a peg but misshapen, a piece of old rag and two big, rusty pins. And there were the three rings."

"One ring to rule them all, one ring to bind them." They all turned around and saw Jack standing in the doorway in a theatrical pose.

"Wow, son, that's impressive!" Maggie grinned and folded her arms. "I mean, you've read an actual book!"

Jack slouched into the conservatory. "Ha! Ha! I'm ready to go."

Maggie went to get up, but he stopped her. "Actually, I was hoping Zelah could give me a lift. In the Spider?" He beamed a hopeful wide grin at her. Zelah stood up.

"I presume we're impressing Pip's father?"

"Yep," Jack replied.

"Then let's go." She stood up. "Talk amongst yourselves. I'll be back in ten minutes."

"Tea, anyone?" Without waiting for an answer, Nick wandered

off into the kitchen.

"And then there were two," Maggie muttered to Bob, "Do you really want to work with me?"

"Look, you know I'm only here for a week, and I could get called back. Unlikely, but well… yes, I'll work with you. But Maggie, there are other important things we talked about for this week."

She sighed and sat back in her chair. "I know. I thought a lot about it last night. I faced up to it. I've needed to. You already know about Nick's background. They've formed a bond, Nick and Alice and I think Alice had ideas about me and Nick being a couple. I suspect that she thinks you've spoiled that. But, honestly, it was never there. Not for me, anyway. He's my friend and colleague, but that's all. But I think she's still hoping and maybe she thinks she can put you off me, if she tries hard enough."

"She's a stubborn little git, I'll give her that."

"That's my daughter you're talking about."

"Which explains where she gets it from."

Maggie sighed. "I didn't think I was that bad. But perhaps I was when I was her age. Whatever. I can't remember. But I have had a thought." She grimaced at his look of misgiving, then continued, "How about, when Nick gets back on Tuesday, we go for an afternoon out, to visit the Cheesewring on Bodmin Moor? I'll be there and I'll try to persuade Jack and his girlfriend to come with us. And I'll try to manoeuvre it so you and Alice can talk together. Worth a try?"

He chewed his bottom lip for a few seconds, then nodded. "OK, and Zelah probably ought to come too. Can't leave her here alone."

"Maybe not her thing," Maggie said.

"What's not her thing?" Nick had returned with a tray of tea and biscuits.

"Nothing," Maggie gabbled, "just talking about Alice."

Nick put down the tray and was about to comment when they all heard Zelah's car.

Maggie looked at her feet, as Zelah walked in, pausing in the doorway. "Did I miss something?"

"No," Maggie replied, too quickly. "Let's get back to where we were. Nick has made tea."

Zelah took a cup and sat down. "Where were we? Yes, there were three rings. You've seen them all. There were also two letters, well, one was more of a note."

Zelah had left a file on her chair, which she now opened. Inside were plastic wallets. From one of them she extracted with the tips of her fingers a fragile looking, faded piece of paper.

"This was with the rings, and with me: 'I am sorry to do this,' she read, 'But I have no choice. Please look after my baby for me. I will return as soon as I can. Keep her safe. And keep my bag and its contents safe, they are precious too, but never put the rings on.'"

She put the paper down in the centre of the table. "Before any of you say anything, let me read you the second one. This was the letter from Tracy for me to have after she died." She took another piece of paper from another wallet. This one was typed. Again, she read:

"Dear Zelah, I am dying, which I am sure will not concern you in the least. I still dislike you as much as you disliked me. Let's not pretend sentiment that was never there. My father's last wishes were that we should return the items left with you. He burned the cot and the filthy rags found on the altar the night before he found you in the graveyard. My solicitor will return the rings and the note left with them. My darling father could barely bring himself to touch those rings. He almost threw them away. I wish he had. I wish he had thrown you away. You were nothing but trouble, you bunch of no-good vile unwanted brats. If you ever wondered what happened to your friend Jay, I think you already know the answer. But what you don't know is that it was me. Good luck finding him. Tracy Jones née Hopton."

Zelah looked at her friends and saw shock, disgust, and puzzlement. "Not bad coming from her," she said. "You should have heard her when she was being unpleasant," and that broke the tension.

"There's a crime in there." Bob was moving from puzzlement to anger. "A bad one."

"Yes. I think they killed my friend. Whether it was deliberate or an accident... I don't know, but now you have a flavour of Tracy. I always thought it was just the vicar. He was good at handing out beatings and Jay never gave in to him; so, I thought they must have gone too far. I never suspected Tracy. But if it was her, then I think it was deliberate. Maggie, you're unusually quiet."

Maggie got up and walked to the door to the garden. A gust of warm wind hit her as she stepped outside. She clenched and unclenched her fists to stop her hands shaking. It didn't work. She heard a footstep behind her. "Zelah needs you back in the room," said Nick quietly from behind her.

"I need a minute," she said, "so I say nothing that will upset her."

"She's hard as nails," Nick replied. "And anyway, if she gets upset, so be it. It's her right. Don't think it will be anything to do with you. You know her well enough to know that if you say the wrong thing, she'll tell you, but without malice. Come back in, please."

Maggie glanced quickly at his frown. Her face was burning. "Sorry, I've just made it about me, haven't I?"

"Just go back in there."

Zelah and Bob were talking. When Maggie sat down again Zelah said, "Bob will investigate what happened to Jay. He's asked me how I knew that Jay hadn't just run away and it's because of this." From the file she took something from another wallet and put it on the table. It was a photograph at the seaside of a young woman and a boy. Both were giggling, each with a hand over their mouth, looking at each other as if sharing a joke. The woman had an arm around the boy's shoulders. He looked about ten years old.

"Jay and his mother," Zelah said. "This was his most precious possession. It's all he had of her. He left it with me because if Tracy had known he had something precious she would've tried to find it and destroy it. He would never have left without it."

"So how did he end up with the evil vicar?" Maggie asked.

"That's for me to find out," Bob interrupted. "Zelah, carry on with your story." He didn't look at Maggie. She suspected he was cross with her, too.

Zelah reached across the table, took Maggie's hand in hers and squeezed, then winked at her. "Here's what I know about the rings. First, the spoon ring. It dates from the late seventeenth century and it's solid silver. There's a crest. The jeweller I spoke to didn't recognise it but thought it might be from a family. The Roman ring is just that. Probably from the first century AD. There's just one marking on the inside which looks like the letters I and V which could be the Roman number four. It's too worn for me to make out. The third wedding ring, well that's an interesting one. It's Welsh gold twenty-one carat and rare. Has the assay mark of the Birmingham office. Made in 1917. But none of them has anything that links to an owner. As far as I know now. Thoughts, anyone?"

"We don't know much. How can we get started?" said Nick.

"Actually, we know quite a lot, and there's plenty to go on with. May I?" Bob looked around the table. "You probably know this stuff, but I can sum up a few lines of enquiry."

"Help yourself, Inspector Clouseau." Zelah grinned at him. Maggie bit her lip to stop herself laughing at Bob's open-mouthed hesitation.

He turned to look straight at Zelah, avoiding Maggie. "Well, first, the original letter. Whoever left you at the church intended to return. They left you there because they believed they couldn't take you. And the rings were also special to both of you. Could be a familial thing."

Zelah shook her head. "Supposition."

"At the beginning, most investigations have as much supposition as fact. Make educated guesses from the evidence you have, so you have several lines of enquiry. Every little thing gets followed up. I thought you wanted my expertise?"

"Sorry," said Zelah.

"OK. The note says about the rings that they are precious too. As precious as the child. That says to me this writer wasn't planning on abandonment. Then, when you go to Tracy Hopton's letter, she says the vicar burned the cradle and blanket he found on the altar. My next supposition is that they left you in the church, probably asleep, in some kind of small bed, with a blanket. That says care. Now, you were about three, yes?" Zelah nodded.

"You would have been mobile. You woke up in the night and wandered out into the graveyard, looking for whoever left you. And you took your little bag of rings. So, at this stage, I believe that you were left for a short time by someone in trouble, who didn't want to involve you, so left you with someone they thought was trustworthy. A bad decision as it turned out. But, for some reason, didn't, or couldn't come back. An accident, perhaps? Fatal? Worth looking into. Do you know the exact date they left you?"

"Of course, I do! I always called it my birthday. No one ever celebrated or cared about my birthday until Martin came along. It was the twenty-fifth of June 1953." She saw Maggie's surprised expression. "Yes, I know, I said my birthday was the twenty-first. I didn't want the actual date, so I chose something noteworthy close by, the Solstice. Seemed significant enough."

Bob continued, "I can check police databases and records for any fatal accidents, probably unsolved, that might have taken place shortly after that date. Before you say anything, it's a long shot and, yes, based on supposition. And maybe the records no longer exist. But trust me, yeah? If nothing comes of it, then you have lost nothing. And another thing before you interrupt again. You couldn't have been local. Someone would have missed you. So maybe it was a holiday maker. But that still seems odd. You don't go on holiday and suddenly clear off without your child."

"Oh, I don't know…" Maggie muttered, "It's tempting."

He frowned at her. "But it might have been someone itinerant and passing through."

"Oh my God, he thinks I'm a Gypsy!" said Zelah in mock

surprise.

"No," Bob said. "Are you lot ever serious? I was thinking of a different kind of traveller. The predecessors of the hippies. It wasn't flower power, but there were wandering groups around then, post war rootless young people. I might ask around the local force. Might be a retiree who remembers something. And I can check into the vicar and his – what was it? – vile unwanted brats. See what records I can sniff out."

"Fair enough. Impressive. Good start. What else?" asked Zelah.

"I'd like to follow up on the spoon ring," said Maggie. "I was thinking I might try the local radio station. In the past they've invited me to come in and do a spot if I was ever in the area. Thought I might talk about the story, Zelah, of you as a child. No names. I could mention that they left you and talk about the spoon ring. Not all three rings, not yet. But I can say this is a case that Maze is investigating and it might have a Cornish link."

Zelah paused for a moment. "OK, but absolutely no suggestion it's one of us. And I agree, nothing about the other two rings for now."

"I'd like to take on the Roman ring," Nick said. "As I'm going back tomorrow, I thought, if you don't mind Zelah, that I could take it with me and go into the museum in Caerleon. See if anyone there could help."

"Can I go too? I'd like to help." Alice stood in the doorway with Janine behind her.

"I was thinking we could all go for a day out on Tuesday," said Maggie. "Visit somewhere we haven't been to yet?"

"I'd rather go to the museum with Nick." She turned to him. "How long are you planning to stay at home?"

He shrugged. "Just a day or two, then back here, we are on holiday. We're supposed to be relaxing and enjoying ourselves, not working."

"But we came here knowing we'd be involved in Zelah's ring research at some point," Maggie replied.

"I am enjoying myself," said Alice. "There's lots more to see.

Standing stones, circles, monoliths, barrows, quoits, fougous—"

Bob interrupted. "Have you seen the Mên-an-Tol, Alice?" The girl had turned her head away but paused.

"No… not yet. What is it?" Curiosity won.

"It's a strange stone, and close by. It's a round stone with a perfect circle cut or worn out of its centre. No one knows how. There are standing stones around it, too. Legend says it cured children's ailments and diseases. And some have said when they look through the circle, they can see into another dimension." There was a sharp intake of breath from Alice.

"Then we have a plan," said Zelah, standing up. "Let's go eat."

As everyone headed to the garden, Maggie touched Zelah's arm and nodded to the kitchen.

"Sorry I walked off… and thanks for the support back there," she said as she switched the kettle on.

"Forget it. They don't know what you know. And they aren't going to know. Right?"

"Absolutely," Maggie said. "But, Zelah, it will get difficult at some point. I mean, if Bob digs up something that has a family connection…"

Zelah paused, hand on the fridge door. "Yes, I know. Don't think I'm not constantly thinking about it." She took food out, banging it down on the worktop. "You know me best, Maggie. I'm a stubborn old woman. I've thought about this the same way all my life and told myself I would never change. My stubbornness protected me. From what? I guess my answer would have been 'from life' or 'from other people who might know what they're talking about'. But I couldn't sleep after I told you all about me." She turned around to face Maggie. "Is it possible to change this much? To let go of everything you've clung onto forever?"

Maggie leaned back against the cupboards and folded her arms. "That's a question, isn't it? My gut reaction is 'yes'. If you can see a need. If you have faith that it will be better for you. You don't have to know how, just that it will be."

"Hmm. Well, I've decided I'll let it unfold. I won't block it, at least. Best I can do, for now."

"And that's good enough. Now, shall we make something edible? You've emptied half the fridge."

"So I have. But it's mostly meat, fish, and salad, so I was subconsciously thinking 'barbeque'. Let's go."

Chapter 15

After dinner, Jack came back and he and the girls went inside to play computer games, leaving the four adults sitting in the garden watching the sunset.

"I don't think I could ever tire of this," said Maggie, one hand on a coffee cup, the other resting on her chin on the table. "It's so peaceful."

"And getting hotter," Nick remarked. "Going to reach thirty degrees tomorrow."

"Just as well we're all spending some time indoors. What time are you planning on leaving with Janine?"

"Early. About eight. What do you think about Alice coming with me?"

"Do you mind?" Maggie asked. "It means you'll have to stay at the house with her."

"Fine by me. She and I can visit the museum once we've dropped Janine, then stay overnight and come back Tuesday afternoon."

She glanced at Bob, who returned an imperceptible nod. "Yes, OK. I'll tell her to pack some overnight stuff."

"I think you'll find she already has," Nick replied, gazing at the blazing orange of the sun as it dulled to a deep red on the horizon.

Zelah laughed aloud. "This is so instructive to sit by and observe. Parenting, huh?" Then she stood up and marched into the house, which took them all by surprise.

"What did we do?" Bob asked.

Before anyone could answer, Zelah returned, carrying the three ring boxes, which she placed on the table, opened them, and took the rings out to hold in her palm.

"I've been thinking about this all day. I've been introduced to some strange things since Maze came into being and enjoyed all of them. And I know that I have an outlandish theory of my own about inherited memory. But, as you all know, I've never been one to take anything at face value, or just do what someone else says. So," she paused and took a determined breath. "Remember the note says the rings should never be worn. Why not? Haven't we assumed that something bad will happen if one were to put them on?"

Their expressions confirmed agreement.

"Well, let's see if that's right."

Giving none of them time to comment or object, Zelah pushed each of the rings onto the ring finger of her left hand and let out a huge scream.

Maggie jumped up and Nick went to reach out when Zelah laughed. "Sorry, couldn't resist. See? Nothing. Not a single thing. No changes. No feelings. Sorry, Maggie." She stopped when she saw the look of horror still on Maggie's face. "I had to do that, as much for me as for any of you. Sorry."

Maggie sank back into her seat and Bob put an arm around her shoulder.

"That was harsh, even for you," Nick said.

"I've said I'm sorry. Don't push it," Zelah growled. "But I had to find out. And if I'd asked your advice or your permission, you'd all have said no. Am I wrong?"

No one disagreed.

"Exactly. And now we know there's no problem for me with these rings. But, going back to what I said earlier, Bob talked about being cared for, because the rings were 'also precious'. What that told me was, if you're right Bob, I have nothing to fear from them. But, Maggie, you told me you felt you couldn't put them on, right?"

"Yes," said Maggie, calmer now. "It was like two magnets repulsing each other. But two things. One – just because the rings are OK for you, there is something not right about them and you don't know what you might just have set in motion. Two – you scared the shit out of me."

"I know, I know. Look, just because I'm better than I used to be doesn't mean that I've changed everything. It felt like a challenge. And if I have set something in motion, well, maybe it's something that needed to happen. But I am sorry, OK? Don't make me keep saying it."

"Apology grudgingly accepted," said Maggie, and she stood up. "Let's clear up here. We have a plan. And I have to go talk to Alice."

**

Three hundred miles away, a man stood in the middle of an open green field, pointing a shotgun towards the sky, and paused. A shiver ran down his back and turned into an ice-cold shudder that ran through his body. There was no cold wind blowing. It was the end of another glorious day. The cold was inside. It had reared up from a deep place that had remained undisturbed for seventy of his ninety years.

He turned to his companion, who was staring at him. "Are you all right there?"

"They've come back." He spoke without moving the gun. He flicked the safety catch off, shot twice, and watched a bird plummet from the sky. He put the safety back on as the dog raced off and brought the carcass back to his feet.

"They've come back," he snarled, and with the heel of his right boot smashed his foot into the dead bird over and over.

Chapter 16

Maggie's early morning call to Radio Cornwall was productive. At midday she was in a café close to the station in Truro, with the programme presenter, Melissa Wilkes.

"Phew, it's a warm one today," said Maggie, taking her coffee mug to a seat as close as possible to the large fan on the counter top.

"Best bit of weather we've had here all summer. Probably won't last," Melissa said. "Now, tell me about your case."

OK, no small talk, Maggie thought. "It's an interesting one. It involves a woman abandoned here as a child, aged around three. She had nothing to identify her, except a note asking whoever found her to look after her until the writer could return. And there was an old ring. But they never came back. Our client has a family involvement in the case, and now wants to find out what happened."

"Real human-interest story, too." Melissa had sat up as Maggie had spoken. Her journalistic nose was twitching. "Can you identify the client?"

"No, we've guaranteed her anonymity as far as possible, sorry. But I can tell you she was left in Sennen and that the person who found her was the local vicar, a man called Hopton. It was back in the fifties. And the ring is called a spoon ring." Maggie reached into her bag and brought out the box, opened it and put the ring on the table in front of Melissa.

"May I?" asked Melissa.

"You may. But don't try it on." Maggie and Zelah had agreed that she should show the ring but say little about it.

"Will I become invisible?" joked Melissa.

Maggie grinned. "You have no idea how many times we've heard that. No, you won't. But the note left with the child said not

57

to wear it, so we haven't tried."

Melissa held the ring up to the light. "It's lovely," she said looking closer, "What's this on the inside, on the flat end?"

"We think it's a family crest, but we don't understand what it might be, or whose. I'm planning to take it to a jeweller later to see if he can make anything of it."

"Let me know, will you? If there's any ID, we can add it to the story. So, when can you come in? I can offer you a five-minute slot tomorrow or Wednesday. I've already announced this morning you'll be featuring on my show in the next couple of days."

"Tomorrow would be good. What time?"

"Ten-thirty on air. We can have a warm-up, then I'll introduce you and ask you some questions."

"That's fine," Maggie replied. "But nothing about the identity of the client, OK? And could we ask for listeners who might have information to be put in touch with me?"

"Naturally," Melissa replied at once. "If we can agree that if you get more information, you'll share it with us? On air?"

"Yes, if I can, if our client agrees. No problem."

Melissa stood up. "Good. Must go, got an interview to record. See you tomorrow at ten-fifteen. Sign in at reception ten minutes before, they'll show you where to go."

After she had gone, Maggie put the ring back in the box, but not before looking at it again for a few minutes. She put it at the top of her ring finger, but, as always, felt a repulsion. *"What happened to you? What secret do you know?"* she whispered to it. She returned the unresponsive object to her bag, and left the café to find the local jeweller.

Chapter 17

There was still a half hour before her appointment. Maggie hadn't been to Truro for some time, not since before her children were born. She decided to wander in the sunshine, perhaps pick up a sandwich and find somewhere to sit outdoors to eat. She had forgotten that it was such a small city, its central streets mainly dating from Georgian times. Today the elegant buildings were sparkling in the sun. She found a small artisan deli, bought her lunch, and went outside to sit on a bench on the cobbled, traffic-free narrow street. As she ate, Maggie wondered how the others were getting on.

Nick had left just after eight, with Alice and a tearful Janine, whose gratitude was overwhelming. She had never been on holiday for two weeks in her whole life or even away from her family for more than a few days. Maggie thought she had thrived on it.

"You've had a successful time, too. So, live up to your reputation as a mega-cool surfer," Maggie had said as she levered Janine from a vice-like hug.

The girl nodded. "And you," Maggie turned to hug Alice and tweaked her nose, "do what Nick tells you. I'm trusting you."

"I won't let you down," Alice replied. They looked knowingly at each other, silently acknowledging that behind the words was a deadly serious threat. The last time Maggie had left Alice in Nick's care, the girl had allowed everyone to think Janine had run away, but in reality, had hidden her in the garden shed. Alice knew there were no second chances.

Bob had also left early for Penzance to visit the local police station. Maggie hadn't heard from him. She wasn't sure if that was good or bad.

It had surprised her that Zelah had stayed with Jack. The two of them got on well, with their mutual interest in sports cars, and

Zelah's expensive car in particular. But why would Zelah sacrifice a day of research?

Glancing at her watch, she saw it was almost two. She had to find the jeweller. When she looked up at the street sign, she saw that she was already on the correct street, and it wasn't far to walk before she found it.

The shop was tiny. They displayed few items in the window, but Maggie could see at once that this was no ordinary jeweller. This was a place to buy something special; commissioned items or rare pieces that would have to be searched for by an expert. A bell tinkled as she entered. A welcome rush of cool air immediately met her. Inside there was just enough room for two glass counters, at ninety degrees to each other, each with a glass-fronted display case. The items were exquisite, no two alike. There were rings, bracelets, necklaces, and watches.

A curtain swished at the back of the room. A tall, wiry, white-haired man brushed it aside and reached her in two steps. He held out his hand, took Maggie's, and gave it an earnest squeeze.

"Mrs Gilbert? I'm John Bottrell," he beamed at her. "Now, your story sounds interesting, doesn't it? I have been looking forward to meeting you since you called."

Maggie took her hand back and sat in the chair he indicated, next to the counter on which stood an old-fashioned manual till.

"Let's have a look, then." He cocked his head to one side, his eyes shining with anticipation.

"I hope I haven't led you astray into thinking this ring is something special. I'm not sure it is, you know," said Maggie. She produced the box from her bag. He took it from her, withdrew the ring, then picked up an antique magnifying glass from the counter and moved the ring towards it, then away, then back again. Then he reached down into a drawer and retrieved a jeweller's eyeglass - that looked like a tiny telescope - which he thrust into his eye socket where it seemed to sit comfortably. He brought the ring right up to the lens.

"Well, I never!"

Maggie sat up. "What?" she said.

He continued to examine the ring, ignoring her outburst. "Sixteen-ninety, when the spoon was made. It's solid silver. Just a small spoon." He took out the eyeglass and looked at her. "Did you know about the crest when you called me?"

"I knew there was one, but we couldn't make it out. Why?"

"It's the crest of the Vyse family. An ancient family that died out in the eighteen-hundreds. Interesting. Nothing left of them now."

"They must have been a well-known family, if you've heard of them down here."

He looked mystified, but then the penny dropped. "Ah, no. Not that well-known. The Vyse family is, or rather was, pure Cornish. From down south, Penwith peninsula. In fact, I think that's what they called the house, Penwith House, or Penwith Manor."

"Well, I never," Maggie said. "I didn't see that coming."

"If you want to sell this, you'll make a good profit, I can assure you. There's a market round here for such a traceable piece."

"I… we don't want to sell it, thank you Mr Bottrell. I'm doing this for a friend." Maggie held out her hand and took the ring back, put it back in its box and into her bag, and stood up. "She had no idea it was Cornish, or at least that its origins were Cornish. It's a family heirloom. I guess if the family was well-known I should be able to find out some information about them in the library, or the Records Office?"

"I'm sure you'll find something, yes indeed. Thank you for bringing the ring to me." He whirled round and disappeared behind the curtain.

Back out onto the street, a wall of heat hit Maggie. The temperature had risen to over thirty degrees as Nick had predicted. She stood in the shade of the awning that covered the front window of the shop, pondering what to do. It was already two thirty. There would be time for a quick visit to the library, but she wasn't sure if she wanted to rush into this, remembering the promise they had all made to Zelah to consult first. No, she should head back to Sennen and report her news. Besides, it would be cooler beside the sea. This inland heat was choking. She could do the initial research on the internet, then follow up with library and archive visits. Decision made. But, as she turned to head back towards the carpark, she felt something solid hit her from the side, knocking her off balance and she fell to her knees, dropping her bag. Shaking her head, she looked up to find a woman standing over her, scowling.

"You should mind where you're looking," she said, and strode off.

"I'm so sorry," Maggie replied, not able to focus and aware of a sharp pain in her right knee. Maggie couldn't see her bag and was panicking when another woman held out her hand to help.

Back on her feet, Maggie saw that this second woman had her bag. "Thank you so much," she gasped, taking it back and checking the contents, first her purse, then the ring box. Both were there.

"That was rude," the second woman said, watching the perpetrator of the accident striding away down the street. "I thought for a minute she was a bag snatcher. But I think she's just a disgruntled local. Amazing how some don't like tourists. Are you OK?"

"Yes, thanks," Maggie replied. "I turned around rather sharply, so I can't blame her for being cross. But it was like walking into a brick wall." They both giggled. "Still, no damage done."

The woman walked back to her family, who were watching from a nearby bench, and Maggie headed back to the carpark.

Chapter 18

An hour later she was back at Sennen, but no one else was there. Zelah's car was gone and there was no sign of Bob.

It was sweltering inside, so Maggie pulled back the folding conservatory doors. She went to the kitchen, poured herself a glass of cold rosé wine and took her laptop and glass back into the conservatory where there was now just enough breeze to be comfortable. Before she started her research, she walked out to the edge of the small garden. The sea was an extraordinary shade of blue. Somewhere below she heard happy surfers and swimmers, which was probably where Zelah and Jack had gone. Gulls wheeled and screamed above the cliffs to her right. To her left she saw the rocks that jutted out into the sea at the far end of the small harbour near the old redundant lifeboat station. She drew a deep breath in and out. This was contentment. But, work to do.

There was little on record about the Vyse family of Penwith. Of the Penwith peninsula itself, Maggie found more, discovering that it was not originally part of the Duchy of Cornwall, but belonged to the Arundell family, an ancient Cornish pedigree dating back to the Norman Conquest. She found a few references to the existence of a house called Penwith and the last known Vyse: Sir John Vyse. But the sources told Maggie little except his year of birth and death, and that he had married twice. However, when she looked at the National Archives Discovery site, it turned out that there were some documents relating to Penwith House at the Cornwall Archive at Truro. She should add that to her trip tomorrow. Sir John hadn't been born at the dating of the silver spoon, which meant it was his parents or grandparents who had commissioned it.

Glancing at her watch, it shocked Maggie to discover that it was almost six. Still no one had returned. A little anxiety crept in, until she heard the unmistakable sound of Zelah's sports car coming up the drive. But not its usual roar, it was jumpy and hesitant before spluttering to a halt. Thinking something had gone wrong with the car; she left the conservatory and went to the front door. She opened it to find Zelah and Jack sitting in the car laughing uproariously, with Jack in the driving seat.

Seeing Maggie, Zelah got out and put her hand up in a 'stop' gesture, walking towards Maggie. "Before you say anything, he didn't drive on any public roads, just around an empty car park then up the private road here."

They stopped in front of each other, eyeball to eyeball. "He isn't old enough to drive," Maggie said.

"He'll be seventeen in December," Zelah replied. "And I guess he'll have his provisional licence ready and waiting on his birthday. Look, he's had a lot of fun, and so have I. What's your problem?"

"I don't have one," Maggie replied and turned back to walk into the house. Zelah gestured to Jack to get out of the car.

"Is she angry?" he asked. "Don't see why she should be."

"I don't think so," Zelah said, linking arms with him as they entered the house. "But let's find out."

Maggie was back in front of her laptop, her back to the door. "It's OK," she said as they entered the room. "I know you want to drive, Jack." Jack glanced questioningly at Zelah who nodded him out of the room.

"He's gone," she said to Maggie's back. "Look, what's the matter? If you think I'm pushing myself too far into your parental geography, say so."

Maggie sat back in her chair, stretching her neck, and relaxing her head on the cushioned headrest. "I never wanted to teach him. But I think I never wanted him to drive, either. I'm over-protective, I know that. It was just the shock of seeing him behind the wheel of a car. I still think of him as a child. But he's not, is he?"

"He's at the turning point. Lots of childish things still, but desperate to grow up. Look, I've never had the responsibility, but I think… let go more, Maggie. He's got a nice girlfriend. And good friends at home. And remember what I told you about me. At seventeen I was selling myself on the streets of Cardiff."

Maggie caught the tension in Zelah's voice and spun the chair around to face her and found Zelah standing bolt upright, arms folded, and displaying her belligerent face.

"I don't want an argument—" Maggie began.

"Then think before you react."

"Look who's talking," Maggie murmured, turning back to her laptop. Then she relented. "OK, let's talk, shall we?" She shut the lid down, stood, and walked into the garden.

Zelah had to uncross her arms to hold on to the door to get out and tripped. Maggie caught her elbow, at which Zelah pulled away sharply. "I don't need help."

"We all need help. And understanding," Maggie replied as she sat in one of the garden loungers. "So, understand that I'm afraid. Not of anything tangible. Just the world and how it might attack my children."

Zelah flopped into the chair beside her. "He had a lot of fun," she repeated.

"So did you. Why did you do it without telling me?"

"We didn't plan it," Zelah bristled, "but Pip's with her parents today and he doesn't have Janine to surf with. He'd been on his computer all morning and I think he was bored. It was boiling, and he asked if we could go for a drive in my car with the hood down, so off we went. When we came across an abandoned industrial site over near Penzance, it came to me. Would he like a go? He jumped at it. And that's all there was to it. It was spontaneous. Are you saying I shouldn't have done it?"

"No, absolutely not saying that. It's just... oh I don't know!" Maggie was trying, but failing, to gain coherent thought on the subject, when the sound of another vehicle arriving at the front of the house interrupted. "Bob's back," she said, standing up and leaving Zelah to stew.

She only got as far as the door when Bob bounded through. "Got some very interesting information," he began, then looked at both of their faces. "What now?"

"Nothing," said Maggie quickly. "Zelah let Jack drive her car on an abandoned industrial site. Then back up the drive here."

"Is that a problem?" he asked. "It's legal, and I bet he loved it." He looked at Maggie again. "Let's go for a walk before dinner." Taking her by the elbow he led her to the gate that opened to the footpath down to the beach. As they reached it, he called back to Zelah, "Dinner in an hour," then turned and mouthed, '*I've got this.*'

Chapter 19

They returned an hour later to the smell of something delicious coming from the kitchen. The garden table was laid ready for dinner and strings of lantern tea lights hung around the umbrella shade over the table and garden fence. As Bob closed the gate, Zelah and Jack came out with steaming tureens and Zelah told them both to sit down. A bottle of white wine was chilling in a bucket at the side of the table.

"Good timing," Zelah called to them. "Sit, let's eat, and discuss your day." She paused. "If that's OK with both of you?"

"It still freaks me out when you ask first," Maggie replied, "but yes, that's fine. Really, fine. And Jack, if Zelah's willing to give you more driving lessons, that's OK with me."

She could tell by the huge grin that lit up Jack's face that he was both pleased and relieved. The conversation with Bob (at a fast pace up and down the steep hill during which she had had to listen because she wasn't fit enough to walk and speak at the same time), had allowed her to understand the dilemma she had caused her son. She wanted him to grow up but hadn't realised how much she wanted to have control over what he experienced. She had to let go.

"Anyway, I've been dying to tell you what I found out today, and Bob has too..." She glanced across at him as he spooned in a huge mouthful of chicken and pasta, "and it looks like I should go first."

Maggie recounted her visit to the jeweller. She went into the house, retrieved the ring from her bag and handed it back to Zelah, with a large magnifying glass. "If you look at the crest again, you can see it more clearly. Mr Bottrell recognised it at once. The family was called Vyse and yes, they were Cornish. The last one in the line appears to be Sir John Vyse who died in 1755 without issue. There's little about them on the internet. Minor nobility, probably a Baronetcy. The title dates to medieval times, but mainly, King James the First sold them to finance his Irish wars, in return for the promise to maintain and keep a number of soldiers that he could call to arms. He made the title hereditary, but it had no political influence. I haven't been able to find anything about what happened to their house, yet. But I'm hoping the library and archives will bring up something tomorrow."

They passed the ring and the magnifying glass around.

"So, what about you, Bob? You have any news?" Zelah asked.

"I do," he said, sitting back from his empty plate. "That was fantastic food. So, I went into the station in Penzance, introduced myself and said I was looking for any archive material from the early fifties. There's nothing on site; if there's anything left, it's at the London Criminal Records Office or at the Archives in Truro. But they pointed me at an old boy. Used to be the local bobby in these parts. Turns out he lives close to here. I went to visit him this afternoon, down on the Lizard at Cadgwith. Lovely place, that. He's still pretty spry although he's almost ninety. Puts it down to a daily diet of fresh fish and beer." He chuckled. "Name of Archibald King. Archie. Anyway, I asked him about Sennen in the mid-fifties. He was a newbie then, based in Sennen for about eighteen months, including through the summer of fifty-three. He covered his patch by bicycle. And, he remembered Zelah: a child found in the churchyard. It caused quite a stir at the time. He wanted to know why I was asking, so I kept to the story of Maze and a client and me helping out. Interesting thing, he didn't like vicar Hopton much. Thought he was sanctimonious and shallow. Apparently made a lot of offering to take the child in. But this old guy suspected that there was money involved. And he thought there might have been money left in the bag, with the rings. A lot of money."

He had been looking directly at Zelah as he spoke, and saw that her expression intensified in its concentration. "And there's more; do you want me to go on?"

"Of course I do," Zelah snapped. "Why would you not?"

"Because you said you wanted to decide about progress. Just

making sure you're OK." Maggie brushed her hand against his arm, with a slight warning squeeze, but Bob shook his head and folded his arms on the table.

"Well, there was trouble that summer, between locals and a group of Travellers. Not gypsies, before you get snotty with me. These were the precursors of the hippies and summer of love, that kind of stuff. Just drifters from what I gathered. They turned up in two clapped-out old caravans and some disused army vehicles. Lived in them. They went onto private land, just scrubland, belonging to a local farmer. They camped out, made camp fires, hung around. Archie just remembers them being a bit pathetic. This was long before the actual hippies and the psychedelic stuff. This lot were more into alcohol than drugs. Archie thought they were just lost; couldn't accept that everything should just go back to how it was before the Korean War and World War II, but had no other focus." He paused and took a gulp of beer.

"The locals didn't like them and tried to get them off. Tried burning one of their vehicles, threatened the women, nasty, petty stuff. After a few months, the group moved on. But their moving on coincided with the kid being left in the churchyard. By the time anyone thought to ask them, they'd gone. Local police chased them down and found them after a month in Dorset. Seems a few of the women had drifted off, with children in tow. No one knew exactly when or where to. So, it turned out to be a dead end."

"Could they identify anyone by name?" Maggie asked.

"No," Bob replied. "No identities, no stories. They accepted anyone who turned up. They picked up strays and dropped them off when they wanted to leave. All Archie could remember was that there were three women who dropped out some time over that month of moving from Cornwall to Dorset. He says the investigation files still exist, they'll be in London. Long shot, though."

"We can try the local archives tomorrow, can't we? There might have been something in the newspapers." Maggie asked. "What do you think, Zelah?"

She paused a moment, then said, "The vicar used to say

sometimes that the gypsies left me. I thought he was just talking figuratively. I didn't know about these Travellers, which explains why Tracy sometimes called me a filthy Gypsy. Back to your question. It's worth a shot. Anything else?"

"I didn't have time to look for reports of accidents and fatalities, not yet. Perhaps you could do that tomorrow when Maggie and I go to Truro?"

Zelah shrugged. Maggie leaned forward and spoke in a whisper to Zelah. "This is your show. We're in your hands."

"I never thought it would be like this. I've never been the emotional type. Great at telling everyone else how to think and act. But I haven't felt like this in a long time." She sat back in her chair and closed her eyes.

No one spoke. Maggie was trying to think of a suitable comment when Zelah sat up. "Did you say Cadgwith Cove?"

"If you mean where Archie is now, yes," Bob replied. "He lives in a small cottage down by the harbour."

"I want to speak to him. Do you think that'd be OK?"

Bob shrugged. "Can't think why not? He's frail, but his memory is excellent. I presume you want to talk about the vicar?"

"Yes," Zelah said, her expression grim. "I want to know what he remembers about the other kids, too. I want to find out if he was around when Jay disappeared."

"I broached the subject," Bob said. "I thought it would have been around the early to mid-sixties. But if you can give him some better details, you might stir something. You should explain that it's not about one of your clients, though. And please tell him I didn't lie deliberately."

Zelah nodded. "He's a copper, he'll understand. And look, just keep going with this, OK? I'll decide if I want to call a halt… and I don't. Yet."

Maggie nodded, but Bob seemed to want to say something, which Zelah didn't miss. "What? Spit it out, Inspector Clouseau."

"You're opening a can of worms, Zelah. Once it's open it won't close, no matter what you want. If you're going to stop, it has to be now. Because something tells me that after tomorrow it will be too late to pull back. In fact, it may already be too late."

"So, you're saying that I have to decide now to let go of any control I have, is that it?"

"Pretty much, yes." Again, he paused, and Maggie got a feeling that something ominous was about to happen.

"Look, I can't ignore what I've heard. I'm a detective. It's not clear, but that letter could be a confession. If that's what it was, and you've a strong suspicion that there was foul play, then I'm bound to report it. Can of worms, in many ways."

Chapter 20

Throughout the night Maggie woke at the sound of footsteps on the stairs, the sound of the kettle boiling in the kitchen, the conservatory doors opening. On one occasion she glanced out of the window and saw Zelah in the moonlight, sitting, then standing, then pacing around the garden. Sometimes she stopped for a few seconds, shook her head, sat, stood, and carried on walking up and down.

At four Maggie wondered if she should join her, but Bob, woken up by Maggie, said to leave it. "This is a massive decision for her. She's got to think it through, all of it. The implications are far-reaching."

"Perhaps she needs someone to listen, so she can talk it out. That doesn't mean a conversation."

"It's nearly dawn. If she's still there in an hour, go down. See if she wants you."

Reluctantly, Maggie climbed back into bed and hugged Bob. "I'm glad you're here. You've laid it out plainly for her."

At six Maggie got up. She had only dozed and now Bob was snoring gently out of the side of his mouth. She sensed that Zelah was still downstairs, and she found her in the kitchen.

"How many cups of tea does that make?" she asked as Zelah stirred the pot.

"Lost track. You want one?"

"Yes, please. I heard you pacing. How are the worms?"

Zelah grunted. "Out of the can, I think. Don't think I could put them back now even if I wanted to."

"But you don't want to?"

They had strolled into the garden towards the cliff edge. The sky was a pale grey, the sea a calm silver, the air still.

"It's why I never came back. I always knew I'd have to do it, if I ever came back. So, I kept away. But when I got that letter, and she admitted what she'd done, I knew that was it. I've tried to keep it contained. I thought I could control it. But it's like spilling water. You can't get it back in its container."

"Are you here for the history of the rings, or for Jay?"

"Can they be separated? I don't think so. They're different and unconnected stories, but I can't follow one without knowing the truth about both."

Maggie could see that Zelah was trembling. She put out her hand but Zelah shook her head. "Lack of sleep," she said. "That's all. I've decided. It all has to come out, whatever it is. It's just…" She stopped, biting her lip. When she spoke again it was harsh, angry almost. "I've been OK with who I am. I regret nothing I've done. I'm a hard woman and I thought I was supposed to be that way. It was my way of coping, and fair enough for how I grew up and what I went through. But now…" she turned to look at Maggie. "I may have been wrong, and I don't know if I can handle that."

Maggie wanted to say something consoling, but the profundity of Zelah's emotions would have made any comment seem superficial, patronising, even. Maggie knew how much Zelah hated being patronised. And, how much she hated to think she might be wrong.

"Hindsight," said Maggie, smiling at Zelah. "Bloody wonderful gift. If only we had it. You were lied to, deceived, and abused. They kept crucial personal things from you. Even if you'd suspected there was something, they would have denied it. Tracy Hopton only confessed to what she did to hurt you from beyond the grave when she knew you couldn't retaliate, and there were no consequences for her. She didn't care about your friend Jay or about justice for him. They were terrible people, Zelah. I've only known about this for a few days and I can see that. You made decisions based on what you knew and what you believed. It's all any of us can do. Now there's more information. That doesn't make what you thought or did wrong. But it gives you a chance to find out the truth. Don't judge yourself. That's the only wrong thing."

"Big speech."

"A Maggie Gilbert speciality."

"Let's find the truth then and damn the consequences." Zelah took Maggie's arm, and they headed back to the kitchen as the sun appeared over the eastern sky.

Chapter 21

Maggie, Bob, and Jack were ready to set off for Truro when Maggie's mobile rang. She could see that it was Nick but couldn't make out what he was saying. After shouting into the handset for a few seconds she yelled, "Whatever it is, send me a text."

She turned to Bob to signal that they should leave. "It sounds like he's on a train. Terrible connection. What's going on?" Then the text arrived, which she read aloud:

On the train to London. Going to British Museum and Museum of London. Try to find Roman ring expert. Cwmbran tonight, Sennen tomorrow. Will call later. Alice fine.

"I wonder why he didn't go to Caerleon?" Zelah muttered in the background.

"I guess we'll find out later. I'll try to call him at lunchtime. Come on, let's go."

Jack went with them to help with the research at the library and at the Records Office and because he wanted to watch Maggie do her piece at the radio station. Bob also declared an interest in watching her. They decided that Bob would begin the formal declaration of a potential crime with the police.

Zelah was feeling the effects of the night before and didn't mind staying behind to catch up on some sleep. She proposed a nap and then a further exploration of the Vyse family online, followed by anything she could find out in newspaper archives about fatal accidents at the time of her abandonment. The visit to Archie King could wait another day.

Chapter 22

Maggie's latest information about the spoon ring delighted Melissa Wilkes, and it thrilled her that the connection was local. She used all her wiles to get Maggie to name the client, but Maggie wasn't having any of it. She resisted leading questions and remained vague about age and description of any kind. She sensed Melissa's frustration, but soothed her with the promise that, if she put out an appeal for information, she would allow Melissa to follow up.

They left the studio just before midday, Melissa saw them to the door and promised again that she would call Maggie if any news came in.

"You're good, Mum," Jack said as they walked towards the city centre. "I thought she'd got you cornered a few times about Zelah, but you got out of it every time."

"Practice," Maggie said. "Let's hope now that someone hears it and we get some useful information."

They split up after lunch, Maggie went to the Records Office and Bob and Jack to the library.

"I'm not thinking there'll be a lot at the library," Bob said. "So, when we're done, I'll text you. If you've got more to do, we'll come to you."

Maggie called Nick. He and Alice were en route from the British Museum to the Museum of London.

"We're walking to the Tube," he said. "Eating ice cream as we go. It's thirty-five degrees here."

"What made you go to London?" Maggie asked.

"We went to Caerleon yesterday, but the expert was away for the day, so rather than just come back with nothing, we made a new plan. It's general information we're getting here. Lots of Roman rings and jewellery to look at. But not much about custom and practice and ritual. But I called the Museum of London yesterday and they said they would have someone there this afternoon who could look, see if there's anything special to tell us."

"Sounds good," said Maggie.

"We'll be back on the train tonight, then tomorrow morning we're going back to Caerleon. Might as well make the most of what time and expertise we've got. Then we'll head off back down to you tomorrow afternoon. Is that OK?"

"As long as Alice is enjoying herself, which I presume she is?"

"Very much so. Here, I'll hand her over to you."

There was a vague mumbling. "Sorry, Mum. Just had a big mouthful of ice cream."

"No problem. How are you getting on?"

"Brill. I love the British Museum. We went to take a quick look at the mummies, and the Rosetta Stone. Can we come back here sometime?"

"Certainly. We'll try to have a proper visit sometime this coming term. Shall I call you this evening? How's Janine?"

"She's OK, I suppose. Bit sad. Don't bother phoning tonight. See you tomorrow." And she ended the call.

"She's fine," said Maggie, then remembered there was no one else with her.

After checking in at the archives' reception, having already confirmed that her Reader's ticket was accepted here, they gave her a quick run-through on how to access documents. She set to work on a potential list of documents to view from the archive index, searching for the Vyse family.

She started with the Vyse family tree. Working from the little knowledge she had and, knowing that the family had died out long before the introduction of civil registration in 1837, Maggie searched for parishes in the Penwith area. She found three that might match the area: Sennen, St Just, and St Leven.

She came up trumps with Sennen. The records were excellent. The first Sir John Vyse she could find was baptised in the parish in May 1680, the son of Sir Edward Vyse and Maria Teague. This John was the fourth child of the marriage and had three older brothers, Charles, Richard and Edward, and a younger sister, Isabella, born in 1682. It struck Maggie that this was a small number of children for the time. Families often numbered above eight children, sometimes as many as twelve or even more. Perhaps the mother had died at the birth of Isabella. She made a note to look for the death of a Maria Vyse in 1682 if she had time. If the family had adopted the standard naming conventions, then John would have been named after his maternal grandfather. The first three boys would be named after their father's father, then mother's father, then, father. Again, something to check out later. For now, she assumed adherence to the naming convention, which told her that going further back there should be a Sir Charles Vyse, possibly the purchaser of the Baronetcy title, but no time today. She could also check out Maria Teague's birth to find out if her mother's name was Isabella. As usual, the lines of research spread like an octopus' tentacles.

She suspected the first three Vyse children, born in 1675, 1676 and 1678, would have had to have died young, for John to inherit the title. A quick check found the records revealed their fate. Each baby had barely survived birth, dying between three and nine months. Although this was not unusual, it was still sad. Maggie had never believed that people then grieved any less for their children than now, despite the high infant mortality rate.

Next, she needed to find out what she could about Sir John. Given he was born in 1680 she looked for a marriage somewhere around 1700. She found he'd married Johanna Arundell in 1701. This was interesting, her quick reading up on local history the previous evening having revealed that in the 1700s the Arundell family were one of the most influential families in Cornwall, owning much of the land on the Penwith peninsula. In marrying into this family, John Vyse must have been, or then become, an influential man himself.

On to the son John – the last in the line. Again, parish records were excellent. He was one of six children born to John Vyse and Johanna Arundell. Edward, the eldest, died in infancy, and was most likely named after John's father. The next boy born was the final John Vyse.

Of the six children, three – Edward, Maria, and Roger – died shortly after birth. Simeon died in his teens. Apart from John, the only survivor was Johanna, born in 1708. Maggie couldn't find a record of her death, so she might have moved away.

The burial records told her that the elder John died in 1715, of a 'swelling of the brain' and that his son inherited the title at the age of ten. But Lady Johanna Vyse, née Arundell, survived into old age. Maggie thought about her bringing up her two surviving children, nurturing young John into his inheritance. Lady Johanna eventually succumbed to influenza in 1735 at the ripe old age of sixty-three. Ripe for those times, anyway.

Finally, she found the marriage records of this last John. He married Emma Trelawney in 1737. He was thirty-two years old. Emma was twenty, which seemed an unusually late marriage and significant age gap; until she saw that he was recorded as a widower. It took further digging to find his first marriage, to Mildred Denys of Exeter, Devon.

She had two choices: to look for children of either marriage to discover clues why the line died out; or to look at the death of Mildred Vyse née Denys. She decided on the former. She found that there had been no children of the marriage to Mildred, but that with Emma Sir John had had four children, none of whom survived childhood, and the birth of the final child, Johanna, caused Emma's death at the age of twenty-six in 1743. Sir John died in 1755, three years after the death of his second son, also named John, at age twelve (they had also called the first son, born in 1738, John but he had died within three days). Maggie thought the death first of his daughter Johanna, then his only remaining child John three years later must have been terrible blows for the poor man. He had been left entirely alone. His death was from a fall from a horse. It finished the direct line of the Vyse family.

She checked her watch. It was already an hour and a half since she had started, and she only had a family tree. But she had the final generations of the direct line of Vyse, from the as-yet unresearched Sir Charles Vyse who would have been born around 1600, to the teenage John Vyse who had died of smallpox aged twelve.

From the dates, she now knew that the spoon would have been the property of, and its making commissioned by Lady Johanna Arundell Vyse, and passed on at her death to John and Mildred, then to Emma. But with no further descendants where would it have gone next? And still no clue about why it had been turned into a ring, or who by.

A glance at her phone told her that there were no messages from Bob and Jack. They must still be at the library. She took a breather before continuing, and to see if she could find a connection to Penwith House.

Outside, the heat was still suffocating. Maggie spent five minutes before hurrying back indoors to the research room, where she could breathe in without fearing that her nostrils and throat were catching fire.

Next task: to find out if there was anything odd about the death of Sir John Vyse. He had fallen from his horse, but was that just an unfortunate accident? It was just a chance, but if he was alone when he fell, there might have been a coroner's inquest. Given that the Cornish records were so good…

She went back to her computer terminal and searched for records. An hour later Maggie sat back, stretched her back and, with a grin of satisfaction, packed up her bag and went back out into the sunshine. A text arrived from Jack as she was getting into her car.

How u getting on?
Great. How about you?
Excellent. on our way over. wait there.

Five minutes later they pulled into the carpark of the Old County Hall. Jack leaned out of the back window and said, "Jump in - lots to share!" Maggie dutifully got in the front seat.

"We've found stuff about Penwith House. Lots of stuff. The library sent us to the Family History Society, and they had good stuff there." Maggie turned her head back and saw that his eyes were sparkling.

"What?" she asked.

Jack looked to Bob who nodded. "It was less than a mile from where we're staying. We could probably walk to the spot. Can we go tomorrow?"

Maggie looked across at Bob. "Do we have an exact location?"

"Close enough," he replied. "But it is completely gone. Destroyed by fire about two hundred years ago. And it was derelict when it burned."

"We have a lot to talk about. You've got the building. I've got the people," Maggie said. "Lots to share."

"It'll have to wait until I get back," Bob said. "I'm off to Penzance Police Station. I called up earlier, told them I was coming in. I'm meeting someone there."

Jack and Maggie took the cue to get out of the car.

"Jack and I will go back, but yes, we'll wait for you. Jack, calm down." Jack had been opening his mouth to protest but closed it again. "OK, but this is so cool."

"He's got the Maze bug," Maggie winked at Bob as he drove off.

Chapter 23

Maggie and Jack arrived back at Sennen at five, to find Zelah underneath a sunshade, on a lounger, fluttering breaths coming out of her mouth, with intermittent snores.

"We're back!" Maggie shouted from the house, causing Zelah's head to shoot up and poke around for the source of the voice.

"Oh, it's you." She got up, stretched, picked up her shoes and walked barefoot across the grass and into the conservatory. "Just a quick nap," she grunted. "Find anything interesting?"

"Indeed, we did," Maggie replied. "But we're going to wait for Bob. He's at the police station in Penzance."

Zelah gave a curt nod at this news. "What about Nick? Heard from him?"

"He and Alice are visiting museums in London today. Tomorrow morning they're going to Caerleon. Then they'll drive back."

**

Two hours later, as they sat in the shade to avoid the scorching hot late sun, they heard Bob's camper van pulling up. He walked round the house, armed with a plastic bag full of fish and chips.

"I know it's more nasty fast food," he said, addressing the comment to all of them, but looking at Maggie. "But there's a lot to do, so I thought we'd not waste time in the kitchen." He dropped the bag on the table and went into the kitchen to get crockery and cutlery.

Once they were all seated and dishing out the food, he said, "OK. Where do we start?"

"With something interesting," Zelah cut in first. "Historical."

"Let's start with Penwith House," Jack said. "Can I go first?" He looked at Bob, who nodded.

"Well, as you know, it burned down two hundred years ago."

"Actually, I didn't know," Zelah interjected.

Jack looked nonplussed, fork in mid-air.

"When you do this reporting, it's best to assume that the people for whom you're doing it know absolutely nothing, zilch, nada," Maggie explained. "Try to organise your thoughts from the beginning. Think about the story."

"Oh, right." He scowled, speared, and ate a few chips, then tried again. "I think the story begins in the fourteen-hundreds. The books and accounts we found said it probably started as a working farm and land. As the Vyse family got richer, they rebuilt bits, mostly in Tudor times. It ended up as a Tudor E-shaped house. Is that right?" Again, directed at Bob, who nodded encouragement.

"Whereabouts was it?" Zelah asked.

"That's the good bit," Jack said, half standing. "See over there?" He waved his fork towards the end of the bay looking north. They turned their heads. "There was a hamlet called Penwith, close to the sea, and the house was about half a mile inland. If it had still been there, we might even have been able to see it from here. How good is that?"

His enthusiasm made Maggie smile. "Go on with your story."

Jack sat down again. "They built it of grey stone, and it had tall chimneys. We'd have definitely been able to see them. Anyway, they modelled it on a house called Trerice, near Newquay, up the coast. That's still there. And I was wondering, could we go to see it, too, and the site where Penwith was? We could walk up there tomorrow."

"Don't see why not," Maggie said. "And we can fit in a visit to Trerice in the next few days. Everyone up for that?" Bob and Zelah said 'yes' together.

"I know Trerice," Maggie said. "It's beautiful, and very old. And it belonged to a branch of the Arundell family, which fits in with my story. Anything else we need to know, Jack?"

"Yeah, the last Vyse to live there was Sir John Vyse and after he died it fell into a ruin. No one lived in it for about seventy years. Then, it burned down. Completely gone. The end." He smiled contentedly and dived back into his fish and chips.

"Anything else?" Zelah asked Bob.

"Yes," he replied. "There was a well on the site and when it was excavated about a hundred years ago, they found a skeleton in it. Broken neck and two broken legs. And evidence of a disability, a club foot. Examination by a forensic anthropologist confirmed that it was a male, of middle age, probably around thirty-five."

"Accident?" Maggie asked.

"Hmm. Could have been. He fell in and died instantly. But, if the house was inhabited, he should have been missed, and the well checked. If he wasn't missed, someone may have pushed him in and told a cover story. So, murder."

"Your profession does lead you to some gruesome conclusions," Zelah said.

"Certainly does," Bob replied. "Don't suppose we'll ever know. The last thing: Sir John Vyse closed one of the main bedrooms in the north wing. It remained sealed. He thought it was haunted by the ghost of his dead first wife, come to get him."

"And I think I know why he might have thought that," Maggie said.

"Don't tell me: he killed her?" Bob smirked.

"Very possibly," Maggie replied.

"Your turn, I think," Zelah said to Maggie. "Remember your own advice. Assume we know nothing."

Maggie put down her cutlery, sat forward and rested a hand on her chin. "My story doesn't go back as far as yours. I found seven generations of the Vyse family, back to Sir Charles Vyse, born around 1600. I'm guessing that from the date of his first son's birth. The son who inherited was another Charles, born about 1625 – I've had to make a guess at that one too. Followed by Edward, born in 1654 – I saw his baptismal record. This was the time of the Commonwealth under Cromwell. So, I'm conjecturing that the family declared for Cromwell, because they got to keep their house and lands.

"I don't know exactly when Edward died, but he married a woman named Maria Teague, and his son John, who was born in 1680, followed him. John was the fourth son. The first three, Charles, Richard, and Edward, all died as babies. So, John Vyse inherited the title and the house, and it was before his marriage. When he married Johanna Arundell in 1701, he was already 'Sir John Vyse'. This marriage was significant. The Arundells were the most powerful landowning family in Cornwall at that time. They owned most of this area, which was in the 'Penwith Hundred'".

"What's that?" Jack asked.

"No interruptions," Zelah growled.

"No, it's OK. It's important to understand the context." Maggie turned to Jack. "A 'Hundred' is an ancient name for what we now call a District. It's an administrative area for governing. They divided English shires into Hundreds. The crucial thing here is that throughout the whole of Cornwall, the Duchy of Cornwall owned all the Hundreds, except Penwith. It gave the Arundells significant wealth. They could try certain court cases themselves, they received rents from Manors, profits from gold and silver mines, and wrecks. They even kept their own debtors' jail. Lots more. Hugely wealthy and influential. So, joining the Arundell family was significant."

"It took the Vyse family up in the world?" Jack asked.

"Very much so," Maggie replied. "Johanna Arundell would have brought a dowry with her to the marriage that would have included property and money. But history repeated itself. The first son, another Edward, died at birth. Then came Louis, died in infancy, then John, followed by Maria, Johanna, Simeon, and Roger.

"As far as I can tell, this Sir John was a good man, but not a particularly good land manager or administrator. He spent a lot of money improving Penwith Manor. It would have been unrecognisable from the farmhouse it started out as. If he based it on Trerice, it was an impressive property. It would have been a stately home if it had survived today. But, crucially, he sold Johanna's properties to raise the money for the building and soon only Penwith Manor remained. But it had enough land attached to bring in rents and get income from farming. Lady Johanna Vyse seems to have been nice. I found a testimonial that described her as 'a good and kindly woman, much given to charitable acts.'

Anyway, her husband Sir John died young, in 1715, when his now-eldest son John was just ten years old. He inherited, but his mother held the purse strings.

"He didn't marry until he was thirty, when he married an heiress. A woman called Mildred Denys, from Devon. But she died a year later and there were no children. He married again another two years later, this time to a woman called Emma Trelawney. She wasn't an heiress, so perhaps it was a love match. Unusual, but it did happen. They had four children. John, who died in early childhood, then another John, who also died young, then Emma, then Johanna. Emma died giving birth to the second daughter Johanna. And neither girl survived beyond their teens. So, no descendants and the end of that branch of the House of Vyse. The property went to the descendants of another Johanna Vyse, who was the second daughter of Sir John and Johanna Arundell. She had married a Charles Williams of Somerset. I have found out little about how it was passed down, but I found a will of a Frederick Williams, in 1810. It confirms that the house was gone, but the land was still in ownership."

"Do you have a chart?" Zelah asked, "Even for me that's a lot to take in. There's a lot of Vyse's called John."

"I've drawn it out in rough, here." She passed a piece of paper across the table. "Anyway, that's the history of the Vyse family as far as I got." She paused for a few seconds, to draw breath and to prepare for her big announcement.

"Now, the good bit. The Sir John on whom we're focussing, died by falling off his horse not long after the death of the last of his children. Not that that's good, but you know what I mean. I don't know if there was anything suspicious about that. There doesn't seem to have been an inquest, just a coroner's report. But what was suspicious was the death of his first wife, Mildred. How do I know this? From one line in a report from the coroner's private summary to Lord Arundell, written after his decision of 'the suspicious and unresolved death of Mildred Vyse'. Regarding Sir John Vyse, it says: 'his reputation being tarnished after the unresolved and unspeakable death of his first wife, Lady Mildred Denys'. That tells me there's a big story there. We need to check how the house burned down. May not be related, but it's a loose end."

"Anything on proceedings from inquests?" Zelah asked. "Mildred Denys' death sounds significant, more so than her husband's. She's the wife who would have inherited the spoon from Johanna Arundell. Is there anything at the archives? If it was a suspicious death, there must have been an inquest with a jury."

"I didn't have time to look yet," Maggie replied. "It needs another visit."

"Agreed. I'll come with you." She turned to Bob. "Your turn."

"Not so exciting. I've spoken to a detective in Penzance. He's not thrilled about an old cold case, but he knows he has to follow it up. He'll come to speak to you, Zelah. I said I'd call him in the morning but give it a day or two so he can do some preliminary investigations into anything from the time Jay disappeared. You and I should talk tonight. As much detail as you can remember, and I'll pass it on in the morning." Zelah nodded, then fell silent.

"Right," Maggie said, jumping to her feet. "I'm going to clear this," she swept her arm at the dishes on the table, "then we'd better talk about a plan for the next few days. Things are building up. And, this is week three of four." She grabbed an armful of plates and Jack jumped up to help her. "We'll be home by the end of next week."

"A lot to get in," Bob said. "I have to go back on Sunday. Zelah, how about meeting the detective here on Friday? ...Zelah?"

"Sorry, miles away. Friday?" she said.

"Yes. What time?"

"First thing. About nine. That will give us more time to plan around the rest of the day."

"It's gone quickly, hasn't it?" Jack said as he and Maggie walked back to the kitchen.

"This is what it's like when you do what you love," she replied. "Time moves in mysterious ways."

Chapter 24

They had made their plan. Maggie had insisted on including holiday leisure time, which no one else agreed with. Zelah insisted that they cram in as much research as possible, which both Jack and Bob agreed with. But Maggie persisted.

"We have to consider Nick and Alice. Nick's the one who reminded us about holidaying, before he left. He's deliberately ignored his 'big project' while we've been here. And Alice isn't as enthusiastic about Maze as we all are. She needs to enjoy her time here, too. And that means visiting prehistoric sites."

Jack groaned. "We can't make everything work around her, just because she wants her own way all the time."

"No, but we can fit in what she wants to do and where she wants to go, and it'll be interesting for us, too. We can still spend time on the beach. I'm assuming you haven't gone off surfing?"

"I haven't," he agreed. "But it's better when you have company. Pip's going home on Friday."

"I know. And we've decided that after Zelah has talked to the police on Friday, we all go up to Trerice, which Alice can come along to, then we all head over to Bodmin Moor to hike up to the Cheesewring. Which we might all enjoy, too."

In a nod to the holiday spirit they agreed on a 'no computer day'.

Zelah was going to Cadgwith Cove to meet up with Archie King. "I have my memories, but between us we might jog something else," she said over breakfast. "And it's a beautiful place. I might stay for lunch. I think there's a good pub restaurant close by."

"How about we all join you there, then?" Maggie asked. "Jack and Pip are going to the beach this morning, to get some surfing in. Bob and I will put our feet up here in the garden and read, with shade and cold drinks. I think Jack and Pip are agreeing on tactics for getting their GCSE results tomorrow morning. Who goes first, who calls who, et cetera."

"I'd forgotten about that," Zelah said. "How is he?"

"Remarkably calm. Which means in denial. Nothing to do, now. Just wait for the morning. But I think it would be good to keep his mind off it as much as possible." She paused for a moment. "How about, if we bring swimming and snorkelling gear, we head over to Kynance Cove after lunch? I remember it being a cracking place, easy to swim and azure-coloured water at the foot of high cliffs. But that was a long time ago."

"OK with me," Zelah replied. "Apart from swimming. It may be beautifully blue, but it's unbeautifully bloody cold. I'll swim when I'm in the Med, should we ever get there."

"I'll put a tenner on you getting into the water," said Maggie.

"Done," replied Zelah, grinning wolfishly and putting out her hand to seal the bet.

Chapter 25

The beach at Kynance turned out to be just as Maggie remembered. What she had forgotten was the long walk down steep steps to get there. But it was worth the struggle. White sand, Caribbean-clear, light blue sea, and gentle waves. The tide was coming in by the time they got there from the pub.

Bob and Jack had carried down beach umbrellas and bags, Jack complaining not only as he slipped down, but with the anticipation of taking it all back up again. But even he had to agree that it was an exquisite seashore.

Maggie noticed that Zelah had been quiet throughout lunch and wasn't talking much now, just replying vaguely to comments about where they were and how good it was. Maggie guessed that Zelah's discussion with Archie King had given her a great deal to think about and instinct told her not to push. During lunch, a text came from Nick, telling them he and Alice had had an extraordinary visit to the museum in Caerleon and that they had some significant information to share when they were all together later. That would also give time for Zelah to process her thoughts and decide what she wanted to share.

Bob, Maggie, and Jack rushed into the sea as soon as everyone was set up on the beach. Jack and Bob, both keen snorkellers, headed out for the offshore rock that divided the two halves of the cove, but Maggie just swam up and down, revelling in the warm currents of water. She was a strong swimmer and, after two lengths up and down the beach, she glanced up and saw Zelah, standing thigh-deep, pouting at her. She swam up.

"Easiest ten quid I've ever won," Maggie said, flicking wet hair out of her eyes. "Sure you won't come in any further? Make it twenty?"

"This will do nicely," Zelah replied. "I'm thinking. It was too hot under the umbrella. I can think in here. You keep swimming,

I'm fine." She turned and waded up and down, splashing water over her back.

Maggie went to say something, but again, sensitivity told her to leave it alone.

Another couple of hours and they'd finished, packed up, and were heading back to Sennen, tanned, tired and contented.

Nick had said he and Alice would be back at around seven. As his car pulled up, Maggie, Bob, Zelah and Jack were in the garden, sipping cocktails. Alice was first to appear, rushing through into the garden and jumping onto Maggie's lap.

"Hey Mum, you'll never guess what we've found out!"

"OMG, you're heavy. Lovely to have you back." She kissed the top of Alice's head. "No, I won't be able to guess. We need a big catch up, all of us. Dinner's ready, so let's get ourselves settled and we can all share our news. Although, I think yours will have to come first."

Nick appeared, having dumped bags in the hall. Maggie poured and handed him a cocktail.

"Perfect, thanks. Has she spilled the beans yet? She hasn't been able to contain herself, the closer we got."

"Not yet," Maggie replied. "We'll start now. Sit yourselves down."

Alice talked almost at once. "In Caerleon we met John, the curator, and he told us…"

"Hold on," Maggie interrupted. "Tell us what happened in London, first".

"I'll do that," Nick said. "Alice, you eat, and I'll talk about the museums. Then I can eat, and you can do the interesting bit." Alice nodded.

Nick put his elbows on the table and linked his hands together under his chin.

"We went to the British Museum, as you know," he began. "It was a good introduction to Roman jewellery. We mainly spent our time in the 'Romans in Britain' room. An excellent display of artefacts and lots of hordes, including jewellery. We found one just like yours, Zelah."

"Then we went to the Museum of London. Superb displays again, but more about how places would have looked. And, there was a lot of information about life and customs. That's where we met an expert who told us about marriage customs. We showed him the ring. It impressed him. He thought it was Welsh gold. And high status. He said the bride could have been any age from about twelve, but more likely to be fourteen to sixteen.

"That's the point we reached at the end of Tuesday. This morning we were at the museum in Caerleon at ten when it opened. We met the curator and showed him the ring. Alice will now take over the story," he said, flourishing his arm in her direction.

Alice banged her fork down on her plate and sat up, taking up the same pose as Nick. "This is the interesting part." For a moment she paused and turned to Nick who, realising what she wanted, took the ring box out of his pocket, opened it, and put it at the centre of the table. "This ring," said Alice as if lecturing a group of admirers, "was probably made in Britain around AD 100. It could be made of Welsh gold and be rare. A high-status family or individual probably commissioned it – that's posh people who could afford it."

Jack laughed but Maggie scowled at him and smiled and nodded at Alice. "So far so good. Keep going."

"They make the carving out of ivory, not bone, which was more usual. There have been such finds, often in bathhouses where items were dropped, sometimes in other places. The filigree is incredibly special. Probably made by a master craftsman, somewhere in Britain." Her eyes shone, and Maggie guessed that she had been rehearsing this and was building up to an announcement.

"Caerleon has a bathhouse that was discovered and excavated in the nineteen eighties. Lots of bits and pieces found there." She paused again and looked slowly round them all. "But someone found this ring before that."

Zelah noticed what Alice was about to say and interrupted at once. "And where was it found, Alice?"

Alice beamed. "It was found in Caerleon during an archaeological dig in 1908. They catalogued it, but then it disappeared, believed stolen by a member of the archaeological team, or by a visitor to the site, or by one of the diggers hired by the chief archaeologist."

She sat back, smirking, pleased with herself. They all started to ask questions.

"How do you know this?" asked Maggie.

"Are you sure?" asked Bob.

"What's the evidence?" asked Zelah. Alice turned to her. "Nick can explain better."

"There was a dig in 1908," Nick began. "There were always a lot at Caerleon. This was a smallish one, about domestic life rather than military, focussed on the area close to the church. Underneath it was the villa of the Roman Commander of the area. Nothing much of the villa remains, but there is a footprint. The 1908 dig concentrated on a corner of the graveyard. Ironic, as it turns out, and fitting."

He had stopped to gaze into the distance at a memory. Zelah called him back. "Get on with it, will you please!"

"Sorry," his head snapped back to his audience. "This was an extension to the churchyard, so there were no previous graves there. That allowed them to get down about five feet – the depth of the Roman buildings' foundations. At the base they found several hexagonal beads, made of emerald. Quite expensive. Probably part of a bracelet or a necklace. The beads were below the floor level of the Roman villa. It intrigued them, so they dug further down. They found a skeleton. It was a girl in her early teens, from the skeleton's development. She was curled up and clutching her hands into her chest. When they moved her hands, they found another bead and – the ring."

"How did he know it was this one? There have been thousands of finds around Britain." Zelah again, sceptical.

"It was a well-documented find, because it wasn't alone. There was also some evidence of scraps of material. And something they thought might once have been a doll. But we know that few

Roman children had playthings. That was more significant than the ring. Few wooden objects have survived from Roman times. It was a national sensation, Roman archaeology being in vogue and exciting much Edwardian interest."

"I still don't understand," Zelah said. "It was obviously a significant find. But it goes nowhere towards explaining how – if this is the same ring – it ended up with me."

"The finds aren't in a museum anywhere," Nick replied, "because they were never recovered. The leader of the dig, an eminent Victorian archaeologist name of Sir Hugh McCarthy Miller, was outraged and humiliated. He had handpicked his team and couldn't believe that one of them might have stolen something so special. He called in the police and detectives, such as the service was, and had them all investigated. They found nothing. He retired, couldn't bear the shame. There was a huge fuss about the theft in the newspapers. It's well recorded. But, none of the finds ever reappeared."

There was silence around the table. Maggie spoke first. "Is the curator certain?"

"Yes," Nick replied. "A photograph was taken of the finds at the time and the museum has a copy, he showed me. It's the same ring. Here, see for yourselves." He bent down to his satchel and took out a piece of paper he passed to Maggie. She studied it, comparing it to the ring, and passed it on. It showed the ring in detail, with the other finds.

"Well, it looks identical," she said as she passed it to Jack, who glanced, nodded, and passed the picture to Bob. He glanced, moved his face closer to the paper, looked up, puzzled, then looked back again. Then he turned to Zelah and passed the photograph to her but didn't look away from her. After a few seconds he said, "Anything occur to you, Zelah?"

She too had been studying the photograph intensely. Without a word she stood up and walked into the house. Bob looked speculatively at Maggie, who shrugged her shoulders.

Within minutes Zelah was back, with a small plastic wallet, which she handed to Bob. "I think this is what you mean," she said.

Bob held it up and now the others could see that it contained a piece of wood, some worn, colourless material, and two steel pins.

"Zelah mentioned that these seemingly unrelated pieces were with the rings. And her note read *please keep my bag and its contents safe*. She said there were a few odd bits of…" he turned to Zelah, "…old junk, I think you called them, in there and I wondered when you said it, if they might have significance. Look now and tell me what you think."

Zelah took the bag back and held it up to the fading light. "But they aren't Roman," she said.

"No, I agree, if they were Roman and put in a paper bag it would have disintegrated almost immediately," Bob replied. "But the owner of the bag thought whatever they were, were precious. And it was the pins that gave it away, for me."

"Are you going to explain?" Maggie demanded.

He arched his eyebrows at her. "I've seen something like this before. And I think it links to the missing Roman finds." He took the bag back. "These are the remains of a poppet."

Maggie's hand flew up to her mouth.

"A poppet?" asked Jack. "I thought that was a name Northerners used, like 'sweetie' or 'darling'?"

"It is," Zelah replied. "But it has another meaning. A poppet was a small doll or a figurine, representing a human being. That explains the pins."

Maggie took her hand away from her mouth. "Witchcraft. No wonder no one was supposed to put on those rings."

Chapter 26

"I see. Thank you… Yes, as we agreed, you will be paid. I will see to it at once. Goodbye." The man seated at the head of the long dining table clicked his phone off and looked up. His companions paused, waiting for him to speak.

He waved his hand airily at no one in particular. "That was an employee at the museum in Caerleon. A man called Howell has been to see the curator there, with the Roman ring." He turned his gaze to hone-in on one diner. "You were right. Bribery works." He was rewarded with a beaming, sycophantic smile. He nodded graciously.

"That now confirms Maze Investigations has two of our rings. They must have the third, and the remaining items. I want them back. I want it all back. However you achieve it." He nodded again to the smiling diner, who nodded emphatically in return.

They all sat still, waiting. The man resumed eating his meal, then paused and looked up and waved imperially again. "Carry on, all of you." As quietly as possible, wincing at every slight scrape of metal on china, they picked up their cutlery and ate.

Chapter 27

It was only after they had all gone to bed and Maggie was dozing, comfortably half awake, that she realised that she hadn't asked Zelah about her conversation with Archie King. She poked Bob in the ribs. "I forgot to speak to Zelah about Archie and what they remembered between them,"

"Yes, I know," he grunted, "but if Zelah wanted to speak about it, nothing would have stopped her. She'll get to it in her own time. Can I go back to sleep now?"

Maggie turned over and left him to it, but she didn't sleep. The conversation about poppets, and the Roman ring found in Caerleon and what it all meant, and how this was turning into a major research project, had taken up the whole of the evening. And now, after she finally nodded off, it infected Maggie's dreams.

An aggressive squawking outside the window woke her. Glancing at the clock on the bedside table she saw it was eight-fifteen. There was no sound of movement from anywhere else in the house. She was wide awake, so she got up, put on a dressing gown, and tiptoed down to the kitchen where she found Jack, sitting at the breakfast bar, mobile in hand and a gloomy expression on his face. For a moment, her heart sank. Then she remembered that the results would be available from eight-thirty.

"How long have you been here?" she asked as she walked past him and switched on the kettle.

"Dunno, about an hour." He paused for a few seconds, in which his expression turned from gloomy to anxious. "What if I've failed them all?"

"Not going to happen," replied Maggie. She walked over to him and put an arm around his shoulders. "Whatever the outcome, as long as you tried your best…"

"I did," he whispered, putting his hand up to squeeze her arm.

"I didn't for a long time. But at the end I did. But maybe it wasn't enough."

"Call them, now. Find out. You can't deal with whatever comes next until you know what you've achieved."

He nodded and pulled out of her embrace. Maggie could see his fingers shaking as they stabbed out the school number on the keypad. She could hear the phone at the other end ringing. Then a recorded voice answered, giving instructions. Jack pressed '3' for exam results. Then he stopped breathing. Maggie thought of something urgent and ran into the office, ignoring Jack's look of panic at her desertion.

As she got back Jack was giving his name and student number. The voice at the end of the phone asked him if he had a paper and pen ready. His look of horror turned to a smile of gratitude as Maggie handed him a pad and a pen. 'Thanks, Mum,' he mouthed.

"Yes, I'm ready," he said steadily into the phone. Then he wrote. Twice his eyes widened in amazement and his mouth formed a 'wow'. Maggie tried hard not to read upside down. Eventually he said, "Thank you very much," and ended the call. He turned to Maggie, with a blank expression.

For a few seconds he said nothing; then, in a great rush: "Two As, four Bs and four Cs!"

It was Maggie's turn to form a 'wow', followed by, "That's fantastic, well done, so proud of you," and she rushed to enfold him in a crushing hug.

"You're crushing me, Mum! Let go, I can't breathe."

Maggie stepped back, then said, "OK, details?"

"I got As in History and English Language. Can't believe it. Bs are Maths, Biology, Geography and Religious Studies. And the Cs are Physics, Chemistry, Art and English Lit."

"I'm almost speechless," Maggie said. "But not quite. I am so proud of you, Jack. You pulled it off. These are impressive results."

She was about to go on when Zelah walked into the kitchen and glared at them both. "Couldn't wait any longer. Heard you talking. Well?"

Jack repeated the results, and again ten minutes later to Bob, Nick, and Alice, all of whom congratulated him.

"Great stuff, bro," Alice said, giving him a rare hug. "Knew you could do it. You're a lazy git but you did it when it mattered."

"And coming from her, that's real praise," he said to Maggie, the smile of joy and relief on his face still stretching from ear to ear.

"Anyone for breakfast?" Zelah moved towards the doorway with pots of tea and coffee and some freshly baked croissants she had been preparing as the others chatted. "Might as well soak up as much of this sunshine as we can. And bask in the reflected triumph coming off Jack."

The sun was up. Everyone tucked in, Jack most of all.

"So, what comes next? A-levels?" asked Bob.

Jack paused mid-bite. "Dunno. 'spect so." He stopped, then sat up and turned to Maggie. "Actually, I've got an idea about what I want to do. I've been thinking about it for a while."

"What's that?" she asked, secretly hoping that he wouldn't say he wanted to join the police force.

"I wouldn't mind becoming a professional genealogist."

The mouthful of tea that Maggie had just put into her mouth came spurting out again. After apologising and mopping up the remains, she said, "What the f—?"

"I didn't expect you to be so shocked," said Jack, astonished by her reaction.

"Now just hang on," Maggie replied. "Just six months ago you were talking about joining the army. Not that I was at all happy about that. But you seemed dead set on it." She softened her tone. "Jack, you play football, and tennis, and you swim and surf, and you hated studying, with a vengeance. You're an outdoors action man. Why do you now want to sit in front of a computer in an office? It would kill you quickly."

The rest of the table had gone quiet. No one moved, each looking wary.

Maggie realised that she had raised her voice too far. But Jack wasn't put off.

"For the same reason that you left a secure job and jumped into this. I've loved what I've helped you with. It's more than that. It excites me, doing research. Look, Mum, I can still play football and tennis and swim and go climbing – yes, that's the next one – but I've watched TV and listened to stories of students getting into huge debt and then just getting jobs in coffee shops, because they didn't have a plan about what to do afterwards. I'm not looking to start right away. I want to do my A-levels, then I might even go to university, but to do a degree that will take me towards genealogy. There are plenty of courses I could do."

Maggie said nothing. Zelah jumped in. "Is it such a bad plan, Maggie? If he'd said he wanted to be an archaeologist, you wouldn't have batted an eyelid. He could help us out in his holidays. Let's give him some grunt work to do. If he really wants to do this, finding out the downside of researching wouldn't be a terrible thing, would it? And we can always do with the help." She turned to Jack. "And if you get bored or find out it's not for you , well that's OK. At least you tried."

"Sounds good to me," he said, still looking at his mother.

Maggie leaned forward and rested her forehead on both hands. "Too much to take in right now. Let's go for that walk, then talk again."

"There's something else, actually…" Jack began, but a warning scowl and a poke on his shoulder from Zelah shut him up. "But it can wait." At that moment, his phone rang.

"Saved by the bell," Zelah muttered as she picked up crockery from the table and headed into the kitchen.

"Kids are hard work." Bob was walking behind her. "Tough being a parent these days."

They deposited the breakfast remains in the kitchen and walked into the garden where Maggie was sitting with her arms folded across her chest.

"Not now," she said without looking at anyone.

"Wasn't going to say anything," said Zelah. They might have

started to debate, but Jack came back out, having finished his call. "That was Pip. She's got eleven GCSEs, all A-star, and A-grades. Brilliant. Makes me look ordinary."

Maggie's head shot up. "You've done brilliantly. Don't sell yourself short."

To her surprise, he walked up and kissed her on the cheek. "Thanks Mum, nice."

Nick and Alice had taken no part in the Maze discussion and were now talking about which stones to visit, which distracted Maggie. "I thought we might visit the Cheesewring tomorrow, after we've been to Trerice. Something for everyone, yes?" she said.

This delighted Alice. "Can we take a picnic?"

"Yes, why not," Maggie replied. "Today, we'll walk the coastal path to where Penwith village and the house used to be."

"And we should celebrate, with lunch or dinner, for Jack," Zelah added. "Where would you like to go, Jack?" she asked. His answer was instant. "Down to the beach café, please. It's the last chance for Pip and me to go surfing. How about we do that after the walk, then all eat together?"

Everyone agreed, and Jack called Pip to make the arrangements.

Chapter 28

An hour later, before the morning became too hot, they walked around the back of the garden, onto the coastal path, and up towards the headland. The sky was again cloudless, and Maggie pondered as they walked on how long this could last. It was so liberating to live in shorts and tee-shirts, sandals, and flip-flops, to swim whenever they wanted, with no wetsuit. They had all developed a tan despite not spending much time exposed to the sun. The outdoor living had done that, and it was what she would miss the most; the carefree, laid back, free flowing lifestyle. And how work had fitted in seamlessly around their leisure.

The headland was on the highest ground and as they made their way towards it, Land's End came briefly into view. The sea was not just azure blue today; it was sparkling with a million droplets of sunlight. As the breeze caught her hair and whipped it across her face, Maggie did a little hop and jump, and Bob, who was walking behind her on the narrow path, laughed and put his hands on her shoulders. She turned and smiled at him, then put one hand up and briefly covered his hand.

Behind them, Alice had seen the gesture. She put her head down and slowed her pace, causing Nick, who was bringing up the rear, to bump into her. They both came to a sudden stop that no one else noticed.

Immediately understanding, he whispered, "Alice, we have to get used to it."

She waved him away as if he was an angry wasp buzzing around her face, looked up, and marched. Undaunted, Nick kept up with her pace. "So then, you think your mother doesn't deserve happiness? That any happiness she has, she can only have if you approve? Don't you think that's selfish? I thought by now you might have left such childishness behind and started to think like a young adult."

She stopped abruptly again. "He doesn't like me."

"No; he doesn't dislike you, it's different. He's never had children of his own and he doesn't know how to deal with your emotions, which are deeply ingrained. But you don't want him to like you. Which would be a validation of your reason to get him out of your mother's life. She doesn't deserve that, not from you. Aren't you feeling, somewhere inside, the least bit of shame?"

She drew a shuddering breath. Nick thought she would cry, but she marched on. "OK, you don't want to talk about it. But just remember you're in danger not only of losing sympathy from everyone, including me, but of turning into a selfish brat. Beware."

He sensed that she had held her breath for a moment but decided enough was enough. No point pushing it. She needed time to take in what he had said. Alice had long perceived how much Nick liked Maggie, had hopes of a deeper relationship and that it disappointed him that her mother didn't return those feelings. But he needed to show Alice that life went on. She wasn't losing out because her mother had found a partner. She wasn't being pushed out. He hoped that he could start a conversation with her about what she was afraid of and guide her towards acceptance. That was why he had stayed.

At the front of the queue, Zelah and Jack were deep in conversation. Maggie caught the occasional word or phrase on the wind and knew that they were talking about history, and how to test what they might find at the site of the old house. Maggie was grateful to Zelah for preparing Jack for what they would find, which she knew was nothing solid. She wasn't sure if he was yet mature enough to appreciate a sense of history rather than actual evidence. That would be part of the work they did at Maze. Visualisation and translation of what you could only imagine was an important part of putting a story together.

They grouped together at the top of the headland and discovered a pathway in the flat scrub that headed inland. "This looks promising," Zelah said, setting off in the path's direction.

"It goes nowhere," Alice argued. "Shouldn't we look further on? There might be another path."

Zelah paused and looked around again. She had already surveyed the immediate landscape and the continuation of the coastal path, but she turned to Alice to explain her reason. "Good point. But look further along the coastal path, Alice. Soon it will head downwards into the next cove, then up again. We know that Penwith House was close to this headland, that the hamlet of Penwith was close to the cliff edge and the house a little further on. This is the only place it could be before we reach the next headland. I might be wrong and it is further on, but we'd have to head down towards those rocks," she pointed at a steep, rocky outcrop leading down into the sea, the site of a well-known former tin mine whose chimneys stood on the top of the rocks, "then back up again. I think that's too far."

Alice looked around and nodded. "My bad."

"Not bad," Zelah said firmly. "You made a good point, but mine's better. Let's go."

They dutifully followed Zelah inland in single file. After five minutes and passing down a gentle incline, they found the remains of a cattle hut, and not far away, the overgrown foundations of a larger building.

"I think we've found Penwith hamlet," Zelah said. She walked over to Jack and produced a plastic wallet from the pocket of her skirt. "Look at this. It's a survey map from around 1800. Shows the site of the old settlement." Jack took it and nodded.

"Why didn't you show me that?" Alice asked.

"What, just shove it under your nose to prove you're wrong? That would have been rude of me. And you needed to understand, not just be swept out of the way."

"I like your sparkly sandals," Alice remarked without looking at Zelah. "Do they come in my size?"

"Probably, funny girl. We'll find out later, you and me." She called the others around and put the map in front of them. "Look, the house is marked here, just a little further on. But I think Penwith wasn't much more than a hamlet, half a dozen houses with a little farmland." She glanced around. "Where would they have gone? Probably poverty forced them to move on. There couldn't have been enough work locally to sustain them. Let's move on."

Without waiting, she walked back to the path and marched onward. They followed, again in single file.

After a further ten minutes, when Zelah wondered if she had read the map correctly, Jack stopped ahead of her and pointed to what looked like a clearing to the left. It was flat and there wasn't as much scrub as on the surrounding land. "Could that be it?" he asked.

"Let's go and see," said Zelah.

The clearing was about five hundred yards off the pathway. As they got closer, they saw that it differed from the surrounding countryside in that it was flat, had gorse and scrub, but no natural outcrops of stone, which were such a feature of this landscape. It was also of a significant size.

Zelah and Nick immediately walked around to find the perimeter, Jack following Zelah. Maggie, Bob, and Alice stood and watched. "What are they looking for?" Alice asked Maggie.

Bob replied, "I think they're trying to find the footprint of the house, Alice."

After a few seconds she turned to him. "It's not exactly where the map said it was, is it?" There was no confrontation in the question, and he smiled back at her. Maggie saw in his expression his relief as he answered the question. "These days we make maps by a combination of satellites, lasers and sophisticated devices to ensure pinpoint accuracy. In 1800 they had a few basic instruments, and they drew by sight and from memory. Whoever produced the map that Zelah is holding was off, but not by much. He wasn't to know that two hundred years later the house would be gone."

Alice nodded thoughtfully. She was about to say something when Jack came running over, almost falling over his feet in his haste to get to them. It frustrated Maggie that this tentative beginning of a conversation between Bob and Alice was about to be interrupted, but whatever Jack would say looked like it couldn't be contained even for a few seconds.

He bounded up to her, eyes shining, mouth open. "Zelah says she thinks this is it!" he shouted at her. Maggie smiled encouragement.

"She says there's evidence of foundations, and Nick agrees, but from ground level we can't get a proper picture, so—" he stopped to draw breath, "She says the only way we'll get a proper picture is from the air, and there's a private airfield just up the road and she will see if we can hire a small plane tomorrow with a pilot who'll take us up over the site." He stopped but was still shaking at the prospect.

"Can I come?" Alice asked at once, eyes equally wide at the idea.

"Sure," Jack replied. "We'll have to see how many seats it has, but yeah."

"But we're supposed to be going to Trerice tomorrow, and then onto Bodmin Moor to walk to the Cheesewring, for Alice," Maggie intervened.

"No problem," Alice jumped in, "I'll wait. This is cool."

Zelah and Nick were walking back towards them.

"Argument?" she asked, looking at Maggie.

"Not at all," Maggie replied. "I said we had a plan. But Alice wants to come with you, which is fine with me."

"Excellent," Zelah said. Maggie thought she looked relieved. "Who wants to come?"

"Don't forget your meeting with the Penzance police tomorrow morning," Bob said.

"I hadn't. And I don't know what size plane we can get, or when, or for how long. Might just be a seat with the pilot and maybe one or two more."

"Then it should be you, Jack, Alice, and Nick," Maggie said.

"Not me," Nick blurted, "Not keen on flying."

"Don't be such a wuss," Alice said sharply to him.

"I could do with a second pair of experienced eyes," Zelah said to him. "But if you really can't… Maggie…?"

"Then Nick and I will have to do rock, paper, scissors to decide. I'm as wussy as he is. Remember me on the paddle steamer?

And I puke."

Nick grinned. "OK, I'll do it. I get a bit green, but I can keep it down. Probably."

"Gross," Alice remarked, turning away. "Can we go back now?"

Chapter 29

When they got back to Avilion Zelah went straight to her computer to find details of the local airfield, Alice took a book into the garden and Nick spent an hour on his neglected project. Jack was ready to go to the beach to meet Pip before lunch, and Maggie took him down. Bob had decided at the top of the headland to walk over to the abandoned tin mine chimneys to take photos and was planning to walk straight back to the beach café at Sennen to meet for lunch.

Maggie had an hour before they went to Sennen Cove for lunch. There was so much information now they hadn't had time to catalogue it. She thought it would be good to write everything down in a daily log, then she could add to it each day. She was a few days behind but was sure she wouldn't miss any important detail. She took her laptop into the garden and sat under the shade and was about to type when her phone rang. Sighing, she turned away from the computer and picked it up. It wasn't a number she recognised.

"Maggie? Hello?"

"Who is this?"

"It's Melissa Wilkes. And have I got news for you!"

Maggie sat up. "Fire away, Melissa."

"We still agree that you'll give me first refusal on your story?"

"Absolutely. What's happened?"

"The studio has had two calls in response to your piece this week. The first is a woman living in Cheshire. She picked you up on a podcast yesterday. Anyway, she's done her family tree and is descended from a man called Edward Steelfox. She says he was a servant of the Vyse family around the seventeen-thirties, which was the time that your spoon became a ring, yes?"

"Yes, it was actually made in the 1690s, but it could have been a possession of the Vyse family around 1730-ish," Maggie replied.

"What else did she say?"

"Not much more to me, but she wants you to call her. Says she has a story for you. I've got the number. You got a pen?"

Maggie searched around the papers on the table and found one. "Go ahead."

Melissa read out the number. "She lives near Chester, a place called Great Boughton. That's the first one."

"Her name?"

"What? Oh yes, sorry, Irene Fox."

"I'll call her right away. And the second one?"

"Ah, well. That's another matter. We already know the second one and between you and me, she's a nightmare. She's called Ann Quinn. She lives on the edge of Bodmin Moor, in an isolated place. She's what you might call... eccentric. Scary. She lives with cats, lots of them and..."

Melissa's hesitation intrigued Maggie. "And what, Melissa?"

"The woman is a witch," Melissa rushed out. "Or, at least, she says she's a witch."

Maggie burst out laughing. "Poor old thing," she said. "But what's the connection to the ring?"

"She told our producer she's descended from the daughter of a witch around at the time of the Vyse family. The daughter was called Julia Pencarrow, and she was the housekeeper at Penwith House."

Maggie was silent for a few seconds, taking this in. "Wow. How do I contact her? Do you have her number?"

"She doesn't have a phone," Melissa replied. "She probably walked into the village to make the call. She likes to live in what she called 'the old way'. No electricity or running water."

"Modern enough to have a radio, though, isn't she?" Maggie said. "How do I get to meet her?"

"I can tell you where she lives. You can only drive so far, then you have to walk. But Maggie, be careful with this woman."

"Why?"

"Because she's a troublemaker. Local people avoid her. She likes to curse them. Some of them are actually scared of her."

"I'll take reinforcements," Maggie joked. "You met my friend staying with us who's a police Inspector? He can be my wingman."

"OK. Let me know how you get on. She said to go whenever you like. But be careful. And don't forget to call me back. We have a deal."

Chapter 30

Maggie held onto the news about this latest development until after lunch. It was Jack and Pip's celebration and she wanted nothing to interfere with that. They walked back up the coastal path to the house, leaving Jack and Pip to spend a few more hours together before she left the next morning. Maggie moved up to Zelah to tell her that there had been a development and Zelah was instantly eager to get the details. Any initial reluctance Zelah had experienced was rapidly disappearing. It concerned Maggie that Zelah was allowing her enthusiasm and passion for genealogy investigation to get in front of her own issues. However, when she hinted this, she got short shrift.

"What kind of idiot do you think I am? Of course I'm not getting carried away. This is my story and my history. I want to know what these people know."

"OK, don't snap my head off."

"Sorry. What's your plan?"

"As soon as we get back, I'll make the call to Cheshire, to Irene Fox. As for visiting the Quinn woman, that will have to wait until tomorrow. I'm thinking we must reorganise our plans for the next few days. There's getting to be a lot to fit in."

"You mean you must reorganise your plan. Do let me know what I'll be doing next, won't you?" said Zelah with a smirk which Maggie mirrored back to her.

Back at the house, Maggie went straight to the office to make the call. Zelah was with her, the speakerphone activated. The call was answered immediately. Maggie introduced herself and was greeted by a gush of enthusiasm, to which she replied politely and let it die down before asking a question.

"So, Mrs Fox, Irene, what can you tell me about this ancestor of yours, Edward Steelfox?"

"Well, Maggie… I can call you Maggie, can't I? I've been doing my husband's family tree for about twenty years now and for a long time I'd hit a real brick wall. They're all Cheshire born and bred, my Daniel's family, all been from here roundabouts, for generations. But as I went back, it suddenly stopped, and I couldn't understand why.

"I tried counties nearby, but nothing. Then I went further afield, and that's when I found an ancestor from Cornwall. She married a local Cheshire man, you see. But after he died, there was no trace of his wife. I knew they had had two boys, Edward and Peter. I couldn't find out if either of them had married or had children. But I knew that they had because Edward is Daniel's ancestor. I looked all over, and eventually I found them in Cornwall! Imagine my surprise. But once I knew, I checked on Edward and Peter's mother and found her right down at the end of Cornwall. I can't imagine what took her to Cheshire, but I'm guessing as soon as her husband, John Steelfox, died, she took her boys and went back to her Cornish roots.

"Then, I found that Edward had returned to Cheshire in 1736. He had married a Cornish woman, Emma Lucas, and they came back to Great Boughton. They had three children, all born here."

"And how do you know about the Vyse family?" Maggie asked. She was interested in the story but had a feeling it still had some way to go before Irene got to the point.

"Edward left his family Bible, which has been handed down through the family for generations. You've probably realised that 'Fox' is a shortened version of the original name 'Steelfox' and that it's my husband's family, not mine. In the Records Office in Truro I found evidence of a manor house called Penwith. Some household records still exist, just a few, and Edward is in the early ones. It records him as a servant in 1734 and 1735, along with his wife Emma and his brother Peter. You know about Peter, of course."

"No, actually I don't," Maggie replied. "Maze Investigations is just picking this up." She wagged a finger at Zelah, who was about to interrupt. "Please, tell me about him." This brought a nod from

Zelah, who had been scribbling while Irene Fox spoke.

"Oh, very good. Well, Peter was a groom. He was there in both records, too. But there was a big scandal in 1736. Edward made a note in his Bible. They transported Peter to the American colonies for stealing from the estate."

"Really? How interesting. What did he steal?" Maggie asked, thinking she already knew the answer.

"Oh, I don't know. I didn't go into it." Zelah made a gesture of strangling a throat, with an accompanying wild-eyed look.

"Well, that's something we can follow up. I'll make a guess it was a silver spoon he made into a ring. The date fits. Is there anything else you can tell me either about Edward or Peter?"

"Not really, Maggie. Well…" there was a pause, and Maggie had a vision of the woman cocking her head to one side, thinking. "Well, Edward's note in the Bible said Peter was sent on a convict ship to the American colonies. That's what they called it then, you know." Zelah rolled her eyes. "But he added the words 'But he was no thief. It was allowed to him'".

"Irene, this has been excellent information. Could you send me a photo of the page in the Bible?"

"I'll get my son to do it when he comes home from work, if that's OK Maggie? I'm not great on these mobiles."

"That's fine, Irene." Maggie gave her the Maze email address. "Anything else?"

"No, that's it. I hope I've been useful to you, Maggie."

"You've been brilliant, Irene." Maggie could almost see the woman preening at the praise. "I'll let you know if anything comes of this. Thank you so much," and she put the phone back on its stand before Irene could gush further.

"This means another trip to the Archives in Truro. There might be an account of the trial. In fact, I'm sure there is. Let's hope it contains the name Steelfox. So where does this take us?" said Maggie.

"It pins down the date. In 1736 they transported a man for theft, possibly of a spoon he turned into a ring, from Penwith House. Those words, 'it was allowed to him' could refer to the spoon he turned into a ring and if so, I think it must be my ring. But what happened to it from there?" Zelah mused. She jumped up. "No time like the present. I'm going to check the Truro Records Office website, see if they have Assizes records for that period."

Maggie followed her into the kitchen where Zelah checked her laptop. She punched away at the keyboard, peering at the screen. After some minutes she said, "Yes! They have records from 1735 to 1740. With any luck Peter Steelfox's trial records will be there. Wonderful. I'm going into Truro. You coming?"

Maggie thought quickly. "No," she said. "I want to think through everything we still have to do. We have just over a week left here and right now we have more questions than answers. It doesn't take two of us to check an archive. And what's happening about your plan to hire a small plane to fly over the Penwith site?"

"Helicopter," Zelah replied, grabbing her bag as she headed for the front door. "Five-seater. Tomorrow afternoon at two."

Maggie heard the slam of the front door and the roar of Zelah's car engine as she headed off down the drive.

"Where's she off to?" asked Bob, wandering in from the garden.

"Archive in Truro. Something has come up from the first of the people who responded to the radio piece."

"Useful information?"

"Yes, significant, I think."

"And you?"

I'm taking an hour to work out what we still need to do. This changes the plan – again. Want to help?"

"Sure," he replied. "I'll get us some beers. Alice has asked me again about Mên-an-Tol. I said we could definitely go, so you'll have to factor that in, too."

"At this rate we'll have to stay for another week," Maggie muttered, going into the office for a pad and pens.

"I'm going back Sunday, so make the most of my time."

"That's gone quickly. Doesn't time fly when you're enjoying yourself?"

"Hmm. Next time you ask me to come on holiday, I'm lowering any expectations I had about sun, sea, and relaxation. Anyway, I'm not sure tomorrow will be enjoyable, for Zelah at least."

"Damn, I'd forgotten about that. You will sit with her, won't you?"

"No need to be anxious, I will. Does she want you there, too?"

"No, I don't think so." Maggie replied. "She's being close about Jay's story and she still hasn't told us about her conversation with Archie King. Hopefully, that will come out in the morning."

"Thinking about it, you're on your own with planning and scheming. I'll search in the Police Gazette, have another go at a lead on an accident in 1953 anywhere in the country that might be worth following up."

"Try the British Newspaper Archive too. Use my account," Maggie said. "And I don't scheme, thank you very much!" He dodged her prodding finger, chuckled, and headed for the office.

Chapter 31

As the evening closed in and the sun set, Maggie had her plan, but Zelah still hadn't returned. She held off explaining what they would do with their remaining time, waiting for Zelah. But she was getting anxious until the familiar roar of the Spider's engine assaulted her ears and she got up and with a sense of relief went into the house to meet Zelah.

"You've taken your time. I kept some food for you. Find something?"

"You bet," Zelah replied, dropping her bag in the hall and heading into the kitchen. She poured herself a glass of cold orange juice and downed it in one long draught. "I needed that," she said, wiping her mouth with the back of her hand. "Right, let's convene the troops."

"All ready and waiting in the garden."

Bob and Nick looked up as Zelah dropped herself into a garden chair and declared, "Progress, chaps."

"Lead on Macduff," said Bob.

Zelah snorted at Bob, who had folded his arms and sat up. "Are you winding me up, Clouseau?" she said.

Maggie sighed. "Not now, you two. What have you found, Zelah?"

"I have found that in all probability Lady Mildred Vyse was murdered, by person or persons unknown – isn't that how you say it, Inspector?" Bob nodded. "The coroner took great care to exonerate Sir John Vyse. Two witnesses were Edward Steelfox and Julia Pencarrow. Between the three of them, they backed each other up. Mildred was found dead in bed, strangled by a chain she wore around her neck, on which there had been... a ring!" She paused and looked around expectantly.

"The spoon ring?" Maggie asked.

"Yes, but the ring wasn't there, just the chain. And no one ever found the ring. But who did it? They didn't know. The door was locked from the inside and there was no other way into the bedroom. Each of the three gave the other two an alibi. Edward Steelfox was also spoken for by his wife, Julia Pencarrow by her husband, and Sir John by both. The coroner recorded the death as 'foule murder'.

"Now, the interesting thing is that there was something alluded to but not fully explained. Something to do with an object found in the bedclothes. Something described as a 'vile and obnoxious thing' and no one could explain how it got there. Julia Pencarrow was questioned about it. But she said that she had never seen the thing before and would have nothing to do with it. Any thoughts, anyone?"

Bob uncrossed his arms. "Same thought as you're having Zelah."

"I think I'm on the same lines," said Nick.

"Well, I'm clearly behind you," Maggie said. "What are we thinking?"

"The poppet," Zelah said. "They thought witchcraft killed Mildred Vyse. But no one would say so. And now I think my bits of wood and pins may be what's left of the 'vile and obnoxious thing'".

"And it explains who they thought the witch was," said Nick, "Julia Pencarrow."

"Right! But they couldn't accuse her. By that time, they weren't burning those poor women at the stake anymore. Nor were they dishing out punishment purely based on an accusation," Zelah added.

"What do you mean?" Jack asked.

"In the most hysterical period of witch-hunting," Zelah explained, "an accusation of witchcraft was considered proof of being a witch, and she had to prove herself to not be one. Any idea of 'innocent until proven guilty' didn't apply. That's why they tied women up and threw them into water. If they sank, they were innocent, but if they floated, that was a sign of a witch. And there were other similar so-called trials."

"That's terrible." Alice had been sitting at the table playing chess with Jack. "Were they persecuted because they were different?"

Maggie went to say something but Zelah got there first. "Yes, Alice. Different was something to be frightened of in those times. Usually encouraged and roused by the Church, which didn't like women. It's quite a history. You should read it sometime."

"I'm going to do it now," Alice replied and headed off to sit at her laptop in the conservatory, leaving Jack frowning at the chessboard.

"Now, for the trial of Peter Steelfox. He was accused of stealing the ring and of assaulting Mildred Vyse when she accused him of theft. There were plenty of character witnesses, including his brother and Julia Pencarrow. Even Sir John asked for clemency and was sure his mother would not have wanted a severe punishment. But there was an eyewitness to the assault. A gardener called Richard Weston. Who, interestingly, was invited to sit to give his evidence having an abnormality of the leg that caused him great pain. Remember the body in the well? Besides the injuries he sustained in the fall, it had a long-standing deformed leg, didn't it?"

"What was Peter Steelfox's defence to the theft?" Bob asked.

"He said old Lady Johanna Vyse, who was alive when he took it, knew that he had it and made no objection. Servants were often known to steal a spoon to make a ring. It wasn't unusual. Her Ladyship knew that Peter wanted to marry the kitchen maid, Julia Treseder. She gave him a nod and a wink, or whatever the eighteenth-century equivalent was. As far as he was concerned, he had done nothing wrong. And he strenuously denied the assault. He said when Mildred Vyse saw the ring and accused him, he explained that he had been tacitly allowed to have it. But the old lady was dead so there was no corroboration. I think Mildred Vyse knew and waited until his story couldn't be substantiated. And she must have made the gardener back her up, then pushed him down the well."

"Whoa, there. Hold on. That's a lot of assumptions," Bob snorted. "You're making the facts fit your theory. Peter Steelfox might have stolen the spoon, and he might have assaulted Lady Vyse."

"Then why did he have so many people speak to his character? And why did her own husband ask for clemency?"

"Just because he was a nice guy doesn't mean he wasn't a thief. And maybe her husband liked the lad and didn't want to see him transported, but that doesn't mean that he thought the boy was innocent. He was caught between his mother's good name and his wife's. But, and it's a big but... we'll never know."

"Correct. So, why can't I go with my theory and see if I can find more supporting evidence? No one's life is hanging in the balance, is it?"

Zelah was half standing now, her face reddening. Bob rose from his seat. Maggie decided it was time to intervene.

"Calm down, both of you. We have another lead to follow. Bob, Zelah, neither of you will ever be one hundred percent correct. We need to get as close as we can. Let's leave it at that, shall we? But it gives credence to the Bible note about it having been 'allowed', don't you think?"

They both sat back in their chairs, glaring at each other.

"We're all on the same side here," Maggie persisted, "and we all want to get as close to the truth as we can. Now, I've spent this afternoon working out what we still need to do. And the list is getting longer. Given that we've only got less than a week left, and that tomorrow is the start of the Bank Holiday, I've drawn up a timetable."

She handed round a one-page document to each of them. Bob's glare changed to a look of amusement, as he saw their time worked out, sometimes, by the hour. "You are a very organised woman."

"I am, right on. Now, look at what you're all down to do on each day. Give it a minute, then let me know if anyone has any objections?" She walked into the conservatory with a page for Alice.

"Was she ever in the military?" Bob asked, not looking up from his paper.

"No, just the Mafia," said Zelah. Bob and Zelah caught each other glancing and raised an eyebrow at each other and a reluctant grin.

Chapter 32

Despite the quips no one objected to what Maggie had organised.

The detective who would investigate Jay's disappearance arrived promptly at nine. Zelah and Bob had already had a run-through of what she would say and Zelah had told Bob about the outcome of her conversation with Archie King.

"That will make a difference," Bob said, when she finished the story. "Make sure you tell it all, answer any questions this detective has. And don't get snotty with him, Zelah. He has to do this but may not be entirely on board because it's a cold case, so he's likely to be cynical. You'll have to convince him. Try some charm."

"I presume you make that suggestion more in hope than expectation?"

"I make that suggestion in the hope, yes hope, that we can move this forward and get you some closure on what happened to your friend Jay. It's all on you now."

Zelah shuffled a little but backed off. She and Bob led the detective into the lounge so they wouldn't be disturbed.

They emerged an hour later, with Zelah looking perky. Bob gave Maggie, who had conveniently walked out of the kitchen into the hall, an approving confirmative nod, as Zelah walked outside with the Penzance detective and saw him drive off.

She joined them in the kitchen and poured a mug of fresh coffee.

"That went better than I expected," she said to Bob.

"Yes," he replied. "He seemed convinced enough. He's off to speak to Archie King now," Bob explained to Maggie as he took a mug of coffee from Zelah. "He'll check the story, but he's definitely in, for an investigation. I'll tell you the rest on our journey up to Bodmin Moor. OK with you Zelah?"

Zelah nodded. "According to… what was his name? Mark

Mooney, Detective Constable Mooney, my stepsister wasn't the most popular of people around these parts. She moved to a cottage on the edge of Mousehole when the vicar died. That's where she lived, before she came to Sennen after her divorce."

"Did Tracy have children?" Maggie asked.

"No," Zelah replied, "and she was the vicar's only child, so no more Hoptons. Thank God. And if you're wondering what happened to her estate, she left it all to an animal charity. The solicitor told me when I collected the rings."

"Probably for the best," Maggie mused. "You wouldn't have wanted to touch a penny of it, would you?"

"If she'd left me anything, which she never would, I'd have left it to a charity that works with abused children," Zelah replied. "Which I probably will do. Anyhow, let's get on." She poured the remains of her coffee into the sink, put her mug into the dishwasher and turned back to Maggie with an arch look. "We can't have your timetable getting behind, can we?"

Before Maggie could reply, Nick walked into the kitchen and looked around. "Did I miss something important?"

"Zelah can tell you about the police visit," Maggie replied. "Bob and I are going up to Bodmin. Good luck with your helicopter ride. Have fun. Tell the kids I'll see them later."

Chapter 33

As soon as they were on the A30 Bob said to a distant Maggie, "Does she get to you?"

It took a few seconds for Maggie to realise that he had spoken. "Sorry, what?"

"I said, does the way she reacts get to you? You left abruptly, back there. Was that because of Zelah?"

"No, not at all. I got over that a long time ago, since we had the showdown after Christmas. You have to take people how they are. If she's ever rude, I'm fine telling her. And now she's fine taking the telling. When I first met her, she was feisty. She's calmed down a lot."

"Honestly, if this is better, I can't imagine what it was like."

Maggie smiled at the recollection. "I've never been a reactive person. On the whole, confrontational behaviour amuses me. But I get intrigued by what's behind it. You should know that."

"Yep. Took me a while to figure you out. But, sometimes, I can't stop myself rising to her manners, or lack of them."

"I get that. But I know from everything we've been through that she's a decent, kind, warm-hearted person. Just with an outer shell that would make a hedgehog look cuddly. She keeps people at bay for a reason. Trust me on this."

"I trust you," he said. "So, where are we headed?"

"The closest village to where Ann Quinn lives is St Breward. I'll guide us when we get closer. What happened in the meeting with the DC?"

"Interesting," Bob began. "The lad had done preliminary work to find out about the people and had discovered that Tracy Hopton, or Tracy Jones as she became, was not a popular person when she lived in Sennen."

"Quick question, how old was Tracy when she died?"

"Early seventies. She was about ten years older than Zelah."

"So, if she killed Jay, she would have been, what, late teens when she did it?"

"Yes, I see where you're going with this. She wasn't a kid. She was practically an adult. It might not have been premeditated, but from everything I heard from Zelah this morning and what Mark Mooney found out, Tracy had one hell of a temper. Capable of lashing out suddenly and violently. Seems there was a history of domestic abuse in the Jones' household. But not the usual, this was Tracy beating up her husband. Apparently, she hit him with a hammer one time and fractured his skull."

"What the hell?" Maggie had shouted without realising. "Surely she would have been arrested?"

"She wasn't. The husband pulled out of pressing charges and giving evidence. He divorced her, but the abuse never came to court. She moved back to the vicar's house and ran it as a B&B after he died and before she retired, but she could never keep staff. Lots of stories going around about how she was rude and malicious. One story is that she slapped a woman visitor she didn't like. Guests never came back and gave her a bad reputation. A nasty creature. But…" He hesitated for a moment. "I'm thinking now she was a psychopath with murderous tendencies. If she had killed once, she wouldn't have found it difficult to do it again. But there weren't any more unsolved suspicious deaths. In a small community it would have been noticeable."

"How she taunted Zelah with Jay's death? Surely that's evidence of a psychopathic tendency?"

"Maybe, I'm not sure. She would have had to have been a great schemer to have killed more people and got away with it. Mark Mooney will look though. He's a good copper. It'll be interesting to hear what he gets from Archie King, especially about there being money in the bag." Again, he paused. "Maggie, it was all a long time ago. What evidence there is will be slim pickings. Don't expect a miracle here. I said the same to Zelah."

"I think Zelah just wants justice for her friend," Maggie

replied. "And if the vicar's true nature comes out, well that's justice too for all those kids who he profited from."

"Yes," Bob replied. "Just don't hold your breath about finding out what happened to Jay."

"OK. Anything else I should know about?"

"Archie gave Zelah a good lowdown about the vicar. Mark will try to trace the money. Again, slim chance. But shortly after Zelah arrived, Hopton, who had always pleaded righteous poverty, suddenly came into an 'inheritance', bought a car and took a family holiday in France. But without Zelah who got farmed-out to a member of his congregation. Later on, he also bought out and did up the vicarage. But he was vague about which relative the money came from."

"We can check for a will from a Hopton naming the vicar as a beneficiary."

"Zelah's already done that. There isn't one. But she'll keep looking. Archie King had nothing good to say about Hopton. I haven't looked into the charity that put the kids with him, but I will, or DC Mooney will."

"And Jay's mother?"

"Mark Mooney will do that."

They had driven along the A30 for some time before Maggie took out the map to check the route they should be taking.

"We're getting close to Indian Queens now. We should take the A39; as we approach the moor, we'll see signposts to St Breward, after Camelford."

They had passed Wadebridge and saw the first views of the higher tors in the distance. Bodmin Moor had always fascinated Maggie. A huge fan of Daphne du Maurier, she had visited Jamaica Inn many times, and had always intended to spend part of a Cornish holiday walking on the moor, but the right time had never presented itself and there had always been another stunning beach to visit instead. Today, with no clouds in a deep blue sky it was fascinating, forbidding, dangerous and attractive. Walking had to be carefully planned to avoid the boggy marshes and quicksand.

Bare granite tors stood proud of the coarse scrubland. Maggie knew that there had been prehistoric settlements here, and she felt the dark attraction of primordial nature.

Turning off the Atlantic Highway they drove towards St Breward, surrounded by green countryside with grazing animals and an abundance of trees. However, when they reached the village and drove through it, looking for the rough lane that Melissa Wilkes had described, it was startling how suddenly the landscape changed into a treeless moor, with the undulating bare vista rising in the distance to the highest point on the moor, the tor called Bronn Wenneli, or its better-known name; Brown Willy.

They found the lane behind a small row of houses and drove along it for about a quarter of a mile where they discovered a layby. They parked and walked to the farmhouse belonging to Ann Quinn about three hundred yards off the road.

"Scruffy looking place after such a pretty village," Bob said as they struggled through the uncut grass that had overtaken the footpath.

Behind and around the sides of the house the moor began its upward sweep. The views were spectacular, but Maggie wondered how the woman survived here without basic amenities, particularly in winter, when the land must surely become snowbound and inhospitable. Closer, they could see that the house was probably once a farm, built of granite blocks in the traditional, local way. To one side was a small vegetable patch where beans, onions and potatoes were growing, and a tiny greenhouse with tomatoes and cucumbers. The front door was ajar. Smoke rose from the tall chimney, dark grey and straight like an accusing finger pointing to the sky, with no breath of wind to interrupt its journey. From somewhere at the back of the house they could hear the clucking of chickens.

Maggie called out "Hello," as they reached the door but there was no response. She moved to peer through a window at what was a sitting room. There were some shabby curtains that had long since lost their colour and were now a uniform grey. She knocked on the window.

"I'll go around the back," said Bob, "see if she's there." He disappeared around the side of the house and Maggie went back to stand in the porch. Glancing up, she saw the outline of a pentangle etched into the triangular stone panel above the open door. Inside was a flagstone floor, to the right a closed door and a staircase leading up. An antique, dark-wood cabinet stood against the wall opposite the stairs. On it was a sizeable mirror. At the far end of the hallway was a closed door leading, she presumed, into the kitchen.

Maggie poked her head inside and was about to shout out when the kitchen door flung open. The light that flooded into the hallway illuminated the outline of a tall woman. Maggie couldn't make out her face, but she could see long, white hair and that she wore a dark, ankle-length skirt.

Shouting "Who are you?" the woman advanced in long strides down the hall, head and neck jutting forward, one hand grasping an object that trailed behind her skirt. As she reached the front door, Maggie, who had retreated outside onto the porch, could see that the object was a chicken with its head cut off, dripping blood. She could also now see that in her other hand was a long-bladed knife.

The woman held up the knife in front of her. Maggie held her ground, staring straight ahead although the woman was much too close for comfort.

"I said, who are you? What are you doing on my property?" The voice was low and rasping, like a long-time smoker.

"You invited me," replied Maggie in as calm a voice as she could muster.

"What do you mean?" There was no let-up in her intensity.

"I mean that you rang Melissa Wilkes at the radio station and said I should come out to see you any time." Maggie was feeling annoyed. "But if it's not convenient…"

"Oh, you're that genealogy woman. You'd better come in."

With neither apology nor explanation Ann Quinn turned and marched back to the kitchen. At that moment Bob appeared beside Maggie. "What's going on? You look flummoxed."

"Not sure if that's the right word," Maggie muttered. "But she has invited us in, so I suppose we'd better go. Come on, but take care. She was brandishing a wicked-looking knife." Maggie walked towards the kitchen just as Ann Quinn was coming out, minus chicken corpse and knife. "Who's he?" she asked.

"My colleague, Bob Pugh. You'll be speaking to both of us."

"You'd better be on the level, both of you, or I shall call the police."

"I am the police," replied Bob, matching her tone, "and you don't have a phone. Do you want to see my warrant card?"

The woman turned to Maggie with an expression of fury. "Why have you brought the police into my house?"

"Because he's my colleague and is helping me with this case. Now look, we haven't got off to the best start, but we have information for each other, so perhaps we can sit down somewhere and speak politely?"

The woman considered this proposition for a few moments, then nodded and with a thrust of her head showed them the door on her right. "Parlour," she said.

The room was dark, with the pervading smell of wood smoke and cat pee. This was the room with the faded curtains and Maggie could see that they were not alone in their thread bareness. Cat hair covered the settee and two armchairs. Reluctantly, Maggie sat on the edge of one chair. Bob remained standing.

"Ms Quinn, you said you had a story to tell—" Maggie began.

"Show me. I want to see it. I'm not saying nothin' 'til I've seen it."

Maggie took the box containing the ring out of her bag and opened it. Ann Quinn stood and thrust out her hand, but Maggie pulled hers back.

"No, it's not for examination. I brought it to show you, but you can't handle it." She snapped the lid shut.

"But it's mine," Ann Quinn's voice hit a high pitch between anger and supplication. "It's rightfully mine. Down through the ages, my family. My ancestor was Julia Pencarrow. She was a witch, like her mother. She took the ring."

Maggie drew a deep breath. "Then you had better tell me your story. This ring belongs to our client. You will need to show me proof if you think you have a claim to it."

Ann Quinn stood quickly and walked out of the room, across the hall and opened the door opposite. When she was out of earshot Bob let out a heavy breath. "She's a nasty piece of work. Something very off about her. Did you see what's she's wearing on her necklace? I think they're animal bones. I don't like this."

"Me neither," Maggie whispered, "but let's see what she tells us. We know that Julia Pencarrow was the housekeeper at Penwith House when Mildred Vyse died."

Ann stormed back into the room with a paper file in her hand. "Here, Gilbert. Here's the proof." She took a piece of paper from the file and shoved it under Maggie's nose. It was a family tree, but it was too small for Maggie to read. She reached into her bag and took out her glasses and phone. Then she looked at the family tree, which led from Ann Quinn directly back to Julia Pencarrow, born in 1700.

"This is interesting, but not proof." As she spoke, she activated the camera on her phone. She held it over the document and snapped a photo. In response, Ann Quinn tried to snatch the phone away. "How dare you," she bellowed. "You need my permission. That's theft. Destroy that picture at once. And I want to see you do it."

Maggie looked back at Bob, who nodded. She turned the phone to Ann Quinn and pressed the delete button. "I apologise. But I will need a copy. I… we will have to look this over."

"Think you're better than me, do you? Think you know more about my family than I do?" Ann sneered, sitting down again. As she sat, three cats wandered into the room and jumped onto her lap, purring.

"My friends are interested in you. They've come to look. And they're not saying good things about you." She stroked each cat and murmured to it.

Maggie fought to keep herself calm. "As I said, I'll need a copy. We won't consider any claim on the ring without it. But you said you had a story to tell. If this is it, then we're done, and we'll leave." She went to stand but Ann put out a hand to stop her.

"I can tell you more. What do you know about Peter Steelfox?"

"You mean the boy accused of theft and sent to enslavement in the American colonies? I know that this ring might be the one they accused him of stealing. And I know that his family was adamant he was innocent. But apart from that, nothing. Is he significant? Did something happen to him in America? I presume he died there if he got that far."

"He came back. After seven years, he came back. John Vyse took him back, too." She stopped and sniggered, then became serious. "Does she have the letter, too? Does she have it? Is that where it is. The last letter?" She had become agitated again, jabbing a finger at Maggie as she hurled the questions that were more accusations than an appeal for information.

"I've no idea what you're talking about, Miss Quinn."

"And if you don't calm down, we'll be leaving," Bob added, jabbing a finger back at her.

The woman sat back in her chair and smiled at them. "Zelah Trevear. You think I'm stupid? Client, my foot. It's her. I know all about her so-called legacy."

"Whatever, it's none of your business. Now, what letter?"

"Three letters there were, written by the three after the inquest. It's said they tell the whole story. Of the murder that is. Or the so-called murder. Human hand didn't do it. You should check the inquest. It's all in the Archives in Truro."

"I know about the poppet. But the inquest notes say nothing about letters. They confirm that Mildred was probably murdered, but there was no mention of letters."

"They were written afterwards, stupid," Ann snorted.

"And you know this… how? And please don't be abusive."

"I'll speak how I choose," Ann Quinn snarled. "There's one letter left. I've been looking for it for twenty years. It must have belonged to Julia Pencarrow. She was the last of the three to die. But where is it? Where is it?" She looked away from Maggie and gazed over her head, out of the window, stroking her cats.

"My client has no letter," Maggie said, "and I'll ask again, how do you know?"

"The vicar," Ann Quinn mumbled. "Mr Steelfox. Flintshire."

Then, as quickly as her attention had wandered, she snapped back. "You're a waste of my time, Gilbert. You know nothing. If Trevear has that letter, I want it. Or she had better look out."

Bob stepped in one stride around the chair to stand in front of Maggie. "What do you mean by that?"

Ann Quinn looked momentarily cowed, but stood up to face him, pushing the cats off her lap. "I have my ways, policeman." From the pocket of her skirt she brought out something that she held up in front of him. Maggie also stood and tried to see what it was. When she saw, she stepped back, but Bob didn't move a muscle.

"If you think a bit of wood and material and some pins will bother us Ms Quinn, think again. I don't subscribe to your nonsense."

"More fool you. Now, get out of my house."

Bob didn't move. "You are being officially warned. Should any harm come to Mrs Trevear, or to any of her colleagues, I won't hesitate to come after you." He leaned in towards her. "And I was around the back of your house. Think about it." Then he turned to Maggie. "Let's go. I'm getting fed up with the smell."

On shaking legs Maggie followed him out of the house. He strode so rapidly that Maggie had to run to keep up with him, and he didn't stop until they reached the motorhome, where he turned, and leaned on the side of the vehicle arms folded. Maggie bent down and put her hands on her knees, panting.

"Get your breath back," he said. "Then we'll go into the village and have a drink and something to eat in the pub." Maggie nodded and climbed into the passenger seat. It was a few seconds before Bob pulled himself into the driver's seat.

Chapter 34

Ten minutes later they had found seats in a quiet corner of the Old Inn in St Breward and Maggie was sitting in front of a large gin and tonic. Bob was at the bar ordering food. She could see him in conversation with the barman. He headed back with a cardboard number on a plastic stand.

"Food will take about ten minutes," he said, sitting beside her and nodding at the glass. "Drink that. You're still pale."

"I'd have preferred an orange juice," she replied. "But this will do." She took a long swig.

"I'm amazed that I'm so shaken," she said. "From a distance she looks like a nasty, malicious old woman. But there was something about that house, and the dead chicken, and the knife and the poppet. And did you get a look at the other room, across the entrance hall?"

"No, I didn't. What did you see?"

"It was just a glimpse. But there was a whole shelf of poppets. All with pins sticking out of their heads and bodies." She shook her head to clear away the bad picture. "And there was a table, with a strange-looking cloth on it, with symbols on it. And bottles on the table, black bottles." She paused for a moment. "Whatever that woman is doing up there, it isn't good."

"I wanted to get away from the cats. Have I ever told you I'm allergic to them? I sneeze and itch. Can't stand the damn things. And there were at least another ten around the back. Disgusting."

"You don't sound like you had that much of a problem with her."

"Oh, I had a problem with her. Something's definitely off there, but... witchcraft? I don't think so. My nose tells me she's just a fraud. She likes the power she creates, but I think it's all smoke and mirrors. So, no, she didn't faze me. But, why did she get to you? You're not an easily spooked woman."

Maggie took another swig of gin and tonic. It burned her throat but was clearing her head. "I don't know, now. Maybe it was just the threat against Zelah, but how did she know about Zelah and the ring? We haven't told anyone."

"Maybe she put two and two together. It's no secret that Zelah's from Cornwall. From her name if nothing else. It wouldn't take much to find out she hasn't been back to Cornwall in a long time, so something special would have brought her back. There are lots of ways. But for me, just one significant thing."

Before he could explain, the barman arrived with two plates of sandwiches and gave Bob a significant look, to which Bob replied, "It's OK, you can speak in front of Maggie. It's actually her show."

"I spoke to a couple of the regulars. They're wary of her: been threatened and some weird things have happened. Aches and pains, that kind of thing. Nothing serious, just a sudden need to go to hospital."

"So, they think Ann Quinn has certain powers, abilities?"

"They'd never say so, somewhat embarrassing in the twenty-first century to say a witch lives near your village," the barman replied. "But most people just try to keep out of her way. They think she has the evil eye, so they prefer not to find themselves on the wrong side of her."

"You're not a local man?" Maggie asked.

"No, we came here about two years ago. From the Midlands."

"You've fitted in OK?"

"No problem at all. Lovely people, very welcoming. My wife's local, mind, that helps. And we came here for years, every summer for a holiday and short breaks, too."

He put the sandwiches on the table, smiled at Bob and walked back to the bar.

"So, what significant thing?" She leaned forward.

"What? Oh…" He had taken a mouth full of sandwich, which he chewed on, swallowed, then gulped a mouthful of orange juice, all while Maggie glared at him.

"Right. Well, if she is a witch, there are things she should definitely know about. Like other people with abilities do. Like your daughter and Nick. But she didn't have a clue. And for another thing... Maggie, let me eat first, will you? I'm starving." He ate another mouthful of sandwich as she sat with her food untouched.

"Are you getting cross with me?" Bob asked, as he swallowed the last mouthful.

"I'm not sure. But I'm thinking about what you said. Why would she know about Alice and Nick? What they have is different."

"Is it?" he replied. "Shouldn't someone with heightened sensitivity be able to recognise it in others? Yes, she knew about Zelah. And you said on the radio you were here on holiday with your family. How do you know she didn't do some snooping, find out more about you?"

"What do you think she did?"

"Do you remember you said the night after your broadcast you heard some loud squawking coming from the garden?"

Maggie nodded. "I went out and checked. We sometimes leave the house unlocked and Zelah has been up a lot at night. I said nothing, didn't want to cause a scare. But someone had been in the garden and disturbed the gulls."

"I... I'm struggling here, Bob. You thought we might have had an intruder, but you said nothing, not one word?"

"I've been watching. Don't get mad with me. I've got a suspicious nature, goes with the territory. If something else was going to happen, I've have been ready for it. I locked the doors every night and checked the ground floor windows were closed. But there has been nothing. So, why just the one night? I think it might have been Ann Quinn. She came to see what she could find."

"How did she know where we're staying?"

"That's a good question. Then, I remembered that Melissa Wilkes announced the day before that you were coming on to talk about the ring and the connection with a Cornish family, didn't she?"

Maggie nodded again. "So, you think…?"

"That Ann Quinn was outside the radio station, saw you go in, followed you out, and back here."

"But Melissa told me she lives alone, with no mod cons. You could see there was no lighting, electricity, gas, nothing. I don't even know if there was running water. How could she have followed me?"

Bob laughed aloud. "On her broomstick, she hopes people will think, or that she can teleport. It's the myth she's created. There is running water and there is a power supply. Remember – I said to her I was around the back. There's no sign of anything growing, apart from those few beanstalks and some pathetic tomatoes and cucumbers, nothing. But there was a pizza delivery box and an oil-fired generator. There were electric lamps and… and I'll pause for effect here..." He stopped.

"Don't you dare," Maggie scolded, "What else?"

"There was a garage. The woman who lives off the land, self-sufficiently with nature… has a car! She's actually an oil-burning, polluting, fast food eating fraud."

Maggie sat back in her chair. "Well, I'll be damned. She had me fooled."

"And that's what she's good at. Fooling people. All the rest is show."

"When did you know?"

"Right from the start. Because I'll let you into a secret. The woman has one talent, a real one and it could easily look like something unnatural to the unknowing."

"Bob Pugh, you're messing with me again, and I don't like it." She sat forward and jabbed a finger into his arm.

"You love it."

"Tell me!"

"OK. Ever heard of micro expressions?"

Maggie paused this time and picked up her sandwich. "No, new on me."

"Every person on the planet, regardless of ethnicity, geography, or cultural identity, has identical facial expressions. They give off

135

seven emotions. Which are," he counted off on his fingers. "Fear, happiness, contempt, disgust, anger, surprise and sadness. They are unconscious and they appear in tiny movements on various parts of your face, for about one twenty-fifth of a second. We can't hide them, and most people see them but can't consciously interpret them."

She gave him a look that suggested scepticism.

"And that wasn't one. Too obvious. The thing with micro expressions is that we don't know we're making them. But they are instinctive emotions and if you can read them, you can know if someone is telling the truth or not."

"And you know this... how?"

"It's science. And I've been studying it for about three years now. But I'm not a natural and I have to work hard at it. Some things I can spot, but only when I'm concentrating. Useful in interrogations, but I don't always pick things up when I'm not trying. But Ann Quinn... I think she's a natural. They're rare, but they can read people brilliantly. Thing is with Ann Quinn, I don't think she knows that's what she's doing."

"How can she not know?"

"Because it's an innate ability. If you don't know what it is, you don't know you've got it. You must have seen that before? The thing is, she's attributing it to witchcraft and building her persona around it. But it's fake."

"But thinking about it," Maggie mused, "there must be part of her that knows that she isn't genuine, because of the car and the generator and the fast food."

"Well, good luck if you can get inside the head of someone like her and figure out how she justifies it to herself. I've never been able to."

"At least I've got her family tree to go on," Maggie smiled.

"Yes," Bob replied, "I saw what you did. You cloned it before you deleted it. Clever."

"I'll make a start when we get back." She glanced at her watch. "It's the witching hour," she whispered. He sat up and paused mid-sandwich, giving her a puzzled look.

"Flying. The helicopter flight, or whatever they end up doing. They should just be taking off. Only witchcraft will stop Nick from throwing up."

"Or motion sickness pills, which I hope he had the sense to go out and buy this morning," said Bob. "Another thought, there's a visit we should add to your timetable, Sergeant Mummy."

She decided not to rise to the bait. "And what would that be, Detective Inspector?"

"A visit to the Museum of Witchcraft and Magic."

Maggie's eyes sparkled. "What, here, in Cornwall?"

"Up in Boscastle, about an hour from here, just north of Tintagel."

"Let's go," she said, standing up, taking Bob's drink from his hand, and putting it back down on the table.

"What, now?" he spluttered. "I haven't finished my lunch."

"I'll make sure you get compensation, in the form of a big dinner."

"I'll want more than that."

"Don't push your luck, Buster."

Chapter 35

An hour later they pulled into the carpark on the edge of Boscastle village, taking the last parking space. The village hummed with activity, with crowds of people on the one main street. This was a tourist destination, most of the shops being craft and gift shops and food outlets. Bob and Maggie walked down to a little bridge they had crossed over as they drove in. He led her to a footpath to the right, that led along the side of a stream toward the narrow steep sided cliffs on both sides.

"It's down there," he pointed. "The river leads to the sea. You can't quite see it from here, but it's just around the bend, down at the end. If we walk that far, we'll be able to see it." He looked at his watch. "Sea should wash around that bend soon. High tide in about an hour and a half."

There were a few houses and shops on either side of the stream and Maggie could see a National Trust store. Bob saw where she was looking. "This is all National Trust land and property, on each side of the harbour and the cliffs too. Further on you'll be able to see the first harbour wall."

They strolled in the sunshine, glancing in the shops, looking for the museum. Maggie spotted it, set back from the pathway up against the cliff face. She headed straight for the front door, paid for the entrance fee and a guidebook, and headed for the first exhibit.

"It's a converted house, not a purpose-built museum," she whispered to Bob. As they walked around, they found the rooms had been cleverly transformed into walkways that led from one glass-cased set of artefacts to another. The lighting was dark and the atmosphere a little creepy.

"Somewhere in here they have an exhibition of poppets," Bob said. "I saw a flyer. That's why I thought of it. And there'll be interesting information here too about the history of witchcraft in

Cornwall."

An hour later they emerged back into the sunlight, both reflective and with an armful of books, pamphlets, and posters.

"How about we find somewhere to sit and talk about what we've just seen?" Bob asked.

"Bob, if you don't mind, I'd prefer to walk a little and talk it through." She paused and turned to the path above the stream leading down to the curving harbour wall. "Can we go in that direction?"

"We can walk past it, down to the sea, if you like."

They crossed the arched white footbridge; Maggie took Bob's hand, and they wandered down the path towards the harbour wall where the sea was already pushing in around the bend. The first two boats, marooned in the mud inside the harbour wall, were almost floating. The sea was moving up towards them.

"On a nice sunny day like this it's beautiful, isn't it?" Bob said.

"Must be bleak in winter, when there are few tourists. Very quiet."

"Worst time ever was summer, about thirteen or fourteen years ago. Do you remember the flash flood?"

Maggie paused for a minute then said, "Yes, I'd forgotten it was here. It rose over the banks and flooded these houses, didn't it?"

"It was a raging torrent, following a storm up on the moors, so fast-moving it took everything in its path – cars, caravans, trees and material from collapsed buildings. It's reckoned that in the space of two hours it was the equivalent of the Thames flowing at huge speed down Boscastle High Street, like through a funnel. The worst flash flood in four hundred years."

Maggie glanced over at the tranquil water flowing ten feet below between what looked like solid river banks. "I can't imagine how terrifying it must have been."

"And so fast," Bob said. "It started about midday and by three in the afternoon it had overwhelmed the whole place."

They walked along in silence as an increasing number of gulls wheeled and dived above them, aware of the sound and scent of the incoming water.

"Have we learned anything useful here today?" Maggie asked as they reached the harbour wall.

"Don't know about you," Bob replied, "but I can see that Ann Quinn has all the right props. But... as we think the bits of wood and material that Zelah has may be the remains of a poppet, then we must conclude that witchcraft will play a part in finding out what we need to know."

They ascended the path that led round the side of the hill, away from the harbour and out towards the sea. It wound uphill and as it became rougher and steeper Maggie found she was puffing to keep up with Bob. Also, she could see that there was still a way to go to reach the edge of the cliff that marked the boundary of the coast.

"Let's stop here," she panted and sat down. "We're high enough and look at that view!"

They were opposite the headland of Warren Point on the other side of Boscastle harbour and there was now an endless view of the sea, shimmering out to the horizon, a deeper blue than Maggie had seen before. It was a calm, empty sea, not even the white sails of yachts in the distance.

Bob plonked down beside her. "You need a serious exercise programme when we get back."

Ignoring him, she said, "I've learned that there's a lot more to witchcraft than I ever thought. I agree now that Ann Quinn is a caricature. She's left nothing out. She had one of everything. Except the cats, and she had too many of them. But even in witchcraft there's good and bad. Historically, they were simply weird old women who made potions and simple herb cures and convinced themselves, probably after they'd swallowed a few too many of their own mushrooms, that they could do supernatural things. But the poppets? That's something else. Do you think Ann Quinn is basically a harmless batty old woman?"

"Not at all," he said, sharply enough for Maggie to turn away from her contemplation of the sea and look at him. "I don't think she has any supernatural powers, but I don't think she's harmless. I got a bad feeling around her."

"Experience?" Maggie said, tapping her nose in the gesture Bob used to demonstrate his professional intuition.

"Exactly. A bad feeling. You get to know when they aren't prepared to stop at anything. I'll check out her record with the local nick. She's angry with us because you didn't supply what she wanted. And that stupid little doll made me cross."

She watched him clench and unclench his fists.

"But would you agree that being well attuned with nature could bring about... something unusual?"

"Well, given that Nick can see a human energy field and Alice sees colours vaporising off people, I would say that's a given. There's a lot more that we don't know about and maybe the historical lack of understanding has given people with such powers names like witch or cunning man. Historically it's been dealt with in the way people deal with anything they don't understand: try to destroy it."

"Thank God we're more enlightened now," Bob said, jumping up. "Come on, let's get back. It'll take us at least an hour and a half with the traffic building for the holiday weekend. The sky-riders will be home already. And dying to tell us what we missed."

"I'd forgotten about them! Damn. I'll call as soon as we get a signal."

Chapter 36

It took over two hours to get back to Avilion. By the time they walked into the kitchen, Maggie was hot, tired, and grumpy. "You wouldn't believe the queues we've been in. Half the country is making its way down to Cornwall for the Bank Holiday weekend."

Zelah handed them each a cold drink. "Let's all go sit in the shade and we can exchange stories. Your kids are dying to tell you about the helicopter ride."

"Was it good?"

"Spectacular," Zelah replied. "Although Nick may have a different word for it."

"Did he… really?"

"Oh, yes. But not until we got back on the ground."

"Poor Nick. Was it worth it though?"

"Most definitely," Zelah enthused. "Apart from being a wonderful experience, we could see the footprint of the house clearly. We could even see where the old well used to be. But not much of the hamlet. Can't say it gets us any closer to anything, though."

"We're the same," Maggie replied. "But we picked up one strong lead from Ann Quinn, who, by the way," she stopped to take another drink, "is a very unpleasant woman and Bob thinks a total fraud."

"What do you think?" Zelah asked.

"Honestly, I'm wavering, but in his direction. But only because we went on to the Museum of Witchcraft and Magic this afternoon. It put some of Ann Quinn's stuff in perspective." She lowered her voice. "Bob thinks the woman came here spying on us. She knows that you're the owner of the ring. But she only knew or cared about the one ring. She may have been listening in on our discussions. We will have to make sure every night we lock all the doors and windows on the ground floor."

"Surely not!" Zelah responded. "If she's one of these batty old women, then her bark will be worse than her bite."

"Bob's gone to check if she has any kind of record. He doesn't think it will be serious stuff, but probably nasty and meant to scare people."

"Old bitch," Zelah remarked. "She'll get short shrift from me if she tries anything here. So, what's the lead?"

"It's a vicar, based in Flintshire. According to Ann Quinn he's descended from Peter Steelfox. And she said something about a letter. That was before she clammed up and threw insults at us. I've got her family tree. I snapped it with the phone and sent it to you. She thinks I deleted it. She says she's descended from a witch called Julia Pencarrow. You remember, one name from the trial. I'll get online tonight and check."

Before Zelah could say more, Nick returned from the beach with Jack and Alice, who dragged Maggie into the garden and regaled her with the story of the afternoon, not leaving out Nick's unfortunate bout of air sickness. He joined them and looked sheepish, but Maggie didn't tease him, and she thought he was grateful.

"So, what have you done today, Mum?" Alice asked.

"Bob and I met and interviewed a woman who says she is a witch. Then we had lunch. Then we went to the Museum of Witchcraft and Magic."

"What? Without us!" Alice's mouth fell open.

"Is she really a witch?" asked Jack.

"If there is such a thing as a real witch. But no, we don't think so. She's playing the part rather well, but we don't think she's genuine."

"Did she have a cat, and a broomstick, and a pointy hat?" Alice asked.

"A cat, yes. Not the others. But lots of other witchy stuff. Too much, in fact."

"Did she do any spells, or anything?"

"No Alice. She was nasty, unpleasant, and insulting.

Threatened to curse us if we didn't let her have Zelah's ring."

"What a bitch," Alice replied vaguely.

"Alice!"

Alice shrugged. "Zelah says it about lots of people."

"Well Zelah shouldn't."

As Zelah had walked out to join them, Maggie changed the subject. "So, I have work to start on tonight. Just an hour on the computer," she said. Alice looked glum. Maggie turned to Jack. "Perhaps you can help, to make it quicker."

"Sure. What shall I do?"

"You can get on your laptop after dinner and look at the 1939 register for the property near St Breward, called Quinn Farm. Find out who lived there and let me have the details. OK?"

He jumped up from his chair. "I'll make a start now."

She turned to Alice. "Tomorrow, we're going to Mên-an-Tol, in the morning. Do you know enough about it before we go?"

"Not a lot, not yet. Shall I go look?"

"That would be an excellent idea. You'll be the lead person, telling us about it. OK with you?"

Alice nodded happily and followed Jack into the house. After a few minutes Maggie could see them both in the conservatory, chatting as they hammered out on their respective keyboards.

"Sorry I laughed," Maggie said, turning to Nick. "Was it bad?"

"It was awful."

"Poor Nick," she said, putting a hand on his arm, which he pulled away as Bob arrived.

"I knew I was right." He looked from one to the other, then back at Maggie. "Ann Quinn has previous for assault and for harassment and intimidation. She doesn't like people who disagree with her. Hit one and stalked the other. Right about that too, wasn't I? She was here."

In answer to Nick's puzzled look, Maggie gave him a summary of their visit and of Bob's suspicions.

"Then we must all be careful. Just as well the holiday is ending. We should enjoy the rest, not get caught up in something this unpleasant."

Maggie wasn't sure if this was a rebuke or a sympathetic warning, but carried on, speaking to Bob, "I expect you're probably right, but don't underestimate the power of someone who believes they have powers or gifts, or whatever we call them. The woman has convinced herself because certain things have turned out as she planned. Coincidence? Who knows? But things may happen that we don't understand in the next few days. If we are ready for them, it will be OK." He turned away and gazed out to sea.

**

It had become a habit to take a stroll in the evening, to the top of the road and down to Land's End to watch the sunset at this furthest westerly point in England. Maggie refused to go, pleading tiredness after a long day, but Zelah insisted. If Nick could do it after his day, Zelah said, they all could.

It was a spectacular sunset, the gold of the setting sun rippling out across the water as a breeze scurried around them on the cliff edge. As the last remnants of a huge red sun sank below the horizon they wandered back up, took a last drink in the garden, then locked up the house and went to bed.

As she fell asleep, Maggie smiled to herself, feeling contented and lazy, all being well with the world, or with hers at least, as she drifted out of consciousness.

Chapter 37
Truro, 1736

The Black Dog in the back streets of Truro was not one frequented by decent men, being dark, dingy, and having a stink that couldn't be cleaned away, of piss and vomit. Not that anyone had ever tried. The rushes on the floor were as black as the smoke-stained walls and ceiling. The windows had such a covering of grime it was impossible to see in or out. This was how the customers of The Dirty Dog, as it was known locally, liked it. Their business was not intended to be seen.

This made it an ideal meeting place for Sir John Vyse and his servant, although they took care to conceal as much of their appearance as possible. They had buttoned their greatcoats to the chin, their hats pulled down as far as they would go, and scarves tied up to the mouth. Fortunately, it was cold enough on the day following Mildred Vyse's inquest for their appearance not to be noteworthy.

After ensuring they were not seen or followed, they entered through the broken door of the inn and headed straight to a table in the small parlour off the main bar, in the darkest corner where even the pathetic light given out by the candles about them would hide their meeting.

The barman wasn't attentive. They ordered beer, sat, and waited. From the bar came bursts of raucous laughter, interspersed with the occasional high-pitched scream. This could have been of delight or fear, it was impossible to tell. The prostitutes who serviced the inn's customers were of no interest to them. One approached with a lustful eye on Sir John, but he sent her packing with the clear understanding they be left alone.

Then they sat in silence.

Fifteen minutes later they were joined at the table. This time the barman looked with some curiosity. Despite the black cloak and heavy hood that obscured the face of the newcomer, he could tell it was a woman. Sir John saw him looking and waved a hand at him to mind his own business, which he did.

Having seated herself, Julia Pencarrow removed her hood. She looked from one man to the other and raised her eyebrows.

"I believe it is truly over, now," Sir John began. "Mistress Pencarrow, I am sorry for the way they treated you, but there will be no further consequences."

"I know, Sir John. It's a little hard, but I can bear it. Edmund understands, too. He does not blame me, but he does not truly know. Like your Emma, Master Steelfox."

Edward Steelfox kept his expression blank.

"Your husband is a good man, mistress," said Sir John, "but, we should move on to what we must do next. Are we all agreed?"

They gave a brief, stiff nod.

From his greatcoat he produced three pieces of parchment.

"I have written out three copies, one for each of us. And each of us to sign each one. No one person should ever have to bear alone the responsibility for what we all decided should be done." He laid the three documents out on the table and they leaned in to read, peering in the poor light.

After a few minutes Edward Steelfox said, "I am content. This is a true account. I will bear my share."

He took up the quill that Sir John had produced, dipped it in the small pot of ink, and signed his name. Then, Julia Pencarrow nodded and did the same.

"What is to become of the ring and the... things," he spat out the word, "that she had about her person?"

"I believe that Master Steelfox should keep the ring," Julia Pencarrow replied. "I shall deal with the poppet." She smiled with thin lips at the two men. "I have no fear of them."

Edward Steelfox shuddered. "No, thank you Mistress Pencarrow. You decide its fate. I could not bear to look at it. I shall never see my brother again. I want no reminder of his downfall, or his lost love."

She nodded and turned to Sir John. "And you, my Lord?"

"Destroy everything," he said. "After this day, although we shall all meet in our daily lives, I wish never to speak of this again. I have no secrets from either of you in this matter. I admit I married my wife for money. I did not know she was an abomination."

Julia laid a hand on his arm, which was quickly shaken off. She was still his servant.

"She had no power to do anything with them, Sir John. She wanted to believe she had, and somewhere in her past someone had told her what the poppets were and what they could do. But she could not use them."

"Unlike yourself," he muttered.

Her eyes darkened. "I did what we agreed. I abhor these objects. It was the only time, I told you. I never did such a thing before and I never will again."

"Then I beg forgiveness, Mistress," he said.

"If we are done," said Edward, "we should leave, before we attract undue attention." He flicked his eyes at the barman, who was watching them from behind a pillar.

Sir John took up the quill and signed his name on each parchment, then rolled up each one, tied it with red string, gave one each to Julia and Edward and put the third into a pocket inside his coat.

"On death, to be destroyed and those remaining to be informed of the destruction," he stated. They nodded. Julia pulled her hood up to obscure her face once again, and putting her head down, hurried from the Inn.

"This place stinks worse than the devil's privy," Edward remarked as they followed her. By the time the two men reached the door there was no sign of Julia Pencarrow in the narrow lane.

It rained. They made their way back to Penwith in silence. When they arrived, the housekeeper was there to meet them. They didn't understand how she had reached the house before them, they being on horseback, she on foot. But there were many things about quiet, respectful Julia Pencarrow that they had no wish to know.

Chapter 38

She didn't know what time it was, but it must have been early because there was no hint of the dawn. Was it a noise that had awoken her, a real one or in a dream? Whatever, Maggie was suddenly sitting up in bed, her heart thumping, knowing there was an intruder.

Or was there? Maybe she had just dreamed it. Or maybe Zelah or Nick couldn't sleep and was down in the kitchen. She waited. This time it was a crash, the sound of something breaking.

Now Bob was awake, sitting bolt upright beside her, finger to his lips. Definitely an intruder. Even in his sleep Bob could recognise the difference between good and bad noises.

He slipped on shorts and tee-shirt and crept silently to the bedroom door, opened it, and peered downstairs. Turning back to her, he gestured that he was going down. She shook her head frantically, but he carried on. She tiptoed to the door, watched him disappear down the stairs, round the bend where she lost sight of him. Heard him descend the final three steps with heavier, deliberate footsteps.

There was no other sound. None of the others had woken up.

Then something else crashed, followed by a yell. Unable to contain herself, Maggie ran down the stairs on bare feet, to find Bob standing in the hall, a serious looking stick raised in one hand, his fingers to his lips in the other. Then he whispered to her, "Go back up and call me. Loudly."

Maggie crept back up the stairs and shouted down his name. From somewhere in the house came the sound of a door banging, then, after a few minutes, a little further away, a car engine started and quickly faded away. She hurried back down the stairs and this time found Bob in the doorway to the dining room, looking out through the conservatory at the dark garden.

"What was that about?" she whispered to him.

"No need to whisper now," he replied. "Whoever it was, they've gone."

"But it was Ann Quinn, wasn't it?"

"Yes, it was." He had answered quickly; too quickly, Maggie thought. "Who else could it have been?"

"Nobody. I was expecting something, so I laid a trap, and she fell right into it. I'm just going to check the door, make sure it's properly locked. Then I'll come back up. Go on, I'll be there in two minutes."

Maggie was sitting next to the window when Bob came back upstairs.

"What did you find?"

He got back into bed. "Well, I can't figure out how she got the door open. I know for certain I locked it. But I made sure with all the doors that if anyone got in, they would have a surprise."

"That worked, at least," Maggie replied. She glanced at the clock on the bedside table. "A bit early to get up." She plumped up the pillows. "I'll see if I can get back to sleep, but if not, I'll get up and do some research."

Bob grunted and she realised that he was already asleep. It might not bother him Ann Quinn had tried to break in, but now Maggie was attuned to external noises. It was unlikely that the woman would try again. And hopefully Bob's welcoming surprise would put her off. She thought about what to say to the others. Zelah and Nick had to be told, but not the children.

After half an hour of tossing and turning, Maggie accepted that her brain was not going to magically lullaby itself to sleep. She went quietly and warily downstairs. Glancing out of the east-facing window on the landing, she could see a lightening of the sky. Within minutes of reaching the office, the birdsong began. That was a relief. She went into the kitchen to make herself a pot of coffee while her laptop started up. When it was ready, she took a long gulp of hot liquid and started on Ann Quinn's family tree.

Ann had only followed her maternal line, believing that to be the ancestor of her witch heritage and her 'gifts'. This was a normal belief for witches. Mother to daughter and so on, through the ages.

Jack had done a thorough job on the 1939 register and had gone beyond that. He had found Quinn Cottage – it still had that name. There were six inhabitants, all Quinns. Harold, Anne's father, was present in the household, along with his parents and two siblings, and an old man called Josiah Quinn. Harold Quinn and Susan Percy, Anne's mother, had married in 1943, so Maggie checked Anne's maternal line for authenticity. All she had to do was to check Anne's research, and that appeared solid, until she came across something at the start of the 19th century. Anne's family tree suggested her three-times great-grandmother was Sarah Milligan, born in 1805. But the only match Maggie could find was a Sarah Miller, born in 1778. This would have made the woman almost sixty years old when her daughter Sarah, the next in Anne's line, was born in 1835. This later date was correct. But sixty was beyond the average life expectancy for poor people, so bearing a child at that age seemed beyond far-fetched. This was a case of making the facts stretch to meet the aspiration.

Even more unlikely, she had Sarah's mother as Alice Pencarrow, born in 1765 and married to James Miller in 1798. Maggie checked the records and found that this was correct and that it was in the parish of Penwith. This was likely the first link to Julia Pencarrow. She would have to trace this Alice's parents. But, after Alice, Anne's research was definitely wrong.

Just as she was about to dive into the Cornish records again, the sound of footsteps coming downstairs made her look up, and Zelah poked her head around the office door.

"What the hell are you doing up at seven in the morning?"

"I could ask you the same thing," Maggie replied. "Is it seven? That means I've been here for almost two hours."

"What the hell for?" Zelah looked angry. "Look, Maggie, this is a holiday. You don't need to do this—"

Maggie interrupted her. "That's not the reason." She told Zelah about the attempted break-in. And Nick matched Zelah's look of shock, when he arrived halfway through the story.

When Maggie had finished, Nick shook his head. "I was fearing something like this. But," he paused and looked directly at them, "it should not dismay us. I said yesterday we should be prepared. It's just happened sooner than we expected. Perhaps she was after the ring. Well, forewarned is forearmed. I suggest that wherever we go from now on, Zelah, you take all three rings with you." Zelah nodded.

"I'm not telling the kids," Maggie warned. "We'll all just have to be more careful about locking up when we aren't here. Now I'm feeling angry. How dare she!"

"I'll tell DC Mooney, when he comes back. But we shouldn't be frightened."

"I'm not," Maggie replied, eyes narrowing.

"Anything else we need to talk about before we set off?" asked Nick. "Alice is looking forward to this. She's even written notes for us."

Maggie's face softened. "Then we'll make it special for her. We're leaving at ten, right?"

"Yes," Nick replied, "it's only a twenty-minute drive away."

Chapter 39

Just before ten they were all ready to go, in the hallway, walking boots in hand, sun hats on heads and slathered in sun cream. Alice's excitement was palpable. Maggie had not seen her so happy and animated for some time. No matter how Maggie felt, this was Alice's current hobby, and she was determined to take it seriously and ask intelligent questions.

They took the main road, turned off towards St Just, and then the coastal road north. Mên-an-Tol was well signposted, and they were able to park on the roadside. There were half a dozen other cars. They got out and put on boots.

"It's supposed to be about half a mile along the footpath," Alice said, pointing over the road to where a sign showed a rough path.

The site turned out to be about a twenty-minute stroll from the roadside, but on a beautiful day the scenery was spectacular.

"Is it me, or is the air particularly clear here?" Zelah asked as they walked along the footpath. All around and into the distance was the rough, treeless landscape of the Penwith peninsula. There was more evidence of prehistoric settlement here than anywhere else in the country. Maggie shivered despite the growing heat.

"What's up, Mum?" Jack asked, sensing her unease.

"Nothing," she replied. "It's just... a shivery feeling I get from a place that seems to have been here forever. The idea of timelessness, I think. Look, people over there. That must be it."

Alice had spotted them too and led the party off the path and through the scrub. As they got closer, they could see a few upright stones, then Mên-an-Tol itself, standing between the uprights. The stone was small, and they all obediently gathered together, waiting for Alice. She was ambling around it, gazing from it to the surrounding stones. After three circuits, she stopped. They gathered closer to her. She took her notes out of her pocket, glanced at them, then put them away again.

"It's supposed to be about three thousand years old," she began. "No one knows what it was originally put here for. These other standing stones are part of a circle. There are more, but they're buried under the ground. There are lots of stories and folktales about the stone. Some say it would cure sick children if they passed through it. That's a bit rubbish. Infertile women came here and performed a rite, to get pregnant. That probably didn't work, either.

"Maybe it was once a burial place. But it was special to the people who put it here, and it's only one of two this size in the whole country. The other one is in Cornwall, too. There are stories it's a gateway into other worlds." She finished and looked around at them.

Bob was the first to speak. "That's fascinating, Alice. Is there any evidence of how it might have got here?"

"None," she replied. "Lots of theories, but just guesses. That's what's so odd about it. I mean, we know what the quoits and circles are, but not this stone."

"I'm not sure what a quoit is, Alice?" Zelah said.

Picking up her notes again Alice said, "It's a set of three or more stones, two or more uprights, and one across the top. The top stone is called a capstone. It's a burial chamber and supposed to be part of a burial ritual, up to five thousand years old. The best known in Cornwall is Lanyon Quoit, further north. Close to here is Zennor Quoit, but it's a collapsed one. Nick and I saw it last week."

"And this one, Alice, is the hole in the centre manmade or natural?" Maggie asked.

"No idea, no one knows how it came to be like this," Alice said. She stepped around it again, her hand on the smooth stone as she walked. Again, she walked around it three times. Then, in front of the hole she stopped, knelt and put her head through. After less than a second, she pulled it back with a sharp intake of breath. Nick noticed and hurried up to her to ask if she was OK. Alice shook her head and whispered, "Later." He nodded quickly.

Bob organised photos, with all of them gathered next to the

various stones. Maggie put her arm around Alice. "This has been wonderful," she said. Alice smiled wanly. "Anything wrong?" Maggie asked. Alice shook her head and wandered off to look at the stones from a distance. "It's a haunting place," Maggie said to Alice's back.

Alice whipped around. "What do you mean?"

"Nothing. Just the atmosphere. You know, very ancient and all that. A people who didn't understand our meaning of time. What did you think I meant?"

Alice shrugged, and Maggie knew something was wrong, but this was not the time to ask.

After ten minutes they all walked back to the cars. "Shall we go somewhere else?" Maggie asked as they reached the roadside.

"No, let's go back," Alice replied before anyone else could speak. "Are we going home now?"

Chapter 40

Back at the house Bob was quiet. "I thought I'd found something she'd like," he said to Maggie when they were alone in the kitchen.

Maggie put an arm around him. "She was enjoying it. Something happened. I don't know what, but I will find out." He pulled away from her and put both hands on the counter, his head down. "Do you think this will work out, Maggie?" he asked without looking at her.

She froze. "You mean, you and me?"

He nodded.

"Do you want out? If so, let me know now. You knew I had children and that one of them wasn't easy."

"I don't want out!" He looked up at her from the counter. "But I want her to accept me, even if she doesn't like me much. Is that too much to ask?"

"No. We said we'd talk about her father." She folded her arms and leaned back against the counter. "I've been thinking about it, but it's been a surprise. I've realised that I can't define David's relationship with his children. He wasn't a bad father. He was kind and polite; he always listened to what they had to say. But it always felt like he wasn't part of the family setup. But then I ask myself am I feeling like this with hindsight? Now I know he was leading a double life I think we were just part of his elaborate disguise. You know already that if he hadn't died, he'd probably have been in jail now. I haven't ever discussed this with the kids, they're still too young. I don't know what she thinks about him, if she misses him, or not. I want to talk, but I'm not ready."

"Fair enough," he said. "You must, eventually. It will eat you up if you don't. And they will ask, eventually. But if they haven't, then they aren't ready either. Best leave it at that." He moved closer to her. "I want it to work between us, I really do. You don't know everything about me, either and I'm not ready. I think we trust each other. But I am concerned that if I can't get on better with Alice, it might become a choice for you."

"No," she replied firmly, "I will talk to her. But first, I must find out what happened this morning. What disturbed her? Can you wait for that before we decide anything further?"

He drew a deep breath. "Yes. I'd like to know too."

Maggie went to look for Alice and found her sitting in her bedroom, cross-legged on her bed, staring out of the window. Maggie sat beside her and went to take her hand but found Alice had balled it into a fist and was rhythmically punching her leg. Instead, she put her arm around Alice's shoulder. The punching continued, but Alice moved her head onto Maggie's shoulder.

"Do you want to tell me what happened this morning?"

"What's wrong with me, Mum?"

Maggie felt her stomach tightening. "There is absolutely nothing wrong with you. Why?"

"I don't know what made me do it. It was like…" Alice stopped and swallowed, her body tensing.

"Just spit it out," Maggie said, squeezing her shoulders. "What was it like?"

"It was like a voice next to my head telling me what to do. To put my hand on the stone and walk around it three times." She exhaled like a deflating balloon, moving closer to Maggie, and opening her hands to put them into her mother's.

"But that wasn't the end, was it?" Maggie sensed there was more.

"Then I put my head through the centre, but I was still holding on."

"Yes, I saw that. What did you see?"

"How do you know I saw something?"

"I saw your face when you pulled your head out. And I saw Nick speak to you."

A deep sigh. "OK. There was a man, across the other side of the field. He turned and looked at me and put his hand up and did this." She lifted one hand out of Maggie's and crooked one finger in a beckoning gesture.

"Why did you pull back? Did he look dangerous?" Maggie hadn't noticed anyone else on the other side of the field, but she wasn't particularly looking.

"I couldn't tell. He was wearing a long coat, with a tie around his middle and the sleeves were big near his hands, and he had a hood up, so I couldn't see his face."

"He must have been very warm. It was hot this morning."

"No, I think he was cold. He must have been."

"Why do you think?"

"Because on his side of the stone it looked cold. It felt like I was being sucked through." She put her hands back into Maggie's and Maggie squeezed them tightly.

"Alice, first, I will repeat; there is nothing wrong with you. If there was something wrong with you then we'd have to say there's something wrong with Nick too, wouldn't we?"

"I suppose."

"Can we agree that there is absolutely nothing wrong with Nick?" Alice nodded her head several times.

"Then perhaps we should talk to him and see what his take is. What do you think?"

Alice nodded and jumped off the bed. "Let's do it. I wasn't going to tell anyone, but Nick will understand."

"One more thing before we go." Alice stopped in the doorway and looked around.

"Bob thinks whatever went wrong is his fault. It was his idea to go there."

Alice frowned, then turned and left the room. Instead of going to find Nick, she went to the kitchen where Bob was still standing, gazing out to sea.

"It wasn't your fault. It was nothing to do with you." She half turned around but stopped still and turned back. "That came out wrong, sorry. It was a good place, I liked it. Mum will tell you." She went into the garden and Maggie joined Bob.

When she had explained to him what Alice had told her, he folded his arms and leaned back against the counter, shaking his head. He was about to say something when his phone rang and he answered it, indicating to Maggie to wait with him.

His responses were short; "OK", "I see", "Yes, I will", and "Not a problem, see you in half an hour."

"That was DC Mooney," he said, and Maggie nodded. "He's got an update for Zelah and he's coming over. That OK?"

She was about to say something sarcastic about asking for approval after the fact, but his expression told her to hold it in. "Sure. I don't know where Zelah went. Let's tell her. Any idea what it is?"

"Not a clue," he said as they walked outside into the sunshine and saw Zelah coming up the path from the beach. When Bob told her that DC Mooney was on his way, she didn't react but walked into the house. As Maggie and Bob sat soaking up the sun, Zelah returned five minutes later with a pot of coffee and several cups.

"I think this is the warmest day yet," she remarked. "Help yourselves. Not as humid as yesterday."

Bob went to speak, but Maggie stopped him with a light touch on his leg. She knew Zelah was preparing herself.

"I passed Nick and Alice walking down to the beach. I went down with Jack. He's surfing."

"Thanks," Maggie replied. "We have nothing else on this afternoon, so he can take his time. Did he take his phone?"

"No," Zelah replied. "It's a scrum down there today. He was afraid if he left it on the beach it would get nicked. I said I'd go down again in a couple of hours and give him a lift if he hadn't come up."

This confirmed Maggie's suspicion that Jack was talking to Zelah about the next step in his education, and for a moment she felt pangs of anger and jealousy. Alice talking to Nick, Jack talking to Zelah. Was she being replaced? Didn't they trust her with their important stuff anymore? Her eyes welled up. She closed them and leaned back in her chair pretending to soak up the sun, but Zelah saw it.

"Now what the hell?" she demanded. When she didn't get a reply, she fell silent for a few moments, then said, "Look, I'm just not his mother, that's all. He needs another perspective. I expect he's talked to Bob, too."

Bob blushed. "Yeah," he said, turning to Maggie. "He wanted a 'no frills' discussion about school. He wanted to be sure he'd thought everything through before he talked to you, that's all. Like Zelah said, we're not his parents. We don't have the same emotional attachment. We can give an opinion. But he gets how much you love him and want the best for him."

He took her hand. Maggie sniffed and Zelah handed her a tissue. "They're growing up. They need space. They're seeing the world from an independent viewpoint, not through your eyes."

Bob scowled at Zelah. "Harsh, Zelah. Maggie, you've been through a lot in the past couple of years. You got them through their father's death and moving them away from the world they loved. Most of it has worked, all credit to you, but some hasn't. School hasn't. You'll have to face that when you get back. Ask Jack to talk to you. He's doing a lot of thinking right now."

Before she could reply the doorbell rang. "Mooney," Bob said and got up to let him in.

"I'll leave you and Bob to it," Maggie said to Zelah, jumping up. She passed Bob and the detective in the hall. "Just going for a swim," she said and ran upstairs.

Maggie changed and set off with her towel in hand. She didn't pass Nick, Alice, or Jack on the way down the cliff path, which was just as well. She didn't want to speak to anyone. The beach was the most crowded she had seen it. The perfect weather had brought out local people and visitors and the beach café looked to be doing a roaring trade. Passing the surfers, Maggie saw Jack sitting on his board and waved, but he didn't see her. She walked to the far end where it wasn't so crowded, put her towel on the rocks and walked into the water. The waves weren't strong today, enough for surfing and body boarding but not too much to interfere with swimming. With a deep breath she dived under, revelling in the cool water and she struck out in a course parallel to the shore.

Chapter 41

Maggie didn't see Nick, Alice, or Jack on her way back up to the house, half an hour later. She had looked again for Jack in the surfers' area but couldn't see him and assumed he had gone. Reaching the house, Maggie saw she was right. DC Mooney had gone, and the others were in the garden. Her hair had dried on the way up the path, but she felt salty, so she went to shower, tidy herself up, put on shorts and a tee-shirt and go back to the garden.

Nick had made a heap of sandwiches of all varieties and put out plates of salad. Maggie immediately grabbed a plateful and waded in.

"Hungry?" Bob asked, after watching three sandwiches disappear without a word.

"Swimming and thinking gives me an appetite."

"Better?" he asked.

"Much." She paused and took another sandwich. "What did I miss?"

"A lot." said Zelah, but there was no antagonism just what seemed to Maggie a fatalistic acceptance of bad news.

"Can you tell me now, or should I wait?"

"No point in waiting. It is what it is. The detective has been following up Jay's mother. Her name was Doreen Stanley, and she lived in Exeter. She had an alcohol problem, which was why Jay was taken from her. He was in a children's home more than once. I knew that. He told me about it. But the last time was with the vicar. Around the time Jay disappeared, she got herself sober, but she had an abusive boyfriend. Apparently, she'd decided to bring Jay home and got up the courage to tell the boyfriend to leave. His response was to beat her up, so badly she ended up in hospital. After a few days she discharged herself, saying she would get her son and went back to the house in Exeter. After a week because of her discharging herself when she wasn't well – she had broken ribs and lots of bruises – the police went to see her. They'd arrested the boyfriend for Grievous Bodily Harm. She must have been in a right state. But she wasn't there. She'd only had a handbag with her when she left hospital, no suitcase, no clothes. Neither she nor Jay were heard of again."

"Did anyone report her disappearance?" asked Maggie.

"The hospital told the police, because of the beating. They were expecting her to press charges. But it doesn't seem like they followed anything up. They made enquiries and found that someone had seen her at the bus station. But they didn't follow it any further. The boyfriend was released stayed in the house for a few months, then he disappeared. Case closed."

As she stopped talking Zelah blew her nose.

"What do you think, Zelah?" Maggie asked. "Do you think she got away with Jay? It doesn't fit with what Tracy said, but perhaps she wanted to dig in a twisting knife. From what you've told us, that kind of cruelty would delight her. If Jay got away with his mother, Tracy wouldn't have liked that, would she?"

"I don't know what to think. He left the photograph with me, but maybe they had to make a run for it. Tracy was so evil she could have set it up for me like this. Maybe she knew that Jay's mother got him. Jay and I were close, we only had each other. Us two against the horrors of our world. I can't believe he left without a word or a message for me. Or never got in touch again."

"That's the bit that leaves me with a question mark," Bob said. "Why did he never get in touch again? It was a lot easier to disappear in those days. Early sixties, wasn't it Zelah?" She nodded. "No internet, no mobile phones, no electronic signals to give away your whereabouts. They could have changed their names and started again. But," he paused, rubbing his chin, "I've come across these cases. They nearly always contact someone they know will be frantic about them. Someone they trust. Same as women running away from domestic abuse get a message to a close friend. Disappearing and never being heard from is unusual."

"How long exactly was it before you ran away?" Nick asked Zelah.

"Another five years," she replied. "I think... that if Jay had been able to, he would have let me know that he was OK. It was something we talked about. I knew that the charity had no interest in me. I was a hundred percent in the hands of Hopton. But Jay? He could have been moved at any time. We agreed that if that happened, we would have a code for him to let me know. If he got put somewhere good, or if he got back to his mother, he'd try to get me there, too." Zelah's voice broke into a fierce whisper, "I waited and waited, but nothing came. And none of them ever spoke about it. I asked once, and the wife hit me hard on the head." She rubbed her ear and shook her head. "Told me Jay was wicked, had run away and I would not speak his name again in her house. It isn't right!"

"I agree," Bob said.

Zelah's head shot up. "It's not right, none of it. Something happened, but how can we find the truth now?"

Maggie had a thought. "Do you think it's anything to do with the rings, and the other stuff?" She couldn't bring herself to call the poppet by its name.

"Absolutely not," Zelah replied. "I knew nothing about them."

"But could Jay have known?"

Zelah considered. "No. If he had, he'd have told me. Apart from Martin, Jay was the best friend I ever had. We didn't have secrets." Her voice had recovered its strength.

"What next?" Maggie asked.

"Mark will keep digging. He wants Zelah and Archie to get together again, to see what else they can produce," Bob replied.

"In the meantime, I will get on with my 'unpaid domestic duties', as the work of a housewife was referred to in the 1939 register." Maggie stood up and walked into the house but halted in the doorway.

"Zelah," she said, "who did the housework in the Hopton house? Was it Mrs Hopton?"

"Definitely not," Zelah replied. "Much too snobby. I hadn't thought about that. Someone must have come in. I can't remember. I'll talk to Archie. He might recall something."

"Must have been someone local," Maggie mused.

"Excellent point," Bob said, beaming at her. "Upload the memory programme, Zelah."

Chapter 42

Bob's last evening with them gave a sense of the holiday being over, and dinner was a quiet affair. Maggie's timetable included a visit to Trerice the following morning and as they were all still up for it, they agreed that they would all go but afterwards Bob would carry on back home.

"I was thinking," Maggie said, "let's cancel Monday and Tuesday, and do something we want to do for enjoyment, not for Maze. We'll be leaving first thing Wednesday. And it's not that far if we need to come back. We can do Cornwall in a day, at a stretch, or an overnight at the most."

"I agree," Nick replied. "Look where we've ended up."

"What do you mean?"

"Zelah, I've enjoyed myself and I'm grateful. In fact, it's been excellent, best holiday I've had for years. But I would prefer to end on a happy note. The amount of stuff that's hanging over us now will leave us with memories we'd prefer to forget. I'm not criticising anyone. But think about it. We have a legacy mystery that's nowhere near resolved; a woman who thinks she's a witch after us; an attempted break-in; a missing man who may have been murdered; and something more complicated for Alice."

"Are you saying we stop everything?" Zelah demanded.

"No. I'm just saying, let's take a breath. Look, this is a wonderful place. But do you remember what we talked about when you first suggested this holiday? I do. We all had things we wanted to do. Maggie wanted to revisit the Lizard and go to Helford. Jack fancied a visit to the listening station at Goonhilly. I thought about going back to Tintagel, to stand on the headland like I last did when I was a boy. I don't know about you, Bob. We have done none of those things. Cornwall has always been a favourite place for all of us. Lots of good memories. Can we try to fit this in before we go back? If we can, we'll return to research with more energy and determination once we're back."

"What do you think, Bob?" Maggie asked.

"Not for me to say. I'm off tomorrow. But I will say this: I've had an exciting week. I've enjoyed your company, even Zelah's scary moments. I like Cornwall. Don't let what's happened spoil any of this for you."

"Then let's rip up my schedule," Maggie said. "I got carried away. Nick's right. I'd be disappointed if I didn't get back to Helford to see the river. It's my favourite spot bar none. Don't know how I could have forgotten that."

Zelah muttered, "This is my fault."

As one they sat up and protested. It wasn't a question of fault; they were a team. She had something needing a resolution. That's what friends did. She held up a hand to silence them.

"Group hug, anyone?" Bob asked.

"Now you are getting on my nerves, Clouseau," Zelah grinned.

They sat for a while in silence, enjoying the balmy evening, the fairy lights around the garden and what had now become a more harmonious atmosphere. Eventually they wandered off to bed, feeling that nothing could now interfere with the enjoyment of their final days of holiday.

Chapter 43

They set out early the following morning. It was hot again, but there was a level of humidity in the air that hadn't been there before. By eight the temperature was already over thirty degrees. There was no breeze, and the humidity had become cloying.

"At this rate we'll have to go back to the Eden Project and go inside the Rain Forest globe to cool down," Maggie complained.

"I think it's the beginning of the end," Bob said as they pulled out of the driveway. "When it gets humid like this at the end of a long spell of hot weather, there may be a storm brewing, so this weather will break."

"We arrived in a storm," Maggie mused. "Perhaps we're destined to leave in one."

"Let's hope it's just the weather," Bob replied.

**

Having re-grouped at Trerice, they took a tour, explored the gardens, and sat in the café to have brunch. Jack was chatting enthusiastically about the likeness to Penwith to anyone who would listen, and Alice was reading a book about the Cheesewring.

Before going to bed they went with Nick's plan, of 'do what makes you happy.' He was going alone to Tintagel, to revisit the castle and walk on the headland. Zelah and Jack would revisit the disused industrial site to do more driving, then go to Goonhilly Station. Maggie, Bob, and Alice would drive to Bodmin Moor and walk to the Cheesewring. Maggie had been pleasantly surprised that Alice hadn't objected to Bob replacing Nick. She was so keen to see the standing stones she had decided that compromise was acceptable. Anyway, Maggie was happy that it would just be the three of them, giving Bob and Alice a chance to talk to each other. If aching feet and blisters could advance that cause, she would stoically suffer.

They drove from Trerice to the village of Minions where they left the car and began the circular walk. It was a little under four miles across some rougher parts of the moor. When they reached the path below the Cheesewring, they had to walk uphill to reach the stones. It enthralled Alice. She climbed to the top of the pile of flat granite stones that looked as if it might overbalance any minute. Big stones were heaped up on top of smaller ones. Bob joined her and obligingly took photos from all angles, Maggie declining to make the climb despite both of them offering to haul her up and telling her that the view across the moor was spectacular.

On the way back they explored the standing stones called The Hurlers, and eventually collapsed into the village pub in time for a final cold drink before Bob took off in his camper van back to Wales.

"I'll probably get caught up in the nightmare traffic up the M5," he said as he gave Maggie a goodbye hug. "But worth it."

Maggie nodded. Alice was beaming at him and stood with Maggie to wave goodbye before they got into Maggie's car to head back to Sennen. A breakthrough? Hopefully.

They were the last to get back. Jack and Zelah had had an enjoyable day at Goonhilly and Jack had almost got Zelah's car into third gear. Nick reported being invigorated by his walk at Tintagel.

The only thing that dampened their spirits was the weather. During the early evening the sky, instead of the usual fading celestial blue they expected, had become a dull grey. Humidity had increased and by nine the first rumble of thunder announced itself.

"Going to be a big one," Nick remarked, quickly clearing up as the first fat raindrops hit the table. "The south coast is expecting flash floods. Not as bad here, but a lot of rain."

"Well, if it clears the air I shan't mind," Zelah said. "A few degrees lower won't kill us."

"Just two days," Maggie said. She turned to Zelah. "Despite where we've ended up, this has been fantastic. I had such a good day, one of the best so far. I expect to drop into a coma tonight after I've soaked my feet."

They all headed to bed early.

The storm got properly underway just after midnight. A lengthy crackling flash of lightning, followed at once by a crash of thunder that made the windows shake awoke Maggie. She had believed as a child that this changing interval would tell her how close the eye of the storm was. But after the next flash there was no time to count as the rumble came immediately.

"Oh my," she said aloud, wondering if she should get up and have a look, torn between fear and appreciation of the spectacle. As she gave herself a minute to decide, there was another flash and smash, but this time a strange, wailing sound accompanied it. Maggie listened carefully and it came again from the garden. She wondered if it was a distressed animal. And again. She couldn't leave it. She got up, went to the window, and peered out.

The garden was in complete darkness. In better weather they left paper lanterns on. But these had been taken inside. She could make out nothing and the noise had stopped. She would have to wait for the next flash of lightning to see if it happened again or if whatever it was, had run away. She hoped for the latter. If not, she'd have to go downstairs and find a torch to try to see better from the conservatory. At that moment, a long fork of lightning filled the sky, and the land was lit in an alien blue-white hue. Just enough time for Maggie to see that it was not an animal. It was a human, female, and it was wailing again. Maggie's stomach lurched. The woman looked full of vicious excitement, howling, and screaming, holding something up above her head. Maggie's heart pounded, and she wasn't sure whether to keep watching or raise Nick and Zelah. It amazed her that no one else was moving around.

She stared intensely at the spot where she knew the figure was standing and within seconds the lightning lit up the figure again. This time Maggie saw properly. And what she saw changed her fear to disbelief and then to gut-churning anger. It was Ann Quinn, howling and chanting at the house. Maggie banged on the window, but a loud thunderclap rendered it useless in getting the mad woman's attention.

Maggie ran back to the bedside table, grabbed her mobile phone, and waited for the next burst of lightning. She didn't know what the camera might pick up, but it was worth a try. Enough was enough, she would call the police. She was poised with phone in hand and when the next flash came; she clicked randomly a few times.

The rain, which had eased off a little, built up again and it must have soaked Ann Quinn. Maggie got a torch, but as she watched, the woman stopped and cocked her head to one side as if listening to something behind her. She looked up at the far end of the house, towards the other turret, then behind her in sharp, bird-like movements. Then she turned and walked at an urgent pace out of the garden. A flash lit up her exit, and the garden was dark for a few seconds. When Maggie's eyes adjusted, she glimpsed the woman disappearing along the coastal path.

Maggie paced from the bedroom door to the window and back. Each time at the door she opened it and checked the hallway, but there was no sound of movement. Surely, she couldn't be the only one woken up by the sound of hell arriving on earth? She carefully opened Alice's door and saw her in bed, deeply asleep. She had kicked off her bed covers. Silently Maggie crept across the room, put the covers back over, watched her daughter sleep for a few moments, and went back to her own room. She paused at the top of the stairs to check for any sound below.

Maggie went straight to the window in her room. The storm was passing. A few stars had appeared between the racing clouds. The volume of the thunder faded. The moon broke through and under the light she could see no sign of a human presence in the garden.

No matter how hard she tried, Maggie couldn't get back into bed. She kept vigil in an armchair by the window for several hours. Eventually she closed her eyes for a few minutes, then opened them and sprang up when a noise outside the window disturbed her. It was the chirruping of an early bird. Dawn was breaking. The clock on the bedside table read five. She decided it was safe and crawled back into bed. But sleep came fitfully. At seven she got up, dressed, and went downstairs. Maybe she could get on with some work. It would be cathartic to lose herself in research. Half an hour of trying but failing to concentrate told her that there was no relief to be had.

It felt safe now to walk in the garden. The first thing she noticed was the smell of wet grass, pungent and verdant. The table and chairs wouldn't be useable for most of the day, but the sun was coming up, and it looked like it would be sunny. She shivered and realised that the temperature had dropped by what felt like at least ten degrees. It might be an hour yet before Zelah or Nick appeared.

She still hadn't decided what to tell them and her head felt thick. A swim might help to clear her thoughts. The sea would be cold after the storm, but that would help. She ran back to her room, put on her costume, grabbed a towel, left a note to say where she was, and ran down the path to the beach.

The sea was remarkably calm. More like a pond than an ocean. There were signs of life in the beach café as Maggie ran down into the water and dived in. Damn! She had been right; it was freezing. After a few minutes she was swimming up and down and thinking. As her strokes became more methodical, her mind took over. She would tell Zelah and Nick exactly what had happened as soon as she got back but keep it from Jack and Alice. Lucky that they must both have been so tired out by the exertions of the previous day they had slept through the night. Maggie remembered her mother, who had slept through the infamous hurricane of 1987. She and David, living in the South East of England, had trembled in their beds throughout the night, thinking the roof would disappear, or it would take a wall out. Her mother had been unaware of and unmoved by what she had missed.

She expected that the kids would be the same this morning. But she would report what had happened to the police. Ann Quinn couldn't get away with such appalling behaviour. Witch, indeed! She was a nasty, vicious, evil woman who liked power and frightening people. Whatever legal sanction she ended up with, serve her right.

After half an hour Maggie was tiring and made her way back towards the shore. The beach lifeguards had arrived and were setting up. She waved to them and they waved back, but she noticed that they were spending more time looking at the beach café than getting on with preparing for the busiest day of the summer – Bank Holiday Monday. And there was more activity there than when she had arrived.

As she walked up the beach and retrieved her towel, Maggie noticed that there were two police cars in the carpark. They were cordoning off an area of the lower cliff behind the café. Perhaps the storm had dislodged rocks. She watched as she towelled herself down. Now one policeman was turning away a group who had arrived for breakfast. If the café was affected and needed to be made safe, she imagined the owners would be furious.

She walked towards the café and could see its staff standing in a huddled group to the side of the decking. Out of curiosity, Maggie walked towards them.

"What's wrong?" she asked as she reached them and saw that one girl was crying.

"There's been an accident," a boy said. "Someone must have been out walking and slipped on the path."

"The storm was bad," said Maggie, "perhaps it washed away part of the path. It was OK when I came down this morning. Is it someone local?"

"No," the boy replied. "I didn't recognise her. I found her, caught on a bush just above where we store stuff at the back. She's dead."

"Poor you," Maggie said, "and poor her. Out for an early morning walk, I expect. What a terrible thing."

She turned to walk away as the café manager appeared. They were on first-name terms, having been welcome patrons for the last month. "Heard our news, Maggie?"

"'Fraid so, Helen. How awful. That lad, Jonathan, says it was a tourist, out for a walk."

"Oh no," Helen replied. Maggie's gut churned, knowing what the woman would say next.

"She wasn't from here, but we know who she is. She's from up-county. Her name's Ann Quinn. I spoke to one of the police, local bloke. It might not have been an accident."

Chapter 44

It took over an hour for Maggie to talk to the police. They had told her to stay put at her house as an officer would come to her for further questioning.

Everyone was up and pottering around when Maggie returned. The usual routine of breakfast in the garden wasn't possible due to the weather, so it spread them amongst various rooms. Zelah, who was in the kitchen, greeted Maggie with a comment about long-distance swimming and how far she expected to get towards America, but one look at Maggie's face stopped her in her tracks. Without a word she put a cup of coffee into Maggie's hand and took her into the conservatory.

"How bad?" she asked.

Maggie took a deep breath and asked Zelah to get Nick, which she did without question.

She took them through the entire story: being woken by the storm; finding out the body on the beach was Ann Quinn; and that the police would come to interview all of them.

"And it was such a good day yesterday," Zelah said. "Damn that woman."

"She's dead, Zelah. Have compassion," said Nick.

Zelah was about to reply when Jack and Alice arrived. Maggie hoped they hadn't heard, but no such luck.

"Who's dead?" asked Jack.

She repeated the story, but in less detail.

It made for a quiet morning. Maggie felt she couldn't allow Jack to go down to the beach, or Alice to go for a walk along the cliff path. They complained, but to no avail.

"We didn't even see her," Jack complained. "I could have passed by her anywhere and I wouldn't have known who she was."

Alice also had an opinion, but Maggie asked them both to button it until the police had been to see them.

A squad car and an unmarked vehicle pulled up twenty minutes later.

The next hours were uncomfortable for all of them. They were interviewed separately. They'd agreed to be honest, not hold anything back; they had done nothing wrong. The officer in charge, DI Fergus Jordan, had Maggie text copies of the photographs she had taken on her phone. He had wanted to take the phone, but Maggie had protested that they'd been the victims of Ann Quinn's stalking. It didn't take much questioning for Maggie to realise that the adults were suspects in Ann Quinn's death. She remembered that she had set the house alarm before going to bed and that it was sufficiently sophisticated to show times on and off. She showed the screen times to DI Jordan. She had been the person to turn off the alarm, at seven thirty. But she could tell that, although Ann Quinn had been dead for some hours by that time, it still didn't rule them out. She was unnerved when members of the forensic team then searched the house.

Others from the forensic team were combing the cliff-top, and the path was closed. Several bystanders came to watch the CSI team, but soon found that there was nothing interesting to see and went away.

DI Jordan had said that they would have to go into Penzance to each make a formal statement, including Jack and Alice. Maggie had insisted that she would sit with Alice, but not until the following morning.

"Not a great start to our last days," Nick remarked, when they gathered in the conservatory for lunch. Jack and Alice had been in and out all morning watching the forensic officers at work, but now they had gone, and the path had opened again.

Maggie was shocked to learn from a call with Bob that he had been summoned to give a statement. He would arrive during the evening. "Do they really suspect one of us?" she asked anxiously.

"They must rule us out. The alarm report shows no one went outside during the night. Might be they think one of you could have already been out there. But that would have meant someone getting a soaking. That's why they searched the house. Don't worry

176

too much. If your statements are honest and they match, they'll rule you out. They'll have checked for fingerprints belonging to Anne Quinn."

"This is horrible," Maggie replied.

They'd made plans for things to do and places to go on their last day, but now no one wanted to do anything other than packing up ready to go home. Maggie abandoned her visit to Helford. The weather had cooled. It was still sunny, but the draining atmosphere of the previous day had given way to a breeze.

"Just as well we're going," Zelah remarked when Maggie found her on her laptop mid-afternoon. "I checked the next ten days. Good weather fading out, uncertainly ahead."

"Well ain't that just on the nose?" Maggie replied, flopping down onto a settee. Then she sat up. "Sorry, Zelah. What do you want to do now?"

Zelah stretched her back and rolled her neck, pinching and rubbing, trying to release tense muscles. "Carry on, for now. We've come too far to drop it. I think I'm getting Bob's copper's nose for a *situation*." She sat back onto her settee. "Do you think someone really murdered Ann Quinn?"

"If the police say so, they must have a reason. But I can't think why. She was a mad old bat, but essentially harmless. I mean of causing actual bodily harm. She threatened a lot, but nothing happened, did it?" She put her feet up. "If we can't go out anywhere until they say so, I'm going to find something to do."

"We'd better think about what to do when we get back. I've been finishing the book for the Parsons family. After that I've got one book to finish, but nothing much then. What's happening to your radio broadcasts?"

"I will have to break the news to Melissa Wilkes that I can't do any follow-up for the time being. She won't be happy, but the police said I can't."

"You'd better hide from her, then. Because when Melissa Wilkes finds out that Ann Quinn's suspicious death took place near our holiday house, she'll be the next person to stalk us."

"Hadn't thought of that. Bugger. You're right. I hope we won't be prisoners here for the next couple of days. Did anyone ask them how long they expect us to stay?"

"I didn't, don't know about Nick."

"What about me?" asked Nick from the door, walking around the back of the settee and sitting next to Zelah.

"Didn't see you standing there," said Zelah without looking up. "Is this stalking thing catching?"

"That's not funny," said Nick.

"I was asking if any of us had asked how long we're expected to stay here," said Maggie.

"I didn't," he replied. "But there is something I told the police I need to tell you."

"I hope you've done nothing that might compromise us," Zelah said.

Instead of being indignant, Nick looked at his feet. "I think I might have done."

"What have you done?" said Zelah, glaring at him.

"On my way back from Tintagel I went to St Breward."

"That was out of your way," Maggie said. "Did you go to see her?"

"Not directly. It was more that I wanted her to see me. Be in her presence. See how… if she reacted. I tracked her down in the village shop. I stood behind her. Then beside her. Then in front of her. I stared at her."

"Wow," Maggie said. "Bold, for you, Nick. How did she react?"

"She didn't, absolutely nothing, except to ask me why I was staring at her. She should have been able to pick something up. They often do, they watch and acknowledge. But there was nothing. That's what convinced me that Bob was right, she was a charlatan, and she was way overdressed."

"So, Bob was right," Maggie mused. "She convinced herself she was a witch and descended from Julia Pencarrow, but I know she isn't. I checked out the tree I got from her. At one point she's descended from a woman who would not only have been sixty-something when her child was born but was already dead. But

178

something interesting did come up in Julia Pencarrow's line I want to follow up."

"What?" asked Zelah.

"Not saying, for now. In case I'm wrong. It's just an atom of an idea. I was looking for something to do this afternoon, so I'm going to pick it up, see where it goes." She stood up, and said, "I am thinking this holiday is over. Would you agree?"

Nick nodded and Zelah said, "Yes, and I hope we don't have to spoil it by hanging around here if we can't go out. Let's find out as soon as we can."

Maggie's phone rang. She looked at it, mouthed 'Bob' and walked to the kitchen. Zelah and Nick waited pensively until Maggie returned.

"He'll be here in about two hours. He's arranged to meet DI Jordan here at six. Seems they have something significant to tell us."

"Oh, for God's sake!" Zelah exploded. "What the hell is that supposed to mean?"

"We'll find out at six," Maggie replied. "I'm off to get my laptop. Alice is reading and Jack is back to gaming. I think they'll be happy to go home too."

Chapter 45

Bob arrived just before six.

"Whatever's the matter with you?" Maggie asked when he came in and put the kettle on without greeting anyone.

"Pulled an all-nighter. Surveillance. I'm knackered. Then I got the call to come down here, and I've got to go back tonight."

Before Maggie could ask any more, the doorbell rang. "OK. Let's get this over. You can stay for dinner though?" she asked. He nodded.

Maggie tried, and failed, to keep Jack and Alice away from the meeting, so they were all seated around the dining table. The atmosphere was tense. Maggie felt as if another storm was about to start – indoors.

DI Jordan sat at the table, a closed file in front of him, and began by bringing them up to date. "I'm still waiting for the official report from our police doctor. But both the physical and medical evidence so far suggests that Ann Quinn was dragged to the edge of the cliff and pushed over."

"Where on the cliff?" Maggie asked.

"About a hundred yards further along, in the direction of the beach. That's how she ended up in the bushes just above the beach café."

"Poor woman," Maggie said. "She was a nasty nuisance, but she didn't deserve that. What does this mean for us? We're presuming that I was the last person to see her? Does that mean we have to stay here?"

"Actually, you weren't," he replied. He opened the file and took out a series of photographs. Maggie recognised them at once.

"I took these from the bedroom window," she said.

"Yes. We've had them blown up and enhanced. Look closely."

They all leaned in to see. It was Alice who spotted it first.

"What's this?" she asked, her finger pointing to the top right-hand corner of a photograph of the path behind the garden.

"We wondered if you could tell us?" the Inspector asked.

At the edge of the photograph, staring into the garden and behind Ann Quinn's back, was a figure, head covered in a peaked cap and wearing a raincoat. In other photos the figure had its back turned.

Maggie was the first to speak. "Now I am completely flummoxed," she said.

"And there's this," DI Jordan continued. He produced an evidence bag.

Maggie recognised what was inside. "That's what she was holding up when she was shouting and waving her arms," Maggie said.

"Yes," he confirmed. "We found it in her pocket."

The object was a poppet – in the likeness of Zelah.

"That's meaningless," Nick said flatly. "We know she was a fraud. That's part of her box of tricks to frighten people."

"Well, if she meant to frighten me, she picked a fight with the wrong woman," Zelah said, standing up and walking around the table, beating her fist against the back of each chair she passed. "No, I'm not frightened, I'm angry. Stupid bitch!"

"She's dead, Zelah," Maggie hissed.

"Like I care," Zelah snapped back.

"Zelah, the best thing we can do now is to focus on who this other person is. That's what matters. There's nothing else we can do now but follow the evidence."

"What do you mean?" DI Jordan interrupted.

"I mean the genealogy, the family history," Maggie explained. "The death is your territory. You know about Zelah's legacy, the rings, what we've been doing. It looks like someone else may be interested. Someone that as yet we know nothing about."

"And someone prepared to kill," said Bob. They all turned to look at him, and his face was as grim as Maggie had ever seen it.

She knew what would happen if she didn't speak up. "We all agreed that we were in on this. We started it; we will finish it.

Right, Zelah?"

Zelah smiled wanly. "Even if it puts us in the firing line?"

"I'm still in," Nick said. "Doesn't matter what we think now. This has pushed us past the point of no return."

"It's also pushed us past the point of holiday," Zelah replied. "How about we pack up and go home tomorrow, instead of Wednesday?" She had turned to DI Jordan and added, "If that's OK with you? You know where to find us. We can easily come back if you need us."

He thought for a moment, then nodded. "OK. You can go. I'll call you if I need anything further. I need formal statements and fingerprints from all of you, for elimination purposes. If you come into Penzance at some point tomorrow, you'll be free to go after that."

"How long will that take?" Maggie asked.

"A few hours, probably, Mrs Gilbert."

"We'll be there early," she said. No one disagreed.

**

Dinner was a quiet affair, indoors as the garden was still wet. Afterwards Jack and Alice went upstairs to pack and Maggie saw Bob off.

"Any idea what he's thinking?" she asked Bob.

"I don't think he sees any of you as the murdering kind. But, currently he doesn't have any other leads. It's early days."

"I've never been suspected of anything illegal before, never mind murder. None of us have. It's horrible."

"You know we haven't done anything. Just stay calm," Bob replied.

"We'll be home this time tomorrow," she said.

"Pity it ended like this. But it's not the end, is it?"

"Of course not," she replied. "Can you join us Wednesday morning? I think we'll need a pow-wow."

He nodded and hugged her. It was a tight, lingering hug. "Be careful," he whispered to her. "You are precious to me."

Chapter 46

Alice and Jack found fingerprinting exciting, but the adults less so. Once they were finished, and statements taken and signed, they returned to Avilion to finish packing. They had expected to leave Penzance together, but Zelah had taken a call from DC Mooney. He wanted to see her. She explained about the death of Ann Quinn and that they had planned to go home later, but he persuaded her to wait to see him. He couldn't get there until six that evening. So, Maggie, Jack, Alice, and Nick went home, while Zelah would meet Mooney, stay overnight, then lock up the house and travel back first thing Wednesday morning.

"I want to hear what he has to say," she said. "And I must let Mabel know that we're leaving, so she can arrange for her agency to take over the keys and sort out the cleaning."

Nick left early before the others. Jack wanted to go down to the beach one last time. Maggie let him go for his final surfing session, but after about twenty minutes he came back out of the sea to where she was watching on the beach.

"It's not the same," he said, picking up his bag and surfboard, and walking back to the car.

They arrived home around seven o'clock on Tuesday evening. Maggie threw their bags into the hall. Unpacking could wait until the following day.

**

Maggie slept fitfully, interrupted by dreams of weird dancing and sudden screams. When she awoke, she wondered if the screams might have been hers. She took a cup of tea and sat looking out over her thriving garden. She had paid a neighbour's son to water the plants and grass for her whilst they were away, and he had done a decent job.

By eight she had unpacked, put everything away and started on the washing. The holiday was morphing into a dream-like memory. Happiness, liquid warmth, and sunshine were no more. They would soon head into autumn. On their first day back, the weather changed. Although the morning was warm, there was a build-up of cloud and the forecast said to expect rain later in the day.

Zelah, Nick, and Bob were expected after lunch, later in the afternoon to allow time for Zelah to travel back. She had left Jack and Alice sleeping. They weren't due back at school until the following Monday. That was the next big issue, but not for today.

She sat in the kitchen with a notebook and listed outstanding lines of enquiry they had to follow up. For Zelah, they needed to hear the latest news from DC Mark Mooney about Jay and his mother. Had he found anything significant? What about Bob's investigation into unsolved deaths in the days after Zelah's abandonment? She didn't think he'd had time to do anything about that yet. Zelah needed to follow up on Archie King's information about the girl who had cleaned for the vicar. Had she seen or heard anything that could be useful? And there was the money that Archie believed the vicar had stolen. How much was it, and was it significant?

Maggie had also been thinking about the third ring on and off but concluded that there was nothing they could do about it. However, she believed that its significance lay in finding its connection to the other two rings. There had to be a connection.

The spoon ring had several paths leading off its story. Now she had her teeth into this she wanted it as her project and hoped that the others would agree. The beating heart of this mystery lay in the past and in the story of Julia Pencarrow, Sir John Vyse and Edward and Peter Steelfox. She needed to contact The Reverend James Steelfox in Flintshire, to find out what he knew. From Ann Quinn's information Maggie had found a retired Reverend, James Steelfox, in Nercwys in Flintshire, who was an active and enthusiastic online genealogist. Could she learn more about the story of the ring, the letter, and the death of Mildred Vyse. How was witchcraft involved, or was that a red herring? And there was the strange coincidence in the family tree of Ann Quinn.

The Roman ring should stay with Nick. She didn't think there was much of interest in that one. Nick might want to investigate but she couldn't see how, without the help of a professional Roman archaeology expert, he could find anything else about the girl who died with the ring clasped in her hand. But Nick, being Nick, might think of something.

She sat with the pen in her hand, musing over each lead when a voice behind startled her.

"Need to talk to you, Mum." A pyjama-clad Jack was standing in the doorway, hair tousled, looking like the outcome of a bad party, with a serious expression.

She showed him a chair which he pulled up next to her and sat down.

"I'm not going back to school next week." He folded his arms and sat up straight.

For a moment, Maggie wondered if she was still asleep. She blinked a few times. "Did you say what I think you just said?"

"Yes."

"And what are you proposing to do instead? Is the local burger-flipping joint looking for new recruits?"

"OK. That didn't come out right. I'm not going back to that school. I've signed up somewhere else."

Maggie rubbed her forehead. Was she missing something? She decided not to go for the confrontation she guessed he was expecting.

"Can you please explain, Jack? A little more detail if you don't mind."

"I want to go to a sixth form college in Cardiff. I've been in touch with them and they're happy with my GCSEs and they'll take me for 'A' levels. It's all sorted." This was delivered with a grimace and a jutted chin and the expectation of an argument. Had she pushed him to the point he felt this decision was like a declaration of war?

"Surely any school needs my permission, as you are still only sixteen?"

He jumped up. "I knew you'd be like this!" Jack had put his

hands in his pockets and walked to the door.

"Like what? You creep up on me and mug me with this information and expect me not to react? I'm trying to stay calm so I can get the full picture. Just sit down and talk without the attitude. Please."

The 'please' did it. He stopped. "Will you listen?"

"Yes. Come back and sit down."

He dawdled back to the chair and threw himself onto it, without taking his hands out of his pockets. "You have to agree, of course. You have to sign the forms, Mum. But I really can't go back on Monday. That stupid uniform. Since when does anyone wear a blazer? And a tie? They treat the sixth formers like they're bigger kids, that's all. You're allowed to leave the premises at lunchtime. It's prehistoric. I hate the place."

He put his head down, resting his chin on his chest, and folded his arms.

"Where's this college, exactly?"

He sat up again, eyes brightening. She hadn't said no. "It's on the outskirts of Cardiff, this side. I'll have to go by bus, but it goes from the stop just down the road, and it's just one bus, right to the college gates. It's good, too. They get consistent results. And there's no uniform; you wear whatever you want. With some rules, naturally. Can I go?"

"What 'A' levels are you thinking of doing?"

"History, English and Psychology."

"Do you know anyone?"

"Yes, there'll be four of us. You know them. Their parents have all agreed already."

"Can I visit?"

"Yeah, we must, but soon. I should get the forms signed. It's already late."

"Tomorrow?"

He looked at her as if he couldn't believe what she was saying. Then he jumped up and hugged her. "You're the best," he said, and ran out of the kitchen.

This must have been what he had been talking to Zelah about.

And probably Bob. But he hadn't felt able to talk to his mother. Had she really been so controlling? Yes, she had, this was all her fault. But would she have reacted differently if he had tried to have this conversation with her at the start of the holiday? Again, yes. She would have put a stop to it. Maggie realised, shamed; in trying to be two parents, she had failed at being one.

"I heard all that." Another voice from behind, this time Alice.

"I expect you did," Maggie replied, staring out at the garden. "And I expect you have an opinion you will now share with me."

"He told me at the weekend. He was scared about speaking to you. I think he should go for it and I told him that. Do they have second-form colleges anywhere? I don't want to go back either. Especially if Jack isn't there."

So much for not having to think about school today. Maggie beckoned her over.

Alice was also in pyjamas, bare-footed, hair rumpled. Maggie felt a lump in her throat. Alice might be on the verge of being a teenager, but right now she looked like a small, frightened, vulnerable child who'd been told Christmas was cancelled.

"Not a lot of call for that," Maggie said. "But Alice, there are always alternatives, and we should talk them through. They may not turn out to be any better. But we can consider them. Would you like that?"

"Yes, please."

"OK, what are you going to do today? Are you planning to see Janine?"

"She's trying out for the Cwmbran girls' netball team. I might go to watch after lunch. I'll get dressed now."

Maggie tightened her grip on her coffee mug. Jack's news she could handle. A shock, but he was thinking for himself. But Alice? A knot in her stomach clenched like a tourniquet. What would happen to Alice? Especially without Jack. Maggie had to do something, but she didn't know what. And that signalled the beginning of dread that would inevitably lead to panic. She clamped down on that. Nothing would happen for a few days, and she had friends to talk to. Something else to go on the agenda. For now, she should concentrate on what was happening with Maze, to keep her mind occupied, and hope that something would occur to help solve the Alice-school-problem.

During the morning she chatted easily with both of them, called the college and arranged a visit for herself and Jack the following day, which Alice would attend with them. After lunch she dropped Alice at the sports centre where she met up with an excited Janine. Then she dropped Jack at a friend's house, who would also be one of the boys going to college.

Chapter 47

Nick was the first to arrive to start work, and she sensed that something wasn't right as soon as he walked in the door. Maggie asked him to wait until the others arrived. Ten minutes later Zelah zoomed up to the front door, followed by Bob on his motorbike.

Nick was sitting at the office table drumming his fingers, glancing around. Maggie cleared their interactive whiteboard, ready for action. This had been a wickedly expensive purchase of Zelah's and had taken an electrician and an IT specialist two days to install, but it was a great advance in their ability to look at charts, timelines and other documents, then move them around the board, add notes, and print out what they had done. It had taken Maggie a month or so to get used to it, but now she wondered how they had coped without it.

As Bob divested himself of his helmet and leathers, Maggie wrote up the headings she had set out, and the issues she felt they needed to follow up.

"Before we start," she said as Bob finally sat down, "Zelah, how did the meeting go with DC Mooney? Did he find out anything more for you?"

"You could say that. He found out that Jay's mother was found dead not long after she left the hospital; that the whole charity thing that the vicar got the kids from was fishy and was closed down; and that he stole about fifty grand in today's money."

"Wow!" said Maggie.

"Cause of death?" asked Bob.

"Drowning. And apparently she had a full load of alcohol."

"Where?"

"Land's End."

"Was anyone suspicious at the time?"

"No, apparently not," Zelah replied. "But Mark is now. She was clean. He says he would have asked a lot more questions about how she got there, and how the alcohol got into her system. Where did she buy it? Was she seen drinking it anywhere in the area?"

"And the rest," Bob said. "Sixties, wasn't it?" Zelah nodded. "I expect they took it at face value. Woman with a history of alcohol abuse, et cetera."

Zelah looked uncharacteristically miserable. "He said they made enquiries, checked the abusive boyfriend who had an alibi. But they never linked it to the vicar. Or Jay."

Bob got up and went to Zelah, putting a hand on her shoulder. "Shoddy," he said. "Sorry, Zelah. They could, no should, have done much more."

She didn't look up from the table. "I keep wondering if Jay saw her. If she let him know she was there, that she'd take him away, then never turned up again."

"I wonder if it's linked to Tracy Hopton," Bob said.

"So does Mark," Zelah replied. "One good thing, though. Archie remembered the name of the cleaning woman. Susan Blessing. Unusual name, which is why he remembered. She cleaned for a few people. Archie says she married and went up-county, and he thinks there's a chance she's still alive, hopefully with all her marbles. Mark will follow it up."

"Did Jay ever give you any indication he'd seen his mother?" Nick asked. "I imagine he'd have been excited, and he'd confide in you."

"He always said she'd come for him, and that he'd try to get me to go with them. But I don't remember him being especially excited, no."

"Then he probably knew nothing," Nick said.

"Or maybe he did," Zelah replied. "Maybe he heard about her body being found, knew it was his mother, and confronted Tracy."

"Try not to speculate, Zelah, it'll drive you mad," Bob said, reaching out to cover her hand with his. "There are too many possibilities. And it's likely, with so few people left, you'll never know. Be prepared for that, but let Mark do his job. He'll find as much as he can for you." He walked back around the table and sat down again.

"I'm trying, OK? He's tracing the other children. The so-called charity got shut down in the early seventies. Most of the records are gone, but he'll try Social Services, see if there's anything left to go on. He's going to put a story out to local press, ask for anyone who knows anyone placed with the vicar. Anyway, let's get on." Zelah sat up and addressed Maggie: "I presume you've got it all worked out on paper?"

"Of course," Maggie replied. She dragged the first heading forward to the front of the whiteboard and, marker pen in hand, stood beside it to add notes.

"My idea is that we concentrate on the two rings, the spoon ring and the Roman ring. That's where I think we have the most leads. Anyone disagree?" She waited. "No, OK. Let's start with the spoon ring." She pulled the picture of the ring forward and wrote underneath.

"We know that the disappearance of the ring happened at the time of Mildred Vyse's death and that one of three people probably took it." She wrote John Vyse, Edward Steelfox and Julia Pencarrow on the board. "I'm thinking we can eliminate Sir John Vyse." She crossed through his name, "and Edward Steelfox. This is the copy of the Bible page that Irene Fox sent me. It arrived last night. There was more to it than she told us, but maybe she didn't think it was significant." She enlarged it to fill the board. The writing was small and spidery.

"Irene Fox told us it said Edward believed his brother was not a thief. But, as you can see, there's an addition from someone else, maybe his wife or son. It says they destroyed the letter, as Sir John Vyse had instructed. But, there's nothing about a ring."

"Seems reasonable," Zelah said. "Sir John died with no one to pass the ring to. Not sure about Edward Steelfox though. It might have been him; it was his brother who made it from the spoon."

"If Edward kept it, he could have passed it down. How would it have been on the instructions of Sir John Vyse, when they were back in Cheshire?" Nick mused.

"If he passed it down, it would probably have come to Irene Fox's husband. But she knew nothing about it. Ann Quinn picked up a lot of information from the vicar in Flintshire, James Steelfox. I traced him on Monday through a Facebook group. He's in the phone book. I had planned to call him in Cornwall, but I kept getting distracted. I think this is a priority."

"When do you think you'll go?" Zelah asked.

"I must call him, see when he can see me, but I hope in the next couple of days. But," Maggie added, "I have school things to sort out. As I think you all know?" Her friends assumed shamefaced expressions. "Was anyone actually planning on telling me?"

"Jack was," Zelah said. "He made me promise not to say anything until he had told you."

"Me too," Bob added. "And don't give me that look, Maggie Gilbert. You'd like it even less if I'd let him down."

"I'm not cross, well, not now I've got over the shock. Jack and I going tomorrow. Alice is coming too. That's my next problem, and I wanted to get your opinions, but later."

"You've got a lot on your plate," Zelah said. "How about I go to Flintshire tomorrow, if the vicar's willing? You can do your college visit and then get on with research."

"OK, I suppose. I want to carry on with Ann Quinn's family line. I said before we left that there was something there that was bugging me. I need to follow it up."

"Can you tell us anything about what you suspect?" Nick asked.

"I think it's something that may connect these two rings. But it's too important to get us all excited, then find out I'm wrong."

"You probably aren't," Nick replied, "but, fine." Zelah shrugged and nodded.

Maggie turned back to the whiteboard. "So, if we rule out Edward Steelfox that leaves Julia Pencarrow. She was suspected of witchcraft and the last to die. If she had the ring and the letter and the poppet, then she could have passed them all on together."

"A reasonable theory," Zelah said. "You carry on with the research, I'll go give the Reverend the third degree. Let's hope it adds something useful."

Maggie nodded. "Next, the Roman ring. Nick, are you going to carry on with that?"

"Yes, but where do we want to go next with this?"

Maggie pulled forward her notes. "I think the theft is what we need to concentrate on. Can you find out who were the members of the dig headed by Sir Hugh McCarthy Miller? And is it worth going back to the museum at Caerleon to speak to the expert again?"

"Yes, and no. There's plenty of information online about the dig. But I don't want to speak to the assistant again. Not sure why, just a feeling. His energy was higher than it should have been, made me uncomfortable; and Alice noticed that he was dark. He was too keen for me to get back in touch with anything I knew. I got the impression he knew more than he was telling me. I don't want to alert him yet."

"You have good instincts," Maggie said. "We'll go with that. Odd, though. Bob, can you look at anything that might explain why no one came back for Zelah?"

"I'll get back onto the Police Gazette, pick up again on what I started in Cornwall. I'll see what records might still be available, that might be digitised. But don't hold your breath, any of you."

Maggie went to speak again, but he stopped her. "Look, I don't want to put the frighteners on you, but you'll all need to be careful. Watch your backs. Something dangerous is going on. You're all still suspects, and the only link between Ann Quinn and you is the spoon ring. She knew it was about Zelah, not some anonymous client. You all think she deduced it. I think there's a possibility that someone told her. On Sunday night it looks like someone else called her name. The story of those photographs says someone interrupted her. Whoever that person was, probably killed her, and they'd been to the house before."

This was news. Zelah went to speak but Maggie got in first. "What do you mean? How do you know that?"

"Remember the night of the break-in, when we went downstairs and after a few minutes heard an engine starting up and heading off?"

"Yes. But that was Ann Quinn, wasn't it?"

"Not unless she used another car. She had a Ford Fiesta, and on Monday it was in the carpark at the beach, so she used it to come over on Sunday night. But the car that drove away that previous time wasn't a Ford Fiesta."

"How do you know? We didn't see anything."

"Are you asking me if I can't tell the difference between the sound of a high-powered, expensive engine, probably German, and an old Ford Fiesta?"

"No, I'm not questioning that. But I am asking why you're only just telling us now! This means you've known for almost a week that there was someone else involved."

"And it's what's got you out of Cornwall; they were going to hold you longer, so don't get arsey with me, Maggie. I knew something, but it didn't fit anything then. Now it does. When I told the Inspector, it gave him another line of enquiry. And it told him that there might be more to this than just crazy Ann Quinn." He paused for a moment, sat back, and put his hands on his head, rubbing briskly at the stubble. "A woman is dead. It's connected with you. As far as I'm concerned, you're in danger until we understand what's going on. Keep investigating but keep me and the Cornish police informed. Understand?"

"I suppose so."

"And don't be sulky."

She was about to snap back at him, but Zelah said, "Maggie, sometimes he's right. Let it go, will you? And don't start on me. He told us back in January to be careful; we didn't, and I got my head bashed in. I don't want a repeat of that. Don't think my skull could take it."

"Oh, all right. I get it. Bob, you and I can speak later. What does this mean? How do we keep each other safe?"

"You go nowhere without telling someone else and arrange a time to check in," Bob replied. "Doesn't matter how trivial it seems, a trip to the shops, whatever. And that includes the kids, Maggie. Where are they now?"

"Alice is with Janine, watching her netball trial at the stadium and Jack is at a friend's house."

"I'll talk them through it later, in my best Inspector's voice."

Maggie knew he was right. "We'll both go pick them up."

"Is there anything else we need to talk about?" Nick asked, standing up. "I'd like to get started."

"Me too," Zelah added. "I will phone the Reverend Steelfox. I'll use the kitchen."

They both left the office. Maggie heard Nick close the front door on his way out.

"Is he OK?" Bob asked. "I'm not trying to cut him out with Alice, you know."

"He's fine. He understands. He needs his own space. A lot of it."

"Fair enough." Bob had been scribbling notes as they talked. Now he was reviewing them. Maggie offered to print off what was on the board, but he shook his head. "Old copper, old habits. I prefer to read my notes." She left him to it and went into the kitchen where Zelah was finishing her call. She gave a thumbs up.

"Nice old bloke," she said. "He'd be delighted to talk to me tomorrow. Excited, actually. I don't think he gets out much. I'll leave early; it's a long drive. You worried ?"

"No. Well… a little. Didn't know where this might go, but murder was not something I ever ruled in. I haven't been around murder before. It's… I don't know… unnerving. What about you, Zelah? You worried?"

"Hell, no! I don't have your sensibilities. I think it's intriguing. But not about Jay. That's different."

"Well, try not to get too enthusiastic about murder in front of Reverend Steelfox."

"Do my best. Look, Bob knows what he's talking about. I'll be checking in with you throughout the day. You check in with Bob, and Nick is likely to be here. We'll recce again at the end of the day. Compare notes then, OK?"

"OK," Maggie said. If she had been honest with Zelah, whom she suspected of being more perceptive than she let on, Maggie was experiencing stirrings of doubt about what was happening. She had started off full of enthusiasm, secretly hoping that Zelah, who had been initially so reticent, would get more involved. Now that was reversed but she didn't want to share yet.

Bob's head poked around the door. "Ready to go?"

She picked up her jacket. This train was now thundering ahead under full steam and it seemed like she was the only one who wanted to put the brakes on. But then the others only had themselves to think of.

Chapter 48

After dinner Maggie and Bob sat with the bi-fold doors open, looking onto the garden. The evening was cool, but the flowerbeds didn't look as if they minded. Maggie had spent a half hour watering and now the pot plants were standing to attention.

Maggie was in shorts but the goose bumps on her legs were getting bigger. Damn it, it was still August, just. *Trousers are for wimps,* she thought.

The discussion with Jack and Alice had gone well. Bob had given the situation gravitas and had somehow got them to take it seriously without frightening them.

"They both agreed to think before they go off anywhere, which was all I wanted," he said. "Whoever shares our interest in those rings will know about the kids, too. They're a way to get at you, if they have to."

"Yes, I know. You've told me at least ten times today."

"Snappy, aren't we?"

"There's a reason for that. Something the boy said, the kid who's been watering the garden. There was a car here a couple of weeks ago. An Audi. Don't smirk."

"I wasn't going to. Sorely tempted, though. And 'I told you so' is fighting to get out."

"Well, fight back. And a woman was asking about us."

He sat up. "He got a good look at her?"

"I suppose so, yes."

"Then I need to interview him. And before you go off on one, this is officially a murder investigation. I'm not formally involved, but I can carry out an interview if Cornwall thinks it's worthwhile."

"Fair enough. I'll warn his parents tomorrow." *And won't they be just thrilled?* she thought. *Their kid waters a garden and gets involved in a neighbour's murder enquiry.*

"Shall we close up and sit inside?" Bob asked. Maggie jumped up and shut the glass doors.

Bob left an hour later. He was working at six the following morning and didn't want to disturb her on his way out.

Before she went to bed, Maggie thought through arrangements for the following day. She had agreed checking in times with Zelah throughout the day. Nick was arriving at eight so she could set off with Jack and Alice at nine to visit the college in Cardiff. He would stay until she got back. Then she had the afternoon to get into the research she thought was going to launch them a good few steps further forward. She had agreed to Jack and Alice spending the afternoon on computers so she could keep them under observation in the house. They needed to get this concluded as quickly as possible. She set the house alarm and checked all the windows and doors three times before feeling secure enough to go upstairs.

Chapter 49

Nick arrived as expected at eight. Maggie was already up and chivvying Jack and Alice out of bed. They got away just after nine and left Nick tapping away on his laptop. Zelah had already done the first of her check-ins when she left at seven thirty. She expected that it would take around three hours, traffic permitting, to get up to Flintshire. She was due to text when she arrived at the Reverend James Steelfox's house in Nercwys village.

The college visit went well, much to Jack's relief and delight. The teacher who showed them around would be Jack's personal tutor. The campus, he explained, centred around a nineteenth-century house, with added buildings for laboratories, classrooms, an impressive gym, and a swimming pool. There would be around two hundred 'A' level students starting in the new term, covering a wide range of subjects including equivalent exams in technical subjects.

"Changing times, Mrs Gilbert, we have to branch out, embrace all aspects of educational attainment," the tutor explained. "We'll be doing 'A' level equivalent apprenticeships next year."

Maggie signed the forms and Jack was handed his induction reading material. He had to be at the college at nine the following Monday morning.

"You will be around next week, won't you Mum?" he asked on the way home. "I mean, I'll be fine, but…"

"I will," she said. "Wouldn't miss your first week. Or Alice's. There's bound to be stuff come up as we get back into the swing of work, but I'll try to keep it to day trips for the first few weeks. OK?" He was happy with that.

As she drove home Maggie thought over the conversation that Alice had had with the tutor. It had surprised him to learn that she still had four years to go at secondary level.

"She's a dazzling girl," he remarked to Maggie as they walked across the grand, mosaic-floored hallway to the main entrance of the core building. "Will she be on accelerated development for her GCSEs?"

"Nothing has been said about that yet," Maggie replied. "But I hope so. She doesn't like school, or at least not the school she's in. It's a pity you don't take younger children. She seems quite taken with this place."

"I suspect she'll do well. We'd definitely take her here when she has her first set of exams under her belt."

Maggie hadn't talked to Alice again about going back to school although she assumed that Alice was taking it as fact, she had to go. But the thought it wouldn't last was growing stronger. It was becoming more urgent to look around for an alternative.

Nick left after lunch for an appointment. He said no more about it, but Maggie suspected that he was meeting Stella Bell at Llanyrafon Manor. Nick and Stella had become friends in the months since Zelah had been hit on the head coming down the stairs at the manor. Stella was one of the few people who knew the truth about what had happened that night. That she had taken the story so calmly was a tribute to her unperturbable character. Maggie didn't know how much Nick had shared with her about himself, but their continuing friendship suggested that whatever Nick had told Stella it was not a problem for the tough, competent, manager of the manor.

Neither Jack nor Alice showed any interest in venturing outdoors. They'd had their share of interest for the day and were happy to be retiring to play what they called 'soothing computer games'.

That gave Maggie the afternoon to research the line of Julia Pencarrow and work out how Ann Quinn had made her mistake. It soon became clear that Maggie's first cursory glance at the timeline had been correct. Ann descended not from Julia Pencarrow, but from a relative of Edmund, Julia's husband. This was a typical case of taking a piece of evidence and making it fit the required story. When Maggie had first looked, it had seemed that the woman to whom Ann had aligned herself was too old to have given birth. Two hours of researching the online parish records showed without doubt that Ann Quinn descended from a much older brother Jude Pencarrow and his wife, also called Julia. But this Pencarrow family had no record of witchcraft.

Maggie's main intention was to look down the line of Julia Pencarrow – housekeeper to Sir John Vyse – to the descendant called Alice Pencarrow, who became Alice Miller. However, as so often happened, Maggie, obsessed as usual with finding out how far back she could get, searched Julia Pencarrow's heritage. It became more than a passing interest when she found that Julia was born Julia Williams in 1700. Her parents were Marjorie Williams and Gabriel Williams. Marjorie had married a man with the same surname so had been retained her birth name – Marjorie Williams. Not uncommon, especially with such an everyday surname. Further investigation revealed that Marjorie was the daughter of Peter Williams and wife Mary. Peter Williams was the son of Hepzibah Pearce: born 1641, married Thomas Williams, died in 1691 at Exeter Gaol, hanged for witchcraft.

So that was where Julia Pencarrow's reputation came from. When Maggie referred to the books from the museum at Boscastle, she found that Marjorie Williams, Julia's mother, was also a notorious Cornish witch, but hadn't been tried or tortured or hanged. Luckily for Marjorie that time had all but passed. But they knew her for her 'cures'. She could diagnose sickness in animals and cure them and the same with humans. Maggie wondered if she had passed this knowledge to her daughter. And her other gift, if that's what it could be called, was the 'evil eye'. If Marjorie Williams didn't like someone, dreadful things happened to them. There was no mention of her making poppets, but Maggie guessed at the possibility.

This was interesting information about Julia, but it didn't help with the spoon ring. If Julia did inherit certain gifts from her mother and great-grandmother, could she have used these to bring about the death of Mildred Vyse? The clue might be that the bag holding the ring left with Zelah also had the remains of a poppet. Was this the 'foul object' found with Mildred Vyse and did it mean that Julia was the person who had kept both ring and poppet?

A persistent ringing of the doorbell roused Maggie from her thoughts. She thought it might be Nick. Although he had a key, he sometimes didn't use it, when he knew that she was in. Try though she might, Maggie could not cure him of this. It wasn't Nick, but a courier, with a box for her to sign for, which she did.

Once in the office she found that she would need tools to get it opened. Someone had taped it heavily and wrapped it with string. Perhaps she had left something behind in Cornwall. She knew that Zelah's friend had returned to the house just after they left, to organise the cleaning. She found scissors and a penknife in one of the desk drawers and she hacked off enough of the brown wrapping paper to see that there was a plain, black shoebox, also with its lid taped down. She cut the tape and took off the lid.

It took a few seconds for Maggie to realise what she was looking at, but it felt that she had spent a long time staring at the contents of the box, mouth open, breath held in, before she stifled a scream, dropped the box onto the table, jumped back and covered her mouth with her hands.

She wanted to run away, lock the door, pretend it wasn't there. But she had to look, to face the thing. Slowly she forced herself to look inside. They were still there. Three wooden doll-like carvings, each had a face made from a photograph stuck onto the front of each of the three heads. Zelah, Jack, and Alice. Each had a miniature dagger of a steel pin pushed through the throat.

Tentatively she touched the sides of the box. She couldn't bring herself to touch the things that were lying on the black velvet material. She shook involuntarily. It could have been shock or anger or fear, or all of the above.

She couldn't do anything but stare. No thoughts came. At that moment, the office door burst open. "Sorry, I should have let you know I was coming," Nick said as he walked in, "but I — Maggie? What's the matter? What is it?"

She turned her head slowly towards him, then back to the box. He walked around the table, looked down, exhaled a long, shocked gasp of air. He quickly reached out and took her hands away from the box and held them in his own.

"Don't look. I'm putting the lid back on now. OK? Don't look."

When he had re-covered the poppets, he picked up the box with his fingertips, holding it like an unexploded bomb, and left the room. Maggie didn't follow.

After a few minutes he returned with two mugs and closed the door behind him. "Here, drink this. I put extra sugar in. Shock."

She took the mug and raised it to her lips, sucked up some tea, then put it down on the table. "I don't know what to do, Nick," she mumbled. Then she burst into tears. Nick put his arms around her, gently pushing her head onto his shoulder, patting and soothing her as she sobbed.

From the hallway came the sound of the front door opening and banging closed. Maggie glanced up as the office door opened and Bob came into the room.

"What the hell —?"

Nick gently shook his head and frowned at Bob's glowering face.

"Maggie, I'm going to show Bob. You don't want to see where I put them, so you stay here for just a few minutes. Then we'll both be back."

"Put what?" Bob half-shouted, but Nick shushed him with a finger to his lips, then crooked it at Bob to follow him. They left Maggie standing at the desk. When they came back two minutes later, she was still there, and she saw that Bob was holding the box in a pair of kitchen gloves.

"I've called this in and I'm taking it down to the station. Is that the packaging for this?" He pointed to where it was lying. Maggie nodded. He picked it up and put it into a transparent plastic food bag he had also been holding. "Not as good as an evidence bag, but it'll do. I'll be back. Don't go anywhere. Nick will stay with you."

Bob left, and they heard his car race off.

"Let's go and sit in the kitchen," Nick said, taking Maggie by the arm, and leading her out.

He put the kettle on again and got more mugs from the cupboard.

"We left perfectly good ones in the office," Maggie said.

"No matter. I'm good at tea. Gives me something to do while I'm thinking."

She didn't argue.

"I won't ask stupid questions like 'Who might have sent them?' or 'Why?' We need to just breathe for now. We'll know when to start thinking."

"Zelah," said Maggie, panicked. "She's supposed to have checked in."

"I'll check your phone. Is it in the office?" She nodded.

He returned with her phone. "She's fine and on her way back. Back about nine, so she will go home, then come over in the morning, about eleven."

Again, Maggie nodded.

Nick stood in front of her, uncertain what to say or do, when the sound of Jack and Alice coming downstairs distracted them both.

"Are we eating soon? I'm starving," Jack said as he sauntered into the kitchen. He stopped and stared at his mother. "Something wrong?"

"No, we're fine. Just talking about having a takeaway, isn't that right, Maggie?"

She forced a smile. "Yes, busy day and I don't have enough in to feed all of us. So, Chinese, I think. OK with all of you? And Bob's coming back soon. He won't mind." She sounded bright, she thought, but the suspicion on Alice's face told her otherwise.

"What's happened, Mum?"

There was no point in telling an outright lie. "Something about the Ann Quinn case has upset me, but I'll get over it. Now, who'll order and collect?"

That was Nick's cue. "Come on Alice, let's get on the phone. The usual?"

He steered Alice out of the room. Jack looked puzzled, but Maggie turned away to the sink to put the kettle on. "I'll make us some tea, shall I?"

"Not for me, thanks. I'm going back up to my computer. Call me if there's anything I can do, Mum."

She turned her head and smiled vaguely over her shoulder.

The slam of the front door signalled the departure of Nick and Alice. Maggie was alone in the kitchen. She went through the motions of making more tea and stood at the sink with it in her hands. But they were trembling so much that suddenly she couldn't control them, and the cup slipped and smashed on the kitchen floor. She didn't know if it was the noise or the shock, but something broke in Maggie. She picked up another cup from the sink drainer, raised it above her head and smashed it down, then another, and another.

The sound had been loud enough to alert Jack, who came flying down the stairs, to find Maggie crying on her knees amid a mound of smashed china.

Without a word he went to the corner cupboard, picked out a broom and swept the shards away from her into a heap to one side. When he thought it was safe enough, he knelt beside her. "You're scaring me, Mum. What's happened? I'm not a kid anymore. Please tell me."

She told him about the poppets in the box, how Bob had taken them away and how she had put them all in danger.

"No, you haven't, actually."

Maggie lifted her head and turned to face him. "I have. Those horrible things are about killing people. There's no other purpose to them."

"Someone wants to scare us, Mum. And they've succeeded, haven't they? Look at us."

"I'm scared, Jack, yes."

"But think about it, Mum. When witches made their voodoo dolls, they danced and chanted with them in their hands, like Ann Quinn did outside the house. Then they stuck a pin through them, or put a noose around their neck, or whatever. They didn't put them in a box and send them to the people they wanted to kill? That wasn't the point, was it?"

"No," she said, considering his words. "No, you're right, Jack, they didn't." She scratched her arm where a piece of china had scratched up a blob of blood. She rose and Jack stood beside her. "Someone is trying to frighten us. There was a note in the box, too. It said STOP NOW. I was so shocked I'd forgotten that."

She was gazing at him with a look of deep concentration. "I've really pissed someone off this time."

"Mum! Language!" They both chuckled.

"But seriously," Maggie said, as she retrieved the broom from Jack and swept furiously around her feet, "it was the most nauseating thing I've ever seen. And I thought I'd seen some nauseating things. This was a scare tactic, and a vicious, spiteful one at that." She paused in her sweeping for a moment. "Please, don't tell Alice? I'm trusting you. But she's too young for this."

"You'll have to change colour then, won't you. You can't fool her."

"I know. Get me the dustpan and brush, please. I'll get rid of this before anyone gets back. In fact, let's not tell anyone else about this. Our secret. OK?"

"What, you mean the broken cups?"

"China is replaceable, and I wasn't that keen on these anyway," she replied, tipping the broken pieces into the bin. "Your dad's Aunty Veronica pushed them on me years ago. They've finally served a useful purpose."

He hugged her. "Get better, please. We need you. You and Zelah and Nick and Bob will work it out." He paused in the doorway. "I won't be nervous if you aren't. Are you?"

"A bit, but Bob has gone to the police station and I know they'll take this seriously." She sighed and shook her head. "We'll all have to be careful until we find out who did this. But I think we must be getting close. Closer than whoever did it wants us to be. Don't you worry too much, we'll make sure you're well protected."

He smiled uncertainly and went back upstairs to his computer.

Maggie wondered if she should have told him at all. They had agreed he wasn't a child, but still, he also wasn't an adult. She decided what was done was done. Parenting continued to be complicated.

Chapter 50

After Jack and Alice had gone to bed, Bob told Maggie and Nick that the police both locally and in Cornwall, were taking the matter very seriously.

"They're checking for fingerprints and DNA. Probably no prints, but you never know with DNA. Unfortunately, it will take up to a week. Not as instant as the TV would have you believe."

"So, they believe that this links to Ann Quinn's death?" Maggie asked.

"Definitely," Bob replied. "They know from the photos of her in the garden she had a poppet in her hand. And it was Zelah that she was trying to curse, wasn't it?"

"Yes, she put Zelah's face on it," Nick replied. "It was about the ring. Do you think someone may have put her up to it?"

"It's a possibility, but what makes you say that?" Bob asked.

"It wasn't chance that there was someone else on the coastal path, in the early hours of the morning, in that storm. There was a widespread appeal, but no one came forward. I think someone egged her on, then followed her."

"But why push her off the cliff?" Maggie asked.

"Your camera had a flash, didn't it?"

"Yes. Do you think they saw it?"

"Possibly," Nick replied. "And if they think the photograph shows them, then they couldn't take a chance."

"Interesting theory," Bob said. "Could be right. For now, keep on with the research. I've arranged for a squad car to pass by the house throughout the night. Maggie, can you be sure that Jack and Alice are never on their own, until we sort this out?"

"Teenage boys roam in packs, so not much chance of Jack ever being alone. But Alice? It will be difficult. It's more unusual if anyone else is with her when she's in school."

Bob raised an eyebrow. "Does she have any other friends

besides Janine?"

"No," Maggie replied, flatly.

He changed the subject. "I thought I'd stay tonight, so I can be here when Zelah comes over tomorrow. What time is she due?"

"Eleven," Nick replied.

"I have one thing to do in the morning, but I'll be back by then."

"Me too. I'll let myself out," Nick said, and left them at the table.

"How bad is this?" Maggie asked Bob when Nick had gone.

"Honestly? It's bad. If it hadn't been for Ann Quinn's death, I would have described it as a nasty, spiteful nuisance, but now… I'll admit I'm worried. But," he added, standing up, "even more reason to get on with finding out what's behind it. You set something in motion, Maggie."

Chapter 51

Maggie awoke drenched in sweat from dreams punctuated by shouting and crying and talking dolls. She thought, as she lay trying not to disturb Bob, that whatever the dolls had been saying was critically important, but she couldn't remember what it was. She came to full consciousness realising that the dream dolls had been Jack and Alice.

She was sufficiently unnerved to get up although it was only six-thirty. She made tea and folded back the conservatory doors. It promised to be another warm day. There was a covering of dew on the grass and the sun was already rising. She took off her slippers and walked around the garden, stopping to smell the flowers. The last day of August; tomorrow would feel like the beginning of autumn.

A heavenly scent arose from the grass as she stepped on it in her bare feet and walked to the bottom of the garden where the canal ran towards Newport. The water was inky, but a few dragonflies were hovering above the surface, sunning themselves as they darted about on flashing wings. She spent a few minutes breathing deeply, finding calm in the meditation.

Returning to the house she switched on her computer. There was no sound from anyone else. Jack and Alice were unlikely to surface for several hours but Bob would be up soon. He was an early riser, from habit. Before the others arrived at eleven, Maggie wanted to check out her theory and suspicion.

She began with Julia Pencarrow. Julia had married young, to Edmund Pencarrow, but they had only had one child, Edward, born in 1740. Maggie wondered if Julia had more children that had not survived. She checked either side of 1740 for four years, but the parish records mentioned no births to an Edmund and Julia. Perhaps they moved away? It didn't matter for now.

Edward Pencarrow had married in 1764 a woman called Johanna Trelawney. They had four children; three sons and a daughter, Alice. It was the daughter that caught Maggie's attention. This daughter was on Ann Quinn's tree, but in the wrong place. She was on an outlying line when she should have been a central character. This Alice Pencarrow, born in 1765 had married a man called James Miller in 1798. The first of James and Alice Miller's children was Johanna Miller, born 1799. And here was the decisive factor: Johanna Miller married Edward McCarthy in 1825. Their first and only son was Hugh McCarthy Miller, born 1835, the archaeologist, knighted for his role as a philanthropist and social benefactor and his professional talents, who led the dig at Caerleon in 1908 – when the Roman ring was found and lost. Here was the connection between two of the rings. What this might mean raced around her brain including one thought that did not shed Sir Hugh McCarthy Miller in a good light.

She heard the first sound of stirring upstairs as Bob padded across the bathroom. It was eight. That was a long lie-in, for him.

She searched for more about Sir Hugh and found that he and his wife, the Honourable Eugenia Fawcett Fitch, had three children, a daughter, Johanna, and two sons, Hugh and Thomas. Sir Hugh died in 1920.

Bob called down to her, and she answered that she was in the kitchen and about to make them both breakfast but he came bounding down fully dressed and ready to go out. "Someone I have to talk to," he said, grabbing the cup of coffee she thrust at him as he headed towards the door. "Tell you about it later." He was gone before Maggie could say anything.

So, she was on her own for another three hours before anyone came to join her. What to do next? She thought she might as well find out more about the McCarthy Millers. She ploughed straight in, giving thanks to the internet where there was a plethora of information about Sir Hugh McCarthy Miller, including the dig at Caerleon and the infamous theft of the Roman ring.

His mother, Johanna Miller, had supported the family's growth towards an affluent life. Having married the solicitor Edward

McCarthy, she had lived a comfortable life. At some point the family had moved to Bath, where Edward McCarthy had first joined a partnership, then become an independent solicitor. They lived in Gay Street, which Maggie knew well from her previous job. One company she had worked for had taken a house in Gay Street and converted it into an office. But as a Grade One listed building all the remaining original features were unchanged, including the grand staircase that led up to the double room on the first floor that must once have transformed into a small ballroom for parties and soirées. She had loved that house - straight out of a Jane Austen or Georgette Heyer novel. Her secret, guilty reading in school when she should have been concentrating on the classics.

She checked the house on the census returns from 1841 to 1891. They must have become a prominent middle-class family in Bath, as they had established their life there, with a batch of servants, right up to Edward McCarthy's death in 1882. Maggie knew that these were big houses, but Johanna had continued to live on there alone, recorded as a 'Widow of Independent Means' in 1891.

In 1901 there was a different family living in the house. Edward and Johanna's son, Hugh, had married and moved away between 1851 and 1861. He had gone to University in London, married the Honourable Eugenia Fawcett Fitch, daughter of Sir Henry Fawcett Fitch. The couple had lived in the Bloomsbury area of London, where his three children, Johanna, Hugh Junior and Thomas, were born. He became an eminent scholar and received his knighthood in 1905 for his academic work and his extensive philanthropy, fifteen years before his death. The unfortunate incident of the theft of the Roman ring had affected neither his fortune nor his reputation. But was the philanthropy a deliberate distraction from an archaeologist with a questionable incident in his past? He was still an eminent archaeological scholar right up to his death; he was a man who had scholarships named after him, and he was renowned for his patronage.

Because he was a prominent figure, there were many photos of Sir Hugh McCarthy Miller, mostly taken in his later life. They depicted a typical Victorian gentleman, elegantly suited and shod, with the usual accoutrements and additions that represented comfortable wealth; the gold pocket watch on a chain on the waistcoat, the signet ring, the high collar with an intricately knotted tie and gold tie pin. He had mutton-chop whiskers and a walrus moustache and, naturally, the grave, staring, and haughty look that was de rigeur in Victorian photography.

But… what was it about the images that didn't impress her? She transferred them all onto the whiteboard, side by side, filling the screen. She looked at him, face-on, head turned slightly to one side, in profile, staring at them, going from image to image. What was it?

As she sat back and stared, she heard footsteps on the stairs, into the kitchen, then around the hall. "I'm in here," she called out. It was Jack. He stumbled into the office, yawned so widely that it seemed his jaw had dislocated and threw himself onto the settee.

"Morning, Mum. What you looking at?"

"That's Sir Hugh McCarthy Miller, the archaeologist. He's a descendant of Julia Pencarrow."

"Unlike Ann Quinn," Jack replied. "Why are you looking at so many photos?"

"I'm not sure," she said. "He was famous and eminent. But there's something bothering me. I'm trying to figure out what."

Jack sat forward and stared carefully at the board. "They're pompous, aren't they? Like, they're not real. Not like our photos."

"The exact opposite of selfies," said Maggie, grinning. "It was about managing what people would think when they looked at the image, not who the subject really was."

He stared at the screen. "Maybe that's what's wrong. Whatever it is, it's leaking out, somehow. Something he can't hide?"

"Hmm," she said. "I think you may be right. But that's instinct, or worse, suspicion, based on what we know. If you want to see something, you'll find a way to see it. I have a suspicion forming about this man. No, it's more of a bad feeling but no idea why, yet."

"Leave them up there. Maybe the others will spot something. See if they agree with you. I'm going to get breakfast." He stood and wandered out of the room.

"Good idea," she said to his departing back.

She turned back to her laptop and looked for details of Sir Hugh, when he changed his name. He had been born Hugh McCarthy. That was an Irish name. Victorian upper-middle-class hypocritical society did not associate Irish with respectability unless it came with a title. And a double-barrelled surname would give him more gravitas. It was a change that had taken place when he was about thirty years old.

Alice arriving in the office put an end to any further searching. "I've been thinking," she began. She flopped down on the settee in the same place that Jack had just vacated. "How about we look at other schools? I know I have to go. I like school, really. I just don't like that one."

"Did you have anywhere in mind?" Maggie asked, knowing she did.

"There's a private school, up near Abergavenny. It's small, about three hundred kids, and it's got a sixth form. Could we take a look?"

Maggie folded her arms and leaned forward. "Yes. We can. Tell me the name and I'll look it up. But Alice, that's a long journey there and back each day. Never mind what the school's like, it will lengthen your day by at least two hours. It would have to be by bus."

"I know," Alice said with a theatrical sigh, "but I'd go anywhere to get out of that place."

"I'll look at it, that's all I'll say for now. Same as Jack. Come back later. What are you doing today?"

"Going over to Janine's, I think. We're going to the cinema later, if I'm allowed?"

"One of us will take you and pick you up to bring you home. Sorry, but that's how it is for now."

Alice shrugged. "OK. I'll sort it out with Janny. I need breakfast." She jumped up and went to the kitchen where Maggie could hear the start of a conversation between Alice and Jack. She sat for a few minutes, thinking about a new school. It had to be the answer, but she was wary about ending up moving from school to school, which was the wrong answer. She'd have to look at what Alice had found and see what she thought. She checked her watch. It was almost half-past ten. She had thirty minutes until anyone arrived. How to best spend the time? Whatever the answer to that question might have been, the ringing of the bell ended any chance of pursuit. It was Nick.

"Can you please use your key?" Maggie grumbled as she led him into the office.

"Sorry," he mumbled. "Miles away. Didn't think." He stopped dead when he saw the whiteboard.

"Why are you looking at Sir Hugh McCarthy Miller?"

"You recognise him?"

"I've been looking at him because of the dig at Caerleon, and I've found out some interesting things about him." He paused, then asked "But why is he up there?"

"Can we wait until Bob and Zelah arrive?" Maggie asked. "I've got a feeling we've arrived at a watershed moment. We all need to hear about everything at the same time."

He nodded and sat. Maggie went into the kitchen to put on a pot of coffee. The front door opened again, and she heard Zelah's voice, followed by Bob, who came to the kitchen to find her.

"We're getting somewhere on several fronts," he said.

She nodded. "I've got that feeling this morning, too. Let's hope we can put it all together. Pick up the tray, will you? Let's get started."

Nick and Zelah were already sitting around the conference table in the office, and Nick was discussing Sir Hugh McCarthy Miller with Zelah.

"Is he going to move to a role centre stage?" Zelah asked as Maggie walked into the office.

"I think so," Maggie replied as Bob set the tray down on the table. "But we'll be able to confirm what that role is once we've shared what we've learned in the past twenty-four hours." She poured out coffee for each of them and passed the cups around the table. "Who wants to go first?"

Zelah began. "OK. I was going to say that we'll need to work out how what we've each learned adds up, but I agree with Maggie, let's get it all out on the table first. So, my bit. Reverend Steelfox. He's in his late eighties, but he's got all his marbles. He realised that Ann Quinn was wrong, tried to tell her so when they spoke on the phone, but she gave him an earful of abuse, so he put the phone down and hasn't spoken to her since. But he's followed her on Facebook. That's where he found her originally. Seems she's posted a lot of news about her quest for the Pencarrow inheritance. He said she'd sounded excited recently. Talking about new leads." Zelah pulled a wry face. "A Facebook account, eh? Another legend smashed about how she lived."

"I'll tell the Penzance police about him," Bob interrupted. "He'll probably have to give a statement."

"I thought so," Zelah replied. "I told him that might happen, and he seemed excited. Appalled at the murder. But I think little happens in his life these days. Anyway, on to what he told me. Maggie, how about you make notes for the board as we go along?" Maggie nodded.

"He has worked out his descent to Peter Steelfox, Edward's brother. And he knows Peter's story, and the bits that interest us. They accused Peter of theft and assault. He was sentenced to death, commuted to transportation. They took him from Bodmin Gaol to Bristol in 1736 and on a transportation ship to America, which was still a British colony then. He landed in Maryland where the captain sold him to a plantation owner. He was there for seven years. But here's the thing, unlike most of the convicts, Peter Steelfox did well for himself. He was good with horses and the plantation owner was a decent person, despite running his plantation off the backs of slaves, convicts, and indentured servants. He used Peter's skills and allowed him to learn how to read and write.

"After seven years Peter was free. He spent the next couple of years setting himself up as a horse expert – don't ask me what that means – then came back to England. He wanted to know what had happened to his family."

"Do you know what year?" Maggie asked.

"Not exactly, but it would have been between 1746 and 1750. The info James Steelfox has doesn't confirm the exact dates. What he could tell me is that Peter arrived in Cornwall to find Edward and Emma had gone back to Shropshire, Mildred Vyse had been murdered, and Sir John had married his secret mistress, Emma Trelawney."

"That's new," Maggie said. "I found that he had married again, but I didn't know that he was carrying on with her before Mildred died. That's a motive for murder."

"Could have been," Zelah agreed. "But I don't think he did it. This is where the story of the letters comes in."

"Does he have the letter?" Nick asked.

"No, he doesn't. But he's put a lot of time and effort into finding the last remaining letter and he's made an interesting supposition about what might have been in it. Can I carry on now?"

Nick nodded.

"When Peter Steelfox came back to England, he went to Cornwall. Sir John Vyse hired him to look after his horses. And this is where we can pin down a date. In 1753 Peter wrote to his brother Edward to say he had returned and would travel to see him, with the permission of his employer, Sir John Vyse. The Reverend believes, and I agree, that he would have had to have been working for Sir John for at least a year to get permission for such a long absence. The letter stayed in the family. It's amazing. Very worn and delicate and the vicar treated it like the Holy Grail. Anyway, off he travelled. But when he got to Cheshire, he found that Edward had died. He stayed with the widow, Emma. She hadn't expected him as she had received the letter but couldn't read. She gave it back to him. That's how the family still has it. He asked her about Edward's copy of the letter as, he says, Sir John asked him to do and had confirmation that it had been destroyed as agreed. This was the reference in the family Bible. And, while he was there, he married.

Chapter 52

"That was quick," Maggie said.

"Wasn't it just? Probably because only six months later, out popped another Steelfox. And that's the vicar's ancestor."

"How reliable is this story?" Nick again.

"I looked through all of his research," Zelah replied, "and I have to agree that he's done a good job. He had to join up some dots. But I would have done the same and come to the same conclusions. It's not like Ann Quinn. And there's more."

"This is fascinating stuff," Maggie said.

"After he married Alice, who was Emma Steelfox's sister, he left before the baby was born, to go back to Cornwall and prepare for her to join him. But she never did." She paused until Bob asked, "Why not?"

"Two reasons, I think. First, perhaps, marry in haste, repent at leisure. Then Sir John died suddenly in 1755. We don't know what would have happened to Peter's job, as there was no direct heir to the Vyse estate. And the decisive factor? He was already married. Perhaps on his trip south, the realisation he was now a bigamist caught up with him."

"Wow, what was that about?" said Maggie.

"He had married a local girl in Maryland, before returning to England. And, guess what? After Sir John died, he went back there, without Alice, who most probably never heard from him again."

"How did the vicar know about this?" Nick asked.

"An American family tracing their family history contacted him. They came to Peter Steelfox, but only to his second arrival. They couldn't figure out how, according to the dates they had, he had married before he arrived in the country. At first, they assumed that his wife had arrived with him. But then they found that she was born in Maryland. So, they tried to trace him back, found the vicar online, and the rest is history."

"But where does that get us in relation to the spoon ring and the letter?" asked Maggie.

"That came from the American family," Zelah replied. "Peter Steelfox became a prosperous man. He passed on his ability with horses. These days the Steelfox family in Maryland owns and breeds racehorses. Anyway, Peter left a lot of papers. In amongst them is a letter to a business partner and friend, in which he describes the outcome of his meetings both with Sir John Vyse and his brother's widow. This must have been a trusted confidante because it's someone who knew the true story of his original reason for being in America. I read a copy. The language disguises it well. But if you know, you can work it out. He had always wanted to know what became of Mildred and John Vyse and that was his main reason for returning to England, but only when it was legal for him to do so. I suspect he wanted to stick it to them. But Mildred was dead. Reverend Steelfox and I suspect that Sir John let him in on part of the real story, maybe out of guilt, who knows? But he agreed to travel to see his brother to confirm the status of Edward's letter, which he found out was destroyed. He describes how, when he informed Sir John, he seemed 'mightily relieved' and then asked Peter to be sure that whenever he, Sir John, died, Peter would ensure that his own copy, which was with his solicitor, would also be destroyed. Those were his instructions, but Peter says Sir John was 'most concerned' that it be done and that Peter would be handsomely rewarded."

"That must have put him in a quandary," Bob said. "Sir John could have lived for years."

"Probably," Zelah said. "But, as it turned out, Sir John died. Peter did as he was asked, collected the reward money, which was five hundred pounds, a fortune back then and hot-footed it back to America telling no one in his family where he had gone."

"Poor little Alice," Maggie said. "Courted, married, made pregnant and deserted, all within months. But I still don't understand how this gets us any further forward."

"The final bit I haven't told you, yet. In these American letters, correspondence covering six months, Peter asks his friend to keep his secrets. He doesn't want his wife to know even though he did nothing wrong."

"Apart from the bigamy," Nick interjected.

"Yes, and stop interrupting, all of you. And the final bit. When he talks about Sir John's reaction to hearing that Edward's letter had been destroyed, he tells Peter that after his death a woman may come to ask if Sir John's letter had also been destroyed. He would know the woman. He was to tell her it had been done, and that she was the inheritor and the 'last one to know the truth'. She sat back and picked up her cup. "Now, questions?"

"That must have been Julia Pencarrow, mustn't it?" Nick asked.

"I agree," Zelah replied.

"Does the Reverend know that?" asked Maggie.

"No, he doesn't. He only heard about Julia Pencarrow from Ann Quinn. He checked out Ann's line and came to the same conclusion; that she did not descend from Julia. But it had given him a lead as to who the woman that Peter would know could have been. So, I gave him some of our information and I told him I would keep him in the picture. I told him I have the ring, but not about the letter."

"Fair enough," Bob said. "But you and the Reverend have a theory about what's in this blasted letter?"

"I do now. It's his theory, but I think he's right. All three were involved in Mildred's death and they alibied each other. They conspired to record the events of the night, why it came about and what happened to the ring, who had it, and why."

"Is there more to your theory, Zelah? Because there's still nothing clear about why this is important," said Bob.

Zelah hmphed. "Isn't it obvious?"

"If it was, I wouldn't be asking."

"Don't get snarky. James Steelfox and I believe that the death wasn't just brutal and nasty. There was witchcraft involved. If the poppet was connected to the ring that will be explained in the letter. Mildred Vyse died in a room locked from the inside, strangled by a chain around her neck that held a ring that has disappeared."

"There's lots of ways to explain that," said Bob scornfully.

"Yes, Mr Detective, in the twenty-first century there are. But as we know that Julia Pencarrow was supposed to have gifts. At the inquest they highlighted her as being present when the door to the bedchamber was opened, which made her one of the first to enter the room, so she's a solid suspect. Who else would have been so trusted?"

"Emma Trelawney, for a start," Bob replied.

"That would mean that it was all on Sir John," said Maggie, "and Emma was already dead by the time Sir John spoke to Peter Steelfox. She couldn't have been the woman who would come to find out about the letter."

"OK," he conceded. "But we have no idea who else was in the house, do we? Or who else might have been involved. I concede she's a good prospect. It's just the witchcraft thing. That's a stretch, for me."

"Try suspending disbelief," Zelah said. "Hard for your profession, but possible. You know about Eira Probert and you saw Morgana Hywel for yourself."

"If it was Julia Pencarrow, and she had the ring, why wasn't the letter with it when the three rings and the remains of the poppet were in Zelah's bag of goodies?" Maggie asked.

Nick sat forward. "Just because it wasn't doesn't mean to say it hadn't been previously. Perhaps whoever took the rings and the poppet didn't value the letter in the same way."

"Possible," Maggie replied. She glanced at the clock. It was midday. "Shall I go next?"

After a brief nod from each of them, Maggie began her story.

"I've been concentrating on getting into the detail of Julia Pencarrow's history, to ensure that I was right about Ann Quinn being wrong, but also to find out more about the woman. I agree that she must have been a key player in the death of Mildred Vyse, and she was suspected of witchcraft. So, I took a longer and deeper look at her. What I found is that her history is littered with witchcraft. Her mother was a well-known witch, and her great-grandmother was a woman called Hepzibah Pearce, who was hanged in Exeter for witchcraft. By Julia's time the hunting of witches was over, but there was still a lot of suspicion. Julia merited no recordable deeds, but her mother did." She stopped to pick up a book from a pile on the desk behind her.

"Bob and I went to the museum in Boscastle, as you know, and we bought books. Both Hepzibah Pearce and Marjorie Williams are mentioned as famous Cornish witches."

"What did they do, or are supposed to have done?" Nick asked.

"In Hepzibah's case, she was a scryer, meaning they supposed her to be able to see the future in a dark mirror. We saw one of those at the museum. Odd thing, a black mirror. And she had the evil eye, meaning she could curse people who upset her and make them ill, or their family or livestock."

"That doesn't sound far removed from making poppets," Zelah said. "Any evidence?"

"No," Maggie replied. "But the cursing got her hanged. And they also supposed her to be able to make objects fly."

Zelah sat up. "What objects?"

"I hadn't thought about it," Maggie said. "Does it matter?"

Zelah shook her head and sat back in her seat.

"Anyway," Maggie continued, "I then looked at Julia's descendants. Her grand-daughter, Alice Pencarrow, married a man called James Miller. They had a daughter, Johanna Miller. She married a lawyer called Edward McCarthy."

"Aha!" Zelah clapped her hands. "The link."

"Exactly," Maggie replied. "Their son, Hugh McCarthy at some point combined both his mother's and father's names, to become Hugh McCarthy Miller. This man, it now turns out, was a direct descendant of Julia Pencarrow."

Chapter 53
Penwith House, Penwith Hamlet. 1755

The news arrived at six in the evening. Julia Pencarrow had been in the kitchen, checking over the accounts, and now she sat in front of the remains of the fire. The other servants had gone to bed. There were only two other servants now. Since the death of Lady Emma Vyse, Sir John had plunged into an eternal state of mourning, made worse by the death first of his daughter, then his only son, John, three years before.

His loneliness had made him eccentric. He closed the entire east wing of the house, claiming it unfit for habitation, then haunted. He kept night hours and could be heard muttering and swearing as he paced the corridors, accompanied by his two hounds.

He would ride out and not return for days, never explaining where he had been.

This time it had been five days. Julia hadn't concerned herself. She had continued to keep house for him, and her husband Edmund had moved in to help with the management of the estate. The earlier estate manager had left, declaring madness had affected Sir John.

The sound of rapid horses' hooves on the cobbles didn't trouble her. Sir John often returned at a great pace, running into the kitchen to find out where everyone was, looking for Lady Emma. She waited for his heavy footsteps, characterised by a limp following a riding accident some years before. But none came. Then, the sound of running footsteps. Not Sir John. Master Wendwort, the house servant who had replaced Edward Steelfox, followed by a young lad carrying a flaming torch.

"Madam," he gasped as he saw her, "an accident. Sir John has been thrown from his horse." He was breathing heavily and having struggled to get the words out, paused for a breath. Julia knew what was coming. "Broken his neck, ma'am. They're bringing him now."

The sound of the cart's wheels bumping over cobbles reached them through the open doors. Julia stood. Edmund went to stand beside her as three men carried the body of Sir John into the kitchen. She pointed to a long table where they placed the corpse. Then they stood around, unsure.

"How did it happen?" Julia asked.

One man stepped forward, cap in hand. "It was a strange thing, Mistress. He was riding his horse fast, pushing it. He rose like they were approaching a wall. He urged the horse to jump. But there weren't no wall, not at all. Right in middle of field, it were. Horse stopped sudden, threw him right over its head. Flew he did, landed on the back of his neck. No hope, Mistress, none at all." She nodded.

"Don't know what he see'd, ma'am," said another from the back of the group. He gave her a suspicious look.

"We will never know." She turned to Wendwort. "We must fetch the priest and inform the constable. Something spooked him. An animal, perhaps."

A side door opened, and two men walked in, chatting and laughing, cutting off when they saw Sir John's body on the table. They both approached and Julia stood beside them.

"He is at peace, Peter."

"At last," Peter Steelfox replied. She put her arm around him. He had tears in his eyes.

"Nothing to be done, Edward," she said to the second man. "We must give him a Christian burial. It was a terrible accident."

"He was a good man, mother," Edward Pencarrow whispered, his head on her shoulder.

"Yes, he was." She turned to the men. "Thank you. Please wait and speak to the constable. Give him your accounts. Wendwort, when you have spoken to him, go to the village and find the carpenter. Ask him to come to measure; we shall need a coffin. And ask Marjorie Watter and Jayne Zeneith to come here. We shall lay him out."

The men dispersed. Julia didn't move. There was just one thing left to do. She summoned Peter Steelfox.

"You remember that when you returned from your brother's home in Cheshire his widow gave you a message?"

"Yes, Mistress."

"You must go to Sir John's lawyer in Truro. First thing. His name is James Trennen. The message is: 'destroy the letter'. And you must watch it happen. He will burn it in your presence. Then you will return and tell me it is done."

"Yes, Mistress." He turned to leave but paused. "There's no heir, Mistress. What will become of us now?"

"I don't know, Peter. The lawyer will inform us." He nodded and left the kitchen.

She sent Edward to his room, leaving just Edmund and the corpse.

"What do you suppose happened, wife?" he said.

"His head was full of frightful thoughts, husband. It is a blessed release for him." She smiled at him, knowing he didn't understand but would not ask for understanding. Now, at last, she was alone with the secret. Unto death.

Chapter 54

Nick stood up suddenly and stared at the whiteboard, at the photographs of Sir Hugh McCarthy Miller.

"I have the next piece of the puzzle," he said to the board. He stood staring at the board for several seconds until Zelah, unable to contain herself, said, "And are you going to share it with us?"

"What? Oh, yes. There are two parts to this story. I was working out which one to start with." He paused again, nodding to himself. "I'll start with the story of the Roman ring." He walked around the table, eyes flicking back and forth from the pictures on the whiteboard to objects in the room.

"I've been speaking to a Professor William Fitzsimmons at the School of Archaeology at Cardiff University, on and off for a couple of weeks. They've done several digs at Caerleon and made a lot of finds, but nothing like this ring. He's an expert on the site, not just the fort and the amphitheatre, but what would have been the town, including the various temples and the other buildings."

"Did he know about Sir Hugh McCarthy Miller?" Maggie asked.

"Oh yes," Nick replied. "He's also something of an expert on the man, and after years of study and research his opinion of the man is low. Not because of the actual work he did, you understand. But because he believes that Sir Hugh kept certain finds for himself. Stole them, in fact. And he thinks it was Sir Hugh himself who stole the ring." He reached into his pocket, took out the box, opened it and put the ring on the table. "He was thrilled when I showed it to him. But before I get into his theory of what happened, I want to tell you about the story of the ring, or at least this professor's theory."

"You mean, whose ring it was?" asked Maggie.

"Yes. He's been interested in the ring since he got involved in digs at Caerleon, over twenty-five years ago. He's pinned it down to a rough period and has identified some characters who could have been involved." He stopped and went back to his seat, putting his hands in front of his face in a prayer-like gesture, thumbs resting under his chin. Maggie thought Zelah would explode and was about to say something calming when Nick began to talk again, slowly.

"There was a legionary Commander in AD 255, a man called Titus Flavius Postumius Varus. The Commander's house is under what remains of the church and graveyard today. The professor pinned down this Commander by examining documents, monumental inscriptions, and so on. These included a few brief descriptions of the villa and how it changed during the years of the Legion at Caerleon, or Isca, as it was then. The depth of the burial of the girl's body helped to determine the time, too. There was just one Commander who's known to have had female relatives of the right age. Professor Fitzsimmons thinks the remains are likely to have been this man's niece. She disappeared, you see. The Commander had a daughter, called Flavia, who was about thirteen at the time of her disappearance and the niece was believed to be around fourteen or fifteen. She was the daughter of his wife's brother. And he was a Julian – a high-status Roman family. He died and left her to the care of Titus Flavius. The marriage age then was about thirteen. Commander Flavius was an ambitious man and foresaw a wonderful opportunity in marrying off this niece to someone who could be a good contact for him back in Rome. So, he arranged for his niece to marry a Senator, a much older man. She was supposed to be sent to Rome for the marriage, but she never arrived. Commander Flavius had sent his wife to go with the girl, but eventually she reported back that the girl had died en route. They never proved where, how, or of what she died. There's an inscription to her dated AD 255, on the Caerleon site, but only fragments remain. It was her uncle Flavius who erected it, dedicating it to her memory."

"Who's to say she didn't die on the journey?" Zelah demanded. "How on earth can anyone be sure, from two thousand years ago?"

"Oh, he's not sure, of course. But there's also a record of sorts in Caerleon about a young soldier who died of a broken heart when he lost his love. Again, pieced together from fragments of graffiti scratched into stonework. He was a young man of a good Roman family, so he must have been important in the Legion. He begged his girl's father to allow them to marry but was refused. He went to look for her, but couldn't find her along the route, nor could he find any of the servants supposed to have gone with her. He wrote to his father but was told to keep his suspicions to himself. He returned to the Legion and shortly thereafter he died. The evidence of this story sits in Rome."

"Sounds a stretch," Bob interjected.

Nick continued as if he hadn't heard. "This was a political marriage. They used young Roman girls from good families as political pawns. They were tradeable goods for important alliances. But supposing this girl refused the marriage? If the soldier was broken-hearted, it's possible they made a promise to each other. The Commander had his eye on returning to the Senate in Rome, that's documented. What if the Commander found his alliance was about to be scuppered and he was to be made a fool of by the girl? He couldn't have stood for that, so he committed an honour killing. The ring, probably given by her suitor, somehow ended up in the ground with her."

"A very big stretch," Bob repeated, drumming his fingers on the table. "Was that done then?"

"It used to be legal, but by this time was outlawed. But the Commander, who was the senior male, had what was called *patria potestas* over his family, which gave them the legal status of possessions."

"But I agree, it's a big stretch. However, there's circumstantial evidence and we must do what we, as self-respecting genealogists, never do. We have to make the facts fit the story we want. But I think it has merit. And one more thing, and this is the real stretch: the girl was a Julia, Julia Drusilla."

"So, you're guessing that they may have secretly married?" Maggie asked.

"No, I don't think that. Perhaps it was a secret betrothal, but it wouldn't have had any validity. Roman high society didn't work like that. The Commander had already given his approval for the marriage to the Senator and the girl would have had to prove that his choice was in some way unsuitable. I doubt she could have done that."

"But you think that the soldier gave her the ring?" Maggie said.

"It's an explanation of how it was found with her. It wasn't on her finger; it was clasped in her hand."

"If it's true, it's a shocking story, and a sad one." Maggie sighed and sat back. "Honestly, I don't think it matters, if it isn't true. There's no one to dispute it."

"I thought honour killings were more of an eastern thing?" Zelah noted.

"Not at all," Nick replied. "They've been going on since the times of the Egyptian pharaohs. And they're found in a lot of European cultures. But, as I said, its legality was dubious in AD 255. The Commander covered it up, but probably felt justified in what he had done."

"You learn something new every day," Zelah muttered. "What next?"

"I haven't finished," Nick said in a flat voice, still strolling around the table. He stopped at the whiteboard.

"Oh, sorry. What else do you have?"

"This," he said, pointing at the board. "This man, Sir Hugh McCarthy Miller and his descendants. I will take up where Maggie left off." They all sat up in anticipation as Nick looked at the photographs on the board.

"When I arrived, Maggie said there was something... what did you say, 'unsettling', about him? That was interesting." He looked directly at her. "You couldn't put your finger on what it was. But as you knew nothing else about him, you were going entirely on what you saw. Well, I can tell you now that there was something very unsettling about this man." He turned back to the board.

Zelah sighed, loudly. "I wish you would get out of the habit of doing that." Her voice had a brittle edge, which reminded Maggie that, for Zelah, this was personal.

"I'm sorry, Zelah," Nick said. "I know that this is affecting you deeply. I want to make sure I explain clearly."

He took the small upwards snap of her head as confirmation he should continue. "I've been researching as much as possible since we got back, made phone calls to people in the history and archaeology fields. The information about him was never mainstream, but it was widely suspected in academic circles. Sir Hugh McCarthy Miller took the Roman ring and other artefacts from the dig himself. And it wasn't the first time."

"How do you know that for certain?" Zelah demanded.

"It was a well-known rumour. When the Caerleon artefacts went missing he organised a witch-hunt, and named two members of his team as suspects, ruining their careers. There was no evidence against them. Turns out it wasn't the first time this happened. People put two and two together and came up with him as the probable thief. But it couldn't be proved. Nothing in writing, you understand. He had a formidable temper to match his reputation. He bullied his staff, so no one challenged him. There was a lot of ill-feeling, but nothing went further than muttering behind his back and spreading gossip. That's what got him in the end – gossip."

"It's the eyes," Maggie said in the pause. "In every photo, from every angle, it's the eyes. He thinks he has composed his face, but his eyes are… vicious, possibly? Calculating?"

"Yes," Nick said. "He was known for his arrogance. Never thought he'd get caught."

"He wasn't," Zelah said. "Caught."

"But the gossip finished him off." Nick countered. "He had to retire, and he gave lots of money to charity. He set up a foundation."

"I suppose charities couldn't refuse his patronage," Maggie added.

"What about who came after him?" Zelah asked.

"He and the Honourable Eugenia had three children. A daughter, called Johanna, then two sons. The first was another Hugh, then Thomas. As the elder son, Hugh inherited the estate and he has an interesting history."

"We're all ears," said Zelah.

Nick smiled. "And so you should be. This next Hugh married when he was twenty. His wife was Mary, an Irish girl and the younger daughter of an Earl, and they had two sons, Hugh and Edward. Tragic story. They both joined up in 1914, officer rank, of course. Both were killed. Hugh in 1916 at the Somme and Edward in 1917. In 1919 Mary died in the Spanish flu epidemic, leaving Sir Hugh alone. In 1920 his father Edward died, and he became a recluse and a bit eccentric. Mary had come from a wealthy family and Hugh inherited everything. Her father had been instrumental in getting Hugh a title, before Mary died, so she could be Lady Mary and he became Sir Hugh. He also inherited land in Ireland in County Cork from Mary's family where they lived from the time they were married until he died. He bred thoroughbred horses."

Nick leaned over the table and picked up a glass of water, gulped it down, coughed and continued, "Also living at the farm – I'm calling it a farm but from what I've found out it's a property of significant size – was his younger brother, Thomas. Thomas was the third of the elder Sir Hugh's three children. He was much younger than Hugh Junior. After Mary's death Thomas took up much of the responsibility of running the family business when Sir Hugh shut himself away. But then came the big shock. Remember the son, Edward, killed in the First World War?" They all nodded.

"He had a friend called John Radcliffe. John was also a local Cork lad. And John was to be married. The date had been set; preparations were made. John was due to leave for home. The girl had only just turned eighteen. On the eve of the marriage, John was killed… on the very same day as Edward. Same battle. The girl had no family left alive, so the McCarthy Miller family took her under their wing. Sir Hugh, Edward's father, was very fond of her. After the death of both of his children he looked on her as his daughter."

"What's shocking about that?" Zelah interrupted. "It happened to many families, I expect. What was her name, by the way?"

232

"Her name was Julia Noble. She was the daughter of a man who had been a business partner of old Sir Hugh in the horse breeding business. The shock, Zelah, is that in 1930 when Sir Hugh was sixty and Julia was thirty, they married."

"Wow," Maggie said. "That moved on from the father-daughter relationship."

"Yes, it did. In 1931 they had a daughter, Margaret. But Julia didn't recover from the birth and she died in 1932 of complications. Sir Hugh was distraught. He shut himself away entirely. Wanted nothing to do with the child. Blamed her for killing her mother."

"What happened to her?" asked Bob.

"She died, too," Nick replied, "but there are questions about the circumstances of her death."

Maggie went to say something, but Bob got in first. "What happened to the property and the inheritance?"

"All went to the brother, Thomas, or rather, to his descendants. They all stayed together in the house. Must have been a big house. Thomas had a son, also named Thomas, in 1928. He's still alive. The horse breeding business is going strong. Thomas is still very much the head of the household. He's ninety but active and mentally fit, but nowadays his children, Noel and Norah, run the business and the grandchildren are also involved. The current Thomas also got a knighthood. He's now Sir Thomas McCarthy Miller."

"Just a minute," Zelah said. "I can understand how a lot of this is available from internet and book research, but you can't have got all of these details that way."

"No," Nick replied. "I got a lot from Stella Bell. Her grandmother comes from Fermoy, in the Cork countryside. She was brought up in a village just outside Fermoy which is close to where the McCarthy Millers live. They're the subjects of much local chatter and chinwag. They employ a lot of the village. Angela, that's Stella's grandmother, likes to keep up with what's going on at home. She told me some fascinating stories about the current crop of McCarthy Millers."

"What kind of stories?" Bob asked.

Nick shrugged. "Some just blether about their goings-on. Some, interesting, particularly about Norah. She's not a person to be crossed. She's inherited the family temper. But on the whole, they are good employers, they do a lot for the village, and are big supporters of the Church, and so on. Philanthropists, nothing bad."

Bob sat back and folded his arms. Maggie noticed that his attention was fixed on the ceiling. She leaned over to him and spoke softly enough for Zelah not to notice. "Something occurring to you?" He didn't speak but nodded with a small jerk of his head. She decided not to push. He could put in his two-penneth when he was ready.

She noticed that Zelah was also ruminating. "Bob, I think you have an update, yes?"

He returned his attention to the group. "Yes, but I want to think a bit more on what we've just heard. All of it."

"And that's seems to be a good point to pause," Maggie said. "Jack said to me earlier that something was leaking out of the photographs up there. Seems he was right. And I thought that we were about to reach a watershed moment. Why don't we stop and have some lunch, give ourselves time to think? I've got to check on activity upstairs. I think I'm on taxi duty soon." She left the room.

In the hallway she realised that the usual buzz of conversation was absent. Lots of thinking going on.

Upstairs Alice was on her phone to Janine, agreeing that Maggie would pick her up in half an hour and take them over to the cinema. Maggie nodded agreement when she heard and went to see Jack. He was on his computer, as expected, still in pyjamas.

"You going out today?" she asked.

"No," he replied after a couple of seconds during which things exploded on the screen. He kept his attention rigidly fixed as his fingers jumped over the keys. "Just chilling with the guys."

She left without comment and went down to the kitchen where she found Bob, Zelah and Nick. Bob and Zelah were making lunch and Nick was folding back the doors so they could eat on the decking, where the sun was now shining relentlessly.

"Take whatever chances we get to be outdoors," he said.

"Agreed. I must take Alice and Janine to the cinema in about half an hour. Gives us time to eat and chat a bit."

"This garden is coming on nicely," Zelah remarked as they sat in the shade looking over the garden and the canal to the sharply outlined mountain beyond.

"I'm getting better at it," Maggie agreed.

"It's the only thing I miss about our house in Caerleon, mine and Martin's house. He was a great gardener. I'm crap at it. But I did like to sit and admire his handiwork."

"He was a creative man," Maggie said, "and I imagine that he had a great eye for colour."

"Didn't matter what season. It always had something coming into bloom." Zelah's voice had taken on a softness that Maggie seldom heard. It didn't last long. "So, what do we think about these McCarthy Millers?" She said, raising her voice sufficiently to make sure she got both Bob's and Nick's attention too.

"I have a question for you, Zelah," Nick replied. "When you had the third ring dated, the gold wedding band, when was it made? Remind me of the date."

"It was 1917... damn!"

"I thought so," Nick said. "If my theory is correct, this is the ring that John Radcliffe had made for Julia Noble, for their wedding. It might well have been returned to her with his effects when he died."

"And there's the connection between the three rings." Maggie said, blowing out a long breath. "This is a big leap forward."

"I think there's more," Bob said. "Alice is calling you."

Maggie turned her head, to find Alice in the doorway, ready to go.

"I'll be back in half an hour. Please don't discuss anything new before I get back!"

Chapter 55

After she had dropped the girls and fixed the exact time and place for collecting them, Maggie drove back, forcing herself to keep to the speed limit. Back at the house the others were in the office sitting around the table. Maggie was interested to see that Jack had joined them.

"We have said nothing," Zelah said as soon as Maggie entered the room, "Except to get Jack up to speed and to talk about the bloody weather, which none of us cares about any longer. Now, shall we get on?"

"My turn," said Bob. He stood up and walked round to the whiteboard. He looked as if he was going to deliver a grim lecture. "I've been looking for suspicious deaths at the end of June 1956. I've come up with three. One in London, one in the North of England and one in Swansea. I based this on the premise that whoever left Zelah was intending to come back but couldn't. I've ruled out the first two. One was claimed three months after the death. The other was too old to have a small child. Could have been a grandparent but the date of the death didn't fit with when Zelah was abandoned. It happened on the same day late morning and by any reckoning, it would have been difficult to get from the end of Cornwall to Newcastle in that time. Unless we now believe in teleportation, it's safe to eliminate that one.

"The third one in Swansea is more interesting, especially after what I've heard this morning. This was a young woman, aged around twenty-five. Someone killed her in a hit-and-run about two or three days after Zelah was left at the church. The vehicle was known to be a white van with no identifiable markings. And a witness thought it drove directly at her, rather than being an accident. The witness said a man got out, picked up something that might have been a handbag or a travel bag and then got back into the van and took off. The van sped off after the incident and wasn't found."

"Same question as before," Zelah said. "What's significant about this one?"

"There was no means of identification," Bob replied. "The bag was taken. But… what the suspect didn't know when he took the bag was that in her coat pocket the girl had a ferry ticket. She was going to Cork later that day."

"Did she die right away?" Maggie asked.

"Yes," Bob replied. "The witness called the police and ambulance at once, but she didn't make it to the hospital. She never regained consciousness. The injuries were catastrophic."

"Is there anything else that we know about her?" Maggie asked again.

"Possibly," Bob replied with an arch smile. "This is technically still an open case, although it's now also a cold one. They thought her to be in her early to mid-twenties. She had dark hair and green eyes. Her clothes, and they kept them, suggested a Bohemian lifestyle. They can't say what happened to them, but Swansea can't confirm they've been destroyed. If they can find them, then with the technology we have now, they can check DNA."

He turned to Zelah. "If this woman was a relative, Zelah, and you're willing to give a DNA sample, then we can compare."

"Assuming you can find the stuff in the first place, and if you do, it hasn't been corrupted by time," Zelah replied. "But, yes, I'll give my DNA. I suppose this is one of those paths we have to go down."

"It's an outside chance," Bob replied. "But, as you say, we can't ignore anything, no matter how preposterous. That's your guiding principle anyway, isn't it?"

"Yes," Maggie said. "Rule everything in, then try to rule it out."

"Sherlock Holmes!" Jack interjected. "'When you have eliminated the impossible, whatever remains, however improbable, must be the truth'. That one?"

"Yep," Zelah replied. "That one."

"I can arrange for your DNA to be taken in the next few days, Zelah."

"OK, Clouseau. Get it over as soon as possible. When are they going to let you know if they find the evidence?"

"Can't say," Bob said. "I couldn't give them a reason to expedite it. It's not like we have any idea who she is and there's no evidence who ran her down. It might never lead to anything."

Zelah shrugged. She went to speak, but Bob put up a hand to stop her. "One more thing. I heard from DC Mooney last night. He's on a roll. He tracked down the cleaning woman, Susan Blessing. She remembered something. Just before Jay disappeared, a woman came to the vicarage looking for him. But she had the misfortune to be met by Tracy who told her that he was no longer there."

"Is she sure? That the person was looking for Jay? Really sure?" asked Zelah.

"Yes, Zelah, she was sure. She's an old lady now, but all there. She remembered Jay. Says she liked him a lot. He was handsome and funny, and kind. She always thought it was a shame a nice family couldn't adopt him."

Zelah sat still for a few seconds, then said, "He was all of those things, and more. Who was the woman?"

"She didn't know. But it's a coincidence, and I don't believe in those. I suspect it was Jay's mother."

Zelah stood up so suddenly that the chair fell back and hit the floor. "Tracy was an evil bitch! How could she? How could she?" She stormed out.

Bob went to call her back, but Maggie put a hand on his arm to stop him. "She needs a moment."

"There's more," he said.

"Is there any chance it's good news?"

"No."

"Tell us now what it is, and I'll find her and tell her. I think that would be better than hearing it in front of all of us. It's rare that she shows her feelings like this."

"It's tough hearing and I suspect that piercing brain of hers has already put two and two together and come up with a conclusion that's probably right but horrific."

Maggie paused for a few seconds, preparing herself for whatever she was about to hear, then said, "OK, off you go."

"DC Mooney thinks there's a link between Jay's mother's so-called death by drowning and Jay's disappearance. It was assumed that she drowned whilst drunk, because people knew she had an alcohol problem and there were two empty gin bottles in her bag. The autopsy was conducted with an expected outcome. These days, it would be much more thorough. When he checked what notes there were, he found that she had sustained a head wound, on the back of her head. They assumed that she hit her head going into the water. Mooney wants it re-examined. He's going to re-open the case, and he will petition to exhume her remains for a more detailed forensic examination."

"Are you saying that Tracy Hopton could have been involved in Jay's mother's death? Why? She sent the woman away. What possible reason could she have had?" Nick asked.

"There's still more," Bob said.

"Oh, dear God, how much worse does this get?" Maggie demanded.

Bob shook his head. "You remember DC Mooney was looking for other children placed with the Hoptons, and find out what happened to the charity that put them there? He hasn't had time to get to the charity yet, but it turns out that one child, who was there at the time Zelah ran away, stayed around and never left the area. A local family fostered her shortly after Jay disappeared. She still lives in Sennen, just half a mile from where we were staying. Her name is Maureen Delaney. Back then she was Maureen Meers. She's about sixty now, I believe."

"And she remembers something important?"

"It would seem so. She's agreed to speak to Mark, over the weekend. She would have been about seven at the time Jay disappeared. That's just about old enough to remember something that might be valid."

Maggie stood up. "I'm going out to find Zelah and tell her

about this."

She found Zelah in the garden, walking slowly around the flowerbeds, pausing to put her nose into some flowers. She didn't look up. "Lovely scents, these roses. I see there are stocks still going, too. They'll be heady at twilight. Best time to smell them. Tell me."

Maggie recited the news and finished with the discovery of Maureen Meers.

"Little MoMe, that's what we used to call her. She was a quiet kid, but always seemed to be there when you looked around. I'm not surprised that she may have overheard something Tracy said. Exhuming Jay's mother's body, eh? That's a bold step." She moved on to another flower and bent over it. "How long is that going to take?"

"He's applying for permission. It requires someone high up in the Church to agree when the body is buried in consecrated ground. It's an involved process. He will make sure that Bob knows. It'll be at least a week or two, I would guess, to get it approved and to get the autopsy done. I mean, I'm no expert, but it won't happen tomorrow."

"Of course not. It has to be done properly. But if she didn't drown accidentally, then we must be looking at foul play."

"Looks that way," Maggie replied, keeping two steps behind Zelah as she made her way down the flower beds. "Come back in when you're ready. We have to decide what comes next."

Back in the office Bob and Nick were talking, but they stopped when Maggie arrived.

"I was just asking Bob if there's any news on the poppets and if anyone has spoken to the lad next door yet about the woman who was here asking about you," said Nick.

"And the answer to both is 'no'. My colleagues are trying to trace the journey of the package. A courier delivered it, so there should be a trail. But it probably won't tell us much. DI Jordan from Cornwall is coming up to speak to the lad. He's OK'd me being present. He's asked me to ask you to let the parents know that he's coming, and he'll confirm with them when."

"Is there any more news about Ann Quinn's death?" Maggie asked.

"Not really. Forensics have gone over her car, and they're checking for DNA on her body and clothing. But nothing significant yet. They're following up on my suggestion about the car I heard being a bigger one than Ann's. There's not a lot of CCTV in that part of Cornwall, but if they headed back on the A30, or stopped somewhere for fuel, there might be a lead. It was the early hours of Bank Holiday Monday, so there won't have been much traffic, assuming they left Cornwall right away. Shouldn't be that difficult to find a big car on the road during the night. Anyway, how's Zelah?"

"Quiet, which is unusual, but—" Before she could elaborate Zelah joined them. She plonked herself down in the seat she had earlier vacated, folded her arms and asked, "What's next?"

"Not sure," Maggie replied. "I'll write up a full set of notes from what we've learned today and what to expect over the next few days. But something you asked earlier, is whether Sir Hugh McCarthy Miller will take centre stage. My feeling is yes, for now, but what do you all think?"

They all turned to look at Zelah who shrugged to show that she wanted to reserve what she had to say until she heard other opinions.

Nick sat forward, his fingers steepled in front of his mouth. "I agree. But we need to learn more about the current family. So far, we only have Stella's grandmother's gossip to go on. We need more. For a start, we need to know who they officially are."

"I can get some of that information from official sources," Bob said. "I think we have enough reason now to consider them persons of interest. It won't be in much detail, though. And I'll keep on top of Jay's case. Plus, Ann Quinn's murder… and the hit-and-run in Swansea."

"Not sure what there's left for me to do," Maggie mused. "I can help with the research. Zelah, we have ongoing cases, don't we? We can't afford to let them get behind. If you want to give me an update, I can make sure we're on top of all of our other work. And just one thing, everyone. Next week is big for me and the kids. I want to be around as much as possible for them."

"Of course," Zelah said. "That's what I want to do right now. It's all moved extremely fast. Let's just slow down, take stock and see where the research gets us. But I'll just say this once, for the record." She stopped and closed her eyes for a moment, took a deep breath, then opened them, sat up and put her palms down on the table. "When this started – when I let it get started – I thought I'd prepared myself for whatever would come of it. How bloody naïve was that? And I thought I could control it. Madness. But I am now totally committed to whatever the outcome is. I've realised that some of it will be terrible. But, whatever. It's rolling. Let it go ahead. OK?"

She didn't stop for an answer, instead going to the garden, where Maggie found her five minutes later, staring into the dark water of the canal.

"We've just agreed to have a quick get together each day, at around ten, to catch up and see if anything should change. But otherwise, we let it roll."

Zelah nodded without looking up. "Bring it on," she said, in what Maggie thought was a sad voice.

Chapter 56

The next few days were quiet, by Maze standards. Each knew the others were working on their agreed assignments, but no one was talking much, which meant no breakthroughs.

On Sunday they had a ten o'clock catch-up by conference call. There wasn't much to report.

Nick had done some thorough research into the McCarthy Miller family and found they were living on a private estate a couple of miles outside Fermoy in County Cork called Rosscarbery House. They had interests in racing as well as horse breeding. Sir Hugh McCarthy Miller Senior's career in archaeology didn't seem to have continued in the family.

"Mark Mooney is meeting Susan Blessing today," Bob reported, sitting next to Maggie in the office. "He's going to call me when he's done, probably this evening. And he's started on the exhumation request. He thinks he's got enough probable cause to get a certificate from the judiciary and the Church."

"Nothing from me," said Maggie. "I've got to concentrate on getting Jack and Alice into school and settled for the next few days. Anything else, anyone?"

"Yes," Zelah said. "We have to think about how to approach the McCarthy Miller family. The rings are leading directly back to them."

"Hang on a minute," Bob interrupted. "I haven't got anything yet from Ireland. We know nothing about these people, except that they have a dodgy ancestor who was probably a high-class thief. Yes, someone has died, most likely because of one of those rings. But we don't know that the present McCarthy Miller family has anything to do with it. We need more information."

"Well, get on with it then," Zelah snapped.

He went to snap back but Maggie got there first. "Cool it, Zelah. He's doing his best. We all are."

"And I'm joining the interview with Maggie's neighbours tomorrow, with Fergus Jordan up from Cornwall, see what we can learn about the person in the Audi who was nosing around here," Bob added.

"OK, OK, I get it," Zelah replied. "Didn't mean to upset you, Clouseau."

Maggie heard Bob's sharp intake of breath next to her, and again got in quickly. "He thanks you for the apology. Can we all agree to keep going, see what we can find out, and meet up tomorrow? Zelah, Nick, we need to be getting on with normal work now, anyway. No reason you shouldn't come here in the morning. I'll be back by half-nine."

They agreed. "Good. And you'll be here to get Bob's info on what he and the Inspector find out."

After they had signed off, Bob turned to Maggie. "She's getting on my nerves."

"If you mean calling you Clouseau, it's her way of showing approval. Try to see it like that."

"If you say so. Feels like ridicule to me."

"Zelah doesn't do bad ridicule, not to people she likes."

He sat back and his shoulders sank. "I'm keeping on top of this as much as I can, you know. But I have a day job, too. She forgets that. I'm not part of your business."

She leaned across and planted a loud kiss on his cheek. "You're wonderful."

He tried to keep a smile off his face, but failed, so changed the subject. "How are the preparations going for tomorrow?"

"They're both ready, in terms of what they need. Shoes, bags, clothes, so on. But mentally?" She sighed. "Alice is saying nothing, just grimacing as she checks things off her list. We're picking up Janine at half-eight. As for Jack…"

"Sorted," Bob said. "A colleague, who'll be very discreet."

"Thank you. He's so excited and nervous. But the last thing he wants is to have his mates thinking that he's being baby-sat. Just until he meets up with other boys at the bus stop and gets on the bus, yes?"

"Yes. But I still think we should tell the other parents and the boys. If they're as good friends as he says, they'll want to watch his back."

"Let me talk to him tomorrow night, once his first day is over."

"Fair enough. And now, I have to go to work."

"Call me later," she called, as he headed out.

Chapter 57

Despite all of Maggie's preparations Monday morning was a nightmare. Jack only just made it to his bus, hassled out of the house by Maggie, whilst being told that they would review his morning timetable.

Alice got ready in silence but couldn't find her shoes. Maggie's suspicions led her to a box at the back of Alice's cupboard, thwarting her daughter's final attempt not to have to go to school.

"Sorry," she said as she pushed Alice out of the front door. "Janine is expecting us. We can't let her down today." They had agreed to pick Janine up so that the two girls could enter the school together, even though Janine lived less than ten minutes' walk from the campus.

By the time Maggie got back to the house, to find Zelah and Nick both waiting for her, she needed a strong cup of coffee and five minutes to sit back on the settee with her eyes closed.

A prod from Zelah roused her. "That bad, eh?"

"Worse," Maggie said, eyes still closed. Then she sat up. "Bit of a shock for Jack, not being in charge of his morning timetable. We can do something about that. But Alice… I don't know, Zelah. I can only wait to see what it's like when I pick her up later."

"It's not going to work, is it?"

"No. I'm going to have to go look at the school she found up near Abergavenny, and quickly."

"Have you given any thought to private tutoring?"

"Yes, but I don't think that's the answer either. I can't see how they can cover the full range of subjects she needs. And, despite what she thinks, she does need social contact. But in an environment where her differences are appreciated, not mocked and ridiculed."

"Tough one. Come on, let's get on with something we can do."

In the office Nick was already on the internet. He looked up as they walked in and sat down. "I'm finding more information about the McCarthy Millers. Ready to hear some of it?"

"Yes, please," Maggie replied.

"Sir Thomas McCarthy Miller is ninety and very sprightly. He still rides out most weeks. He fishes and hunts. He's the patron of a number of local societies and the Catholic Church is in raptures about him."

"That's no indicator of a good man," sniped Zelah.

Ignoring her, Nick continued, "His children are Noel and Norah, twins. Noel was married to Sorcha – she died a couple of years ago of breast cancer – and they have two sons, Stephen and Niall. Norah is a widow. She has one daughter, Emer. All three grandchildren live at home. None are married, although the two boys are both heading towards thirty. Emer, Norah's daughter, is twenty-five. All three have graduated from university. Emer was at Oxford, got a First. Her subject was Medieval History." He sat back and folded his arms. "There's nothing I've learned so far that gives me any feeling of concern, or any feeling of anything. I'm wondering if they even knew about the rings."

"The old boy must do," Zelah said. "Hugh was his uncle. Julia Noble became his aunt, and the baby Margaret was his cousin. And most importantly, his grandfather was the thief."

"Doesn't mean he knew," Maggie countered.

"Think about this," said Zelah. "If his grandfather stole the Roman ring and was suspected of stealing other finds from archaeological digs, would he have hidden them away? No, he took them because he desired them. He wouldn't then have hidden them, would he? He'd want to see and appreciate them. And the spoon ring? If he inherited that, isn't there a chance that he would have kept it with other precious things that came into his possession?"

"Supposition," Nick said.

"Well, I'd love to get into that house to take a look. Wouldn't you?"

"I would," Maggie said. Nick shook his head. "I can't think that they'd be brazen enough to display stolen goods."

"Think about this, then. Somebody took all three rings and the remains of the poppet, which might have belonged to Julia Pencarrow. So, they must all have been together and retrievable."

"They could have taken them one by one," said Nick.

Zelah shook her head. "If that happened, surely the first one would have been noticed. Your way would mean returning to the scene of the crime four times. I can't see how that's possible, to get away with it, I mean."

"There's sense in that," Maggie said, "but how do we find out if they know anything?"

"Easy. Ask them. Don't bugger about. We'll go and ask them."

"Whoa! Hold on there, Zelah. You can't just turn up at someone's house and ask if they know about stolen items and systematic theft by a relative. Apart from anything else, that's police business."

"You can be such a wuss, Nick. What can they do?"

"Push you off a cliff?" Maggie said.

"Their house is landlocked. OK, OK. Don't look at me like that. No, I haven't thought it through. But I can't see why we couldn't make an approach of some kind. The live ones don't have a criminal background, unless Bob turns something up. And anyway, we don't have anyone else to speak to, do we? They might be able to give us some useful information if there's anyone else looking for the rings."

"There are three things to think about," Nick said. "First, if the family did have the rings and they were stolen, why didn't they report it? We know that they certainly didn't tell the local police, or at least no one did in the fifties when the rings came into Zelah's possession. Second, it's possible that the current Sir Thomas might not have known, so the rest of the family is innocent and might be outraged by our turning up accusing their esteemed ancestor of theft. But the third thing, if they've hidden the fact that the rings were stolen all this time, what else are they hiding? And don't forget, someone else is trying to find the rings now the cat's out the bag. If it's not the McCarthy Millers, then they're likely to be under a watchful eye, too. And we don't want to alienate them if they can help us, do we?"

"Well, what do you suggest? We can't just sit here," said Zelah.

"Yes, we can, for now," said Nick. "Eventually all of this information gathering is going to turn up something significant. It always does. I'm going back to see Stella, see if we can get her grandmother on the phone. We'll ask more questions about each of them. Please, Zelah, don't get carried away and do something foolish."

Maggie knew 'foolish' was not an appropriate choice of word. She knew the signs of Zelah bristling and working up to an outburst. "Zelah, I know that you've got the most personal interest in this, but please don't forget that my children have been threatened. Before we go off anywhere, I want to be sure that it's safe. That's all Nick is asking."

Without answering, Zelah sat at one of the desks and typed, hammering the keyboard. Maggie looked at Nick and shrugged.

A ping from her phone alerted her to a text. "Bob's next door, with DI Jordan. He's chatting to the lad now. He'll come in here as soon as they're done."

Zelah hadn't stopped hammering, but Maggie was sure she'd heard.

"I'm going into the garden to water the plants. Might as well keep them going for as long as I can." She left Nick and Zelah with their backs to each other, each appearing to be engrossed in their respective screen.

Maggie was glad to get away from them. The morning was pleasantly warm, good enough for summer clothes. As she made her way around the garden, she thought about Zelah's words. She could understand, to a certain extent. They had suddenly seemed to make progress and now it had all come to a halt. Wasn't that always the way with their cases? But this wasn't just one of their cases and she had to admit that she was holding back, waiting for something more concrete to reveal itself, to show that it was safe to move in any direction. The poppets had created a nervousness she hadn't felt before. And there had been little opportunity since they came home to sit quietly and gather any thoughts about the whole experience so far. It would be better to do so, for a couple of days at least before they went haring off again, chasing some elusive lead. Bob would demand safety before they approached the McCarthy Millers. Nick also was uncertain about such a move until they had something more conclusive.

She watered the last basket of geraniums and trailing lobelia of which she was particularly proud. She was about to get herself a coffee and sit down near the canal, when she heard a door slam, signalling Bob's arrival. She hurried back up the garden. He was already in the office and was twitching up and down on the balls of his feet. Both Nick and Zelah had turned to face him. She took a seat.

"There have been two interesting developments," Bob began. "Firstly, the evidence bag from the Swansea hit-and-run death was located and sent for DNA testing on Friday. They know that there's potential that this has always been a murder investigation, so it's going to get priority. Which means we might get a result before next weekend. Secondly, the interview with the lad next door. I can't share too many details with you. But the woman who came looking for you here said she was looking for Maze Investigations and had information to share about a case Maze was investigating."

"What's interesting about that?" Zelah asked.

"She specifically said Maze?" interrupted Nick. Bob nodded.

"We've never given this address to anyone, nor have we ever shared it online, or anywhere else," Nick said. "In fact, we've gone out of our way to protect it. It's not the registered company address."

"True, but it probably wouldn't be difficult to find out," said Bob.

"Zelah, why would anyone want to track us down here? Maggie, maybe, on a personal basis as it's her home. But not Maze." Nick turned back to Bob. "Anything else?"

"The boy called her an 'old woman', which could mean anything from forty to eighty but probably around sixty-ish. And she had an accent."

"What accent?" Zelah asked.

"The best he could say was 'sort of soft and sing-songy'. Not much to go on."

"Would he recognise her again?" asked Maggie.

"It was hot. She was wearing a floppy hat and sunglasses she didn't take off, so probably not. But... she was driving a big German car. He couldn't say what, he's not much of a car buff, but he was able to describe the badge on the front of the car; it was an Audi."

"So she followed you on to Cornwall."

"Not by chance. She asked the boy if he knew where you were and when you might be expected back. He told her you were on holiday in Cornwall. It wouldn't have taken much to find you there if she found you here. Right, I've got work to do. I'll let you know about anything else that crops up. I'm expecting to hear from Mark Mooney later. And I'll make sure that someone sees Jack home from the bus." He gave Maggie a quick kiss on the cheek but followed it with a scowl and a shake of the head that he hid from the others and left.

Zelah was drumming her fingers on the table. "Irish accent," she said.

"Or Swedish, or Italian," Maggie replied. "You're the last person I expected to be making suppositions to fit your story. But finding the Swansea evidence is exciting, isn't it?"

Zelah stood up. "I'm off," she said. "I need to think." Her phone rang, and she answered it as she walked out.

Maggie sighed as the front door banged closed. "She's worrying me."

"She's never been patient," Nick replied, eyes fixed on his computer screen. "But I've always thought that she's sensible. She won't do anything stupid."

"I'm not so sure. The strain is telling. If we get the DNA result and it matches, and if it's a close familial match, then it will change her entire world. That's a lot for anyone to cope with. We're going to need to stay close to her." She paused. "Anyway, you getting anywhere?"

"Nothing direct. I've been looking at Facebook profiles. The only one of the McCarthy Millers with a public profile is Emer. Look." He swung his screen around, and Maggie put on her glasses.

The photo was of a laughing girl, with long black hair and green eyes, looking like she was in the middle of an exchange of jokes with the photographer. Her head was cocked to one side. Standing behind her was a small group of older people.

"Pretty girl," Maggie said. "Can you enlarge that?"

Nick zoomed in.

"Not on her so much, on the group behind her. Do you think that might be family?"

"Maybe. Or it could be college. Is it an argument, do you think? The woman in the background doesn't look very happy."

"She looks like she finds smiling difficult. Face like a bag of spanners. I had a teacher looked like that. I don't think I ever saw the woman smile once in seven years. Miserable old bag, she was." She moved closer to the screen.

"What?"

"I don't know. There's something familiar there, but I can't place it." She shrugged. "Probably that teacher I'm thinking of. We used to have competitions to see if we could force a laugh out of her. Never managed it. It'll come to me. That reminds me. Alice is finishing at two today. I'll have to be there in good time."

They worked on for the next two hours, Maggie working on a new case in Liverpool and Nick hunting for information about the McCarthy Millers. At one-thirty Maggie packed up.

"Found anything else?" she asked as she grabbed her keys and headed for the door.

"No. They're very private. No more photos on any social media. Nothing much in the press apart from publicity shots. Highly successful businesses, though. Enough to have just given a big donation to a charity for rough sleepers in Dublin."

"They sound like decent people. Right, I'm off. Wish me luck. Will you be here when I get back?"

"No. I'm meeting up with Stella to talk to her grandmother."

"Let us know how you get on. You coming back to find out what progress Mark Mooney has made?" He grunted agreement. "And please, lock up, won't you?"

Chapter 58

Maggie parked the car outside the school and waited on the pavement. It was too warm to sit in the car and she wanted to see Alice walking out, if she was with anyone.

She was getting anxious after ten minutes as most of the students had streamed out of the campus, but there was no sign of Alice. Ever since the incident with Eira Probert, she felt a gnaw of fear when Alice was late leaving school. As the last of the stragglers made their way to the gate, she spotted Alice, walking slowly up the path, head down, alone. This did not bode well.

Alice acknowledged her with a flick of her head and walked past her to the car. Inside, Maggie turned to her with a questioning look, but Alice shook her head and said, "Can we go home, please?" Her eyes were red-rimmed. Not good.

The drive home was in total silence, Alice staring ahead, Maggie trying to think how to get the information out of Alice without a scene. As soon as they were indoors Alice turned to her. "No one will sit with me. Every class I went to, when I sat down, they moved." She started to cry, raggedy breathing in the attempt to suppress the sobs.

Maggie took her into the sitting room, sat in an armchair and pulled Alice down onto her lap. Putting her arms around her to let Alice sob it out, she silently fumed.

When the sobbing slowed to steadier breathing Maggie said, "That sounds organised."

"It's that Lizzie girl, she's the one who was onto Janine all the time. But Janine is OK now. She was on the stage in assembly this morning, after the surfing thing. She has lots of admirers. And she's on our year's netball team."

"So, they've moved on to you?"

"Yes. Lizzie has told everyone to pretend I don't exist. Not to have anything to do with me. And when I put up my hand to answer a question in class, they laugh."

"Didn't any of the teachers stop that?"

"A few did. But one just told me to go sit at a desk at the side of the room on my own."

"Did Janine help?"

"I haven't seen her. She's been too busy."

"I'm going to get you out of there, Alice. As soon as possible. Can you give me a couple of days? Please?"

"Just a couple of days?"

"Promise. Pinky-promise." Maggie put her hand out. They linked little fingers and shook three times. This had always been their sign of a promise that could not be forgotten or broken.

Alice stood up. "I'm going to get out of this stinky uniform."

Maggie didn't have the heart to tell her off. She wanted to cry herself. How could this be allowed to happen? Where was the humanity? Pointless question. She had learned that this school didn't have any. It was all about publishable results. But Alice had the makings of a brilliant student. Maggie would be at the school first thing in the morning. But in her heart, she knew it wouldn't make any difference. That was the culture and it wasn't going to change, not under the current regime.

She went to her computer and looked up the number for the school in Abergavenny, dialled and made an appointment for the following day at lunchtime. At least that was something she could do.

Jack returned at five o'clock, flung his bag down in the hall and collapsed onto the settee in the living room.

"How was your day?" Maggie asked, handing him a mug of tea.

"Brilliant," he muttered, eyes closed. "They treat you like an adult. I'm knackered."

"Get used to it," Maggie replied. "You're travelling for the next two years."

"Thanks for the sympathy." He sat up. "How did the mini witch get on?"

"Badly. Seems like she's been sent to Coventry."

"What's that?"

"That's what we used to call it. Happened to me, once. No one is speaking to her. Organised by one girl."

"Why?"

"I have no idea, neither does Alice. But Janine is no longer available for bullying, so Alice seems to be next in line. Alice is different. She thinks and speaks differently. That is a good enough reason in their nasty warped little minds."

"Can you get her out of there? I know she can be a pain, but that's disgusting."

"As soon as I can. I've asked her to give me a couple of days. Can you be a bit supportive, Jack? Anything will help now."

"Of course. What do you want me to do?"

"If she gets snippy, don't rise. And maybe give her a hug?"

"OK." He closed his eyes again but was frowning.

"And don't do anything stupid. Retaliation won't help."

Chapter 59

Bob had promised that he would let them know the outcome of Mark Mooney's meeting with Maureen Meers. Zelah arrived after dinner. Nick had joined them earlier. Maggie and Nick were in the sitting room discussing the McCarthy Millers again when Bob arrived. Zelah hadn't joined in any of the conversation but was sitting staring grimly at the blank whiteboard.

Bob sat next to Maggie and turned to Zelah. "Your old friend Maureen has a good memory. She remembers Jay. Liked him. Had nothing good to say about Tracy Hopton. Hated her. But she was an observant little girl. She remembered a lot of detail about old man Hopton and his wife. She remembered the woman coming to the house looking for Jay. But better still, she remembered more of the conversation the woman had with Tracy. Some of the words didn't mean anything to her then. But as she grew up, she realised that Tracy had made some ugly threats against the woman and against Jay. She threw her out of the house and laughed at her. The woman said that she'd go to the police, do whatever she could. Tracy said that would be a very bad idea, or something like that, that the woman would regret it. That's when Tracy said she would make sure the woman never saw Jay again."

Maggie shook her head. "And that was just out of spite? It seems incredible behaviour. I mean, I know from what you've said, Zelah, that she was a foul person. But—"

"She liked it," Zelah replied. "She liked any opportunity to hurt someone. It gave her a feeling of power. And I think she wouldn't have stopped at anything to exercise that power. If someone challenged her, which Jay's mother seems to have done, yes, I believe she was capable of killing her."

"The exhumation is going to happen in two days' time. It will probably be in the early hours. Again, he'll let me know the result."

"But none of this tells us what happened to Jay," Zelah said to Bob.

"Mark and I are talking about possibilities. That's all I can say."

"You have a theory?"

"Just an idea. We want to hear about the outcome of the exhumation first."

"Oh, come on, tell me what you think."

"No," Bob replied sharply. "Not yet." Then he turned to Zelah. "I have her phone number for you. She said she was sorry she didn't know you were so close this summer. She'd like to speak to you again. She said to tell you that she remembers Little Jay, or LJ as they used to call you. She says you were like his mini-me." He smiled, but Zelah looked puzzled. "Did I get something wrong?" he asked.

"No," she replied. "But it's just–" Then her expression changed. Maggie thought Zelah looked like she'd seen a ghost. Her eyes had widened, and she was staring into space, lips moving slightly, muttering over and over, 'Little Jay, LJ, LJ, LJ,' as if a memory was fluttering around her head, but she couldn't catch it.

"Zelah, are you OK?" Maggie asked.

"Of course I am. Stupid question." But her face was pale and her eyes staring.

"Anything else, anyone?" Maggie asked quickly. No one answered. "Then I'm going to get ready for tomorrow. See yourselves out."

She went upstairs to talk to Jack and Alice and after ten minutes Bob called up to her. "I need to go, Maggie. Can you come down for a minute?"

She joined him in the hall.

He kept his voice low. "How do you think Zelah is coping?"

"I think there's a lot more going on in her head than she's prepared to say. Something just rattled her."

"Yeah, that's what I thought. Do you think she would do something rash? Like contact the McCarthy Millers before we're ready?"

"The problem is, Bob, that we still don't have any idea when we'll be ready. And Zelah, although she knows it's sensible to wait, doesn't do patience. She believes in confrontation. She might just up and off. I can ask her, but I don't know if I'll get an honest reply."

He shook his head. "No, leave it. We have just two days until the exhumation takes place."

"She's got so much to think about. I wouldn't be surprised if she explodes," said Maggie.

"Do what you can to contain it." He paused. "Look, something else has happened re- Ann Quinn. Fergus Jordan wants to question Zelah again. He's 'invited' her to return to Cornwall for another interview."

For a few seconds Maggie couldn't think what to say. "He cannot possibly believe that she had anything to do with it?"

Bob shrugged. "I think you and Nick are off the hook. But Zelah… he thought there might be more to it. First he thought it might be because of a financial interest." He put his hand up as Maggie rose to respond. "I know. Then he looked at her financials and dropped that idea. Now, he's wondering if it might be manslaughter. If she followed Ann Quinn down the path, argued with her and accidentally pushed her when the argument got physical."

"That's the most ludicrous thing I've ever heard," Maggie responded. "Zelah is incapable of doing such a thing. The idea that she might not only have killed someone, but hidden it from all of us…"

"I've told him I think it's weak. There's no evidence. She'd have to have been out there all night, as the alarm wasn't turned off until the morning. But he wants to go through with it. He's going to call her tomorrow."

Maggie gave him a piercing look. "Do you actually think it's a possibility?"

He put up his hands. "I don't know her as well as you do. He needs to rule it out. That's all I can say. Don't be angry with me. And you absolutely cannot say anything to her about this."

"Difficult. My friend could not kill another human being."

He leaned forward to kiss her and went to leave, but Maggie caught his arm. "Can you please come back in for five minutes? There's something I want to confront Zelah with and I think it's important you hear it. And I need to speak to Nick with all of us present."

He looked at his watch. "Five minutes." He smiled but got nothing in return.

Back in the office, Zelah and Nick were still talking about the McCarthy Miller family. "Zelah thinks we should be planning a trip to Fermoy," Nick said in his usual soft voice, but Maggie detected tension.

"I agree," said Maggie, hoping to prevent an argument. "We'll have to talk to them sooner or later. But I'd like a few more facts."

"Like what?" Zelah demanded.

"Like the result of the DNA test on the clothes from the hit-and-run in Swansea."

Zelah jumped up. "I don't want to talk about that."

"OK, OK, Zelah," Maggie said. "Please sit down. It's up to you, but you did agree to find out." She paused for a moment, then turned to Bob and Nick. "Could you guys give us the room for a few minutes, please?" Bob scowled and looked at his watch but they both got up and walked out.

Maggie turned to Zelah. "This must be a roller coaster for you. It's an elephant in the room isn't it?" Zelah nodded.

"But, Zelah, if it is… what we are thinking it might be… that doesn't link directly to the McCarthy Millers."

Zelah shook her head angrily but didn't reply.

"Can't you see, it makes sense to wait? It's just a couple of days. There's no reason we can't plan a trip to Fermoy, but let's go armed with information. Because if it is… you know… we need a good reason to approach them, to probe." Again, no acknowledgement of Maggie.

"Look, we all want to get to the bottom of this and you more than any of us. But please, let us be there for you when we meet them. Please."

The pleading in Maggie's voice was enough for Zelah to look at her. Her shallow sigh and tut was enough. Maggie felt a little reassured. "Let's get Nick and Bob back in. There's something I still want to know about the family, and I think it's significant."

"Oh, alright."

Once they were all seated again, Maggie spoke directly to Nick. "You said there were some unanswered questions around the death of Margaret McCarthy Miller. Can you elaborate?"

"She drowned. But her body wasn't found for a couple of months. She had run away to Dublin and got in with a bad crowd. But they were rich, bad people. Lots of drugs, drink, and parties. Story was that Margaret fell overboard from a yacht belonging to one of them in her mid-twenties."

"Do you know the date when this is supposed to have happened?" Bob asked, sitting up. His eyes were piercing in their direct scrutiny of Nick.

"Yes," Nick replied, sheepishly, Maggie thought. "It was at the end of June 1956."

"And when was the body found?"

"Late August."

"What was the evidence of the accident, which we should presume it was, and the identification?" Bob was in full interview mode.

"The owner of the yacht saw her go overboard, and threw out a life jacket and a ring, but she was panicking in the water. He jumped in, but by the time he got to where he had last seen her, she had disappeared. The identification was made by her uncle, Thomas McCarthy Miller. There was a birthmark, but that was about all they could recognise. Just enough to confirm her identity."

"What about her father?"

"What about him?"

"Did he play any part in identifying her? Did he confirm the birthmark?"

"I don't know," Nick replied. "Is it important?"

"At this point everything is important. I'll try to find out. And

I'll get some info from the Irish side about the details."

"What are you thinking?" Zelah asked.

"I'm thinking there are a lot of coincidences. It was within days of the hit-and-run. Margaret was still her father's heir. Two months later her body could only be identified by a birthmark, not corroborated by her father. Her uncle then became heir to a big property and a lucrative business."

"How long before the DNA result?"

"A couple of days at most, but I'm hoping for tomorrow," Bob replied. "And today I'm going to find a contact in Cork to speak to about the family." He turned to Nick. "Email me all of the details about Margaret McCarthy Miller's death, will you? I want to know the name of the yacht owner."

"Of course."

"Right. I have to go now." Bob stood up, nodded to Maggie, and left.

Chapter 60

The following morning Maggie got Jack off to his bus and took Alice to school. She had decided to wait until lessons started, then try to speak to the Head of Year. But she wasn't available, so she made an appointment to return before the end of school. That would give her time to visit the private school at lunchtime. Maggie had allowed Alice to take her mobile phone to school, and told her to find a quiet place to call, if anything bad happened. She left that information with the Head of Year's secretary, who looked displeased, but didn't argue, especially after Maggie referred to 'bullying' and 'intimidation'.

There was no word from Bob, Zelah, or Nick, during the morning and after a little more online research into her Liverpool case, Maggie had just enough time to get to the school viewing appointment. She spent most of the journey there tormented about what to say to Zelah, knowing that by lunchtime she would know about the further interview in Cornwall.

After the meeting she had to rush back to see Alice's Head of Year and was only just out in time to meet Alice as she left the school. Janine and two other girls were with her but Alice looked tense. A group of around ten boys and girls were following them and getting closer. They were shouting to Alice's group, who ignored them and tried to hurry. Then one of the following group threw something that landed on the back of one of the girls and made the followers laugh uproariously. Maggie took out her phone and took photos of the group.

Janine put her arm around Alice, and they hurried towards Maggie. Maggie hustled them both into the car and asked, "Who were those kids and what was thrown on that girl's back, Alice?"

It was Janine who replied. "That's Lizzie Montgomery's gang. And it was a flour and egg bomb."

Maggie fought to keep her voice steady. "When I go to the school tomorrow with the pictures, will you speak up, Janine? Will the other two girls?"

"I will," Janine replied, "and Lowri will. She's the one who got bombed. I'll speak to them when we get in tomorrow."

"Thank you." It was all Maggie could say. Alice was shaking.

They dropped Janine home and Maggie and Alice travelled back in silence. When they got back to the house Alice ran straight upstairs and took off her uniform. After a few minutes Maggie followed her up to her room, where she found Alice, dry eyed, white faced, and shaking, sitting on her bed and staring at the wall.

She enveloped Alice in a hug, stroking her back and for once the girl didn't object.

"That's it. You don't have to go back there again. No more. Don't worry about the uniform, it's going in the bin."

"You mean that?"

"I'll be going there first thing in the morning. I took pictures and video of what they did."

"It won't make any difference." Alice's voice was a whisper. "They know they can get away with it."

"Not if I have anything to say," Maggie said, as calmly as she could manage. "I went to the private school today, by the way."

Alice didn't react and Maggie didn't push it. There was plenty of time to decide what to do about Alice's education. Retribution came first. She had the beginnings of an idea, but needed to speak to Bob.

Then, unexpectedly, Alice said, "It was the turnip badge."

"Sorry?" Maggie asked. "The what?"

"That's what started them. He forgot that he wasn't supposed to ask questions in DT and Mr Smith said he had to wear the turnip badge."

Maggie had to put one hand on the bed to steady herself against the roaring noise that was building up in her head. "Please explain this to me, Alice. I don't understand."

Alice spoke quietly into Maggie's shoulder. "We have this technology thing; it's about making stuff from written instructions.

The teacher says we have to be able to see and interpret how to do things for ourselves, not keep asking questions. He told us how to do it, then put the instructions on the wall. Anyone who asked again had to wear the turnip badge. He does it to all of the Year Seven classes."

"What does the badge look like, Alice?"

"Duh. It looks like a turnip."

"What does that mean? Why a turnip?"

"Because it means stupid, of course. Don't you know that Mum?"

"Yes, but I wanted to know how you understood it. Do the others in your class also understand the meaning of it?"

"Well," Alice replied, "if your teacher explains that if you can't remember the instructions and have to ask a question, you get the wear this badge and all the other kids have to chant 'What's the question? What's the question?' at you, then, yeah, they get it."

"That's what he makes you do?"

"It's what he told us to do. Most of them did it. They're too scared not to. I did it too. But Lowri didn't. She went up to Ryan, that's the boy who had to wear the badge, and put her arm around him. He was all shaky trying not to cry."

It took everything Maggie had to keep her muscles relaxed. "And what happened then?"

"Mr Smith told her to come away from Ryan. He was cross. But she wouldn't, she stayed there. Then he told her she would be in detention for cheeking a teacher. So, she had to spend lunchtime outside the Head's office."

"Was she there, the Head?"

"No, I don't think so. Lowri said she didn't come out of her office, anyway."

"What happened next?"

"Nothing. She came back to class after lunch. But the ones you saw, started to tease her about Ryan. Calling him her little boyfriend and making kissing noises. Then after school, they waited and did the same. What they threw at her, they called it confetti." She sat up, pushing away from Maggie. "I've had enough of it, Mum. I waited to walk out with her. She was laughing at them. She's strong. I'm not, I was scared. What if I get the badge next time?"

"Yes," Maggie replied, letting out her breath. "You won't be going back there. I'm going there first thing tomorrow." She put up her hand in response to Alice's gaping mouth. "Don't tell me not to. Someone must stand up to this. And as you won't be going back there, it doesn't make any difference to you, does it?"

Alice shook her head. "But where am I going to go?"

"We have an appointment to see the private school tomorrow afternoon. I was going to take you out of that school anyway. This has just confirmed it's the right decision."

"Will it be better?"

Maggie paused. "Honestly, Alice, I don't know. But we can only go and see. The Head wants to talk to you. And you need to take a walk around, see how it feels."

"OK. I'll give it a go."

Maggie couldn't sense enthusiasm, but given what Alice had just been through, that wasn't surprising.

"I think I'll read for a while," said Alice, picking up a book from her bedside table. She opened it and stared at it but glanced up at her mother. "I suppose this means I don't have to do the shitload of homework I've got?"

"If you use that kind of language, I'll make you do double," Maggie replied, with a smile at the edges of her mouth.

"Jack says it."

"But not to me. I know that doesn't make it any better. But still... I'm going downstairs. I have a few things to finish."

Alice settled herself down on the bed as Maggie left the room.

Maggie went into the office, then the kitchen, then the garden to walk around, but she couldn't settle. She was in turmoil. On one hand she was furious, beyond furious. This was the worst kind of bullying, adult on child. Teacher on pupil. And using the other children to enforce it. The man should be sacked. On the other hand, she admired the girl who stood up against the teacher and defended the boy. And Alice had joined the group walking out of school with her. But none of it should have happened and now the die was cast in terms of school. Whatever she was to do about Alice's education, it had to be done quickly.

She needed time to get her head straight to challenge the school in the morning. At least she could get herself ready for that. She went back into the office, phoned the school to make an appointment to see the Head. The Head's secretary tried to refuse on the grounds that Maggie wouldn't tell her what it was about. But she stayed firm and said that it was an issue of bullying involving a teacher and that the Head was the only person to speak to. The appointment was agreed for nine the following morning.

She was still pacing half an hour later when the doorbell signalled a visitor. It was Bob, which surprised Maggie as she wasn't expecting him back. He looked exhausted and intense and was carrying a folder.

"You've not had any sleep, again," she said grudgingly to him.

"None," he replied. "But that doesn't matter. I've... what's the matter? You don't look great."

"Alice and the school. I'll tell you later. I need your advice... and some wise counsel."

"OK... are we OK?"

"I haven't heard from Zelah yet."

"I've heard from Cornwall. She didn't take it well, but she has agreed to go, with her solicitor. But, I'm here because I have the results of the DNA testing from the clothing from the accident, with the comparison to Zelah's DNA."

Maggie drew in a sharp breath. "That was quick. And?"

"We need to get Zelah here. Pronto."

"Just as well I decided to come over." They both spun around. Zelah was standing in the doorway. Maggie hadn't heard her or her car.

"Shall we all sit down?" Bob asked.

"No, I don't want to sit down. Out with it."

Bob opened the folder. "It's a match, Zelah."

"What kind of match? You asked for the matriarchal comparison, didn't you?"

He took out a piece of paper and held it out for Zelah's inspection. "Yes. Whoever she was, she was your mother."

Chapter 61

The visit to the private school near Monmouth hadn't gone well. Maggie had watched Alice as they were shown around. Alice had acquitted herself well. She was polite, had answered all the questions asked of her by the Head. But nothing either of them saw sparked enthusiasm. The classes were small, the discipline seemed strong.

But afterwards, back at the house, they both agreed that it didn't feel right. Having given Alice sandwiches and allowed her to go to her room, Maggie sat in the kitchen, staring out at the garden, wondering what on earth she was going to do.

The visit to the Head at Alice's current school hadn't gone well, either. She had refused to believe Maggie's story, saying that children exaggerated, that the teacher had an excellent record, that there was probably a simple explanation. And she put off the story of Alice's deliberate exclusion as 'girls being girls'.

When Maggie informed her that Alice would not be attending again until the matter was investigated and that she would be making a formal complaint to both the Governors and the Education Authority if the Head didn't act, she found herself on the receiving end of a threat.

"In my school," the woman began, "children do not dictate terms. Nor do their parents."

"Sounds like neither group gets a fair hearing, then," Maggie retaliated. "And it's not your school. It's the children's school. And I am not dictating anything. I am asking for a fair hearing. Alice will not be returning until I have had assurances that she will not be bullied, either by other children or by teachers." She spoke calmly, but her stomach was clenched. "As soon as you have any news, please get back to me." With that, she stood up and left. At least she'd had the last word. But she knew two things. First, it wasn't going to get resolved in any way to her satisfaction or to

Alice's. And second, Alice was never going to set foot in those grounds again.

Maggie returned to her Maze research. She had received an email from the client on whose case she was working and had to admit that she hadn't made enough progress. Time to get her head down. Zelah had gone silent, which didn't bode well either.

Later, when she had finally come to the hoped-for breakthrough, the slamming front door announced the arrival of Jack's homecoming from day three. He poked his head into the office.

"Great day. I'm hungry," and took himself off to the kitchen. Maggie followed. "Started on my main subjects today. It's going to be interesting. I like the way they teach. We sit around, not in rows. They talk to you, not at you," he said over his shoulder as he grabbed a pile of food and took it to the table, where he began to butter bread and slap fillers onto it. "How was your day?"

"Nice of you to ask," Maggie replied, grinning. "The visit to the private school was a no-go. It's just not right. And I had a meeting this morning with your ex-Head."

His eyes widened. "I'm not going to ask how that went, Mum. I can guess. The whole place is a bitch-fest."

"I'd like to tell you off and disagree, but I can't. So, what are we going to do next?"

"Anyone else got any ideas?"

"I haven't asked, yet. But I'm going to. For now, I'm thinking maybe private tutors."

"Pity she can't come with me. She'd like it. There are some quirky kids there. But no one insults them, or even makes snide remarks. We had a session today on the school's culture. It was all about openness and accepting people for who they are. We talked about being gay, or LGBT, about how people dress and look, and about the way people speak to each other. It's a real atmosphere of tolerance. I got the feeling that if anyone were to do or say anything unacceptable, they'd be counselled, but if it happened again, they'd be out."

"That sounds good," Maggie replied. "Impressive. It's how it usually works in the office, too. Although not always. But I'm glad. Good decision on your part, Jack."

He beamed at her. "I've got some research to do. Not much homework. They say that they don't overburden you." He breathed a deep sigh of contentment.

Maggie left him to his sandwich mountain and went back to the office. A little later she heard Alice come downstairs and go into the kitchen. She left her children to talk together.

She worked for another hour, then made dinner. Alice was quiet but listened attentively to Jack's description of what he was going to be studying.

"Do you still want to be a genealogist?" she asked.

"I think so," he replied, "but I'm going to make the most of the experience in college. I think I'm going to like it."

Alice sighed.

"We'll find something," Maggie said to her. "I don't know what, but have faith."

A little after nine, Alice was in bed reading and, unusually, Jack was already asleep. The phone rang. It was Bob, and there was no preamble. "I've got news from Ireland. When are you all meeting again?"

"Hello to you too. Tomorrow morning, ten."

"Sorry, I'm at work. See you in the morning." And that was that.

Maggie stared at her mobile, shook her head, and went into the office to message Zelah and Nick to let them know Bob was coming. Zelah acknowledged the call without further comment.

Maggie stayed in the office, thinking for some time. She knew that something had happened that had either upset Zelah or caused her to remember something. Or both. It was frustrating that Zelah didn't want to share whatever it was, but perhaps that was unkind. You had to let people come around in their own way and in their own time. Zelah was usually forthcoming, so it would have to wait. Maggie couldn't understand why she wasn't talking about the interview in Cornwall. She couldn't blame them for having been dropped from the enquiry. Could she?

With that thought she realised she was exhausted. She switched off the computers and the lights, locked up, and made sure that the alarm was set. Then she went up to bed, checking on Alice, who was asleep, glasses askew and book lying on the duvet. Maggie quietly removed the glasses and the book, put them on the bedside table and turned off the lamp. She stood for a moment watching Alice breathing. With a brief kiss on her daughter's forehead, she went to bed.

Chapter 62

The next morning Nick arrived early. Maggie was ready and Alice had asked if she could join them in the office at their meeting.

"Might as well have something to do," she said.

"I'll ask the others, but I'm sure they won't mind," Maggie replied.

She left Nick and Alice chatting in the office as she made a pot of coffee and had just put it down on the office table when the front door opened and closed, and Bob came in.

"Sorry I'm late. Got another phone call from Ireland." He glanced around. "Where's Zelah?"

"She's late, too," Maggie replied. "But I talked to her last night and she's definitely coming. But–" She was interrupted by her phone ringing. "It's Zelah." She answered the call and put it on speaker.

"Sorry," Zelah began, "I can't get there this morning. I'll just listen."

Maggie looked at the others, who shrugged and nodded. She gave Bob an inquisitive glance and mouthed 'Cornwall?' He shrugged.

"OK. Bob has some news." She nodded at Bob.

"I've had some interesting interactions with the police in Cork and in Dublin," he said. "I explained our case and told them about the possible connection with the McCarthy Miller family. Cork police gave me some interesting updates on the family. They're powerful, and respected. But not for the right reasons. They have connections in high places, and you don't cross them. My contact warned me to be very careful. There's no evidence of any wrongdoing or corruption. No suspected illegality. But... there have been cases of people badly treated, trying to complain and coming up against a brick wall of bureaucracy. And in the past twelve months one man who tried to take it to them was savagely

273

beaten up. No trace back to them, of course. But, he said, just be careful."

"Not much to go on there," Nick remarked.

"I haven't finished," said Bob. "Then, we come to Dublin. The case of Margaret McCarthy Miller's drowning. On first impressions it looked obvious: she fell overboard. Someone tried to save her but couldn't. Her body washed up months later. She was identified by a birthmark by her uncle. So far, so good. But. And it's a big one. One officer wasn't sure it was that simple. The body recovered had evidence of drug use. Margaret was never known to be a user. Her uncle said after she left home no one knew what she got up to, and it was possible she'd started to use. So that was that. But the officer was still suspicious, and he kept going. Thing was, he couldn't find anyone else who had seen Margaret on the boat in the first place. The guy who owned the boat who supposedly jumped in after her, had financial problems and was facing bankruptcy. Which went away because he came into some money that he said was an unexpected family legacy. The officer tried to trace the money but only came up with an offshore account. Brick wall. He couldn't prove anything suspicious. But he was suspicious – Copper's nose."

"Can we speak to him?" Maggie asked.

"No, he died twenty years ago. But he left his notes in the file. The police in Dublin are curious now and interested in the DNA evidence we have. They don't have anything left from the body in the sea. It was cremated." Then Bob beamed at them. "But the son of the boat owner is still alive. He's going to be interviewed to see what he knows about the so-called legacy. It may not lead to anything. There's enough to cause a spark of interest, but not enough to formally re-open the investigation. Not yet, but I think we're getting there."

Maggie looked at her phone. "Zelah, what are you thinking?"

There was a pause. "What do you mean 'getting there'?"

"I mean that we're closing in, Zelah."

"But not that close."

"Closer each time we find something of interest." He rubbed

his chin and his face, his way of trying to calm his frustration. "We take it a step at a time. The Garda in Ireland can now look at something solid. I've spoken to Swansea this morning. They'll make the DNA available once there's a closer link. It's another country. These things aren't as straightforward as they would be between forces in the UK. Good job we're still in Europe, at least. Things like this will be hell when we're out."

There was no response.

"Zelah, are you still there?"

A few more seconds' silence. "What? Yes. Just a minute. OK, thank you. Sorry, just talking to someone. I have to go now."

"Hold on," Maggie raised her voice. "Where are you, Zelah? What are you doing?"

"Something for myself. Personal. It doesn't involve any of you. I'll be in touch." She rang off.

"I don't like this," Maggie said, turning to Nick. "This is what we were worried about."

"Maybe, maybe not," he replied. "Something has upset her and given her more to think about than she's admitting. But we shouldn't push her."

Maggie glanced at Bob, the unspoken question whether she should tell Nick what she knew, but he shook his head.

"I'm not so sure," she said to Nick. "What now?" She turned to Bob. "Maybe it is time to get in touch with the McCarthy Millers?"

"Maybe. Let me think about it. I only just got most of this information. We need a plan before we set off. We need to decide what to ask and what we want to get out of a meeting."

She nodded and Nick said, "That's fair. Let's talk about it."

"OK," Maggie replied. "But I need a quick break."

"And there's something I want to talk to you about, Maggie, you and Alice," said Bob.

Alice had been staring at the table where Maggie's phone still sat, looking puzzled.

"Then let's talk." Maggie said.

"I'll take this as an opportunity to take a break, too. I'll leave you all alone," Nick said and got up to walk out.

Maggie was going to tell him to stay, but Bob put his hand on her arm. "Just the three of us, to start. Then by all means, talk with Nick and Zelah. By tonight, Zelah should be ready to tell you what happened in Penzance today."

When Nick had gone, Alice sat up at the table and Bob began without preamble. "Alice can't go back to school here and you told me last night that the visit to the private school didn't go well. So, I've been in touch with a friend. Someone I met through a case. A bit like Jeremy. My friend the old vet, you remember?"

"Of course I remember," Maggie replied. "How could I possibly forget Jerry Allen? He brought us together. So, another of your oddballs?"

"Sort of," he replied with a grin. "A lady called Jan. She's a qualified teacher, but she doesn't work in the mainstream system. She runs a… what can I call it? It's a school, but it's called 'Not School'. She works with kids who don't fit into the mainstream."

"Like me?" Alice jumped in.

"Yes, like you," he replied. "Clever kids, kids who'll never be nine-to-five people because they don't think in straight lines. Like you." He smiled at Alice. "I've talked to her about you. She'd like to meet you. Both of you, naturally, if you're interested." He checked Maggie for a reaction, but she sat back with arms folded.

"Well, I'd like to meet her," Alice replied, glaring at her mother. "It's my education."

"Tell me more," Maggie said.

"She has about twenty kids in all, ranging from eleven to sixteen. She takes them through to GCSE. It's private, of course. But she's subject to the usual government inspections and has passed them all with flying colours. Most of her kids go on to take 'A' levels. The difference is, it's pupil led. They study their subjects as they please. No age groups, either. They work together. They sign a contract to say they will adhere to the qualifications' requirements once they reach that stage. But they all seem to get good results. The thing is…" He paused again and looked at Maggie. "They are all very clever kids. Most of them have a high

IQ, but they've all rejected, or been rejected from, mainstream schools because they can't cope in the system. Look, there's no obligation. Just go and see and look around and talk and decide if it's right or not. I just thought I'd ask her."

"Anything else I need to know?" asked Maggie.

"Just one thing." He looked down, then up again. "There is one thing that you won't like."

"Then you'd better tell me what it is."

"It's not local. Jan's place is in Hereford. Alice would have to board."

Maggie jumped up. "Absolutely out of the question. How on earth could you think that I would let her go away?"

She was about to continue, when Alice stood up, walked around the tabled and stood in front of her, hands on hips. "Well, I'd like to go and see it and meet Jan. And if you don't like that, you needn't come. I'll ask Nick to take me."

Maggie opened her mouth, then closed it, looking from Alice to Bob. From her daughter to her lover. Bob went to move towards her, but she put her hand up to stop him. "She's a child."

"I'm twelve. And Bob said there are eleven-year-olds there. I want to go and see."

Maggie's eyes were blazing. "I'll think about it." It was the best she could do with Alice in the room. She had no intention of agreeing.

"OK. I'll leave you two to have a big row now. I'm going to my room," said Alice. She walked to the door but stopped and turned back to them. "By the way, why was Zelah on a boat?"

"What?"

"Zelah was on a boat. Didn't you hear the sound in the background? I 'spect that's why she had to go. She'll probably lose her signal soon."

Chapter 63

Maggie flopped into her seat. Bob stood with his mouth open, as Nick walked back into the room. He took a quick look at them. "It's Zelah, isn't it? What's she done?"

"I think she's gone to Ireland," Bob replied. "Alice heard the sound of a boat in the background during the call."

"That's what it was!" said Nick. "I've been trying to figure it out. Well, not unexpected, I suppose, patience not being one of her virtues."

"She was already on her way before the call. She had no intention of letting us know. If Alice hadn't recognised the sound of the boat, we'd not have even suspected."

"It's been her show from the start, Maggie. Don't judge her," said Nick.

"The problem is," Bob intervened, "the information we've heard suggests that at the very least the McCarthy Millers are not to be messed with. At worst, if the body wasn't Margaret, then they've deliberately misled the law, at least Sir Thomas McCarthy Miller did. The question is – why?"

"No," Maggie replied, "that's just one question. There's also whether he already knew that Margaret was dead. If he did and was trying to hide it, was that because he was the man in the white van?"

"We can't rule it out," Bob said, "but it's a police matter."

"But you said there wasn't enough for them to act. And Zelah is now taking the law into her own hands, if she really is on her way to Ireland. I don't want anything that happens to her to become the reason for them to decide to act." She paused. "I think we have to go to Ireland, at once. Hopefully, we can get to her in enough time to convince her not to approach them alone."

"Who do you mean by 'we'?" Nick asked.

"Not sure." Maggie replied. "Strictly speaking I need to stay here to look after my kids. But I feel like I should go. I don't know if I could just sit here and wait for news."

"Then you go, and I'll stay here and look after the kids," Nick said. "If Bob's able to go with you? You shouldn't go alone."

Bob nodded. "This time, I agree. I'll get a few days emergency leave."

Maggie put her head in her hands. "How could she? I know this is her show. But she must have known we'd find out and follow her. She knows how difficult things are here. I am so angry with her right now."

Bob felt able now to approach her and put an arm around her shoulders. She didn't shrug him off. He said, "I'll check which boat she's on. I guess it's over to Rosslare. Then I'll book us on the first one available. We'll take the camper van. Are you OK with that?"

She nodded. "Nick, Jack just needs to be got out of bed, sent off in time to get his bus, and then fed when he gets back. Nothing drastic. You'll have to explain to him why we left in such a hurry. Alice… it won't do any harm for her to have you to talk to whilst I'm gone. I don't think we'll be more than a day or two?" She looked to Bob for confirmation. "Please talk to her about this school idea. She can explain. I'll go and talk to her now."

"I'll have to go into work. Back as soon as I can," Bob said, rushing for the door.

Alice made no objection to them going off in pursuit of Zelah. "She just wants to know. I can understand. If I was her, I'd want to know, too."

"And you'll do whatever Nick says?"

"Of course, I will."

"We'll be a couple of hours yet before we set off. I trust you, Alice. I know you won't let me down this time."

Alice smiled back at her.

Chapter 64

Maggie packed a bag, worried about food and was calmed by Nick who said they would have the same as last time – takeaways. They wouldn't be fatally harmed by a day or two of fat and fried carbs. She didn't argue. Alice watched the preparations and discussions with a sense of detachment. Maggie guessed that uppermost in Alice's mind was the new school idea and how good it would be to have her mother out of the way so she could talk to Nick.

Then, a thought crossed Maggie's mind. "Nick, if she suggests a day trip to Hereford, don't go." She had told him what little she knew.

"Of course not. It's nothing to do with me. Happy to talk to her, but that's all."

Bob rushed back at three.

"All sorted. But the bad news is, we can't get a ferry until a quarter to midnight. We've missed the afternoon crossing. We'll be going from Fishguard. I've booked the van, two passengers, and a cabin."

"How far behind Zelah will we be?"

"Difficult to say," he replied. "Her ferry left at eleven and is getting to Rosslare about now. I don't know what she'll do. Will she head straight to the McCarthy Miller home?"

"God knows," Maggie shrugged. "I don't know. Nick?"

"Same. Can't say. It's a couple of hours from Rosslare to Fermoy. Would she ambush them? I can't believe she'd be that stupid."

"I can." Maggie paced around the office. "Is there really no earlier ferry?"

"No, 'fraid not."

"What time will we get there?"

"Our ferry docks at six-ish tomorrow morning. It's a slow overnight route. With half an hour to get off the boat and drive to

Fermoy, I guess we could be there before nine tomorrow morning. If Zelah's off her boat by three-thirty, she won't be there until early evening. If she can show even a little restraint, she'll call ahead and ask to see them in the morning. There's a chance, if she does, we could get there about the same time."

Maggie put her hands together in a gesture of prayer. "When are we booked to come back?"

"I've left it open. But I think we could do with one night. If we need to, we can drive up to Dublin to speak to the Garda. I have the name and contact number there and in Cork."

"Are you going to let them know we are coming?"

"Oh yes, I most certainly am."

Chapter 65

By early evening, Maggie had spoken to Jack, who wasn't pleased that she was going away when she'd promised she wouldn't. But he understood that Zelah had to have backup, whether she wanted it or not. Alice had remained stoic, seeming more interested in her potential new school than their trip.

Maggie became increasingly agitated as afternoon turned into evening, and at six Bob suggested they get going. "Let's you and I get something to eat on the way and leave these guys to a takeaway."

"Yes, do," said Alice and Jack together.

**

"Not sure I'll be able to eat," Maggie said half an hour later. She'd changed her mind several times about even going, but now they were pulling onto the M4 motorway.

"We've got four hours to complete a two-and-a-half-hour journey. Either I drive at forty miles an hour on the motorway and piss everyone off, or we stop for half an hour. You can drink tea and watch me, if that helps."

Maggie had tried Zelah's phone over and over, once she was sure that Zelah would have arrived in Ireland. Eventually accepted that Zelah had switched it off.

"She wanted to do this alone," Bob said as they passed Cardiff. "But I agree that she can't be allowed to do that. I don't know the woman well, but I don't think I'll ever understand anyone who acts as recklessly as she's doing. And she'll have really pissed off Fergus Jordan in Cornwall."

Maggie nodded, drummed her fingers on the dashboard, and stopped when she noticed that Bob was glaring at her. "Sorry. No, I don't understand this either. I mean, she's definitely a person for facing stuff head-on. And that's a good trait. But why would she not realise that she might be heading into a dangerous situation?"

Bob was quiet.

"Something you want to say?" Maggie asked.

"I'm just thinking over everything that we've learned in the past couple of days. Something is bugging me, but I can't reach it. Give me time."

"Sometimes, if something is bugging you and you can't remember, stop trying." She glanced across at him. "Your brain relaxes and it's easier to bring the fact back. Just saying."

The next hour was spent in silence until they reached the end of the motorway.

"We'll stop here. I know a decent pub."

Once again, no question of asking Maggie's opinion, she thought irritatedly. But then she relented. He had taken this trip at short notice and taken time off work. He was worried. No value in pointing out that he had, once again, taken charge in a time of stress. On this trip a time might come when that would be a good thing. She got out of the campervan and followed him into the pub.

During their short meal they realised that there was so much information in such a brief time that it was no wonder something that should stand out, didn't. "Something is hiding in plain sight," Maggie said as they got up to leave.

Chapter 66

At the port of Fishguard, having been loaded onto the ferry, they left the campervan for their cabin, and Bob promptly fell asleep. Maggie, despite her tiredness, had a whirring brain. Images came to her, flashing in and out, and fragments of comments.

"Go away," she muttered quietly to her brain. "Go to sleep." And it seemed to work. She was floating on top of waves, water lapping gently around her bed, when suddenly an enormous gush of water flew up and soaked her. She sat up in bed, shaking, thinking the ferry was sinking, her heart beating like a beatbox. She felt her arms. They were dry, of course. The ferry was droning along on a calm sea. Then she remembered her last thoughts as she was drifting off on the sea of sleep. She turned on the overhead light and shook Bob.

"Wake up, I've got it!"

"Got what?" he slurred, trying to shake off her tugging hand on his shoulder.

"I know what it was that was bothering you."

He sat up, gave her a grumpy stare and said, "You've got my attention. Speak."

Maggie was rocking back and forward. "It's the timeline. We've only heard it in fragments and not in the right chronological order. So, there was no reason for it to stand out."

He let out a sigh of impatience. "For what to stand out?"

"When we talked in the pub, we went over everything we've learned about Zelah's life, a bit from her and more from others, re-constructed from memories. You remember what Mark Mooney said about Zelah? She was known as Little Jay, yes?" He nodded.

"Which, we assumed, was with Zelah's consent, or when you think about it, her lack of rebuttal. But when you look at the timeline and think about what happened, it doesn't add up." He was about to protest, but Maggie held up her hand. "Let me finish. Zelah was found when she was about three years old. For a while, she was the only child with Hopton and his family. But later, more children were temporarily fostered with them. Amongst them Jay and Maureen Meers, MoMe. Zelah took to Jay right away and they became best friends. Maureen said when she arrived Zelah introduced herself as Little Jay."

"I can't see what you are getting at."

"What I am getting at is that Maureen only arrived a week or so after Jay. There was a group of them, and Jay was also a newcomer. So, how could Zelah have been Little Jay in such a brief time? She would hardly have known him, and it couldn't have been enough time for them to become bosom buddies. They became friends over time and Little Jay became a fitting nickname for her. But she was already Little Jay when the other children arrived. But what if it was her secret name for herself?"

"Yes, I can see that it fits. But, so what?" He was quiet for a few seconds, staring at the wall ahead. Then he slowly turned to Maggie. "Not J for Jay. J for something else."

"Exactly. Little J. Which I think stood for—"

"Little Julia!" he interrupted. "She remembered. But why didn't she tell us?"

"Because I think she'd forgotten. Remember, she was just three. Hopton kept her because of the money and the rings. But he must have realised there was something not right about the whole situation. Maybe that's what she called herself, but he wanted the money and couldn't afford her to be identified, so he called her after the name on the gravestone. Over time, after she became friends with Jay, she became Little Jay. Bob, I think she just forgot. But now, she remembers. And I think she's remembered some, if not all, of the story behind the nickname."

"When the story of the rings began to unfold, she must have begun to remember fragments. Maybe Maureen Meers' story finally brought it all back. And the McCarthy Millers are at the centre of all three Julia stories. That's why she's gone." He sat back. "That confirms it. We're going straight there when we reach

Ireland. I'll call the Garda to give them a heads-up, but I don't think we should delay. I've got a bad feeling about this."

Maggie nodded and he sat up again. "That's why she's been so withdrawn and grumpy lately. I thought it was her default setting and the suspicions of the Cornish police. But you think she's been worse than usual, don't you?"

"Yes," Maggie admitted. "I've been trying to justify her behaviour because of what she's found out and had to face up to after all this time. But, yes, now I can see that she's been more secretive in the last few days." She paused. "But was she remembering what she might have been called as a baby? It seemed like the answer, but I'm not sure now. Perhaps I'm going over the top?"

"Honestly, I don't know. But whatever, it triggered something for her. Enough to send her scurrying off to confront the McCarthy Miller family." He shook his head, then reached out and switched off the light." Let's get some sleep. We'll need to be alert in the morning."

But neither slept. At six in the morning, they rolled off the ferry and into the Irish countryside, satnav set for Fermoy.

Chapter 67

A thick mist hovered over the port as they drove through the countryside around Rosslare. It didn't evaporate as they reached further inland and the poor visibility caused Bob to drive more slowly than usual, which frustrated both of them. Maggie kept glancing at the speedometer and her watch. So much so, that Bob snapped at her. "I'm doing the best I can, for God's sake. I can barely see. Driving into a ditch isn't going to help us, is it?"

"It's not my fault," she snapped, sitting back and drumming her fingers on the edge of her seat as they sat in silence for the next thirty minutes.

Maggie relented first. "I'm just worried."

"Apology accepted."

She suppressed a grin. "So, where are we? Any idea?"

"We're about to skirt around Waterford, then back down towards the coast to Dungarven, then back inland to Fermoy. About another hour and a half. We should get there before nine."

"Well, if I was hoping for scenic, that's clearly not going to happen. Mind if I close my eyes? I'm not going to sleep, just think."

"Works better for me if you aren't checking my every move. Go ahead. Let me know if you come up with a useful thought. Not that I think that your thoughts aren't usually useful. But I see your shoulders straightening. Back off, Boogaloo."

"Apology accepted," she said, and closed her eyes.

Chapter 68

Despite her best intentions, Maggie fell asleep at once. The sound of Bob's voice brought her around, although for the first few seconds, she had no idea where she was and had to concentrate to recall any details. Then she dredged it up, as consciousness and memory came with a sharp pain in her neck and shoulder.

"Who was that?" she asked, struggling against the discomfort to sit up.

"Garda," he replied. "I've told them what we're doing, and why. While you were snoring, I've been doing some thinking. Getting through the fog, in my head and outside this bloody van."

"Where are we? Why have we stopped?"

"We're in Fermoy. I'd say look around, but you can't see anything except fog."

Maggie peered through the wide front window and could barely make out a few houses and shops at the side of the road.

"We stopped so I could make the phone call and get my bearings from the satnav about where we go next. And I need a pee, now." With that he got out of the van and disappeared into the mist.

Still not entirely returned to full consciousness, Maggie peered around. Still nothing. Was she awake, or was this a dream? She glanced at the dashboard clock and was amazed that it was nine-thirty. Feeling more disconcerted she found her bag on the floor, ransacked through it for her phone and called home. Nick answered straight away.

"Is everything OK?" she asked.

"Good morning to you, too. Yes, Maggie, everything's fine. Jack got his bus. Alice and I are having breakfast and talking about Hereford. What's going on with you?"

She breathed a sigh of relief. "We've reached Fermoy. Bob has gone to… get directions to find the house. We're going straight there."

"Alice says take care, as do I." She heard the scrape of a chair as he got up and walked away from the table. "She and I have a bad feeling about these people, Maggie. It may be that we're putting two and two together and making twenty-two. But, you know, be careful. Has Zelah contacted you?"

"No. Her phone is off."

"Yes, I know. I was hoping she's turn it back on at least to check for messages. But there's been nothing."

Maggie shivered. "It's odd here. It's very foggy. And colourless."

There was no response. Then, Bob opened the door and jumped back into the cab.

"Anyway, got to go. Bob's back. I'll call you later. Love to Alice." She ended the call.

"That's better," he remarked as he started the engine. "I asked in a local shop. I'm OK with the satnav but I needed a guide to what to look for to recognise their driveway." He paused for a moment. "Before we set off, we need to discuss what happens when we get there."

"Can't we do that as we drive?"

"No." He turned the engine off again and turned to her, hands gripping the wheel. "We're in my territory now. You are going to follow my instructions and my lead. I know how these things can go. Do you get that?"

The intensity of the last words hit Maggie like a slamming ball in the chest and she sat up. "Explain, please."

"This could get nasty. I'm in charge. You do what I say without question. That's it."

Everything in her wanted to argue but she could see that would be a bad idea. "OK. Anything else?"

He re-started the engine and began to drive slowly along what seemed to be a straight road, but Maggie realised was a large square. He didn't answer as he turned the van left and along a shop-lined road.

"We don't even know if Zelah is there yet. So, we approach this in a friendly way. We explain who we are and what Maze does. We say that our friend and colleague was planning to speak to them today and we're joining her. Then we see how they react."

"What reactions should we anticipate?"

"Could be anything. We're going into this cold because we aren't sufficiently prepared, so we have to anticipate anything."

"You wanted to wait."

"Yes, I did. But now we can't, so there's no point in thinking about that. But we'll have to think on our feet. Depends on whether Zelah is already there, or not."

Maggie shivered again. "I need my jacket."

"The heating is on. You're just nervous."

"Well of course I am," she snapped. "I'd run away if I could. But I can't. So, I'm putting my coat on."

They left the town behind and drove along country roads. After ten minutes she asked, "How much further?"

"It isn't," he replied. "We're here." He signalled and turned off the main road onto a single-track, well-tarmacked, path. "Here we go," he muttered, taking a deep breath.

Chapter 69

As he drove up the winding approach Maggie thought the fog was beginning to lift. She made out trees lining the track, water shimmering off their lower branches. She strained forward as they rounded yet another bend and the house came into sight, appearing through the mist, its bottom storeys clear, the top of the house still fog-bound.

The driveway gave way to a circular approach in front of the house, with a small fountain at its centre. Bob pulled up to the side and killed the engine. They opened the doors. There was silence. No footsteps or distant voices. No animal or traffic noise. Just silence, which made the sound of their footsteps echo in their ears. And there was no sign of Zelah's car.

"What do we do?" Maggie whispered to Bob.

"Stop whispering, for a start," he replied in his normal voice. "We go up to the front door and ring the bell, or knock."

Maggie's stomach was flipping like wavelets on a beach. "Shouldn't we look around the outside first?"

"What for? Zelah isn't likely to be wandering around admiring the gardens, is she? If she's here, she'll be inside. And we need to get inside quickly." He strode up to the front door and Maggie hurriedly followed him.

The two doors were solid wood, antique, with a large knocker in the centre of one and a bell pull set in the stone wall to its side. The portico was covered with wisteria.

"Ready?" Bob asked without looking at her. Maggie realised that he was anxious too.

"As I'll ever be."

He gave her a quick look and a smile, then pulled the bell handle and knocked as loudly as he could. Nothing happened. They stood there for a couple of minutes. Bob knocked again. Still nothing.

Maggie felt a sense of relief. There was no one at home, and Zelah had found this and gone away. Yes, that was it. A lot of fuss about nothing.

Then she heard echoing footsteps approaching the door, followed by a heavy latch being lifted. The door was flung open. Standing there was a man who looked to be in his sixties, of average height, stoop-shouldered, with a small moustache and greying hair. He was wearing a two-piece navy pinstripe suit with a jumper underneath the jacket. His face was pale, his lips thin. There was something familiar about him, but Maggie couldn't place him.

"Yes?" His voice was barely above a whisper, a timid supplication.

Bob went straight into an explanation of who they were and why they had come and asked if Zelah had arrived. His tone was polite but firm and the man seemed to realise that further questioning was a waste of time.

"Come in Mrs Gilbert, and you too, Inspector."

As she stepped through the door Maggie realised that Bob had introduced himself as a police officer, but not with his rank. The realisation hit her as the door slammed behind them.

We're in trouble, Maggie thought. She glanced at Bob and saw from his cautious expression that he too had picked up what might have been a mistake, or maybe not.

The man gave them a perfunctory smile and said, "Welcome to Rosscarbery House. Come with me, please," and without waiting or introducing himself he turned and walked across the entrance hall towards another thick wooden door.

Glancing around as they walked, Maggie could see the house retained features of its eighteenth-century past. The plaster on the walls was painted white and an impressive chandelier hung from the ceiling. There was a door immediately to their right, covered in hand-painted decorative fruit and flowers. The floor was covered with a Persian carpet, worth thousands of pounds, laid over the original flagstones. To their left was an open room with two Roman style pillars, a piano and armchairs, and a staircase. The walls were adorned with old portraits.

"A beautiful house," she murmured.

The man caught the words and turned back to her as he reached the opposite door, also white and hand-painted, on the opposite side of the hall. He paused and turned to face her, his hand on the handle.

"Yes, Mrs Gilbert. It was built in 1728 and we've saved many of the original features. It was in my mother's family," he said in his half-whisper. He turned back to the door. Maggie guessed this was Noel McCarthy Miller, but didn't have time to guess further, as the door opened. The man held back the door for them. It opened into a long corridor with closed doors on the right, another closed door on the left. At the end of the corridor was a glass-panelled door through which Maggie glimpsed a garden.

"In here please," the man said, opening the door on the left. They walked into a large room, at the back of which were three sets of full-length panelled windows, the middle set being doors that led out onto a patio and garden with magnificent borders and flowerbeds. The left side of the room was dominated by a fireplace of gigantic proportions. The opposite wall was lined with cases and shelves of books. In the centre of the room, facing the fire, were two substantial brown Chesterfield settees and a matching chair. In the chair sat Zelah, ramrod straight. A woman stood behind her, a bone china coffee cup in one hand, a double-barrelled shotgun resting carelessly over her other arm.

Bob stopped so abruptly Maggie walked into his back.

On one of the settees sat an old man. Next to him, a girl, dressed in a flowery shift, with waist-length, flowing dark hair. She had a sweet smile fixed on her face; her hands folded in her lap. It was a picture of posed perfection. But Maggie caught a quick, contemptuous flick of a glance from the girl in Zelah's direction.

The old man sat up in his chair and expanded his arms towards them. "Welcome, welcome," he said with a smile. "So pleased you've joined us. We're just getting to know our latest family member." He turned his head towards Zelah, his eyes calculating.

"How nice for you," Maggie said to him, keeping her eyes fixed on Zelah, who neither moved nor acknowledged their presence.

"Not really," he replied without a change of expression. "I didn't say we liked her, just that we are getting to know her."

"Sir Thomas McCarthy Miller," Bob said.

"Of course," the old man replied. "You've met my son, Noel." As he spoke he flicked the fingers of his right hand at Noel, who scooted to a spot behind the sofa, opposite Maggie, where he bit his lips and wiped his palms on the sides of his trousers, watching her intently. A small tic caused his head to jerk in an unrhythmical nod.

"And the ladies. My daughter, Norah." Sir Thomas continued with a soft, Irish lilt. He pointed to the woman behind Zelah, who neither responded nor moved. "And my lovely niece Emer," waving his hand to his side.

He sat back, crossing one elegantly shod leg over the other and folded his arms. A shaft of weak sunlight came in through the windows and lit up the coffee table between the two sofas, on which sat the boxes with the three rings. It caught his attention and he leaned forward, holding out his hands, but he stopped short of picking up any of the boxes.

"These are beauties, aren't they?" he said, moving his head to one side. "And I presume that, between you, you have the rest of the historic artefacts that my bitch of a cousin stole." He looked up at Maggie but it was Bob who answered. "Yes, we do."

The man waved his arm again, this time at the opposite sofa. "Sit, please."

"No."

"Dear me, Inspector. That wasn't a request. And don't make Norah angry, she has quite a temper."

"We aren't sitting. I presume she has a permit for that weapon. But I want it where I can see it. How about you stand?"

The man shook his head and tutted, his expression sad. "And there was I hoping we could solve this dilemma without too much fuss."

Maggie glanced at Bob. His expression was unreadable, implacable. A tremor went through her knees. She tasted vomit in her throat and swallowed it down. He had asked... ordered her to trust him. She had to.

Sir Thomas noticed her movement. "I don't blame you, Mrs Gilbert. He's not being, what shall we say, sensible? Co-operative?"

"I have no intention of co-operating with you," Bob growled. "How are you intending to deal with us? You must realise there are many people who know we are here."

"Ah, the Gardaí? How do you think we knew you were coming?" His smile was wolfish. "I have no problem with how I deal with you. I'm thinking... you are going to have an unfortunate traffic accident? Do we all agree?" He looked around at his family. Norah nodded, Emer beamed at him. Noel gave a quick tic of his head. "And, of course, the investigation will be conducted by our local... friends." He heaved a theatrical sigh. "So sad." He turned to Maggie. "And terrible for your poor children, Jack and Alice, to be without a mother so young."

They all turned at the sound of a guttural growl, which came from Zelah.

"Oh dear, my cousin's daughter is upset at the thought of more children being left motherless, as was she. A pity, but unavoidable now."

Maggie couldn't find her voice. Her ears buzzed, as the walls of the room swayed about her. Bob took her hand and squeezed hard. The message was 'hold on'. She bit her lip and brought her focus back to the room.

Bob spoke. "So, boyo, we know it was you who mowed down Margaret in Swansea, with a white van. Your father's niece – Zelah's mother. I guess Zelah has told you. But do you know how we found you?"

"Do show some respect, Inspector. I am Sir Thomas to you. Of course it was me. But my father was there too, I can't take all the credit. I suspect, however, when I took her bag and checked her pockets that I missed something?"

"Too right, boyo."

The old man shot forward in his chair and stabbed a finger at Bob. "How dare you, you jumped-up Welsh slob. I earned this title through hard work, which my dear departed uncle Hugh despised. He was an *intellectual*." He said the last word with a sneer. "And I was knighted independently of my uncle. I have dual citizenship, British and Irish. I was honoured in England for my work and my charitable undertakings."

"I don't know about your uncle, but your grandfather was a thief. And I don't care how hard you worked. You don't deserve a title. You killed a woman in cold blood and disguised her death." Bob spoke in the same dispassionate voice, but before anyone else spoke, Norah moved quickly to his side and put the muzzle of the shotgun under his chin. Maggie could see the pulse going in his neck. She thought she was going to be sick.

He opened his mouth to speak again but was interrupted. "Shut up, Bob. Just… shut up." Zelah hadn't moved in her chair but her voice was clear and calm. "I've got this."

"You think?" Emer asked in a sweet, incredulous voice. Sir Thomas reached out a hand to his daughter. "Put the gun down, Norah. Keep it on her," he pointed at Zelah and Norah swung the muzzle around. "I find I am interested in what she has to say."

Maggie thought if it wasn't for the gun this would be a 1970s drawing room farce and wanted to laugh. Seven people in an elegant room, chatting and exchanging information. If it wasn't for the gun. She was getting hysterical. Must get a grip.

Zelah smiled and nodded at him. She seemed calm, despite Norah walking back to her and holding the gun loosely inches from her head. "I know you killed my mother. You've already said so. But you didn't know about me. First mistake of many. You never even considered she might have had a child. But I'm there, in the UK Birth, Marriage and Death records. Julia Miller. With a date of birth. Mother Maggie Miller, no father. And I think she was coming back here to reconcile with her father, your uncle. I guess she wrote to him and you got to see the letter?"

He nodded and signalled her to carry on.

"After you ran her down you took her bag to hide her identity and I expect you checked her pockets. But you weren't thorough enough. You didn't check her inside pockets. That's where she'd put the ferry ticket. That was our clue."

Sir Thomas took a thoughtful breath. "I knew about you, but only recently, I admit. The name gave it away, as soon as you put up your little blog about an inherited ring." He pointed at Maggie. "We were tracking you. Then you went public with your spoon ring story." He turned to Maggie and Bob and sneered. "You call yourselves professional genealogists. You are utterly incompetent. A most important clue, sitting right under your nose and you missed it. If I was a client of yours, I'd ask for my money back."

Emer giggled. Maggie was puzzled, but the expression on Zelah's face told her she should keep quiet. Zelah continued, "We'd have got there. We've only been researching for two months and we found you. You've been looking at the rings for over sixty years and you couldn't find me." She turned to Maggie. "When did we do the blog about the trip to Cornwall?"

"June, I think." Maggie hesitated. "But we didn't talk about the rings, just an inheritance. So how did they know?"

"You underestimate us, Mrs Gilbert. We've been watching for years. The vicar, Mr Hopton, left a will, for which probate was granted to Mrs Tracy Jones. It mentioned jewellery – including rings – to be held in safekeeping and for Mrs Jones to decide the right time for the items to be returned to the rightful owner. That was of interest to us, so we kept an eye on her, along with many other possible leads. When Mrs Jones died earlier this year and her Will was proved, there was information that three rings, belonging to Zelah Trevear, should be returned to her. We knew, then. We've been keeping an eye on you for months. But your trip to Cornwall seemed too good an opportunity to miss."

"That was when you finally made the connection with my name? You'd done the research, but it took you sixty years to find me. I'd call that utterly incompetent. Now, I could tell you my story, but I'm not going to. After all, I wasn't a Trevear for long, I became a Fitzgerald. And that's another of your mistakes. The famous Martin Fitzgerald's widow is as well-known as you are, probably more so. Well, I can't just disappear, can I." She smiled at him and was met by a frozen glare. "So, tell that murdering bitch of a daughter of yours to put the gun down. If she pulls the trigger, you're all done for."

He put his fingers together, steepled in front of his mouth. "She has a point, Norah. But keep it there anyway. We could always say she threatened us."

"And have the story come out about my mother? I don't think so." Zelah paused. "I hope you don't think I just headed here on spec, that I didn't make sure that I left enough information to lead straight to you."

"But you didn't tell them." He pointed at Maggie and Bob.

"No, I didn't. I didn't expect them to work it out and follow me, either, which is a complication, isn't it?" She glared at Maggie and Bob.

Maggie couldn't help herself. "She," pointing at Norah, "killed Ann Quinn."

"Of course I did," Norah growled. "The silly cow was supposed to convince you she was the rightful heir to the rings."

"Then you chose your tool badly," Maggie replied, steadier now. "Ann was eccentric, bonkers actually. But she didn't deserve to die."

Norah shrugged. "She'd become a liability."

"And don't think I don't recognise you. If you thought you could knock me down and get your hands on the spoon ring, that was pathetic," Maggie added. Zelah looked puzzled. "In Truro, as I came out of the jeweller's shop, a woman bumped into me and I dropped my bag. It was her."

"Amateurs, amateurs," Zelah muttered, shaking her head. "So, what are we going to do here? You're all done for. Can't get out of this one, not this time."

"Just one thing," Maggie asked. "Why are we poor professionals? What did we miss?"

"Why don't you tell her?" Sir Thomas said, "Whilst I consider

298

what to do about you all?"

"It's the full family history," Zelah said. "He had years to research. We only had two months. We'd have got there. But… my memory was jolted by something Maureen Meers said. I remembered a lot of things. I truly remembered who I am, and what I was."

Maggie was about to say something, but Zelah held up her hand and hissed, "Not now." Maggie noticed that Bob was further away from her. While they had been talking, he had edged his way towards Norah.

Sir Thomas spoke. "I still like the accident idea. But for all three of you." He nodded to Emer. "Yes, it will work. A fire following a nasty crash. Take them ages to work it out. Get up," he ordered Zelah.

"No," Zelah replied. "That's not going to happen."

"Of course it's going to happen," he said impatiently, getting to his feet with Emer's help. "Get up now."

"No. Not used to people refusing to do what you order, are you?" Zelah smiled. "But those days are over. You are just a stupid, pathetic old man who's going to spend his final years in jail. This place is rightfully mine, all mine. And I'm going to take it apart, brick by brick. And you, cousin, you'll be tried for murder. You and your pointless daughter. I'm going to take you all down, every single one of you."

To Maggie's horror, Zelah sat back in the chair. What was she thinking? She was deliberately taunting a psychopathic woman who had already killed without compunction.

Norah's face turned beetroot. She stared at Zelah as she backed away and raised the gun.

Sir Thomas stayed on his feet, looking worried. "She's taunting you, Norah. Put the gun down. There's nothing to be gained."

Zelah stood up and stepped towards Norah and laughed. "You won't do it. You're a coward, Norah. You crept up on a defenceless woman and dragged her to a cliff edge and pushed her off. That's all you're capable of. A miserable coward." She was eye to eye with the gun now. Just inches away. "Do what Daddy tells you or you'll be in trouble."

Maggie heard Bob take in a sharp breath, just as Norah put the gun to her shoulder. He was going to reach out. Then, in the space of a couple of seconds, several things happened.

Chapter 70

Bob shouted "Now, now!"

A glimpse showed something moving outside the garden window.

The sound of a lever being cocked as Norah aimed the gun.

The sound of two shots.

Something large at the far side of the room flying backwards.

And a smell of acrid, choking smoke.

The noise was deafening, not just the gunshots but the doors of the room and the windows exploding and armed men charging in. Voices yelled, "Armed police!" and "Shots fired!" Maggie and Bob dropped to their knees as the men in black shouted, "Get on your knees! Hands on your head! Now!" Over and over. Maggie coughed and spluttered but could hear nothing through the ringing in her ears. She tried to stand, but her knees buckled, and hands roughly pushed her back down.

People were talking to her, but the sound was as if she were underwater. She looked at them, uncomprehending. The man in front of her spoke again, mouthing his words carefully. "Are you hurt? Are you injured?" She shook her head and pointed to her ears. She couldn't understand what was going on. It was as if her brain was seeing all but taking in nothing. Like a film acted out in front of her. All action, but no emotion. She looked around.

It was Bob putting an arm around her that brought her back. Her ears cleared a little. "Zelah!" she yelled, grabbing at Bob's arm, although she could barely hear her own voice.

Another hand came to rest on her shoulder. She looked up. "I'm here, I'm fine." Zelah's face was smoke-blackened.

"You're not hurt?" Maggie mouthed and gestured, not sure if she could be heard.

"No." Zelah shook her head and pointed across the room.

Maggie turned to see Sir Thomas McCarthy Miller being

picked up off the floor by two Gards. His head was bleeding profusely.

Near the settee, two paramedics were attending to a casualty. One looked up at the nearest Gard, shook his head, and stood up. On the floor, was Noel's body; arms wide, chest bloody, eyes wide open, staring in an infinite expression of bewilderment.

Chapter 71

Over the next couple of hours, the house was a bustle of activity. More Gards, some armed, filled the house and patrolled the grounds. More paramedics arrived, checked everyone who had been in the library, then left.

Maggie, Bob and Zelah had been moved from the library to the smaller sitting room off the hallway. The library was now the domain of CSIs, wrapped head to toe in white-hooded body suits, eyes covered by goggles, feet in disposable covers, and gloved hands. Maggie had seen this so many times on TV, but in real life their anonymity felt menacing.

She watched in silence as Norah and Sir Thomas were taken away in handcuffs and Noel's body was removed in a body bag.

Bob and Zelah spoke to various people who came in and out. But Maggie just sat on a settee, wrapped in a shiny gold blanket, unable to hear anything, watching the hustle and bustle but not really caring. At some point someone handed her a cup of tea, which she took and drank. For much of the time Bob, or Zelah, or both, sat next to her. Neither spoke to her. They understood that, for now, there was nothing to say.

At one point a man in a three-piece suit appeared in front of her and, pointing at her, he argued with Bob who accompanied everything he said with a shake of his head. The argument continued for several minutes before the man went away.

Slowly, she began to hear fragments of sound. A word here and there, bent and twisted. But it brought back a sense of the present and the fact she was in it. She turned to Bob. "What's happening?"

"Can you hear now?"

"Bits. Some. I have an unbelievably bad headache." In truth, the inside of her head felt as if an army of carpenters had taken up residence, hammering and sawing and drilling.

"You may have a perforated eardrum. You'll need to go to

hospital."

"What about you two?"

"We're both OK. Must have been the angle at which you were standing. It's affected you more than us. Look, it needs checking out. If it's perforated, you'll need antibiotics."

"What makes you think it is?"

"It's been bleeding."

She put her hand to the left side of her head, realising it was returning to normal, but from the right she could hear nothing. She felt dried blood on her cheek.

"Where are the others?"

"Thomas and Norah have been arrested. Noel is dead. Emer has disappeared. She got away in the confusion following the shots."

Maggie nodded slowly but stopped as the pain of moving her head was too great. "Where's Zelah?"

"Not sure, she was here a moment ago. She keeps getting up and disappearing."

As she spoke, Zelah returned, not from the door through which Maggie and Bob had entered, but another, next to the staircase, partly hidden by a curtain, to the side of a fireplace. She had something in her hand, a piece of parchment, faded and brown and delicate. She sat on Maggie's other side.

"No point talking to me," Maggie began, turning to look directly at her.

"If you're that angry with me, forget it. I don't want to hear it right now."

"No, I'm not. Not yet, anyway. I just can't hear properly." She pointed at her bad ear. "Bob, shift across. Come and sit on this side." Maggie patted the settee where Bob had just vacated. Zelah sat there. "Better?" she asked.

"Yes. There's a lot we need to talk about. But at the moment talking hurts. It means moving my jaw; which is part of my head, which is totally killing me. Bob says I may have a perforated eardrum. So, most of it will have to wait until I get some painkillers. What's that?" She pointed at the parchment.

"The answer to a lot of questions."

Maggie gave her a wry look.

"There's a secret room through there," she pointed to the curtain. "It's his collection. Sir Hugh McCarthy Miller's that is. Most of it probably stolen from digs over the years. But this... this is what we've been looking for. It's the letter."

Maggie stared at it. "What, the last of the three letters?"

"Yep. It's been well looked after. We shouldn't be handling it. It's too delicate."

Maggie glanced furtively around the room. "Does anyone know you've got it?"

"Nope."

"Where can we hide it?"

Bob interjected, "You can't do that. It's theft."

"No, it's not," Zelah replied. "Not exactly. He inherited it, so by rights it's mine. But if we declare it, it'll be months, maybe years, before we get to see what's in it. I'm allowing myself to get my hands on it earlier than the course of the law will let me."

Bob stared at her for a moment, stood up, and walked across the room to speak to one of the Gards.

"His way of saying he doesn't want to know," Maggie said. "Where can we put it? Is there a bag we can put it in?"

Before Zelah could reply, Bob walked over and handed a plastic bag to Maggie. "Evidence bag. I told the Gard there might be something useful around here and if we saw it, or remembered something we'd need a bag to put it in. So as not to contaminate it. Not that I've seen anything." He walked back to the Gard, turning him away as he talked to him.

Zelah took the bag, slipped the parchment in, and put it in her jacket pocket. "Safe till later. Now, you need to get to hospital," she said, standing up and pulling Maggie up with a hand under her armpit.

Glancing at the clock, Maggie saw it was coming up to midday. Only two hours had passed since they had arrived at Rosscarbery House. It seemed longer and there was more to face.

Chapter 72

The hospital confirmed that Maggie did have a perforated eardrum, but the hole was small. Because of the ferocity of her headache she was advised to spend the night under observation. She refused but agreed to a couple of hours with pain relief. During this time she slept soundly, with Bob and Zelah by her bedside.

"Has someone spoken to Nick and the kids?" she asked on waking and seeing where she was.

"Me," Bob replied. "They're all fine. I've played down what's happened for Jack and Alice. No need for them to know everything. Nick knows."

"When can I get out of here?"

"How are you feeling?"

"The pain seems to have gone," said Maggie.

"They want you to stay overnight. I told them you probably wouldn't want to," Zelah replied. "You can discharge yourself."

Bob scowled at her. Maggie felt the tension arcing across her bed. "What's up with you two?"

"Bob's not speaking to me. He's furious with me for coming to Fermoy alone. And he thinks I almost got all of us killed. I didn't, but he doesn't agree."

"You scared the shit out of me," Maggie said. "I really thought she was going to shoot your head off. But… I don't want an argument. I want to go. Explanations later." She turned to Bob. "What time is it? What's the plan for tonight?"

"You still have to give your statement. But I've said you won't be fit enough tonight. We're booked into a local hotel, out in the country. That's me and Zelah. The Gardaí think you'll be here. You can come too, but we won't tell them until we're there, then arrange your statement for the morning." He looked around. "I'll get the doctor to give you something to help you sleep, along with some pain relief."

Maggie sat up, swung her legs across and put her feet on the floor. When she tried to stand, she wobbled and Bob caught her. "Sure you want to get out of here?"

"Yes, absolutely." She took a deep breath. "It's just the shock of it all. But I want to get somewhere we can get some peace and quiet to discuss what happened. And what's in that letter, Zelah, which I presume you still have?"

Zelah nodded.

"Then let's get out of here."

Chapter 73

Zelah had found a country house hotel a few miles outside Fermoy and by early evening they had settled into their rooms. Maggie called Jack and Alice, who were anxious for an update. She played down her injury and promised they would be home the next day, which she hoped was the truth.

From Maggie and Bob's room they ordered room service due to Maggie's reluctance to sit in a restaurant full of people making a noise. Their room was ornately large and had a small dining table. They ate in silence.

"Let's get started, shall we?" Maggie began after finishing her food and taking painkillers. "And for starters, Zelah, you owe us an explanation. When you got there, how did you introduce yourself? What happened before we arrived? Don't leave anything out." She sat back in her armchair and arranged the pillow behind her head. "I want to hear about it before we even get to the letter. Go."

"Fair enough," Zelah replied. "Although I didn't want your help and I didn't need it."

"That's ridiculous, and ungrateful." Bob sat forward in his chair and pointed a sharp finger at her. "That psychopathic woman – that's what she is, believe me – had a gun pointed at your head. How can you sit there and say there was no danger?"

"I didn't say there was no danger, I said I didn't need your help. And if you're just going to shout, I'm not saying anything else."

Maggie stood up, holding her hand to her head and wincing. "Yes, you are going to say something else. Everything else, in fact. That gun was aimed at Bob's head too. You owe him – us – an explanation. This is no time to get stroppy." She fell back into her chair.

Zelah waited a few seconds, grasping the arms of her chair.

Then she too sat back. "I'll tell you as much as I can. But no shouting."

"Bob?" Maggie gave him an intent stare.

He shrugged, which she took as assent.

"All of the stories we'd put together since we got back from Cornwall pointed to the McCarthy Miller family. There were no other leads. They were involved, somehow. We just didn't know to what extent. For me, there was nothing positive coming out of it. When I got the news about the dead woman in Swansea being my mother, that did it for me. I had to talk to them, not challenge them. That would have been stupid. Just talk." She paused, looked from one to the other. Maggie nodded at her to continue. "I didn't want anyone else to be involved. I told you from the start that all decisions were mine to make, no one else. So, if I was going to jump in with both feet that was up to me. I knew the risks; I knew what I was doing."

Bob snorted. "Had a lot of experience with this kind of thing, have you? Considered all the potential risks? That if this was the family that murdered your mother, why did they do it? Why wouldn't they do the same to you? God, Zelah! You are so fucking naïve." He jumped up and paced around the room, then turned back to her. "And I don't care what you say about it being your decision alone. The three of you at Maze are supposed to be a team. If that's the case, then you should always have each other's backs. And you need honesty."

"Are you saying that I've been dishonest?"

"Too bloody right. I know about the interview in Cornwall. You didn't even tell Maggie and Nick."

Zelah glanced at Maggie, then back to Bob. "If I'd gone down there, they might have arrested me. I avoided that by coming here."

"No, they would not have arrested you. They don't have any evidence."

"I didn't know that, did I?"

"You didn't trust any of us enough to ask?"

They were facing each other like snarling dogs. Maggie

struggled up and pushed her way in-between them. "I'm going to say this for the last time. Bob, listen to the story and keep your anger to yourself, for now. I have things I don't understand to ask you, too. Zelah, stop justifying what you did and get on with it."

They both turned angry eyes on her, stung by the criticism, and were met by a cool, steady gaze. Slowly, they circled back to their chairs.

"If either of you gets out of your chair again, this discussion is over." Her voice was low but filled with intent.

Zelah said, "I called ahead early on the day I travelled. I told them I was in possession of a ring that we, Maze that is, had traced through Sir Hugh McCarthy Miller's ancestry, which he might have come into as an inheritance. And another ring that disappeared during his final archaeological dig. Sir Thomas expressed polite surprise. He told me the rings had been missing for well over half a century, presumed stolen, and that there was a third one. He said he'd be glad to meet me. I said I was on my way to Ireland and could he see me the following day. He said to come at nine in the morning, which I did. I was even early." She paused for breath.

"Looking back now, it was odd that he didn't ask any questions. Not about my intentions or how we'd come by the rings. He should have done, but I missed the obvious connotations."

"I disagree with Bob, Zelah. You aren't that naïve."

"Well, alright. He should have asked, but I didn't miss anything. I knew what I was walking into. I got there just after eight-thirty. Noel let me in, same as you. Norah and Emer were already there with Sir Thomas, but there was no gun. It was an odd scene. Very odd, the atmosphere; they were all so polite. But I knew that they knew me, they couldn't hide it. After the pleasantries he began by asking me what I knew. Wrong question. But I told him. I had been born in the West Country," her gaze returned to Maggie. "Sorry, I didn't get around to telling you that bit yet. I was registered as Julia Miller, mother Maggie Miller, no father. She was a traveller of sorts. We progressed south until we reached Cornwall. We stayed there for almost a year, moving further and further to the end of the county.

"I don't know why she decided to return home. I said I guessed that was what she was doing, or why she decided to leave me with the vicar. I asked him if he could fill in any gaps. He nodded but asked me to carry on. I said I'd been left in the church and in the middle of the night I went into the graveyard and sat on a stone. When the vicar found me in the morning, he couldn't get my name out of me, so he gave me the name of the person on the headstone. Sir Thomas' eyes widened at that. He asked me if I found anything odd about that. I said no, but I couldn't hide the truth. I tried being disingenuous, but it didn't work. It's just not me, as you know. That was when the shit hit the fan."

"I don't understand," Maggie said. "What did you say that changed the game?"

"I know now that there was an additional family connection. That's what he noticed and he realised I knew."

"Which was?"

"You did the research on the family history of the first Sir Hugh that got back to Julia Pencarrow and her great-grandmother, Hepzibah Williams."

"Yes, and that's their family, too."

"You remember he called us amateurs? That's because we didn't get as far as tracing other lines. But we would have done. We had weeks. He had years. What he already knew was that when the family names were combined, McCarthy and Miller, the Miller line through Alice Pencarrow's husband, James Miller, also led back to Cornwall. To Hepzibah Williams, born Pearce, in 1641."

Maggie went to speak, but Zelah cut her off. "Let me finish. Because there's more. Hepzibah had six children, three boys and three girls. We know about Julia Pencarrow's father, Peter Williams. The girls were called Hepzibah, Ruth and the youngest was... Zelah. The youngest of the six children. Zelah Williams, who married Ezekiel Trevear."

Maggie's mouth opened.

"Yep. Double witches. Zelah had a daughter called Mary. She

married Matthew Miller. Their son was Robert Miller. His son was James Miller, who married Alice Pencarrow. And their daughter, Johanna, married Edward McCarthy, as we knew. We traced back Alice Pencarrow's line. If we'd followed her husband, we'd have found Zelah Trevear, on whose grave I was found."

"There was no reason for us to even think of looking at James Miller," Maggie said.

"No, I agree. But if we had looked further at Hepzibah, which I think we would eventually have done, which is what I did, we'd have found Zelah. Then we'd have found the line that re-joined the Pencarrows over a hundred years after Zelah was born. But it wasn't our focus."

"What made you look?" Bob asked.

Zelah sat looking at them for long enough for Bob to ask again, "What made you look, Zelah? Are you just cleverer, more far-seeing than Maggie or Nick?"

"If you're asking if I'm a better researcher than Maggie and Nick, then yes, I am," she bristled. "I've been at this a long time. I know when there's more to be found. But that wasn't the reason. It's more… personal."

She leaned forward and picked up a glass of water from the dining table, took a long gulp, and kept the glass in her hand. They waited.

"I wouldn't go back to Cornwall because of so many bad memories. You know about most of them. You know about Jay. But there are some you still don't know. Hopton was a cruel and vicious man. Maggie, you asked me once if he ever hit me and I said no. But that wasn't the truth. He beat me on several occasions. After Jay disappeared, I put my head down and kept as far out of trouble as I could. It didn't stop Tracy taunting me, but I learned to do what I had never done before: not retaliate. Once I left there, I put it all behind me. I forgot a lot of things. I knew that going back was risky, but there were things I needed to know, and the rings were the catalyst. So, back we went."

She took another long draught of water, draining the glass which she put back on the table, jarring it slightly so that she had to put out her other hand to steady it.

"It was MoMe – Maureen Meers – who said something. Wait, no. I'll have to go back further." She screwed up her eyes, focussed on the ceiling. "When I was a small child, before the others arrived, I had an imaginary friend. She was a beautiful girl, with long, fair hair, large blue eyes, and a beautiful smile. Whenever Hopton treated me badly I went to my room and spoke to her. She was kind and nice to me. She always told me that everything would be OK. Those were her words – *all will be well for you, little... girl.*"

"You mean 'little Julia', Bob said. "Maggie worked it out. Don't forget, we heard Maureen's story too. LJ wasn't Little Jay, was it?"

"No. It was little Julia. But the thing is, I forgot. After the other children came and Jay arrived, they started to call me Little Jay, LJ. I forgot about my imaginary friend, once I had a real one. But when we went back in August, that day I took you to the churchyard and showed you Zelah Trevear's gravestone, that's when it started. That night I heard the voice of my imaginary friend again. I thought it was a dream. Then I thought it was an inherited memory. But it was neither. As the month went on, the memory got stronger. She called me when I was left in the church. I was in the church and she called me out. I was crying, alone and frightened. She put an arm around me and told me to sit with her. She told me not to cry and that all would be well for me. She called me little Julia. When I heard the story of my mother and the Travellers, I thought she must have been one of them. But the memory wouldn't go away. And then, just before I left to come here, I got the final piece. She had called me out into the graveyard and told me to sit with her. On her place: her final resting place. I realised I'd never seen her. I had invented what she looked like from a pantomime we saw in Penzance when I was four. There was a fairy in it, who I thought was the most beautiful person I had ever seen. So, I only ever heard her voice and felt her arm around me when I sat down."

"Was that all she said?" asked Maggie.

"No. The only other thing she said was that one day Maggie

would come back. Funny, when I met you something triggered. I couldn't think why, so I dismissed it."

"You believe it was Zelah Trevear." It was a statement, not a question.

"I think it was."

"And that's what Sir Thomas meant when he asked you if you found it strange that you had been called Zelah Trevear?"

"Obviously. He already knew that the first Zelah was the daughter of a witch and that the lines of the children had come back together again. And he had the letter. When we get to it, you'll see why it's significant in the family history."

"Carry on," Bob said. "We still haven't reached the point where Maggie and I arrived."

"He said not to beat about the bush; we both knew who I am. No point denying it, I thought. He knew I had the rings as a legacy, and he'd worked out they'd been in the possession of Hopton's family for over half a decade. So, it could only have been Margaret who passed them on. Then he explained, in a conversational way, that Margaret had decided to come home, eight years after running away. She'd written to her father to ask if he would forgive her. 'Never mind forgive her, he was absolutely thrilled and excited,' he told me. And she said in her letter she had a surprise for him. That, of course, was me. I think the reason she left me behind was because she wanted to tell him about me first, to see how he would react, not just turn up with me. And the Travellers were moving on, so there was a chance she wouldn't be able to find me when she came back. She left me with the vicar, thinking nothing could be safer. Hmmm."

She clenched and untightened her fists. "That was when he nodded to Norah, who produced the shotgun from behind my chair. I felt something brush the back of my head. It was a shock when I turned around. That's when I knew that something bad was coming. But I was prepared.

"He started to talk again, about himself and his own father, Edward, Sir Hugh's brother. How Sir Hugh had inherited the property and the business but wanted nothing to do with it, just the money. Hugh had lost both of his sons from his first marriage, in the war. Then his wife died of Spanish flu. He became a recluse. But he took in Julia Noble, the fiancée of his younger son's best friend. The boys had died together in 1917. He felt more responsibility towards her, than to his brother. He let Edward take all the financial burden and do all the work. Edward assumed that he was going to inherit. Thomas was born in 1928. He was brought up with a sense of entitlement and resentment. He remembered the shock and horror when Sir Hugh married Julia Noble, and even more when she produced a child, then died. Sir Hugh became a recluse again. Once more, he left it all to Edward and the growing Thomas to run the business. As long as he could have the lifestyle, he wanted nothing to do with the business. I can understand how Edward felt he was the rightful heir, that he deserved something for everything he had done, all the work he had put in.

"Anyway, Sir Hugh blamed Margaret for her mother's death. He wanted nothing to do with her. She grew up resentful and wild. Edward could have helped and supported her, but he didn't. He encouraged her to run away and made sure that Thomas grew up believing that Margaret had no right to inherit. When they heard Margaret had written to her father and was coming back, they decided to stop it at any cost. She said in her letter she would arrive on the boat from Swansea in a week. That gave them all the time they needed. They decided that stopping her meant killing her. They worked out the whole plan: a hit-and-run and the story about her falling off a boat a month later. It was clinical in its conception and execution.

"You know what happened. The big mistake they made, as I said, was that they never considered that the 'surprise' might be me. They suspected a husband who might come looking for her, but no one came. As the years rolled by, they relaxed. But they couldn't relax completely, because they knew the rings were out there, somewhere. She took jewellery too, but nothing special. Probably pawned it. And the money, of course, but that was mostly her own. Five grand. The same amount as Hopton claimed he inherited. He didn't inherit anything; he stole it, from Margaret. They set up a watch for the rings through auction houses, jewellers, plus museums for the Roman ring. That included Caerleon. The Roman ring was the one that would most easily identify them, because of the public story of its theft. They wanted to avoid identification, but they also wanted to know who had it and how they got it."

She paused for a moment. "We must tell Nick that someone there had a hotline to the McCarthy Millers. They also put a watch on probate and that's where it paid off in the end. They missed the full significance of the vicar's will. He wasn't specific enough, although they regarded it as an item of interest. But Tracy gave it all up and she named me. As soon as he saw Zelah Trevear, Thomas knew that something was up. Interesting thing," she turned to Maggie. "You know how you couldn't put the rings on? Well, neither could he. Nor Norah, nor anyone in the family. But he knew as soon as I did. Thought-provoking, eh? I need a drink."

Bob reached out to fill her glass. "No, not water. Is there any whisky in this room?"

He went over to the fridge and brought out a miniature, gave it to Zelah, then called room service and ordered three doubles.

"I don't know if I'm allowed to drink alcohol and take these painkillers, but what the hell, I'll sleep well. Anyway, let me summarise quickly, so I'm sure I've got the full picture. OK with you two?"

Both nodded their assent.

"Sir Thomas McCarthy Miller's entire motivation has been greed. He always wanted nothing more than to keep Rosscarbery and enjoy the reputation that comes with being its owner. He watched his father encourage his niece to run away. I wonder if he might have suggested she take some souvenirs with her. What do you think?"

"Entirely possible," Zelah mused. "Go on."

"But that was where I think he made his greatest mistake. Because what she took had more than monetary value. The historical importance of the rings could lead someone directly back to the family. The money and the other jewellery didn't matter much. If Margaret pawned the jewellery it would never come to anything. But the rings… there was every chance they could be recognised, particularly the Roman ring. And, if they were kept together and treated as a group… how do I put this into words without sounding melodramatic or batshit crazy?" Maggie screwed her face up as she battled to work out what she was going to say and turned her eyes to the table.

"The memories contained in those rings are of deep love. But unrequited, in each case and associated with a tragic outcome. They were never worn for the purposes for which they'd been created. They are beautiful but heart-breaking objects and I think there's an energy to them that prevents them from being worn. Unless…" She looked at Zelah. "Unless it's by someone who has a sympathetic connection with them. It's as if they allow themselves to be attached to a finger. Does that sound stupid?"

"Not at all," Zelah replied, "that's exactly what I think."

"Bob?"

"Hmmm. I can't be objective if I try the rings on, I know the background and it might influence me.

"Why don't you try anyway?" Zelah asked. "Find out."

"No," he replied firmly. "Too late. You need to test them on someone who doesn't know."

"But I didn't know their history when I tried to put them on," Maggie said.

"Still no," he said adamantly.

"That's disappointing. Despite all you've seen and experienced since you've been with me, you're still sceptical."

There were a few seconds of silence, before a loud bang on the door made them all jump. Bob got up. "That's room service." He opened the door to a young girl in hotel uniform, carrying a tray of drinks, a dish of ice, and some mixers. He held the door open and she went to the table.

"Thanks, put them down there please. Actually, would you mind doing a favour for us?" Maggie asked.

Chapter 74

The girl smiled uncertainly. "If I can, Madam."

"You see these rings? We're trying to decide what to do with them. But they don't fit any of us. You look like you have small fingers. Would you mind trying them on, just so we can decide?"

Bob went to protest, but Zelah pointed at him and shook her head. Maggie hadn't looked at him, but she knew he was furious.

"Sure. They're lovely, aren't they?"

"Yes, they are." Maggie smiled. "Up to you which one you want to try first."

The girl leaned over, looked at each ring in turn and picked up the Roman ring. "This looks amazing. Can I try this one? I think it'll fit my ring finger."

"Put it on your right hand," Zelah intervened. "It's not good luck to put someone else's ring on the finger for your own ring."

The girl picked up the Roman ring, looked closely at it, smiled at Maggie, and moved it towards the third finger of her right hand. Maggie and Zelah held their breath. Just as she went to slip it on, the girl paused, frowned, and then moved again. Then, she laid the ring down on the table. She looked at them with a puzzled expression. "Sorry. But I just feel like I can't do it. Almost like the ring doesn't want to be worn. Isn't that odd, now?"

"Not at all," Maggie said, smiling at her. "Some rings can be like that. Never mind. But thanks for trying."

"Thanks," Zelah added, slipping a ten Euro note into the girl's hand.

"We were actually interested more in which one you'd pick, so we can decide which one to sell first, but thanks anyway. We guessed right, didn't we Zelah?" And she gave Zelah a wide, false grin. Zelah nodded and smiled likewise. She went over and opened the door to see the girl out.

As soon as the door closed Maggie turned to Bob. "Well?"

His face was red. "That was bloody disgusting. You shouldn't have done that to the poor girl."

"You're the one who said we should try it with someone who didn't know." Maggie picked up her glass of whisky and knocked it back neat, in one gulp. A burning pain in her throat made her shudder, but she stayed on her feet.

"I didn't mean some unassuming kid."

"Then who did you mean?"

He threw his hands up. "I don't know." He walked into the bathroom and slammed the door.

Maggie sat down. "I thought he was getting used to the idea that not everything in this world is black and white."

"He is," Zelah said. "Give him a break, Maggie. How old is he? Mid-fifties?"

"Fifty-three."

"He's had fifty-two years of black and white. These things take time. Some people don't embrace the 'difficult to explain' as quickly as others."

"I know that, but I'm disappointed."

"Well, button it. Treat him with patience. He'll come around. We've all had a dreadful day. Let it sink in. Probably the first time he's had a shotgun in his face. He'll get over it."

"Something I don't understand," Maggie said, "How come the Gardaí turned up?"

"Bob's doing. He's been talking to them a bit more than he told us. They've had concerns about the McCarthy Millers' 'association' with the local force. So, they hatched a plan this morning. He had them on a live feed. As soon as they heard him shout 'Now, now', that was the signal for them to enter."

Maggie stared at her; eyes wide.

"What?" Zelah asked.

"You mean he knew they were outside all along?" Zelah nodded and stood up. "I'm going to bed now. I don't think I can talk any more. I'm done for tonight." Bob opened the bathroom door and came out as the bedroom door slammed shut.

"She's gone?"

"Yes." Maggie watched Bob as he went to the window and closed the elaborate red velvet curtains. He remained standing in front of them, his back to her.

"Something to tell me?" Maggie asked. "Zelah told me what you did with the Gardaí."

"It saved our lives," he said, still not turning.

Maggie stood up slowly and walked over to him as he turned to look at her. "How dare you?" she whispered.

He stepped back. "Don't get funny with me. I couldn't tell you."

"Really? You couldn't? Somebody ordered you not to tell me? Or was it your decision yet again, not to involve me?" She raised her voice slightly. "I was absolutely fucking terrified. I thought we were all going to be shot, but you knew that the bloody cavalry was waiting. And you chose – yes, chose – not to tell me? Like what I thought didn't matter?"

"You've never been in this situation before. I was afraid you'd give it away."

She raised her hand to hit him, but he caught it and held it away from his face. "I am sorry, truly, but I knew what I was doing. I asked you to trust me."

Tears blurred her vision. "I can't believe you did this." She went back to her chair and fell into it.

For a few minutes neither spoke. Bob moved towards her, but she held up her hand to stop him and he sat on the bed.

Then she said, "I don't understand how the gun moved from Zelah's face to the other side of the room."

"The sound of the armed Gards breaking in?"

"No. I heard shots before they broke down the door. It was a jerking movement, as if someone pushed the barrel. I thought it might have been Zelah somehow."

"I don't think so. She would have said. I think it was the Gards."

"No," Maggie snapped. "Norah would have moved the other

way. They came in from the wrong side."

"Odd," he pondered, "but something made it point away from Zelah's head. It all happened so fast and the noise was deafening. You probably didn't hear it the way you think you did."

He stood and came to her, trying to take her hand but she pulled away. "I'm sorry," he said, "I know I'm supposed to be OK with situations like this, but sometimes I'm not. Please don't be angry with me. I was acting in our best interest."

"If you say so. And if you mean the shotgun, I can't believe that anyone's ever OK with that. And if they are, they shouldn't be. But the other stuff. Well, are you sure you want to be?"

"Look, I want to believe… there's an explanation. But in dangerous situations my instincts and training kick in. It's who I am."

Maggie sighed. "I understand that. But what you've done today? I'm not sure how I feel right this minute. I need to think it through. But there is an explanation of the things that Maze deals with."

He frowned and raised his eyebrows.

"I don't know how to explain properly. In eastern medicine they work on the basis that, in addition to a nervous system and a blood flow system, there's an energy channel of equal importance with critical points that if blocked cause illness. I had an experience once, in my twenties. I was skiing and I injured my knee. I could barely move it. Anyway, I was sitting with a group of people and someone stood on my foot, which caused my knee to jerk and bend. The agony was unbelievable. Sitting nearby was an American. Said he was a doctor who specialised in something I didn't understand then. I was weeping with the pain. He stood in front of me. Asked if he could touch my leg. I think I said he could chop it off if it would help. He smiled and pressed a couple of places on the upper part of my leg. I can't remember where, but at once the pain went away and my knee straightened. After five minutes of calming down, I asked him what he did. He asked me if I had heard of acupuncture, which I had. He said that it was acupressure. That there are certain points in the body that could release energy. Just a case of knowing where they were. He said he suspected that I had a serious injury and should go to hospital, which I did. Turned out I had torn the ligament right through. If he hadn't done what he did, the injury would have taken longer to heal. Now, Western science will tell you that it's not provable, that it's quack medicine. I had no idea what the guy was doing. It was an emergency, for me, and he stopped the pain and straightened my leg. Energy flow, meridians in the body. What do you say?"

"Amazing."

Maggie looked gratified.

"Fancy… you being able to ski," he said with a grin.

She threw a cushion at him. "Bastard."

He caught the cushion and laughed. "Fair enough. But this is a step further than acupressure."

"Yes, I know. And I've said before that most people will either never experience it, or they may just have one tiny moment when something odd occurs that they can't explain within the boundaries of human experience. So, they shrug and forget it. We're just a couple of steps beyond that."

"We're a bloody great flight of stairs beyond it. Anyway, I'm sorry that you think I didn't trust you. It wasn't that at all. How are you feeling?"

"Knackered. And you should stop apologising. It doesn't make anything better or easier to deal with."

"Right. Let's get some sleep."

"OK. Bugger," she sighed. "We didn't look at the letter and now Zelah's gone."

"Tomorrow," he said firmly. "Plenty of time to finish the story. Now, sleep, woman."

Chapter 75

Maggie slept well and awoke early. She pulled back the curtains to reveal rolling green countryside and a weak sun. She pulled up a chair to the window and, with a cup of tea, sat down to consider events of the previous day. It was important for her to take this time without interruption to remember as much detail as she could, who said what, who did what, how events unfolded. She was quite clear that Norah had fired her gun before the armed Gards came in, whatever Bob said. She suspected there would be more than one thing that still puzzled her, but if she could recall everything in finer points then perhaps some of what was not clear could become so. She also had to deal with how Bob had acted. The more she thought about it, the stronger her sense of betrayal became.

Noel puzzled her. He had said nothing from the moment that the library door opened to reveal the rest of the family. She recalled glancing at him a few times, catching his reaction. His expression was of concern, he licked dry lips several times. But he kept his hands clasped together in front of his stomach. And never once looked any member of his family in the eye. Downtrodden and manipulated? She suspected that he hadn't liked what was going on, but had been so subjugated by his bully of a father and psychopathic sister he simply didn't know how to challenge them. He had two sons. She wondered if they knew what had happened. Probably. She suspected that Noel and his sons had, in fact, been the driving force behind the business's success, Noel keeping his head down and getting on with what he loved doing. If Zelah went through with what she'd threatened, those boys were in for difficult times.

Sir Thomas was nothing more than an arrogant liar and murderer. He clearly loved his superior reputation and had assumed that nothing could touch him. She wondered what he was doing now. Still in hospital because of his head wound? Or had he been moved to a local prison? What was he thinking? Impossible to imagine.

Norah had been taken to a women's prison in Dublin. She would be raging, unable to believe that she had been taken down. Threatening anyone who came across her path that she would deal with them. She was going to spend the rest of her life in prison. Or was she? Maggie thought she'd probably end up in a secure psychiatric unit, and hopefully never be let out.

That left Emer, who was now the subject of a national search. Could she have left the country? This worried Maggie. She was her mother's daughter. Her hatred of Maggie and Zelah would be all-consuming. They would have to watch their backs until she was caught.

"You don't look happy," Bob interrupted. He was sitting up in bed, looking at her.

"Just thinking about the family and what will happen if Emer isn't found."

"They'll find her," he said. "They had the airports and ports on high alert before she could even think about which one to try for. What time is it?"

"Just after seven," Maggie replied. "What's the plan for today?"

"Breakfast first. Then we'll have to go back to the police station so you can give your statement. Do you feel up to it?"

She nodded her head slowly and winced. "It still hurts, but nothing like yesterday. We still need to go over the letter. I'm desperate now to know what's in it."

"What we really need is to get back home," said Bob. "You have other priorities."

"I know what my priorities are. If there's a trial, I guess we'll all have to come back here?"

"Yes, but I don't know if there will be. It occurred to me that Norah will probably end up in a psychiatric unit."

"That's just what I was thinking, but–"

A loud knock at the door and a shout of, "Are you up yet?" announced Zelah's impending presence. Bob jumped out of bed, grabbed his overnight bag and headed for the bathroom, as Maggie opened the door and Zelah marched in.

"I thought we'd have breakfast here, so we have the privacy to read the letter and–"

"Just stop there." Maggie was standing with arms folded, one foot tapping the floor.

"What? You want to know what's in it, don't you?"

"Of course I do. But why do we need privacy? It's meaningless to anyone else. I hope you haven't ordered anything?"

"No, I haven't. You have a better idea?"

"Bob wants to go down to the restaurant to have a long, enjoyable breakfast where he can choose whatever he wants. And I think it's the least we can let him do."

Zelah looked as if she was going to object but closed her mouth and nodded. "Fair enough. He can stuff his face and listen to me reading the letter." She turned and made to go back to the door.

"Zelah," Maggie's voice was slow and quiet. "I know this has been a life-changing experience for you. But please don't think that Bob and I weren't affected. Please consider our feelings too, not just your own."

"I wasn't doing anything of the kind," Zelah remonstrated.

"Good. Then we'll see you down in the restaurant at eight." Maggie turned and walked into the bathroom, leaving Zelah to see herself out.

When Maggie and Bob entered the dining area promptly at eight o'clock they found a large, elegant room, rather like a nineteenth-century parlour, bright and cheerful, with floor-length drapes drawn back to reveal a manicured lawn surrounded by luscious flowering gardens where summer flowers still bloomed. The sun was streaming in, but there was also the remains of mist crawling in patches across the grass. A fire blazing in the hearth showed that outside the temperature was not at all summery. Along a windowless wall was a table laden like a banquet with breakfast food to satisfy every possible taste. There were a dozen tables in the room, a few of which were occupied. Zelah had chosen a round table in a corner, next to a window, shaded from the sun. They joined her.

Maggie was about to ask how they wanted to approach things, when Zelah said, "Look, I'm just keen to get all of this over with, OK, so we can go home and get back to normal."

"I'm not sure what normal is," Maggie replied, "But I want to get away from here, too. How about we get some breakfast first, then you read out the letter, and we can talk over the whole history of the Pencarrow family. I've lost track a bit and I still can't hear properly, which seems to be affecting my ability to concentrate. Will that work for both of you?"

Zelah grunted. Bob nodded, stood up and made his way to the breakfast table.

"Is he not speaking to me?" Zelah asked.

"It's not that. He's had to duck out of work, again, for 'personal reasons'. They aren't happy. He's had a shot gun in his face, seen a man shot dead, and is going to have to explain to his bosses about his interactions with the Gardaí. He needs to get home. And he doesn't see any evidence that you are particularly concerned. Before you start yelling," she held up a finger in front of Zelah's face, "I know you are concerned. But I've come to know you. He doesn't. So just cut him some slack. He did a good job in the past couple of days." She didn't tell Zelah yet about her own issues with his behaviour.

Zelah sighed and sat back. "I know, I know. It's hard."

"That's quite an admission from you. OK, what are you having for breakfast?"

"Nothing."

"Don't give me that. You're a hearty breakfast eater. I've seen you put away cream cakes first thing in the morning."

"Not today."

"A drink, then? Your usual, coffee with cream, one sugar?"

Zelah nodded and Maggie realised how hard Zelah was working to keep it together. She nodded back, smiling, and joined Bob.

When they sat back at the table, Bob was in front of a full plate of cooked food. "Full Irish," he said, and tucked in.

Zelah started to sip her coffee, while Maggie launched into a bowl of fruit.

"Shall I read it, then?" asked Zelah.

"Yes, please. I assume you already know what's in it. Does it explain fully the circumstances of how it came to be written?"

"It explains everything," Zelah replied. "Here goes."

"Who wrote it?" Maggie interjected.

"Just listen, will you? Like I said, it explains everything." She read the letter:

This account is written this twelfth day of October in the Year of our Lord Seventeen Hundred and Thirty-six and in the ninth year of the reign of His Majesty King George.

It is written by the hand of myself, John Vyse and is made in three parts, one for my said self, one for Mistress Julia Pencarrow, and one for my faithful servant Edward Steelfox. Each will keep safe our copy until the time of our death. We will arrange with a trusted person for the destruction of said copy. We do this so that, in the event of any of us being accused of the death of my wife the Lady Mildred Vyse, the accuser will know that three persons bear responsibility.

This heavy burden was undertaken by the aforesaid three persons who knew that Lady Vyse was responsible for the unfair trial and transportation of Peter Steelfox and for the murder of a gardener by name of Richard Weston. And that said, Lady Mildred Vyse was in the course of planning further deaths by witchcraft, by the foul use of poppets to bring about pain and suffering to those against whom she bore a grudge. One of said poppets is retained by Mistress Pencarrow. In the event of her early death it will be sent to one of the survivors in receipt of this account.

Mistress Pencarrow will also have in safekeeping the ring, made from a silver spoon and gifted by my own mother to Peter Steelfox, the brother of the aforesaid Edward Steelfox, who was transported to the American colonies, wrongly convicted of the theft of said ring on the word of Lady Vyse and of assault upon her person, both being untruths. The witness, aforesaid Richard Weston having been paid by Mildred Vyse to tell a wicked lie to the Assizes.

The death of Mildred Vyse was caused by strangulation. Her room was entered by Julia Pencarrow using her abilities. She was able to lock the room with the key on the inside of the door, again with her abilities. We will not say how the strangulation was done, except that there was no human hand involved in it.

Lady Mildred Vyse was an evil woman, who delighted in the prospect of causing hurt and grief to those she believed to be her enemies, of which she believed there were many, although in God's Truth there were none. She thrilled at the prospect of the making cursed figures of such supposed enemies and bringing about their deaths. But she was no witch. She had a desire to be, but had no abilities. Her devices were a product of a diseased mind. Her rude plans were brought about by vicious campaigns. She is not missed in this world.

Each of the aforementioned three persons will keep their copy of this account unto death. The last person to remain in this world will decide whether his copy be destroyed or passed on.

Signed here by the hand of each person,

John Vyse   Edward Steelfox   Julia Pencarrow

"And they each signed it," Zelah said, putting the piece of parchment onto the table. For a few moments they stared at it.

"Julia Pencarrow was the last of the three to die, and she decided to keep it, plus the poppet and the ring, and pass them on. There are some unanswered issues, but I think we can fill in the gaps with reasonable supposition. I don't suppose it matters now," Maggie said.

"'Abilities?'" Bob asked. He had been concentrating on his food and didn't look up.

"Exactly what you're thinking," Zelah replied. "John Vyse uses the word in relation to Julia Pencarrow opening a locked door and then closing it with the key on the inside, and Mildred Vyse thinking she could hurt people with poppets. Witchcraft. Julia's abilities came from her mother and great-grandmother. She probably passed them on to her descendants."

"Just the women?" he asked, looking up at her and folding his arms.

"There's evidence and history of cunning men, too," Zelah said in a neutral voice, "but the publicity was always around the women. But think about Aleister Crowley. He believed he had special powers, although he was all about Satanic ritual. Witchcraft centuries ago could be as much about good as evil. They knew how to use plants and herbs for medicinal purposes."

A shaft of light from the window next to their table threw a sparkling beam onto the letter.

"Sun's on the move. We should be, too," Zelah said, carefully picking up the parchment. "What are your plans for today?"

"We have to go into Fermoy, so I can give a statement. Then, I guess we're going to get the first ferry back." She looked at Bob, unsmiling. "I'm keen to get home."

"If you two don't mind, I've done my bit, so I'm going to head off. I need to find a good solicitor in Dublin to talk about what happens to the McCarthy Miller estate and inheritance. I suppose I should contact the police in Cornwall to let them know what's happened. At least we're all off the hook now for that one."

Bob shrugged and Maggie said, "Yes that's fine. Alice's school is my priority. Then I guess we need to re-group. It's Sunday today. How about Tuesday or Wednesday?"

"Make it Wednesday," Zelah said. "I don't know how long I'll be here.

Chapter 76

It took Maggie a couple of hours, longer than she'd expected, to make a written statement. She was questioned in detail about what had occurred in the half hour they had been at Rosscarbery House.

When it was over, she asked about the McCarthy Millers. Sir Thomas was still in hospital with a permanent guard; it turned out that his wound was superficial but he was kept in for observation due to his age. He would be at a committal hearing in a couple of days, then moved to a medium security prison in Cork. Norah was in a women's prison, but due to be psychiatrically evaluated as her behaviour was increasingly erratic and threatening.

Emer was still at large. She had taken enough cash with her not to leave an electronic trail – the Gardaí thought about two thousand euros. Their main concern was that she had headed into Northern Ireland from where she could get over to Liverpool. Every ferry was being checked, but the concern was of a private boat hire. She was now one of Ireland's most wanted subjects, so they were confident she wouldn't remain at large for long.

"Let's hope they're right," Maggie said as they left the station. "With yet another one to watch out for, I'm going to have to get one eyeball transplanted into the back of my head."

"Good job I've got your back," Bob replied, reaching out to take her hand, but she thrust it in her pocket.

Chapter 77

They headed back to Rosslare without hanging around. Maggie thought she would like to come back to Fermoy. This was possibly the birthplace of her own great-grandfather, although she had failed to nail that down one hundred percent. For now, she just wanted to go home.

The ferry trip was uneventful, the crossing calm and there was little traffic on the motorway. Just after eleven that night they arrived home. Bob decided to go home, as he had to be in work at six. On the ferry he had taken a phone call and had taken himself out of earshot to listen to it. Maggie watched him gesticulating, rubbing his head several times, nodding vigorously. Her curiosity aroused, she asked him who the call was from, but he just said work and she left it there. They mainly sat in silence.

Both children were still awake and waiting for her. She hugged them both as they bombarded her with questions.

"Are you OK, really?" said Jack.

"Is your ear going to get better?" asked Alice.

"Are the people going to stay in prison?" said Jack.

"I'm glad you're OK. Can we go to Hereford tomorrow?" said Alice.

Maggie reassured Alice that she would talk to the school in Hereford the following day, then ordered them both to bed.

She sat down to talk to Nick, to fill him in on the details. They sat for an hour or so, watching the embers of the fire he had lit. The night was calm and cold.

"That's it, then?" Nick asked. "All questions answered?"

"From the investigative point of view, I would say so," Maggie said. "I can't think of anything else we need to know."

"I guess it's up to Zelah what she wants to do with the rings," he ruminated, "and the letter and the remains of the poppet. I guess she's not going to involve us in whatever she decides to do, nor with the McCarthy Miller business empire."

"None of our business. And honestly, Nick, having met those people, I'll give her whatever support she needs, but I don't want to know the details."

"Will this change her?"

Maggie considered the question as the logs she had thrown onto the fire popped and spluttered. "I suppose it's bound to. You can't unknow things you wish you'd never found out. But I can't see that she'll become anything other than who she's always been; brash, abrasive, mouthy Zelah. Would you want her any different?"

"No." He smiled. "I've got used to her. Bark worse than bite. And the idea she could have killed someone, I agree was desperate groping by the police for something to move them forward, even if there was no evidence. But Maggie," he added, "Is she really OK? There's something different. A strange energy."

"I hadn't noticed," Maggie replied, "but that's your area of expertise. I'm ready for bed. I'm going to take a couple of days with Alice to find out about this school."

"I did some research while you were away," he said as he stood up and they walked to the front door. "It's different, but it gets officially inspected, same as other schools. The results are good. And there are plenty of positive reports from the parents of kids who have been there. The model is like one that's being trialled in Finland. Mixed year groups, pupil-led learning, and that's in the public-school system. They are miles ahead of the rest of the world. You know, I think it would be good for her." He paused. "I'm more concerned for you, how you'll cope if she goes away."

"Me too," Maggie replied. "But if it's right for her, then I'll have to suck it up. Anyway, Hereford's only an hour away. We'll see." Maggie hugged Nick, which made him blush and look away. "Thank you for being here with them. They have total faith in you, as have I."

Without looking back, he waved and walked away down the path.

Chapter 78

On Wednesday morning, after seeing Jack off to school, Maggie and Alice sat in the office, waiting for the others to arrive, discussing the next steps in Alice's transfer to the school in Hereford.

They had visited on Monday, and again on Tuesday. Each time Alice slipped easily into conversation with Jan, the lead teacher, and the other students. No one called them children: Alice liked that.

Reluctantly, Maggie could see that it was right for Alice and that she would have to let her go. Jan felt that Alice would be a fantastic addition to her student group. Of course, she had to board Monday to Friday. Maggie would drive her up to Hereford on Monday morning and collect her at lunchtime on Friday.

Maggie spent much of her time there observing, in particular Alice's interactions with the other students, and had to admit that, although she found the conversations a bit odd for their age, Alice, by the end of the day, looked comfortable and at home. It had been agreed that she would start the following Monday. There was no uniform, but an agreement that clothes had to be comfortable and practical. No designer labels just for show. Which bothered Alice not at all. There were rules about tidiness, which Maggie liked, and a written commitment to abide by the school principles of inclusion and enthusiasm. Homework was entirely a matter of choice and called 'personal additional study'. The students did it if they felt they wanted or needed to, and most did.

Alice was now a mixture of excitement and nervousness. She was going to have to share a room – something she had never done before, but she had spent Tuesday with her potential roommate, and they seemed to get on well. There was a counsellor, external specialist teachers for dance, art, and biology. Otherwise, all subjects were covered. Alice wouldn't miss out. Maggie had a concern about the quality of the teaching, not based on anything specific, just on the small number of students and the difference in their ages. But time would tell. They had excellent exam results. It was just… so different.

As Zelah and Nick arrived, Alice was going through a list she had made of what she should take with her, Maggie silently crossing off the more outlandish items.

"Well done, Alice," Nick said, giving her a hug. "It will be good."

"Hope so," she said. "Think so."

They sat around the table and Maggie explained that Bob was going to join them, as he had some important news from Cornwall.

"He didn't tell me anything," Zelah said.

"He had a conversation with Mark Mooney yesterday afternoon and Mark went off to check something out. I didn't hear any more. That's why he's coming to tell us this morning." Zelah shrugged.

"Do you have any more information from Ireland, Zelah?" Nick asked.

She shook her head. "They tracked Emer to Cork but nothing since. Sir Thomas has his hearing this morning. He'll be committed to jail to await trial in Cork. Medium security." She put her head down, took papers out of her bag, and studied them. Maggie and Nick exchanged a quick quizzical look.

Maggie was relieved when, after a few minutes' silence Bob arrived. Zelah didn't look up as he entered the office and sat down. Without preamble he began, "I have news from Cornwall. And Zelah, this is mainly for you. Shall we go into the kitchen to talk?"

"No. Say it here."

Maggie held up her hand, sending a disappointed Alice out of the room with a promise she would talk to her later, and nodded to Bob to begin.

"Mark and I have had a suspicion for some time about what might have occurred during those days when Jay's mother came to look for him. We've been able to pin down the date using the notes from her hospital stay, to the time she was found in the sea, and the autopsy report. Now we also have the report from the exhumation. The forensic scientist who examined the remains thinks that the wound on the skull was inflicted deliberately, before the body went into the water. She was probably alive but unconscious when she went in."

"Why didn't they figure that out at the time?" asked Zelah.

"Presumptions, we think. She had a reputation. She had taken in a lot of alcohol, which could have been poured down her throat when she was unconscious, or semi-conscious. No one locally knew who she was or why she was there."

"Except for Tracy."

"Except for Tracy, and she's dead so we can't question her. But Maureen Meers' memory of the conversation was a good lead. And she has since remembered the name of another child who we've been able to track down and contact. A boy called Kevin Elliott. Ring any bells?"

"No."

"He wasn't there long before he went back to his family, but he remembers Tracy. And he remembers a woman coming to ask about Jay. He remembered because there had been a big bust-up between Tracy and Jay after school and it was soon after, that the woman came asking about Jay. He says Tracy's temper got the better of her and she threw the woman out, which we know. But he also thought Tracy was frightened. That was something new. And he was able to add to the timeline. The woman arrived a couple of days after Jay disappeared. We've also contacted the school he attended, for their records and they've confirmed the dates."

"What's the timeline?" Maggie asked.

"As far as we've been able to put together, it went like this... It all happened in early October. Jay goes to school on Monday and has a bust-up with Tracy after school later that day. On Tuesday, the school notices a lot of bruises, but he won't talk about what had happened. They make a note of it and are going to ask

Hopton. Wednesday, he goes to school again. He leaves at the normal time, but doesn't go back to the vicarage, at least that's what everyone thinks at the time. He's reported missing on Thursday, the day Doreen discharges herself from hospital and travels to Penzance, where she was last seen, except by Tracy and the children who were in the house at the time she called. She and Tracy quarrel, and Tracy sends her packing at about five in the evening."

"But there must have been police around, searching for him," Zelah interrupted. "Why didn't she speak to any of them?"

"This is where the conjecture starts on our part," Bob replied. "We think Tracy's second bust-up with Jay was violent and she killed him somewhere between the school and the vicarage. She may have waited for him. It must have been a terrible shock for her when his mother knocked on the door two days later. Which would explain why she seemed frightened. If the woman was around looking for her son, who was the subject of a police search, then she was in deep trouble. So, she couldn't afford for Doreen to speak to the police and she thought if the woman found out he was missing that she, Tracy, would be in the spotlight and her rows with him and his bruises would be looked at more closely. According to the notes we've got, she told the police he had gone off in a temper and said he was going away. She then somehow found Doreen, laid her out with a blow to the head and got a load of alcohol into her. God knows how she did it."

"She was capable of anything," Zelah muttered.

"Anyway, she pushed the unconscious body into the water. And…" he stopped and looked directly at Zelah, "she told her father what she had done."

Zelah's head swung around. "Why do you think that? How can you know?"

"They must have just hoped that whenever Doreen's body turned up, if it turned up, she wouldn't be identified, but they'd deal with it if she was recognisable. But Jay was different. So, they devised a plan. Mark and I talked through scenarios of how you might dispose of a body in a small community without it being found. And we both came to the same conclusion. That's when we put the timeline together, checked out something else and–"

"Oh, my word," Nick interrupted, "that's terrible, truly evil."

Bob nodded and said, "Yes."

"I don't understand," Maggie said. "What happened?"

Bob seemed reluctant to speak.

"There was one about to happen, I presume?" Zelah asked.

"Yes," Bob said. "The following Monday."

"Have you checked it?"

"Yes. We checked the date and opened it up." Bob paused. "He was there."

"You've done all that and not told me?"

"I'm sorry, I couldn't tell you. We've already had one exhumation order. We needed convincing evidence for two. It took time. We could have been wrong and then we'd have a lot of explaining to do."

"Do some explaining for me, please," said Maggie.

"They had a funeral on the Monday morning. A village pensioner. The grave had already been dug. So, they put Jay in, covered him with earth, and the coffin went in on top."

Maggie put her hands to her mouth. She was about to speak, but a low, haunting moan from Zelah stopped her. "He was there, all the time."

"Yes," Bob said gently. "All the time."

"I suppose… I suppose I knew. But there was always, deep inside…" she paused, tapping a fist on her breastbone, "a small light of hope. That somehow, he got away. But I knew, really."

Maggie went over to Zelah and put her arms around her. Zelah remained stiff and upright, but she didn't push Maggie away. She asked, "What now?"

"It's impossible to say how he died. No clear evidence, so we'll never know what Tracy did to him. But his remains will be released for re-burial. We thought you might like to decide how that happens. There are no other family members."

"And what about his mother, Doreen?"

"She was in a common grave. Would you like to have her

moved?"

"Yes. They should be together. Let me think about it."

"Of course," Bob replied. "When you're ready, let me know what you want to do, and we can make the arrangements with the Coroner's Office in Cornwall."

"What else should we talk about?" Zelah asked. "We've plenty of work to do."

"Can we leave it a couple of days?" asked Nick.

"Why?"

"Because I for one think we've all gone through enough. Maggie is coming to terms with Alice going away. You've just got this, and I've... frankly, I've had enough for now. I'd like a couple of days off."

Zelah sat up, thrust out her chin and was about to speak. But she paused and looked around at their faces. "Yes. Good idea. Let's leave it until after the weekend."

Chapter 79

Two weeks later, Maggie, Zelah, Bob, Nick, and Jack stood together on a hillside and watched two small wicker baskets being lowered into the ground.

After cremation, Zelah had opted for a natural burial, having decided that both Jay and his mother had no need of religion in their final resting place. They had attended a quiet memorial in an open-sided shepherd's hut, then walked up the hillside to the edge of a pasture of wild flowers, where Zelah had chosen a plot on the far edge underneath the overhanging branches of a tree, with magnificent views of the countryside towards the Welsh coastline.

"Jay loved the sea and the open country," Zelah said as the baskets reached the floor of the plot. "He used to run around all over the scrubland behind the church, pretending to be an aeroplane. But Cornwall didn't seem like the right place. This is better for them."

"It's beautiful," Maggie replied. "Such a tranquil spot. I didn't know about these places."

"There won't be a headstone, just a marker plate with a number. Their names are inscribed on the wall we passed on the way in. I'll come here, sometimes."

After a few minutes' quiet contemplation, Zelah suggested they go back down and she marched off, leaving them to follow.

They were going to a local pub for lunch, small but well-known, historic with low ceilings and beams and a peaceful ambience, with views of the Brecon Beacons mountain range. While waiting for food they chatted about work, Alice's new school, all manner of things, except for the elephant that sat large and looming. Until Maggie decided that it was time to share her news.

"Sir Thomas asked to see me." The conversations ended and all

339

heads turned to her.

"Why?" Zelah cut through the silence. "Why you?"

"His lawyer says he has information he thinks I want to hear."

"What could he have to say that could be of any interest to you?" Zelah asked.

"I have no idea," Maggie replied. "Maybe something about the history that we don't know? Or the artefacts?"

"Well, you aren't going. I'm getting into a complicated legal situation over my right to the property and I don't want it screwed up by you charging in and compromising it."

Maggie took a deep breath. "I'm not going to compromise anything. I had just planned to listen to what he has to say. If he's trying to do anything against you, I'll just walk out."

"So, you're planning to go?" Zelah picked up a knife from the table and banged the handle down.

"I haven't decided, and of course I wasn't going to do anything without telling you."

At that moment two waitresses arrived with plates of steaming food, halting the conversation. Maggie thought the atmosphere could easily be cut with the knife that Zelah was clutching. Once they had gone, she turned to Zelah. "I am absolutely not going to do or say anything that will compromise you, I promise. But, aren't you just a bit curious?"

"No, not the least bit."

"If you feel that strongly, I'll leave it. But I am curious. I think there might be more to the story. I'd like to think that, as we've got this far, we get the rest."

"I agree," Nick butted-in before Zelah could speak. "What harm could there be?"

"I don't know. But it's my history and I don't want anyone else poking their nose in." The knife clattered on the table.

"Oh-Kay." Maggie gave the word two long syllables. "Let's talk about this later. We shouldn't forget why we're here today. This is more important." She put her head down and started to eat. The others followed suit.

When they had finished the meal Zelah left and Nick followed her, leaving Maggie, Bob, and Jack sitting around the table.

"What are you going to do, Mum?"

"I think I need more information," Maggie replied. "I don't know why he wants to speak to me, and if it's just to be vitriolic then I'm not going to waste my time. He is a vicious old man so he could be trying to stir up trouble. I think I'll get back to his lawyer first and ask some more questions."

"Good idea," Bob said. "But if there is something you think you need to hear, then go. Zelah went off to Ireland without telling us and almost caused us–" he broke off at the warning glance from Maggie. They hadn't told Jack and Alice the full story. "Anyway, go, if that's what you think is right. You'll make a decent decision. I have faith in you."

"I hope so. I don't want to be a snooping old cow, poking my nose into someone else's business, just to satisfy my curiosity."

Chapter 80

Three days later, Bob dropped Maggie off in front of the terminal building at Cardiff airport, ready for her flight to Cork. He had wanted to go with her but couldn't justify more time off.

"Be careful," he said, as she got out of the camper van. "He's dangerous."

"He's also ninety, he's been in jail for almost a month, and there'll be guards. I don't think I'll be in any physical danger. It's the other thing, whatever he's going to say."

"It's just information. You don't have to let it affect you."

"I know, I'll try. Wish me luck."

"You don't need it."

**

At three o'clock, after going through the usual security searches and locked doors, Maggie sat at a table, waiting for Sir Thomas McCarthy Miller.

It wasn't her first visit to a prison. In her earlier corporate life, she'd had occasion to make visits round the country to different prisons, working with the staff. She had seen the rows of locked doors, the tiny cells, the starkness, the security nets to stop prisoners jumping over balconies; or being thrown over. She always found the close intrusiveness of it overwhelming and could never understand why anyone on the outside ever thought prison was soft. She even found the guards who showed her around with their huge bunches of keys, intimidating. Young Offenders institutions had been the worst. The kids had looked so lost.

After a few minutes, Sir Thomas entered the room with a guard. His appearance was shocking. Gone was the dapper gent with the air of spoiled arrogance. His hair was unkempt, his morning shave had left several cuts and not been particularly effective, leaving him with a grey shadow. He stooped as he walked. Maggie didn't stand up. He sat opposite her, lounging back in the chair, arms folded.

"You wanted to speak to me?" Maggie asked.

"I wanted to see you again, Mrs Gilbert. I'm not sure yet if I want to speak to you."

"Then I have been brought here under false pretences." She stood up and turned to the door.

"Wait," he commanded.

"You are no longer in a position to order anyone around, Mr McCarthy Miller." Maggie's refusal to use his title was intended to anger him. She needed to be on the front foot.

"Please," he added, through a gritted snarl.

"Better. You wanted to speak to me. Please say whatever it is you have to say. Quickly, I have to catch a flight home this evening."

"My so-called heir. She's supposed to be your friend, isn't she?"

"She isn't 'so-called'. Zelah is the rightful heir."

"I see you use her false name."

"It's the one she's had all her life. She certainly isn't going to take your name. Just your property."

"Feisty, aren't you, Maggie Gilbert?"

"Get on with it."

He sat forward in his chair, put his elbows on the table, his hands under his chin, and stared at her. In the centre of his eyes, Maggie could see that there was still a glowing vestige of spite.

"You should know about her. Things she'll never tell you. What she did."

Maggie stood up and pushed her chair back, pointing a forefinger at him. "You are nothing more than a spiteful, psychopathic old shit. You killed her mother for money and land. You and your daughter killed a silly old woman in Cornwall. Don't shake your head. Norah may have pushed, but your hand was there too when Ann Quinn went over the cliff. You will be convicted of murder." Her hands were shaking and, leaning forward, she anchored them on the table. "Don't you dare try to affect my friendship with Zelah with your poison."

"Yes, I killed her mother. I've admitted it. I'm not getting out of here. But you should know what she did, and how. I deserve that. She…" he paused as a wave of coughing hit him. Maggie crossed her arms. The brief pause allowed her a few seconds of thought. Should she walk out? Yes. But something was holding her here.

He cleared his throat and started to speak again but as he opened his mouth the cough started again. He couldn't stop it. The warder moved forward.

"Go get him a drink," Maggie ordered.

The man hesitated. He wasn't supposed to leave the room. He called quickly on a radio for someone to bring water. Thomas McCarthy Miller began to clutch at his chest. The warder made an emergency call as the old man fell forward onto the table. He tried to sit up, but was clutching his chest in agony, beating his breast above his heart as if stabbing himself, or warding off something stabbing at him. His lips turned blue.

Two more warders crashed into the room, followed by a nurse, who took one look at him and yelled, "He's having a heart attack. Get the defibrillator. Call an ambulance."

For fifteen minutes Maggie watched in silence, pinned to the back wall of the room, as the nurse, then a paramedic tried to revive the old man. All the time his eyes were on her, his lips moving. Suddenly, he beckoned her over. The paramedic pushed her back but she moved to his side and he grabbed her arm. He beckoned her to his ear and whispered. Then he closed his eyes as the machine recorded a flat tone.

Chapter 81

Maggie made a statement about what she saw and heard, but it had all been recorded on CCTV. She only just made it to the airport and got her flight home, knowing that Bob was waiting in Cardiff. She desperately needed to speak to him.

What should she tell him? Sir Thomas – she could still only think of him as such, even though she had taunted him with the coming loss of his title – had been trying to tell her something about Zelah. But what could he know? He'd only found out about her existence just months before. He knew about the family history and the coincidence of the name. He may have thought it was more than that. But he had met her for the first time on that fateful day at Rosscarbery House.

Her thoughts were interrupted by the steward offering her a drink, which she gladly took. This was definitely gin and tonic time. She felt like asking him to leave the bottle. As the liquid went down and fired her insides she sat back and tried to make sense of what had happened; to guess what he might have said. 'Something Zelah had done.' She closed her eyes and let her mind run free. She wandered randomly over fragments of memories and conversations, pictures, and words. As she was about to drop off to sleep, something jarred. Two things. Could they be linked? How could she find out? For a start she could get hold of Mark Mooney. And then speak to Maureen Meers.

Her brain didn't even want to contemplate for one second what Sir Thomas had whispered to her as he died. She had misheard, definitely. It must have been, 'Norah said to say hello'. He can't have said Eira. Then she fell asleep.

**

Bob held her in a great bear hug for longer than was necessary to greet someone who had only been away since that morning.

"Difficult day?" he whispered.

"You could say that. Let's get home."

"Not an easy thing to watch someone die. Twice in a month."

She sighed. "No, it wasn't. Not that he told me anything, so it was a big waste of time." She paused, then said to him, "I'd like to have a quick chat with Maureen Meers, if that would be OK? Could you get her number for me?"

"Yes," he answered, waiting for more. When none came, he asked, "Anything you want to tell me?"

"Not yet. And another thing, could you find out who visited Sir Thomas while he was there? And Bob, please don't assume we're OK. I'm not sure about that yet."

**

Alice came home on Friday, bouncing like a jack-in-a-box, chattering non-stop and happier than Maggie had seen her in many months. She loved the school, was learning about things that interested her that Maggie hoped were things she was supposed to learn.

They put all ideas of work to one side and had a family weekend, in what were to be the last warm days of the fading summer.

When Maggie drove her back to Hereford early on Monday morning she asked if she could have a friend come to stay sometime soon. That was fine with Maggie.

"How's Zelah, Mum? Is she feeling better about Jay now? And what does she think about those horrible Irish people?"

Just horrible people, Alice. The fact that they lived in Ireland is not relevant."

"I didn't think it was, but I get your point." That was a first, Maggie thought. A concession.

"Zelah was incredibly sad to find out about Jay, but I think she's getting over it. He has a lovely burial place. With his mum. We'll go some time."

"I'd like that," Alice said. "We'll keep them company. Perhaps we could read them a story."

"That would be nice. As for the McCarthy Miller family, Zelah

346

is going to have to go through a complicated legal process to prove her right to the property and the fortune. It's going to take a long time."

"Will she still be part of Maze?"

"Yes, of course."

"That's OK, then. Oh, turn off here. It's a short-cut. By the way, what's wrong with you and Bob?"

Chapter 82

They all finally got together on Tuesday morning. Maggie gave Nick and Zelah a full account, almost.

"So, he never told you anything?" asked Zelah.

"Nothing at all. Whatever he wanted to say about you, never got said. Do you have any idea what it might have been?"

Zelah jumped in quickly with an answer. Too quickly. "I think it was something to do with the name. And the family history."

Maggie didn't think so, and she thought that Zelah didn't believe that either.

"What's going to happen to the McCarthy Miller empire?" Nick asked.

"Not what I originally thought," Zelah replied. "I've found out that the two boys, Noel's sons, had nothing to do with the rest of the family. Noel knew but was too much of a coward to stop it. But he kept it away from his sons. They are decent individuals, with integrity and conscience. They wanted to give everything over to me, but I said no. They won't continue the racehorse breeding. But we're starting a discussion about how we can turn the business into a charity, to use the grounds for holidays for disadvantaged kids, and keep horses there for pleasure and for involvement with the kids."

"That's a nice idea," Maggie smiled.

"It will take time, of course. But I've said that I'm in, if they are. I don't need the money. But I'm still going to take on the legal issues, for my mother. I can at least find some justice for her."

"And the rings?"

"Not sure yet. The wedding band was my grandmother's. Her first fiancée had it made specially. She never got to wear it. I think the Roman ring will go back to Caerleon. I haven't decided about the spoon ring." She turned her head to look at Maggie. "Do you think Jack would like it?"

"I think he might, thank you Zelah. It's a wonderful piece of history and with such a story attached."

"Good. Then, I think we can finally draw the line under this project."

"Bit more than a project," Nick remarked.

"Shall we get on? I now have three stories to write up. Maggie, what about you?"

"I have a long-overdue visit to the Cheshire archives and to Liverpool, the mystery of the missing policeman I told you about?"

"Right. And there are a few bits to finish off, besides. You'll need to draft the reports. Nick?"

"Ended the first phase of my project. Three hundred websites are on the database. Now I'll keep in touch with it. And I'm going to help Maggie with her missing policeman."

"And my radio interviews start again next week. We'd better decide how much I can say about the rings," Maggie added

"They'll make an interesting story for the radio, and for the Maze website. Let's talk it through." Zelah said.

Nick turned to his laptop and began to tap. Maggie and Zelah started to talk about the content of the website and radio broadcast. Business as usual.

Chapter 83

Before Jack arrived home, Maggie was sitting with yet another G and T – she must get a grip on this – looking out at the last of the summer flowering plants in her garden.

After Zelah and Nick had gone she had made a phone call. She and Maureen Meers had chatted for some time. Maggie used the excuse of letting Maureen know how the interment ceremony had gone. Maureen had wanted to attend but had been prevented at the last minute by pressing family business.

Maureen asked how Zelah was, and Maggie had used this pretext to get Maureen talking about the past, about MoMe and Little Jay. They talked for half an hour, MoMe reminisced about Zelah's cleverness and how she could get into locked rooms and how she could do 'magic' by making things fly around without strings. At the end of the call Maggie promised that, if they visited Cornwall again, they would call in to see her and reminisce more about old times. She now knew that was the last thing Zelah would want to do.

Now she understood what had been bugging her. And she knew that Noel McCarthy Miller's death had been an accident. And she knew why Zelah hadn't shown any fear of Norah and her shotgun. But these were not things that she would ever tell anyone.

Zelah was a good person. She didn't need to know that Maggie had guessed what it was Sir Thomas had wanted to tell her. Good riddance to him. Norah was locked away, raving at everyone, threatening them with her abilities, of which it was clear she had none.

It was a worry that Emer had evaded capture, that she was still out there and no doubt determined to do Zelah, Maggie, and Bob as much harm as she could. But they knew that wherever she had gone, it wasn't mainland UK.

She and Bob hadn't spoken for a few days. They needed to talk and it wasn't going to be an easy conversation. Maybe she had jumped into a relationship too quickly. She thought she loved him, but now…? Could the trust return? She felt betrayed by his secrecy but he was still convinced that he'd acted in everyone's best interests.

Maze Investigations was going from strength to strength, even if there were some unresolved questions for Zelah to answer.

But her family was happy, her friends were safe, and that was enough for today.

Epilogue – Part 1
Bonfire Night

The village on the hill, having planned its annual Bonfire Night celebrations months in advance, was about ready to light up. Volunteers had built the bonfire in the centre of the small common. Barriers had been erected. The night was fine. The fireworks display was ready to go.

Zelah had never attended previously, as far as anyone could remember. So it had been a shock when she turned up at seven with a tray of toffee apples and cups of hot chocolate.

"My contribution." She handed the tray to the Chairman of the bonfire committee, who politely thanked her and took it with a puzzled expression. He watched her surreptitiously as she made her way around the bonfire, smiling at people as she passed them. Most had no idea who she was.

At seven-fifteen the Chairman delivered his speech welcoming locals and visitors, then ceremoniously stepped forward to put the first torch to the fire. He was followed by torch bearers who lit the fire at other points, and within minutes the heap of branches, logs, pallets, paper and anything else that would burn was dancing with flames.

Zelah watched, smiling, with a small group of people for ten minutes or so, when the Chairman further announced that the fireworks would start. Everyone turned to look at the far end of the common where the display had been set up.

Once she was sure she would not be observed, Zelah ducked under the safety barrier. From her pocket, as she walked, she retrieved a small black box and took off the lid, which she threw into the fire. She glanced quickly at the main object within the box. Anyone else looking at it would have thought it was some kind of doll. Just a small figurine. A smartly dressed figurine, with grey hair and the face of an old man. She took out some other, smaller loose objects and put them back in her pocket. Then, drawing back her arm and summoning up as much aim and power as she could muster, she threw the box onto the fire. It landed high up and quickly sank through the flames until it was out of sight.

Within seconds she was back on the safe side of the barrier. She glanced left and right. When she was sure that no one had observed her and that they were all looking with anticipation for the next exploding sparks and lights, she extricated herself and walked back in the direction of her flat.

As she reached the road across from her block there was an almighty explosion, loud enough to make children scream, that seemed to come from the centre of the fire. People afterwards said they turned to see what looked like a great human form of flame shoot out of the centre of the fire and straight up into the black sky.

Zelah didn't turn around. At the far side of the road she reached into her pocket again and took out the loose objects. There was a communal bin by the road. She lifted the lid and threw in the three objects clasped in her palm. Long and straight with sharpened ends, they clattered around on the bottom of the bin, then were silent. She rubbed her hands together, as if trying to rid them of something that was stuck. She put them back in her pockets.

What was done, was done. It was all in the past, never to be repeated, never again.

Epilogue – Part 2
The Long House, Penwith Hamlet, 1776

It was almost over. She had survived the worst. Her darling son Edward was safe. She could die in her own bed. But there was one thing to do.

Julia Pencarrow grimaced through the pain. It had spread from her woman's parts to the whole of her body and was now barely allowing her to breathe. She rolled over onto her side and fumbled around under the mattress until she found the folded parchment and its contents. The last letter. She read it again, and was again comforted by the knowledge that the other two copies had both been destroyed.

She didn't know what had happened to Edward Steelfox, only that he had died shortly after his return to Cheshire. He was still a relatively young man. She had heard that it had been a strange accident. She had never tried to find out.

Sir John, though. Poor Sir John. Deprived by childbirth of the woman he adored. For the sake of whose life and reputation he had allowed his first wife to be killed by Julia's special skills. And then the children of his second marriage had all died. It was rumoured that he had taken his own life. Out of loneliness, people said. But she thought otherwise. More likely out of shame.

Now it was her turn. But she had no loneliness or shame. She had done what had to be done. All that remained was her letter and the ring and the recognisable poppet she had taken from the dead hand of Mildred Vyse. The other she had left behind for the coroner to puzzle over. This one had been made in the shape and form of Emma Trelawney, who would become Lady Vyse. Why had she kept them? She thought that, somehow, history needed to know the truth of what Mildred Vyse had been. Or did she believe that God would judge her more kindly?

If she was going to leave the objects they needed to be in safe hands. It would be up to others if they chose to tell her story after she was gone.

Her son would be up to her room directly. She would tell him everything. Although he knew of her gifts they had never spoken of it. She thought, sadly, that he would be horrified. Perhaps he would burn everything, destroy the ring. She would leave it to his conscience.

She heard his footsteps on the narrow, winding, stone staircase. She sat up as far as she could, the items clutched in her hand and prepared herself for what was likely to be their final conversation. How she loved Edward. He would not judge her. She looked up as the young man entered the room with a posset he had prepared for her. She beckoned him to come sit by her bed.

"I have a story to tell you," she whispered.

Thanks and Acknowledgements

My grateful thanks go to my first readers, Cheryl, Rose and Joy who, again, have given me encouragement, excellent feedback and advice on how to get out of plot holes!

My friend and fellow author, John Wake, former police detective, I thank for the check on police procedure. Where there are mistakes, these are of my making.

I am also very pleased to thank Ellen Morrow, who has re-proofed this latest version for me.

My family as always, give me support, technical help and plenty of tea as I type away.

The covers for all of the books in the Maze Investigations series are designed by Alison Morgan of AliCat Design of Monmouth.

A FEW WORDS ON THE WITCHES OF SALEM AND WITCHCRAFT IN ENGLAND

The lithograph on the front cover of this book is of Bridget Bishop, the first woman to be hanged for witchcraft at the Salem Witchcraft trials, in June 1692. This is the only known likeness of her. She was born Bridget Magnus, in Norwich around 1632 and moved to the United States as a young married woman. Her first husband died and she married again three times.

She had previously been accused of using witchcraft to bring about the death of her third husband, from whom she inherited property and land, but this never came to trial, as it was believed that the accusers, the children of that husband, Thomas Oliver, who had inherited little from him, wanted the house and property for themselves.

She was, apparently, rather wild, flamboyant in dress and temper and supposedly an Innkeeper. However, it has now been proved that she was confused with another woman accused of witchcraft, Sarah Bishop, the daughter in law of Bridget's fourth husband, Edward Bishop. Bridget lived in Salem town where she had a house and an orchard, where she also kept chickens. She and Oliver had been taken to court on more than one occasion for their quarrelling and fighting.

She made a number of enemies, whose evidence eventually brought about her conviction, including four women and several families who claimed she had bewitched them and their families. Throughout the trial, Bridget denied all knowledge of the accusers and proclaimed her innocence.

But, the weight of evidence and the fact of a previous accusation meant that the outcome was practically pre-determined. Her trial took just one day. On 8th June 1692 a jury found her guilty and a death warrant was issued. She was hanged on 10th June 1692 and buried at the execution site (because of the accusation of witchcraft she could not be buried in consecrated ground).

The journal "History of Massachusetts.org" suggests that:

"Bridget Bishop was not the first victim accused during the Salem Witch Trials of 1692, but it is believed that officials chose to hear her case first because they felt, given her prior history and reputation, it would be an easy win. They were right and a string of other convictions and executions followed hers before the hysteria came to an end in 1693."

Trials for witchcraft in England began around the 15th century and went on until the 18th century. They are estimated to have resulted in the death of between 500 and 1000 people, 90 percent of whom were women. The witch hunt was as its most intense stage during the Civil War (1642–1651) and the Puritan era of the mid-17th century. The most infamous in England was the trial of the Pendle witches in 1612, which resulted in ten men and women being hanged, amongst them Alice Device and her grandmother.

Overall, some 500 people in England alone are believed to have been executed for witchcraft. The last recorded execution was in Devon, in 1685.

So many poor souls persecuted and killed, all innocent of any wrong doing.

The next book in the Maze Investigations series,
available on Amazon, is:

use.

Printed in Great Britain
by Amazon

23073530R00202